WRATH OF TITAN

A FANTASY ADVENTURE

PAUL MOUCHET

PAUL MOUCHET PUBLISHING

To my wife, who believes in me, even when I struggle to believe in myself. Without her support and infinite patience, I would have never realized my dream of becoming an author.
And, to my big sister Louise, thank you for helping me bring my stories to life.

CONTENTS

CHAPTER ONE

AN ACT OF DESPERATION

Ymir clutched at his bare, frozen chest. A hint of frost thistle hung in the air, enticing Titan's chosen one to inhale deeply through his nostrils. He scanned the perimeter of the expansive room, taking in the multitude of ice-giant statues that lined its perimeter. His eyes fell upon the statue bearing his own likeness, standing a good two feet taller than every other statue. With the slightest hint of a smile, he blew out a frosty breath and stepped inside. With each step, the sound of his bare feet slapping the ice-tiled floor echoed off the walls and ceiling. He smiled as he looked down at a single oval altar that stood upon a dais at the room's center. A tiny Berrat woman lay upon it, tied down with thick, spidersilk ropes. Her tight white braids hung limp across the altar's silver-blue stone surface.

"Hello, Riva." The god rapped his icy knuckles on the altar's granite top, next to Riva's ear. "Come now, child. You cannot feign deafness and expect me to buy into it."

"Do with me what you will, traitor. Get it over with or release me. Either way, your days are numbered." Riva never opened her eyes, and she barely moved as she spoke. A low, menacing growl came out from behind Ymir, bringing a smile to his chapped blue lips.

"I know, Shade. I smell it, too." Ymir sneered at the tiny woman splayed out on the altar. "There is more to her than she lets on. I plan on using that to my advantage."

Riva pulled back her lips in disgust. "What you smell is your own failure. Bringing me here will be your undoing. The ramparts of this grand castle will come crashing down about your ears. Your mongrel friend will perish, and Titan will see that you suffer for all eternity." Riva laughed a hollow, mirthless laugh. "Unless my daughter finds you first, that is."

The lesser deity chuckled at the woman's assertion while Shade's growl increased in ferocity. "You bore me with your faulty visions, witch. Titan will never be freed, and I do not fear your whelp." Ymir reached down and stroked his dire wolf's neck-fur. Without warning, he grabbed a thick handful of Shade's ruff and yanked on it, causing the animal to yelp.

"I do not need a vision to foretell your future, traitor. Already you feel the world closing in on you. It's the only explanation for you dragging me all the way to Jotunheim. What will your brethren think when you bring the celestial's wrath upon the home of the Ice Giants? Do you believe they will come to your aid? If so, you're even more delusional than I thought."

"If only Aurora and her annoying daughter would show up together. I could remove them both with a single wave of my trident. Then there would be nothing to keep me from ruling the northern realms."

Riva chuckled at the ice god's words. "You're delusional. Your insatiable desire for power will be your undoing. You were given everything you could have ever needed, but you wanted more."

"The truth of the matter is, I wanted less. I did not want to bow to Titan. I did not want to be his servant." Ymir rolled his trident in his hand, admiring its yeti-bone tines. With a sadistic grin, he touched the weapon to the altar. On contact, a sheet of ice spread out across its granite surface. "You will speak to me of the future, and do not attempt to deceive me, for I will know."

The little Berrat's body stiffened, but she refused to cry out. Riva's eyes snapped open before rolling back in her head. Her body quaked uncontrollably, as foam poured from her lips. When the episode passed, she drew a deep breath. "Holding me captive will draw my daughter here. If that is your goal, then you will succeed. Sadly, for you, when she leaves, you will be dead and I will leave with her." Ymir grinned at the woman's words.

A tall, thin woman with blue-gray skin and four spider legs protruding from her back stepped from the shadows. Ymir lowered his gaze while Shade cowered behind him. She surveyed Riva with each of her eight eyes, delighted when the Berrat recoiled from her. "You're not telling him everything, little one." Riva gazed at the spider-woman, but she refused to speak further.

"Oh, don't be like that." The woman practically purred. "Perhaps I should introduce myself. I am Arachnielle, God of Spiders." When Riva didn't react, Arachnielle turned to Ymir, regarding him with obvious disdain. "And what am I to do with you? How much help does a god need to take over a swath of frozen wasteland filled with retched vermin? I gave you an army. I gave you elementals. I even lured that little priest, Kit Standing Bear, right into your clutches." Ymir took another step away from the woman, with Shade staying close behind him.

"Arachnielle…" Ymir stuttered as he struggled to find his words. "But, most terrible goddess, the priest is not what she seems."

"She is part celestial," the spider god scoffed. "A small part of her is celestial. Does the tiny girl frighten you? Are you not a god? Are you so weak that you and your mongrel cower from a child?"

"But she has help. She is being aided by Fenrir and the trickster, Tyr."

"And you have me," Arachnielle cooed. She ran her finger along Ymir's chin, allowing it to trace down his neck to his bare chest. The woman rolled her eyes and turned away. "And when we bring down the Veil, you'll have Bael and Gorgaraeth fighting with you as well." Ymir nodded and bowed with an obsequious flourish. "Now, stop playing with this changeling and regain that which was taken from you. We need to have control of Cormorant when those foolish dwarves break through the Veil. I want a front-row seat when Gorgaraeth and Bael arrive and lay waste to the lands."

Arachnielle clutched her hand to her bony breast. "It will be glorious!"

Chapter Two

The Morning After

Kit blinked and then blinked again. What she was seeing wasn't registering in her brain. It made little sense.

Why are there scorch marks all over my ceiling?

She rolled over onto her side and grimaced. Her bed was abnormally hard. Not that it was ever soft, but it felt like she was sleeping on a stone slab. A thick fog was wrapped around her brain, making it difficult for her to process what her eyes and her body were telling her. She patted her bed, expecting to find her straw mattress, but all she felt was cold granite.

Where's my mattress?

A snort from beside her roused Kit's mind a bit more. Maybe it was Runt or Lump who had stolen her mattress, so they'd have a comfortable spot on the floor. She reached out behind herself, expecting to find the thick, soft fur of either Runt or Lump. Instead, her hands found smooth bare skin.

Holy Helja!

Kit leapt from the bed and took a battle stance. When Indie rolled over to face her, the memories of the past night came flooding back. When she realized she was naked, she ineffectually tried to cover herself with nothing more than her hands. Indie's eyebrows shot up at the sight.

"Seriously?" He propped himself up on his elbow. "After last night's *adventures* you're being shy with my seeing you naked?" Indie looked down at his own nudity and grinned. There wasn't so much as a bedsheet around with which to cover himself up.

Kit gathered up one of her priestly robes and slipped it over her head. She scanned her long, narrow cell, looking for something for Indie to wear. Scratching at the door drove her into a panic.

"Where are your clothes?" Kit's head was practically spinning as she continued to search for something for Indie to wear.

"In the bath, I'm guessing. We sort of rushed from there to here. I was covered in scales, and you were wreathed in flames."

"Put something over yourself. There's someone at the door." Indie looked around and shrugged, making Kit's eyes bulge. "Then get in my wardrobe. You can't lie there naked." Indie's playful demeanor disappeared for a moment and his expression became serious. A moment later, he was covered in bright gold scales from head to toe. His hair turned into long, soft spikes. Kit gawked at the man. He was mesmerizing. His body shimmered as the morning light reflected off him.

The scratching at the door was becoming frantic.

With a groan, Kit moved to the door and opened it a crack so she could see who was in the hall. As soon as the latch was pulled, the door burst inward, sending Kit to the floor. A moment later, Lump and Runt were busy greeting her with their wet, slobbery kisses. They were behaving like they hadn't seen Kit in weeks. Amid the jubilant celebrations, Lump caught sight of Indie and the state of the room. He morphed into his human form, his face beet red. "Runt, we need to leave. Now."

Runt didn't pay Lump any mind until he grabbed him by the scruff of the neck and hauled the dire wolf off Kit. "Now, Runt." As he pulled the unwilling pup towards the door, Lump offered a quick apology and left.

Kit locked the door and Indie's scales melted away. He patted the stone slab and smiled sweetly.

"Again?" she asked, taking a seat on the bed next to her love. She ignited a small flame in her hand and touched her finger to Indie's chest. Kit smiled as the heat of her touch summoned his golden scales. She sucked a sharp breath when they radiated outward from the source, like the ripple of stone breaking the still surface of a pond. By Titan, he was beautiful.

"You look happy." Indie scooched a little closer. "Perhaps the happiest I've ever seen." The little priest smiled and shrugged.

"I'm relieved, I think. I feared my father was dead. I feared Father Hoarfrost was dead. Sister Miyuki..." Kit's eyes became glassy as she spoke. The memory of Sister Miyuki reached for her heart and gripped it. The woman was the kindest soul. She didn't deserve to be tortured to death.

"She would want you to be happy." Indie tucked Kit's dark red hair behind her ear, and let his hand linger on her neck. A tear leaked from the corner of her eye and traced a thin line down her cheek. Before it fell, the young man used the back of a finger to brush it away. Kit's heart was thudding in her chest. She wasn't sure if it was from the tenderness of the moment or the memory of Miyuki's brutal death.

Kit took Indie's wrist in her still flaming hand and kissed his scale-covered palm. "If you stop being Fury's apprentice, do you expect you'll lose this gift?" Indie pulled his hand away.

"Why would I stop being Fury's apprentice? He asks very little, and he's given me so much."

"And you don't see the problem with that?" Kit rolled her eyes. "Nobody gives something and expects nothing in return. Besides, you don't need your fire resistance anymore. I have complete control over my flames."

"You do." Indie's voice was soft and easy.

Kit's eyebrows shot up. He had never believed that she could control her daemon self. Why was he being so agreeable?

"You finally believe I can control the daemon? You believe I won't accidentally – set you on fire?"

"No, not that. You said nobody gives something and expects nothing in return. You do that all the time. You constantly give of yourself and expect nothing in return. You do things for people because you want to help. You never ask for recompense. You offered your life to save mine, and you hardly even knew me." Kit's expression went flat as she considered his words. "Besides, if I can help Fury be free of his prison, why wouldn't I want to do that? Especially if he gave me dragon wings..."

"So that you could fly away and be free. Is that what you want?" Indie closed his eyes and lowered his chin. Kit regretted her choice of words. She trusted Indie and his love for her. What had possessed her to act like that with him?

"Do you really believe I would willingly choose to spend even a second away from you? I am yours, for ever. Nothing can change that." He raised his chin and stared deeply into Kit's swirling gold eyes. "I've seen you. I saw the look of pure joy on your face when you and Angel jumped over the canyon. If you were offered the gift of flight, you'd take it in a heartbeat."

"You're right," Kit said, tilting her head to the side. "I would love to have that ability. The feeling of flight is like nothing I've ever experienced before." A sly grin appeared at the corner of her mouth. "Well, almost nothing." Indie reached for her hand, but she pulled it away before he could take it. "But if being able to fly meant me risking my relationship with you, even just a little, I wouldn't want it. I wouldn't risk our happiness just so that I could fly."

An untimely knock on the door interrupted Indie's response.

⤜⥤⥢⤛

Lin waited patiently for the door to open. She spun her old war hammer in her hand, still impressed by its lightness. She had never regretted gifting it to Kit, but now that it held two pieces of the dragon lord, Fury, it made the weapon even more wondrous.

She knocked again, this time with more vigor. Sounds of scuffling and hushed words came from beyond the door. Lin pursed her lips together and beat out a playful rhythm with her knuckles on the thick oak planks.

"Just open the door, Kit." Lin pounded on the door harder. She had considered using the hammer, just for fun, but Fury may not have appreciated being used as a knocker. Frankly, she was surprised that the dragon lord hadn't been furious for having been left unattended outside the priest's bathing room. When it dawned on her why he was not upset, Lin gazed approvingly at the weapon. "You're a classy dragon, Fury. Very classy, indeed."

The door to Kit's room creaked open. A single golden eyeball was visible through the crack. "What?"

Lin stuck her nose close to the opening and smiled at her friend. Beyond the doorway, Indie was sitting on the bed. At least, she believed it was him. It was difficult to tell for sure, seeing as how golden scales were covering his entire body. "I'd like to come in."

"It's not a good time." Kit's voice carried a hint of threat in it. Lin's smile brightened at the comment.

"It's important. Fury invited me to be his apprentice." At Lin's declaration, Indie hopped up from his spot and threw the door open.

"That's not possible. I'm his chosen apprentice." Indie's scales shimmered as he moved, his thick golden mane standing on end. Fury appeared inside the room.

"Your transformation is coming along nicely," the draken said to Indie while he preened his own sky blue scales. "Having multiple apprentices is absolutely possible, even if it is... unprecedented." Indie wheeled around and stormed up to Fury. His face reddened while he clenched his hands into tight fists at his side.

"I am your apprentice. Me. Why do you need her?"

"What happened to your cell?" Lin stepped past Kit, her gaze fixated on the heavy scorch marks on the bed, walls, and ceiling.

"Never mind what happened," Kit snapped. She wheeled around on Fury; her chin raised defiantly at the seven-foot draken who stood before her. "You can't have two apprentices. If you've made Lin your apprentice, you don't need Indie anymore." A feral grin spread across Fury's face, exposing some of his needle-like teeth.

"I don't *need* either of them, and, just to be clear, I can have as many apprentices as I choose. You would also make a fine apprentice if you weren't so... you. I don't expect you could even accept my gifts. Your celestial heritage would likely make it impossible." The comment made both Indie and Lin cringe.

"And what if he demands you stay in his mountain range?" Kit said, directing her question to the two of them. "What of Rusty? Are you ready to abandon your love just so you can have whatever gifts Fury's offering?" The little priest redirected her ire towards Indie. "And you, too? Will you give up being with me just so you can fly?" Kit turned back at Lin. "What of your dream of becoming an enchanter? What of your dream of opening a shop and selling the finest items in all of Arnnor? You'll give up on everything you've ever wanted, for him?" Fury seemed amused by Kit's questioning.

Lin recoiled at the harsh words. She was so caught up in what Fury had offered her, she hadn't considered what she might have to leave behind. She turned to the draken, her heart fluttering. "Is that true? If I were your apprentice, would you make me give up everything just to serve you?"

"Just to serve me? If I *were* your apprentice?" Fury's gaze shifted between Indie and Lin. "You are both my apprentices. I made an offer, and you accepted. The bargain has been struck and there is no backing out of it. Only death forgives you your obligation to me." In the instant that the last word left the draken's mouth, Kit leapt up and kicked him in the chest, launching him backwards towards the cell's window. He winked out before he fell.

A deafening roar filled the room. Fury, his face directly in front of Kit's, screeched out. She dug into the stone floor with her toes and leaned in towards the irate draken.

"You threaten my friends again and I will end you." Kit's eyes were swirling pools of molten gold. "I will have the Hobgoblins split you again, and again, and again. I will throw your pieces into the North Sea, and nobody will ever find you. You can spend eternity shivering on its cold, desolate floor."

Fury's body color shifted from sky blue to a crimson so deep it was nearly black. Billows of smoke blew from his nostrils. He was about to flame the girl when Indie jumped between the two of them. "I did not offer you servitude," he said. "I promised to help you leave your mountain prison. I offered you nothing more."

The deep rumble grew within the draken's chest as he peeled back his scaled lips. "You have a short, selective memory."

"And you're lying." Kit pushed Indie out of the way. Her eyes narrowed as she turned her gaze to Lin and the war hammer that held Fury's soul. Slowly, she raised her eyes back to confront the draken. "And I can assure you, I was not. Am I clear? Is there any part of this threat that you believe I will not follow through with? Do I need to restate it to be sure you understand my meaning?"

Fury's lips slowly relaxed, sliding down over his teeth, but the deep, resonating rumble in his chest never lessened.

"Fine." A small stream of flame flew out of his mouth along with the word. Kit's body was immediately wreathed in flames before his attack struck her, rendering the dragon fire inconsequential. As quickly as her fires engulfed her, they dissipated. "But I will hold you both to your promise of freeing me. Once you have, your debt will have been paid and you will be free to go about your lives without me." Fury gave Kit a quick, sarcastic smile.

Indie and Lin exchanged a glance and nodded at each other. Lin felt there was still a trap wrapped within the dragon lord's words, but she had what she wanted for now.

"Indie," Lin said. "Can you please go put some clothes on? I need to talk with Kit. Alone."

Kit eyed the man and his golden scales. "It's not a bad idea. You're a bit *distracting* in your current state." Without a word, Indie snatched the hammer from Lin's hand and left the room, slamming the door behind him as he did.

⌇⌇⌇◇⌇⌇⌇

"I didn't think it through," Lin said. Kit didn't know how to react. She was still furious with her friend, but she trusted her. "I didn't think of how it would affect my relationship with Rusty, if there is a relationship there at all."

"I understand." In truth, Kit didn't understand, but her friend was hurting, and she would not pour salt in the wound.

"I hate being away from her. It consumes my every waking moment." Kit cocked an eyebrow at Lin's assertion. "Okay, it doesn't consume every moment, but I think about her often, especially when I'm alone in my bed at night. I think back to how I've lived my life. I don't deserve someone like Rusty. She's so... perfect."

Kit sat on her stone slab bed and invited Lin to sit beside her. As soon as she did, the little priest wrapped her arm around her friend's shoulder and pulled her tight. "You are the most confusing person I've ever met, but I know your heart to be true. Your past does not define you." Kit stroked the woman's chin length black hair. She remembered back when her mother, Riva, used to do that and it always made her feel better. "You are worthy of love, and of trust, and of every bit of happiness the world has to offer."

Lin wrapped her arm around the small of Kit's back and hugged her. "Thank you. Thank you for everything. I know I don't deserve you as a friend, but I'm thankful that you are. I won't let you down."

"Don't worry about me," Kit offered. She slipped out of Lin's grasp and stood. "Why don't you follow me to the bathing room? I need to get my clothes and I want to give you my dragon tear. Reach out to Rusty. Tell her you miss her and that you can't wait to return to her."

Lin hopped to her feet and smothered Kit with hugs and kisses.

Chapter Three

Uncharted Waters

Danny stared into the blue and white swirling ball that rested in the palm of his hand. He had been trying to reach Kit for several days and he feared the worst. The only report he had on the girl was from his cousin, Breayn, who had said Kit had left for Aarall and that Father Hoarfrost had been killed. His heart beat heavily in his chest as he waited for the image in the crystal to clear. His face sagged when the visage of Lin came into view.

"Nice to see you, too," Lin said. Even over a great distance, her dislike for him came through. He didn't really understand the woman's attitude toward him. He had never wronged her. In fact, in all the time they had been at the Temple together, he had hardly had any interactions with her. "Is Rusty around? I need to talk to her."

"Is Kit there? Is she safe?"

"Yes, and yes. I need to speak to Rusty. Is she there?"

"What happened to everyone? Breayn told me Father Hoarfrost was dead. I've been trying to reach Kit for days." Lin sighed and rolled her eyes at his questions.

"King Jordain tried to overthrow Aarall. We stopped it. Father Hoarfrost is okay." A lump grew in Danny's throat when Lin's eyes welled up. There was more to this story than she was saying.

"Is Kit okay?" Lin nodded, but the tears came, nonetheless. "Lin, what's wrong?"

"They killed Miyuki. They tortured her in front of Captain Harding to make him switch sides." Lin wiped her nose with her sleeve, her emotions overwhelming her. "Brother Powder did it. He set fire to her feet. He murdered her."

The phoenix surged within Danny's chest. Flames licked from his eyes. The blue and white ball turned to shades of purple and pink, with the image of Lin appearing as bright yellow. "Why? Why would Powder do such a thing?" Flames were now licking the small orb in his hand. Fearful that he might damage the crystal, the Berrat regained control of himself and the fires died out.

"We don't know." Lin snuffled and wiped the last of the tears from her face. "We're going to interrogate him this morning. I expect he won't survive the day. I'm guessing there's a lineup of priests ready to deliver justice upon him."

Danny's heart was still pounding against his chest. How anybody, especially another priest, could bring harm to the Temple's head baker was beyond him.

"Danny, I'm sorry to have to deliver such horrible news to you, but I really need to speak with Rusty. Is she around?"

The words washed over Danny. He heard them, but they didn't register in his mind. A moment later he shook off his grief and focused his attention back on Lin. "Sure, she's in the war room, I think. I'll bring her the seer's crystal."

"It's a dragon tear," Lin said, correcting Danny's choice of words. "My master would be displeased to hear you refer to it as a seer's crystal."

"Your what?" Danny blinked at the tiny sphere. "Did you say *your master*?"

"Fury has taken me on as an apprentice. He promised to teach me everything he knows about enchanting and potion making. In return, I will help him escape his mountain prison." Danny frowned. The deal sounded too one sided. Deep inside, he feared Lin had struck a bargain that would drag her into lifelong servitude. He wanted to say something, to tell her to get out of it, but he decided it was her decision and her life, and he had no right to question her choices.

"I'll find Rusty."

Rusty looked away and wiped her eyes when Danny stepped into the war room. His demeanor was subdued, and his typical cocky grin was nowhere to be seen. She was in no mood for his nonsense and wished he'd go back to brooding about Kit. Then again, she couldn't be too hard on him. She felt exactly the same way about Lin; a love, she feared, that would never be returned.

"What?" she asked, even though she really had no interest in knowing what he had to say.

"Lin wants to talk with you." He tossed the sphere across the room to the general. She caught it easily, but she glowered at him just the same. Had his throw been off the mark or if she had dropped it, the crystal might have shattered, and they'd have lost their means of communicating with the others.

No sooner had Rusty gazed into the ball than the image of Lin swirled into view. She looked nervous. "We need to talk." Rusty's pulse immediately quickened. No pleasant conversation ever started with those words.

"Yes?" Rusty swallowed hard. She hoped Lin hadn't picked up the worry in her voice. Even in the tiny crystal, the woman was beautiful. Rusty had no idea how Lin found her attractive. She was short, overweight, and had a surly demeanor, where Lin was tall, and beautiful, and perfect.

"I miss you." Lin's words caught the general off guard. Rusty had imagined this conversation in her head a hundred times, but never did it start like this. Her lower lip trembled. "I'm worried, Rusty. I'm worried that I'll never see you again."

Oh, sweet Titan. What in Helja did that mean?

"We're at war with the King of Arnnor and King Faol, too, I expect. King Jordain has tried to overthrow Aarall. His people attacked the Temple and the City Watch. We fought them back and retook the city, but it came at a heavy price." Rusty tried to absorb what Lin was saying. That the king would attack his own city was absurd. Lin had said something else, but the words never registered in Rusty's ears.

"Did you hear what I said?" Lin asked. "I thought you'd be more upset."

"I am upset. I don't understand why the king would attack his own city." Lin's face crumpled at her response.

"I said I've become an apprentice to Fury. I don't know what that means for us, but it's something I need to do." Rusty scrubbed her forehead. She was still stuck on the king's attack and now Lin was speaking nonsense about the damned draken. "I promised to help him escape his mountain prison. In return, he's going to teach me about enchanting and potions and dragon magic."

"We're not ready to fight." They were the only words Rusty could muster. The two bits of news that Lin had shared didn't fit together. The look of confusion on Rusty's face only seemed to make the matter worse.

"I don't want to fight." Lin replied. "I want to discuss what this means for our relationship."

"What does the king's attack on Aarall have to do with us? I'm saying my soldiers aren't ready to fight. Your friends, Mukale and Treedale, are doing outstanding work with the new Berrat recruits, but I still don't know how I'm going to use them."

"He's my brother, not my friend."

"What?" Rusty's head snapped back at the comment. "Who's your brother?"

"Treedale. How can you not know that?"

"You never told me!" Rusty was ready to explode. How could her lover have not bothered to tell her that the young man was her brother? Lin had never told her and now, for some inexplicable reason, she was upset. The scowl on Lin's face slowly melted away.

"I didn't? Are you sure?" Rusty growled at the questions.

"Of course, I'm sure. I'd remember if my love told me something so important." Lin's eyes widened at the statement. "You don't believe me?"

"You've never mentioned love before. I didn't think I was good enough for you. I... oh, sweet Titan, what have I done? I promised to help Fury. I didn't think that... I didn't know how you felt about me."

Rusty's face crumbled. Why did this conversation need to be so hard? Why hadn't she ever spoken of love to Lin before? It was at that moment that her emotions came into clarity. "I never spoke of love because I didn't think I was good enough for you. I'm so ordinary compared to you." Rusty still hadn't processed everything Lin had said to her. Every time she had mentioned Fury, the words never sunk in. "Tell me again. What did you promise to Fury?" Her heart started racing. In what way had Lin promised herself to a dragon?

Lin wiped her nose with the back of her hand. "I promised to devote myself to freeing him. I... I'll speak to him. I'll get out of it. I don't want to be his apprentice anymore."

"Don't be hard on yourself." Rusty didn't fully understand what Lin was getting at, but there was more to her own story than she had yet to share. "If I can't find a host for my father's soul, I don't know if we can ever be together. He..." She exhaled and dropped her chin to her ample chest. "He disapproves of my lifestyle choices. He wants a grandson. Helja, he'd even accept a granddaughter, but if you and I are to be together, there would be no babies for him to fuss over."

Lin's head snapped towards Rusty. Ferocity raged in her eyes. "That's not his decision. That's your decision. How dare he force his own views of morality upon you?"

"He can't help what he thinks, and I can't stop hearing him. Unless I use my ring to suppress him, I can't quiet him or his thoughts. I can't leave this ring on forever. It's not fair to him to be permanently trapped in a state of limbo." Lin nodded her understanding. Rusty's racing pulse had subsided somewhat. Their lives were complicated, and a life together might be impossible. Unless her father was returned to his body, she was going to be forced to rule Cormorant in his place. The idea of being the lady of the city thrilled her, and it terrified her, but she could not deny that she enjoyed being in charge, even if she shared the command with her father.

"Can you ask Lin to give the crystal back to Kit? I really need to talk to her." Rusty wheeled around to find Danny standing behind her. The man had been there the entire time, listening in on her deeply private conversation.

"Get out! Take your smug face and your skinny butt, and get the Helja out of here. If you don't leave right now, so help me Titan, I'll take that smug face and ram it up your skinny butt.

Danny ignored Rusty's threat and gave her a thin-lipped grin. "Lin, give the crystal back to Kit! I need to talk to her." The Berrat's eyes bugged out of his head when he looked up. Rusty's fists were clenched tightly while her face turned a deep shade of purple. From the dragon tear within her clenched fist, Lin called out.

"Rusty, I need to go. Something's happening here. Tell Danny I'll return the dragon tear to Kit."

"Thank you," Danny yelled as he hastened towards the doorway with Rusty hot on his heels.

"Get out!" the general screamed, throwing the dragon tear at the Berrat. Her throw was wild, but Danny snagged it before it crashed against the wall. He waved the crystal at Rusty and slipped out the door.

"I see why she likes you so much." Danny's voice carried through the closed door. "You're adorable when you're angry."

⚜

A chill wind blew through the window in Danny's bedroom. Goosebumps raised on his bronze skin, and he shivered briefly. The phoenix burned from within, warming him from the inside out. He was propped up on his pillow, staring intently at the dragon tear resting in his hands. He ran his fingers through his long fire-red hair and blew out his cheeks. He shook his head, letting his locks return to their normal state of perfection.

Where are you, Kitten? Why are you not speaking to me?

A sudden pang ripped through his chest. What if she was with Indie and didn't want to be disturbed? What if Indie had convinced her to break ties with him? What if... His musings were cut short when Kit's image swirled into focus. Sweet Titan, she was beautiful. Her golden skin seemed glossier than the last time he had seen her. Her hair appeared a much brighter red, much like his own.

"Hello, Danny. I'm sorry I didn't reach out to speak sooner. Things have been... difficult here."

"Hello, Kitten. I overheard some of Lin's discussion with Rusty and I feared the worst. I was heart broken when she spoke of Miyuki's passing to the Great

Cycle. Are you safe? Are you well?" Kit nodded weakly in response. Her eyes welled up at the mention of her friend's death.

"We'll deal with Powder, and Rimes, and Lieutenant Karr later today." A hint of *something* crossed Kit's face when she mentioned Lieutenant Karr.

"And what of Indie? I trust he is well." Kit instantly blushed at the question. Even through the swirling blue and white smoke that partially obscured her from view, her skin darkened considerably. A deep shame crept into Danny's heart. He had hoped, beyond reason, that Kit had been hiding her feelings for him and that, if she hadn't met Indie, someday they'd be together. Seeing how happy she was with the young Nomad crushed his soul. But she was his best friend, and he cherished that more than life itself. He smiled warmly. "I see." Kit reddened significantly more.

"Why did you need to speak with me?"

Thank Titan! Her simple question gave him a way out of the awkward predicament he had gotten himself into.

"I heard the king attacked Aarall. Your army here is not fully ready, but we could send them south to you, to help you reinforce the City Watch." Kit tied her mouth up into a perfect pink bow.

"What does Rusty think you should do? I could ask my father if he thinks we need help, too."

"Rusty wants us to attack Faol's army at Ravenlord, or at least her father does. It makes sense to me, too, but that was before we heard the king had turned on his own."

"Then it's probably best to follow Rusty's plans. She's much better at military tactics than I'll ever be." A smile crept across her face. "I'm just a blunt instrument that smashes whatever's in front of me."

"Oh, Kitten. You are so much more than a blunt instrument. Surely you see that."

A light rap on Danny's door brought their conversation to an immediate halt. Before he could speak, the door swung open and Calian stepped in. Her mouth flopped open while she ran her hand over her heavily tattooed bald scalp.

"You're naked!" The woman blinked, unsure what to say or do.

"Your naked?" Kit asked, her voice raising an octave or two. "Why in Helja are you naked?"

"What are you doing with that orb on your lap?" Calian asked. Danny couldn't decide where to focus his attention. His gaze flitted back and forth between Kit and the woman standing inside his bedroom.

"Danny?" Kit said. "What are you doing?"

"I'm not naked," he shouted. "I'm talking with Kit. I'm just not wearing a shirt." He threw back the sheet that had been covering him from the waist down. Calian shrieked and turned away. "I'm wearing trousers," Danny said as he leapt up from his bed. "Kit, I'm not naked. I have breaches on. I'm... just not wearing a shirt."

"Why are you shirtless?" Kit's eyes were bulging out of her head. "You asked me to call you!"

"Kit, I'll talk to you later." Before she could reply, he stuffed the dragon tear into his pocket and wheeled around on Calian. "Why would you just walk into my bedroom without an invitation to do so?"

"Why are you talking to another man's mate, half dressed? That's the more important question."

Danny walked across the room to the chair on which he had tossed his bright green tunic. He snatched it up and pulled it on. When his head popped out of the neck hole, he noticed Calian was watching him intently. "Like what you see?"

It was the woman's turn to blush. Unfortunately, the way her eyes narrowed suggested that the blush wasn't embarrassment. No, not even close. "A moment ago, you were trying to do whatever it was you were doing with another man's woman, and now you're trying to turn your charms on me. Do you have no limits?"

Danny plopped to the floor, sitting cross-legged. He knitted his fingers behind his head and crumpled into a ball. "I'm a fool."

"You won't get an argument from me," Calian replied. Her voice was a bit more tempered than it had been a moment ago.

"I've been in love with her since the day she came to the Temple. When she looked at me, all she saw was a friend." He stared up at the woman who had taken a few steps toward him. "I was content with being friends, at first. As time went by, our friendship grew, but she treated me like a big brother and not as a potential mate. I tried to make her jealous by flaunting my *acquaintances* with her, but it did no good. She was only ever happy for me that I had found someone to be with. She was so sweet and so innocent. When the phoenix chose me, I thought, maybe, she would see that there was more to me than... just me." Calian knelt down beside the man, perhaps offering to help ease his troubled soul.

"But she had already given her love to another?" Danny nodded and dipped his head again, unable to look up at the woman.

"When we first met," Danny said, raising his head, "I thought maybe you and me..." He let the words hang there for a moment. Calian didn't look away. She didn't react at all. "And then I saw her again here. All those feelings I've had for her came flooding back. She had changed so much, and yet, she was still the sweet girl I knew at the Temple."

"And now?"

"I know she'll never be mine and I need to move on with my life." A hint of a grin appeared at the corner of the Berrat's mouth. He locked onto Calian's bright green eyes.

"You think I would want to be with you? Do I look like the type of woman who wants to be somebody's second choice?" In a single motion, the woman popped up to her feet. Danny groaned while his head once again drooped low. "You're wanted in the war room. Let me help you up."

Danny took the woman's outstretched hand and allowed her to pull him to his feet. She was incredibly strong. In the seriousness of the conversation, he had forgotten that she was a dog soldier, a dire wolf shifter.

Chapter Four

Dwarven Artistry

The sounds of steel on stone rang out as Kit and Indie walked down the stairway that led to the rear of the Temple's nave. There were a good deal of angry shouts carrying over the din. Most of them sounded like they were coming from Coldforge.

"No, no, no. Ye can't be tryin' to do that. Just clear the rubble from the outside o' the room. We need to keep the paths to the exit open."

Kit stepped through the doorway and carefully surveyed the activity. Dozens of people were working to clear the debris from the nave floor. She grimaced slightly at those who were busy with the more gruesome task of removing dead bodies. These were the soldiers who had been crushed when Father Hoarfrost brought the statue of Titan down on them. With mop and pail and scraper, others were trying to clean the gore from the tiled floor.

"They got what they deserved," Kit said. "They had to know they were doing wrong." Inside, her stomach was roiling at the sight, but she refused to look away. Coldforge came striding towards the couple. He was covered in dust from head to toe. His bright orange beard appeared nearly white.

"The dwarf who designed this structure was a genius." The dwarven prince stretched his hands toward the domed ceiling. "I think this room could stand without the pillars at all. The way the structure leans in on itself..."

"Would you say that it's a marvel of dwarven ingenuity?" Indie asked. Coldforge's eyes went wide, and the dwarf nodded furiously.

"Triple redundancy," he replied, brushing some of the stone dust from his face. "Never have I seen the likes of this; at least, not outside the halls of Goldstone or Mitril. Truly wondrous it is." Coldforge's eyes brightened. "Ah, Captain, yer timing is excellent. Can ye lend me some of your stronger members? These people who are helping are doing their best, but they lack the strength to move some of the bigger pieces. I've been showing them how to move the stones with oiled sand, but it still takes a strong back to move the blocks. If'n I had me kin, we could do this with ease, but the people here are... well, they're not dwarves."

Captain Harding chuckled as he approached. "Would twenty of my strongest people be enough?" The dwarf stroked his beard as he considered the question.

"Thirty would be better, but if you can't spare that many, I will make do."

"I'll send an acolyte to the barracks," Father Hoarfrost said as he joined the group. "If that's okay with you, Captain." It seemed the hope of stronger backs appeased Coldforge. He turned back to his task, immediately shouting out his displeasure at those who were not doing it *the dwarven way*.

"Kit, we need to talk." Father Hoarfrost said. "We need to discuss the prisoners."

A knot immediately twisted in Kit's stomach. Just the thought of Brother Powder and Brother Rimes got her blood boiling. She wasn't certain that she could hold her daemon self back once she started her interrogation.

Father Hoarfrost turned to Indie and inclined his head slightly at the young man. "We will not be needing you for this discussion. These are Temple matters." Kit felt her boyfriend recoil at the words. She could practically see his heart thumping against his ribs. With each heartbeat, Indie's face became darker.

"But Captain Harding isn't a part of the Temple."

Kit groaned. She had never seen Indie act like a petulant child before. Was he still harboring resentment for the way she had reacted to him being Fury's apprentice? His sudden change in body language announced that he immediately regretted his choice of words.

"Forgive me, Father. Forgive me, Captain. I just..."

"We understand, lad," Captain Harding said, grasping the young man by the shoulder. The captain applied enough pressure to make Indie wince. He would not let Indie's childish outburst off with a simple apology. "Kit wouldn't be invited to attend these meetings either, except we need her special gifts to separate lies from truths."

Indie still looked like Father's words had delivered a solid gut punch, but nodded to the two men before letting his finger slip into Kit's hand. "I'll stay here and help Coldforge. Come find me when you're finished."

⸨⸨⸨◈⸩⸩⸩

Father Hoarfrost led the way down a set of stairs, forced to stoop to avoid banging his head on the low ceilings. Neither Kit nor Captain Harding had ever been here before. They were in the bell tower, below a trap door in the floor that was all but invisible. The air quickly turned cool and moist as they wended their way down the tightly spiraled set of stairs.

"I want to speak with Brother Rimes again," Father Hoarfrost said to nobody in particular, voicing his thoughts aloud.

"You need to keep your emotions under control," Kit's father said to her. "Give the man a chance to talk without interruption. You will learn more from him being quiet than you will if you're the one speaking."

Kit nodded her understanding, drawing a grin from her father. Captain Harding struggled to believe that she could do what had been asked of her. In all the years he had known Kit, even before she'd become aware he was her father, the girl couldn't hold her tongue to save her life. Words spilled from her mouth without consideration of their consequences. Despite this minor fault, he was so proud of the young woman she had become. He could not have hoped for more in a daughter.

Ever-burning torches lit the way as they descended the smooth-cut stone stairs. The temperature continued to drop and yet the air was still fresh; unlike the City Watch dungeons that smelled of rot and mold. The captain wasn't sure how deep they had gone, but he guessed they were several stories beneath ground level when they reached the bottom.

"This way," Father said, as he stooped beneath a low stone archway. Kit passed under it easily without having to bend, which made the captain laugh to himself, especially because he had to hunch severely to make it through. Clearly, this was more dwarven construction. It seemed they'd had their own stature in mind when they created these dungeons.

"These were the dwarves' living quarters," Father Hoarfrost said, as though he had read the captain's mind. He was still hunched over as he walked down the comfortably wide hallway. "Back when they constructed the Temple, they created these rooms for their own purposes. Once the Temple was complete, they returned home, leaving these quarters behind. The ceilings are so low though, they're almost unusable. The enchantments they wove into the stonework were quite impressive. They work nicely as dungeons, not that we have much use for such devices. Holding prisoners is not Titan's way."

The trio walked past the first door. It looked to be a thick slab of granite with a single brass handle. Two angry-looking priests stood on either side of the entrance.

"The next cell," Father Hoarfrost said. "We'll come back for Brother Powder. I want to talk with Brother Rimes first." Kit growled when she heard who was behind the door.

"You're going to have to stand in line to *talk* with Powder, Father." A thick vein had appeared on Captain Harding's temple. It was pulsing hard, turning redder with each beat of his heart. Unbidden memories of how Brother Powder had mercilessly tortured innocents were tearing at his mind. Brother Powder had killed so many people in his efforts to make the captain change his fealty. As much as it ripped the soul from the man to see Sister Miyuki endure such pain, he could not give in to Brother Powder's demands. Had he proclaimed his loyalty to Karr and the king, many more lives would have been lost.

There were two more priests standing outside Brother Rime's cell. They had the same surly disposition as the pair guarding Brother Powder. "Step aside, if you will." Father Hoarfrost motioned with his hands, shooing away the two women who were barring the door. With practiced precision, they stepped to the side and crossed their fists over their chest. With a simple push on its handle, the thick granite slab door swung inward.

Across the nearly empty room was Brother Rimes, kneeling in the far corner, praying. He didn't acknowledge their entrance, other than to bob his head slightly. Captain Harding closed the door behind the group. While Kit and Father Hoarfrost approached the man, the captain stayed back and barred the exit with his massive frame.

"I have committed no crime." Brother Rimes didn't move from his spot, nor did he turn to address those who had just entered his room. Kit recoiled slightly at the comment. The captain couldn't tell if it was in anger because the priest had lied, or in surprise because he had spoken the truth.

"Or so you believe," Kit said. A hint of a grin appeared on Captain Harding's face as his daughter immediately ignored his instructions for her to remain silent. It took Kit even less time than he had expected before she would break her word. If her interjection had bothered Father Hoarfrost, he didn't let it show.

"I took no part in any of the king's actions." Brother Rimes rocked back onto his heels before slowly standing. His face was quite red, and dried tracks stained his cheeks. "Any actions I took during the king's occupation were not voluntary. I had no power over my body, even as my mind screamed at whoever had taken control of me."

Father Hoarfrost turned to Kit; his eyebrows raised. "Was any part of what he just said false?" Kit didn't respond right away. She seemed to consider the high priest's question as she replayed the brother's words in her mind. Kit shrugged without ever looking directly at her mentor. "This is as much as we've been able to get from him, Sister. Do you have questions for Brother Rimes you'd like to ask?"

"If I could, Father, I would like to ask him a question." Captain Harding stepped away from the door and moved within arm's reach of Brother Rimes. The high priest inclined his head.

"If you have not been a part of the king's plans, why have you hated my daughter all these years?" Kit's ears turned bright red. "Why have you made her life here so difficult?"

"I didn't appreciate the special treatment she received." Brother Rimes had to crane his neck slightly to maintain his gaze on the captain. There was almost no emotion on his face as he spoke. "Others could only rise through the ranks with time and hard work. She was made an acolyte the day she arrived. Other children waited years for such an honor."

"And because of that, you hated me?" Kit's ears had become so red they were practically glowing. "I had no control over what benefits Father Hoarfrost had given me. I didn't even know I had received anything special." Captain Harding moved closer to his daughter, silently offering her his support in the conversation.

"I never hated you." Brother Rimes stood taller and cleared his throat. "I trust Father Hoarfrost with my life. I trust him to do what is best for this Temple and for the people of this city. If he felt you were worthy of such honors, then I did, too." Kit's mouth flopped open. Captain Harding's similar reaction followed shortly thereafter. "If you were worthy of his trust, I planned on doing everything I could to make you the strongest priest you could be. The Temple coddled none of its faithful. We priests become stronger through our suffering. It tempers us like a forge tempers steel. If we did not sufficiently challenge you, you would not reach your full potential and you would have squandered your gifts."

"But…" Kit glared at Father Hoarfrost. "Is this true?"

"I do not dictate how the priests choose to conduct their training. I offer guidance when requested, but otherwise, I leave it up to them."

"Why did Miyuki not trust you then? The last time I spoke with her, she seemed to think that you were up to no good." Brother Rimes squinted and rubbed his stubbled chin. He lowered his head for a moment before making an odd clucking sound.

"I remember," he said, crossing his arms over his chest. "That was shortly after you beat me down in the nave. She asked me, point blank, if I was involved in a conspiracy against you. She said there were whispers of a priest who was not acting *normal*. I suggested she speak with Brother Powder, as she might find her answers with him." The man's face sagged, and a sneer appeared. "That was the last time I spoke with Miyuki. May Titan guide her to the Great Cycle."

"Why didn't you say something?" Captain Harding was on the priest like a lion taking a lamb. He grabbed the man by the front of his robes and effortlessly hoisted him off his feet. The priest offered no resistance. His expression remained stoic. "It was shortly after that..." His words faltered as he tried to speak. "It was then I lost control of my body. I became an unwilling passenger in my skin, unable to direct my actions."

Kit placed her hand on her father's side and patted it lightly. "Do you have any idea who it was that took control of your body? Did she ever speak to you?" Brother Rimes' head cocked at the question.

"How did you know it was a woman's voice I was hearing?" Brother Rimes turned to the captain. "I swear, I was not responsible for any of these foul things. If you could please return me to the floor... this is quite uncomfortable."

"It will make you a better priest," the captain said as he twisted his grip on the man's robes. "Suffering is good for the soul."

"Captain," Father Hoarfrost said, his voice not so gentle. "He is innocent of what we are holding him for." The captain turned to Kit for confirmation. When she nodded, he released his grip, letting the priest drop. With surprising grace, he landed softly on his feet. He shook his shoulders, helping his robe to settle over his body.

"What did the woman say to you?" Kit took a step between her father and Brother Rimes. "Did she say her name?"

"No, she never told me who she was, even though I asked constantly. I figured that as long as I had control of my mind, I was going to make her lose hers. I pestered her continuously, mercilessly. It was only in anger that she ever spoke to me. All she ever said was for me to shut up."

Kit sighed and lowered her head. "We should release him, Father. He is innocent in this matter. I find no deception in his words. Everything he said was truthful, to the best of his knowledge."

Father Hoarfrost closed his eyes for a moment before turning his gaze upon the captain. "Ray, my friend, even though this is Temple business, I will allow you to have a say in the matter."

The captain rolled his shoulders. He didn't want this man to be set free. He wanted to exact punishment on him for the crimes done against the Temple and the city. He wanted him to feel what Sister Miyuki went through.

"I see no reason to detain him further." He motioned to the door with his head. "But I will not be so lenient with Brother Powder. I will not allow him to keep his life after everything he's done; after what he did to Miyuki."

Kit's expression turned dark. "Let's do it."

CHAPTER FIVE

THE GOOD, THE BAD, AND THE ESCAPED

"What is to happen to me?" Brother Powder bowed his head while he kneeled in the center of the makeshift dungeon cell. A thick iron collar hung from around his neck.

Captain Harding slammed the granite slab door with a thunderous boom. His hands were clenched into tight fists. The tension in his face and neck told just how desperately he wanted to crush the life out of the man. "You're going to die. I learned a lot while you tortured me and Sister Miyuki. I can bring you to the edge and my daughter can either bring you back or push you into the abyss. I'm hoping it will be the former because I plan on punishing you for days."

Kit's eyes widened. She knew the captain was speaking the truth. She lunged forward, putting herself between her father and the despicable piece of gutter scum kneeling on the floor.

"Tell us everything, and I'll give you a death befitting your station within the Temple." Kit threw her hand up to hold off her father. The cords on his neck strained against his skin while a deep red vein pulsed on his forehead.

"It's Aithlin's fault." The words were barely out of Brother Powder's mouth when Kit's boot found his chin, snapping his head to the side, sending him sprawling across the floor. He laid there, motionless, for several seconds before rolling onto his back. His fingers went to the thick cold-iron collar around his neck. It looked identical to the one Brother Rimes had been wearing. Kit's brow wrinkled.

"What is it?" The captain moved up beside his daughter.

"He believes he's speaking the truth. He believes it was Lin's fault."

The captain took two quick steps, snatched the priest by his braids, and dragged him to his feet. "How? How is this Lin's fault?" The priest offered the captain no resistance. Instead, he simply gave the man a smug, obsequious smile.

"She showed me how easy it was to bend people; how malleable they are." The smug smile turned into a sneer. It was, perhaps, a miscalculation on his part. The big man holding him tightened his grip on the prisoner's braids and swung him into the wall. There was a muffled crack when his face smashed into the stonework. Brother Powder remained standing for a moment before slumping to the floor.

The captain turned to his daughter. "Can you revive him?"

"I can," Father Hoarfrost said. He knelt beside Brother Powder and placed his hand on the unconscious priest's back. A moment later, a pulse of pale-yellow light burst out. The old priest picked himself up off the floor with a groan and nodded to the captain. "You may continue."

Kit kicked the downed man in the ribs. "She taught you that people are greedy, and you figured that was reason enough to torture my father? You figured it was enough to torture and murder Miyuki?" Brother Powder groaned and rolled onto his side, clutching at his ribs.

"No." The priest grimaced as he spoke. "She showed me that fighting against the king was futile. If it wasn't me helping him, it would have been someone else. The king promised me riches in return for my actions. He promised me death if I didn't." Brother Powder's eyes suddenly turned wild. "He has terrible, cruel, vile people working for him. What was the point? With or without my assistance, he was going to take the city. Why die if I didn't need to?"

Kit kicked him in the side a second time. The crack of the man's ribs echoed off the walls, followed immediately by his screams of agony. Father Hoarfrost stepped forward to heal his injuries again, but the captain put his thick arm out to block his way. "Let him live with it for a few minutes."

The downed priest clutched at his ribs and moaned. "Father." His words came out in a hoarse croak. "Father, please help me."

"I'll help you," Kit said as she knelt beside the man. Her father tried to intervene but paused when her eyes flashed golden. "Where does it hurt?" The stricken priest cringed and pointed to where Kit had kicked him. "Here?" Kit asked as she jammed her fist into his side, eliciting another bout of screams. "Is that better?" A crazed look filled Brother Powder's eyes. He muttered something. Perhaps he was offering a prayer to Titan. Perhaps he was calling on him for help. Either way, it earned him another solid jab from the little priest.

"Titan can't hear you." Inky blackness crept in from the corners of Kit's eyes. The swirling pools of gold faded away until her eyes were glistening orbs of pure ebony. A guttural chuckle echoed in her throat. She leaned in close to Brother Powder, her whispering lips brushing against his ear. "Tell me again why you murdered Miyuki." Kit turned her palm upwards next to the man's face. A lick of flames appeared, hovering barely above her open hand. "Why did you need to hang her, to burn her, to make her last moments a living Helja?"

Brother Powder licked his lips. His eyes sought Father Hoarfrost, hoping that he might intervene, hoping that he might show him mercy. He did not. With a honey-sweet smile, the fallen priest turned his gaze back to Kit, his eyes widening. "I needed to prove my loyalty to the king, and to Lord Martelle, as well. He didn't believe I would betray the Temple."

The memory of Lin's childhood friend rushed into Kit's mind. Lin was devastated when she'd learned of Martelle's treachery. There had been no look of satisfaction on the woman's face, though, when she ended his life after blinding the man. With that act of vengeance, a piece of Lin had died that day.

Kit kept her voice low and metered. "You murdered the sweetest person who has ever entered this sanctuary to prove your loyalty to a monster. We would have stood with you against the king. You declared your loyalty to Titan and at the first sign of trouble, you turned your back on him." Kit pressed her flaming palm against the man's cheek. The screams and the acrid scent of burning flesh filled the room.

"Kit, stop!" Captain Harding grabbed the girl by the back of her armor and dragged her away. "Don't, please. I can't watch another person die like that." Through the writhing agony, the slightest hint of relief peeked out from

Brother Powder. Kit immediately acquiesced, allowing her father to pull her away. The captain stepped forward and grabbed the burned priest by the throat and hoisted him into the air. "Take off his boots."

"Enough," Father Hoarfrost said, placing his hand on Captain Harding's forearm. "He can't talk if you're choking him."

"I haven't heard everything I need to hear." Kit grabbed Brother Powder's flailing leg and yanked off a boot. "He has more to share with us."

The high priest tightened his grip. "Captain, release him. Now."

Following Father Hoarfrost's instructions, the captain released his grip and let the prisoner drop to the ground. Kit still had a firm grip on his leg, forcing Brother Powder to fall awkwardly to the floor. He renewed his screams for a moment before his voice went silent. Kit tossed his boot at him and moved to pull off the other.

"Sister Kit." The high priest's voice carried an icy firmness. "Release the man."

"But Father." She looked up, her expression a mixture of rage and resolve. "He may have more information to give us." The old man shook his head, his long gray braid swaying lazily across his back.

"No, Sister. He does not. We do not seek revenge. We deliver justice." Kit's face soured at the man's words. She pulled her lips back in a snarl. With a hateful twist, she yanked the second boot off Brother Powder and tossed it against the wall.

Captain Harding sucked in a sharp breath. "No, Kit. Father's right. You need to stop."

A look of helplessness peered through Kit's hatred. Swirls of gold pushed back the blackness that had filled her eyes. "How shall he be punished? He needs to pay for his sins against the Temple."

Father's expression softened. "What punishment would you mete out? I leave the decision to you."

"He needs to suffer." Captain Harding was beside himself. Like his daughter, he wanted this man to pay for his crimes and he wanted him to pay in pain. Kit's gaze flitted between the two men.

"He will." Kit turned and pressed her palm against Brother Powder's broken ribs. His eyes snapped open, and he screeched out. A deep golden aura burst forth from Kit's hands, her head snapping back as she turned her gaze toward the sky. The glow poured out over the broken man, coalescing around his face and torso. As the glow intensified, Kit's face twisted in agony. When the pain drained from her expression, so did the golden aura. "We will keep this collar on him, and he will spend his life in the dungeons. Without Titan's grace, he is harmless. He will spend the rest of his life regretting his decisions. He will suffer as we do, unable to repair the hole in our hearts left by Sister Miyuki."

Brother Powder's hands trembled, and he let out a huge breath. His look of relief appeared to give Kit a look of satisfaction. Her eyelids slowly dropped while her expression changed to one of pure bliss. When she opened her eyes, they were filled with a golden glow. She leaned over the priest and caught his gaze. The glow in her eyes intensified. As it did, the disgraced priest writhed.

"You will relive the atrocities you committed every minute of every day until Titan frees you of this torment." Brother Powder wailed. He closed his eyes tight, trying to banish the visions that were searing into his mind.

Kit turned to Father Hoarfrost. "That will be the punishment for his crime. He will feel the pain, the despair, the sorrow of every person he hurt. He will relive their experiences, one by one, until his last breath."

"A fitting fate," Father Hoarfrost said. "I didn't know you could do that."

"She is her mother's daughter," Captain Harding said, moving closer to Kit. His chest swelled with pride at his child's decision. He didn't fully understand what she had just done, but the anguish on Brother Powder's face was enough for him. "Let's go see Karr, or what's left of him."

⸺⸺◈⸺⸺

"Karr has escaped." Indie came running through the City Watch barracks' front gate. There were several guards following him. They were all shouting at the captain, their voices frantic.

"Find him. Now." The captain's voice practically knocked his people off stride. Like a stream parting around an enormous boulder, his guards ran past and continued towards the city's front gate.

"What did you do?" Kit yelled.

Indie skid to a halt. He tried in vain to keep his distance from the girl as she continued to bear down on him. He held his hands up in front of himself in a defensive pose, trying to ward off Kit's fury.

"I did nothing. He was gone when I went to look in on him. I swear to Titan, I did nothing."

"Boy, what were you even doing in the dungeons?" Captain Harding was only a few paces behind Kit, his long strides quickly outpacing his daughter's. "You were supposed to be with Coldforge. We came for you, but you were gone."

"And he said you left right after we did." Kit kept pace with her father while Indie continued to back peddle.

"I... I just wanted to do something worthwhile. I wanted to be a part of healing the city." Indie stopped trying to move away, deciding to stand his ground. Kit glared at him as she thundered past.

"Come with me," Captain Harding said, grabbing the young man by his collar, practically hoisting him into the air. "Tell me what we're walking into."

"He's gone." The two words came out sounding like a croak. Indie spun around, trying to maintain his footing while the captain continued to drag him towards the barracks. Several of the City Watch came running up to the group.

The captain looked about to see how many of the Watch were within the range of his voice. "Karr's escaped. A promotion to anyone who can find him. A cycle's extra pay if you can bring him to me, alive." Those members who had been approaching stopped in their tracks and took off at a dead run.

"Are you sure he wasn't just eaten?" Kit asked, pulling her war hammer from its sheath.

Indie struggled to maintain his composure under the intensity of the girl's glare and the iron grip of the captain. He suddenly wondered if this was how

Kit's enemies felt when she bared down on them. Just dealing with her annoyance might be enough to loosen a man's bowels.

When they got to the top of the stairs, the captain finally released his grip on Indie's collar. Kit drew her war hammer and called on its brilliance, instantly illuminating the nearly pitch-black stairwell.

"Not eaten. Escaped." Indie tried to straighten his clothing. "When I went to see him, to see if the vampire had already destroyed Karr, I found his cell door ripped off its hinges. The vampire was cowering in the corner of his cell. When I entered the room, he whimpered and curled up in a ball.

"Cowering?" Captain Harding gave Indie an incredulous look. "That vile creature was frightened?"

Indie swallowed hard. Tension was creeping up his back, twisting the muscles in his neck. "Whatever freed Karr, it terrified the vampire." Indie's head swiveled about. "Where's Father Hoarfrost?"

"He's freeing Brother Rimes and making sure that Brother Powder never again sees the light of day." Kit barely had time to respond before she bolted down the stairs. She continued to pick up speed, taking the stairs two at a time. Both men struggled to keep up. She didn't slow until she made her way to the barracks' dungeon entrance.

Indie hardly remembered wending his way into the barracks' cellar. He was busy processing what Kit had said, how Brother Rimes had been released, and that Brother Powder was still alive. He had expected the Temple to have executed them both for their crimes.

Kit and the captain paused outside Karr's cell. Indie's description of the room's door having been ripped from its hinges did not come close to the reality of the situation. The thick iron door was dented and twisted beyond comprehension. The captain gave his daughter a quizzical look, and they both stepped inside. Indie followed close behind. The pair were standing in the middle of the cell, their faces slack. Just as Indie had said, the vampire had curled himself into a small ball in the room's corner. He continued to whimper, refusing to look up.

"What could have done this?" Captain Harding asked. "I've seen nothing that could mangle a door like that." Fury appeared behind Kit.

"A dragon could have done that. Any of us could have broken this poor creature's mind as well. We dragons are truly wondrous beings of power and awesomeness. Our very presence can instill fear in anyone, even in the gods themselves."

Kit ignored the draken visage and turned to her father, her face twisted with disdain. "If we feed him, do you think he could tell us what happened?"

"Unlikely," Indie responded. "He's too far gone to regain any of his humanity."

"You could mix blood with one of Lin's marvelous rejuvenation potions," Fury offered. "If his mind is twisted beyond repair, it won't help, but it may be enough to allow him to recount what he witnessed."

Kit looked to her father, who shrugged in response. Nobody really had any idea how a healing potion or a rejuvenation potion might affect a vampire.

"I'll get some potions," Indie said. "But where do you want me to get the blood?"

"Use mine," Kit said. "I'm the only one with natural resistance to his compulsion. I'll be able to pull away before he feeds too long."

"You cannot feed him," Fury said, shaking his head frantically. "Feeding him celestial blood may have unexpected side effects. It's not a risk worth taking. Neither you nor your father can feed him."

"I'll do it," Indie said. "After I get back with the potions, he can drink some of my blood."

The captain snatched the young man by his upper arm, his grip like a vise. "No. You'll do no such thing. This vampire isn't going anywhere. Whatever he saw can wait. Right now, we search for Karr."

"Father, he may supply us with clues. Karr didn't escape, he was broken out by whomever got past the guards and did all this. Don't you think it's worth learning more?"

CHAPTER SIX

THE HUNT FOR KARR

The news of Karr's escape reached the Temple in record time. Within the hour, there was a contingent of priests and acolytes at the City Watch barracks, assisting in the search. Captain Harding's small office was bursting at the seams with people, everyone desperate for instructions on how to proceed.

"Where are the boys?" Kit asked, suddenly aware that Runt and Lump were missing.

"They're with Coldforge, trying to pick up Karr's trail," her father said, rubbing the thick stubble on his chin. "They lost the scent in the barracks' kitchens."

"I'm guessing they were distracted by food, all three of them." Indie shook his head. There was a hint of a laugh in his voice.

Captain Harding scrubbed his face with a thick, meaty hand. "You don't give them enough credit. My people made a lot of food last night. Many got drunk. They spilled food all over the floors, but the boys ignored it all. Well, most of it, at any rate. There was one spot that they focused on. There was an overturned kettle of stew. It had poured out in all directions."

"A trapdoor." Lin pursed her lips and nodded. "The kettle was concealing a trap door beneath it. They were still following Karr's scent. It's difficult to ignore your baser instincts."

"How could they put a cast-iron kettle over the door once they were inside?" Indie asked, his voice dripping with skepticism.

"Whoever freed Karr hid him in the cellar and then left another way, or they used magic to move the kettle over the door once they were inside," Silverleaf offered. "I have a scroll of levitation that could do something like that."

"Where would you get such a scroll?" Father Hoarfrost asked, his voice accusatory.

"Not all of us are blessed by Titan as you are, Father." Lin jutted her chin out. "We find other ways to get things done. I make potions and enchantments, and Silverleaf here, well…"

"Even before failing my trials, I didn't think I'd ever become a priest, so I spent a lot of time learning to make scrolls." Silverleaf withered under the high priest's scrutiny; his small, pointed ears turning a bright red. He tried to slide in behind Amara, using her as a giant shield, but she was having none of it. With a quick swoop of her hand, she pushed him towards the high priest. The two glared at one another for a moment.

"Of what happens under the Temple roof, it seems I know half as much as I thought I did," the old man said. "Yet further proof my time here as High Priest has passed."

There was a stunned silence for several seconds before Kit broke the awkward moment. "Maybe we should head to the kitchens?" She gave the high priest a sideways look as she passed him, heading out the door. *What, in the name of Titan, did that mean?* Father Hoarfrost hadn't been himself since he'd brought down the statue on the king's men, but he'd been badly injured and had suffered for a long time before being rescued. Such prolonged exposure to that kind of extreme pain would sap the life out of anybody, even the most revered man in Arnnor.

Lin twirled a finger through her hair before tucking it behind an ear. "Kit, if you and your father want to go check for the trapdoor, Indie and I can go question the vampire." When Indie shook his head, Lin eagerly pressed on. "Come on, Indie. The ring the little blue freaks made for me is exceptionally good, but even with it, I can't fight their compulsion the way you can."

Indie looked to Kit to gauge her reaction. They all knew going to visit the vampire was going directly against her father's orders. Kit also knew it was likely the fastest way to get answers. "Fine, but if he kills you both, I will not speak to either of you ever again."

"What about us?" Silverleaf asked, unsure which group he and Amara should follow. He reminded Kit of Lump when he was confused, kind of sad and super cute.

"Go with Kit," Indie said, not giving the little priest a chance to answer. "The fewer of us with the vampire, the better. If he recovers his full power, he's going to be difficult to resist."

⚬⚬⚬⚬⚬◇⚬⚬⚬⚬⚬

The state of the barracks' kitchen was far worse than Kit had expected. The floor wasn't covered with just food. There was also an ungodly amount of vomit and over a half dozen City Watch guards passed out on the floor. Two of them were covered in messes of their own making.

"I let them sleep it off," Captain Harding said. "They needed a chance to blow off some steam last night." Kit's upper lip curled up at his comment. "I suppose I could have had them taken to a cot someplace, and maybe cleaned up a bit."

Kit shook her head and moved over to one of the drunken guards. She bent low, putting her ear to the man's chest. "Father, this man's not unconscious. He's dead."

"Sweet Titan," Captain Harding said as the duo quickly moved to each of the soldiers and checked for signs of life. "How? Why didn't I see that?"

Silverleaf made a gagging noise when Amara rolled a soldier onto her back. "There are no visible wounds. I have no idea what killed them."

"Look at their eyes," Silverleaf said, pulling open the eyelids of the woman. "They're full of blood."

"Sweet Titan." Kit had moved next to the half elf, peering over his shoulder. "What could cause such a thing?"

The little priest practically jumped out of her skin at the sound of the cast-iron kettle smashing against the wall. "When I get a hold of Karr, I will rip him in two. By my hands or by my sword, the man will die."

Captain Harding was standing in front of a trap door. The outline made plainly visible as the stew's gravy seeped into the cracks around the entrance.

"I can't believe we missed that," Coldforge said as he pushed his way through the crowd that had assembled around the trap door. The boys were by his side. He clomped across the smooth tiled floor over to the trap door and ran his hand along its surface. His eyes brightened suddenly as he pushed on one of the smaller stones, causing it to depress with a loud click. When he pulled his hand away, the door slowly swung downward. More of the stew poured over the lip, splashing down a set of carved stone stairs.

"Ye must have had a good number of me kin helping to build this city. The workmanship is impressive. I wonder what this building's original purpose was. It seems a bit much for a simple kitchen."

"Wouldn't know," Captain Harding said, knocking Coldforge aside as he charged down the stairs. Puddles of gravy covered every step, making the big man's movements awkward. There was a moment of silence before the captain called out. "Holy Helja! There are freshly dug tunnels down here. Firebugs I'm guessing."

Kit and the others made their way to the cellar. The boys barrelled down after them, practically upending Kit as they ran past. Their noses were immediately pressed tight to the ground as they moved around the cavern that was once a cold cellar. Lump barked when he picked up Karr's trail and went bounding down one tunnel, with Runt following close behind him.

"Lump! Runt! Get back here!" Kit called out as the boys quickly outdistanced the rest of the group. Even running at full speed, the others had no hope of keeping up with the canines. After several excruciating minutes, filled mostly by the sound of a gasping Coldforge as he tried desperately to catch his breath, the boys returned.

"Stay with us," Kit scolded. She gave them both a good scratch, thankful they had come when called. "Lump, what do you smell?"

Kit frowned when Lump started barking at her. "Can you change into your human form and just tell me?"

Lump's body morphed into that of a young man with shaggy, golden-brown hair. "We don't know the smells. Some were older, some were newer, easier to follow. The man you seek was among the fresh smells." Lump paused for a moment. "Something was with him. It smelled of ash and something foul. It burned our noses."

Captain Harding scowled. "I'm guessing that foul smelling thing is what freed Karr. After seeing how terrified the vampire was, I'm guessing that whatever that creature is, it's not pleasant." Captain Harding stared down the tunnel, lit up by a ghastly green glow. "Um, what is it that's lighting up the tunnels?"

"That's the leavings of the firebugs," Coldforge said as he inspected the tunnel wall. "The ground here was once full of blightroot. It's one of their favorite foods."

"You know these creatures?" Captain Harding reached up to touch the green slime.

"I wouldn't do that," Coldforge said, pulling the big man's hand away from the wall. "It's a powerful acid. It'll burn through your skin in seconds. The pain is excruciating."

The captain yanked his hand away, putting it behind his back like a child, denying that he was going to touch a hot stove.

"I know these bugs well," Coldforge said, his orange beard dancing on his face. "We use them to help us mine the mountains. So long as you treat them well, they are immensely helpful. They'll even let us ride them once we build up enough trust."

"Their spike tossing friends are definitely not friendly," Captain Harding said. He was still inspecting the green slime. "I lost several good people to those creatures. I built an entire training regime around learning how to defend against them."

"Ah, they're not so bad. They're the bug's protectors. They can sense yer aggression and they respond in kind. If you show them no hostility, they leave you alone." Coldforge rubbed at his beard. "But they get upset pretty easy. It might be best if ye just give them a wide berth, if you get my meaning."

"Good to know," Kit said, cutting the conversation off. "Runt, can you carry our friend here?"

Runt bent down to let Coldforge scramble onto his back. The young dire wolf seemed to take great pride in carrying the dwarf. He was just plain happy around the stocky little man. A pang of jealousy ripped through Kit. She didn't really understand why. She was happy that Runt was happy. Deep inside, perhaps, she feared he was pulling away, ready to live his life on his own. She shook her head, quickly dismissing the thought. From the time she found him as a pup, she and Runt were inseparable, and they'd be together forever.

When Runt bolted ahead with Coldforge whooping it up on his back, the pang returned.

⌒⌒⌒⌒◇⌒⌒⌒⌒

The group followed Karr's trail for many minutes before the tunnel climbed towards the surface. Further up the corridor, the bright afternoon sun illuminated the passageway. It seemed they had finally reached the warren's end. The stuffy air lightened, filling Kit's nostrils with the scents of trees and wildflowers. The rush of relief she felt ended as soon as she stepped into the light.

The tunnel exited between two large monuments. "He's gone," Kit growled.

Silverleaf grimaced when he emerged from the tunnel shortly after Kit. "We're in the city cemetery," he said, clutching his arms around himself. "All this time, we've been wandering around under the graves."

"They're just the remains of loved ones," Captain Harding said, his voice far gentler than one might expect from such a gruff, burly man.

"Ya," Silverleaf said, still frowning. "Until somebody reanimates them, and then they're shambling corpses, looking to suck the life out of you." While the captain grunted at the remark, Amara shuddered.

The Gigas had shared her story of how she and Silverleaf had barely escaped with their lives. She had said how the wailing, mournful cries of the dead still awakened her at night.

Kit turned to Silverleaf and gave him a wide-eyed smile. "And your efforts to destroy a necromancer and his undead minions earned you and Amara the title of priest. You both showed a lot of heart that day."

Silverleaf and Amara gave Kit a withering look.

Exuberant howls brought everyone back to the here and now. The boys had been running about the cemetery, trying desperately to pick up Karr's trail. Runt stopped at a tombstone and began a series of high-pitched barks. Coldforge slipped off his back to move in for a closer inspection.

"I ain't never seen marks like these." The dwarf ran his fingers over two sets of deep gouges on the top of the large granite headstone.

"What do you make of that?" Kit asked her father. Inside her heart, she feared it was the claws of a demon. The memory of climbing to the secret library crashed into her head. Eris had unleashed shadow demons to stop Kit and Danny from reaching their goal. They all had long, stiletto like claws that could have easily made these marks.

"Raptor claws, most likely," Captain Harding said, letting his fingers run over the rent in the stone. "I'm going to guess it was from a great hawk." Somewhere deep inside, Kit was disappointed that they were not from something more exotic.

Kit considered her father's suggestion more carefully. "Hawk riders? From Silverhawk? They're mostly corrupt, except the White Riders, the healers. I guess somebody paid them more than I had offered them. I suppose with the king's backing, gold wouldn't be an issue."

"You've been paying off the Silverhawk Watch?" Captain Harding asked, blinking rapidly at his daughter.

"They've basically turned into mercenaries," Kit said with a shrug. "Willing to work for anybody who puts gold in their pockets. I had hired some to hunt down the slaver-parties working northern Arnnor."

"Commander Eagle Claw would have flayed them all if he'd found out," Captain Harding said. When he saw the blank stares coming from the others, he elaborated. "Kren Eagle Claw was the City Watch Captain here in Aarall before accepting a post as the Wing Commander in Silverhawk. Under his leadership, the Hawk Riders became the most revered military group in the entire kingdom. To be a member of his unit was considered the highest achievement a soldier could make. It was even more coveted than being a member of the king's personal guard."

"Well, things have deteriorated since then," Kit said.

"That could have only happened after he retired. He was the most stalwart, honest man I've ever known. He was beyond reproach."

"You make it sound like he was your hero." Kit's voice was teasing, yet she marveled at the way her father was honoring the man.

"He was a hero. Not for having won some great battle or killing some horrendous beast. He was a hero for being a role model for soldiers and civilians alike." Captain Harding lowered his chin. "Maybe it's time for Kren to come out of retirement and set things straight."

"Father, maybe we should leave. If Karr's been carried off by a great hawk, there will be nothing more to find here. Let's get back to the barracks. Maybe Indie and Lin gathered information from the vampire." Captain Harding's face turned stern at the comment. Kit had never cleared the interrogation with him. She gave him a quick smile and called the boys to her side.

"Silverleaf and I will continue to search the grounds," Amara said, leaning on the haft of her polearm. "We'll return before sundown." Silverleaf nodded furiously.

"I have no desire to wander these grounds after dark." He shivered and grimaced. "Not in the slightest."

CHAPTER SEVEN

INTERVIEW WITH A VAMPIRE

Kit stepped out into the City Watch courtyard. She had just finished coming back through the bug warrens and desperately wanted some fresh air before heading back down into the barracks' dungeons to check on Indie and Lin's progress with the vampire.

"If you want to stay up here, I'll go check in on our guest in the dungeons." Captain Harding brushed Kit's flame-red hair away from her face with his thick, meaty hand. You don't need to do everything yourself. You'll just end up spreading yourself too thin. Kit smiled weakly at her father. She knew he was right but, she wasn't good at letting things go.

Two black wagons came rumbling through the barracks' gatehouse, each pulled by a pair of sable draft horses. Two large men, each dressed in dusky attire, drove the wagons into the courtyard. The captain groaned when he saw them.

"If you're okay to deal with our dungeon issue, I best attend to this," her father said with a heavy sigh. Kit glanced at the wagons and gave her father a questioning look. "Undertakers. My people have likely been preparing funeral pyres for the fallen. I need to be with them for this."

Kit's heart broke for the man. In contrast to his intimidating exterior, he made a point of getting to know every soldier in the Watch. If any of them died while on duty, he treated it like he'd lost a friend. "I should come with you. The prisoner interrogation can wait. This is more important."

The captain shook his head and gave his daughter a warm smile. "It is important, particularly important, but what you need to do is critical. We need to know what we're facing. I'm sure Father Hoarfrost will make his way to the ceremony."

Four City Watch guards came jogging out to meet the undertakers. "We're still preparing the bodies," one guard said. "If you can help us, it will go much faster. We want the fallen to be at their best when their loved ones arrive." The four undertakers nodded somberly and followed the soldiers inside.

Kit was about to give her father a hug when Lin and Indie came running across the courtyard. If she didn't know better, she'd have guessed the two were racing to see who would get to speak first. Indie quickly slowed as he approached, his chest heaving from the exertion.

"Lin was right," Indie said, a healthy dose of annoyance in his voice. "Mixing a rejuvenation potion with blood, well, it practically cured the vampire instantly."

Kit ignored Lin's look of smug satisfaction. "Would he talk with you? Did the vampire say anything helpful?"

"It took a while," Indie said. "He wouldn't give up trying to compel us to release him. He stopped trying when Lin ran him through with one of her flaming swords."

"It wouldn't have killed him," Lin said with feigned innocence, "but it sure got his attention."

"Did he tell you anything useful?" Captain Harding said, his voice now in full commander mode.

"Not much," Lin and Indie responded together, which made Kit laugh and Indie scowl.

"In his previous state, his mind was lost," Indie continued, after giving Lin a quick glare. "The only meaningful words he said were *woman* and *demon*."

"He also mentioned that if we freed him," Lin said, cutting Indie off, "that he'd help us find the woman who had ravaged his cell."

"Apparently, she spent a good amount of time tormenting the vampire," Indie continued, still glaring at Lin.

"I could ask him," Kit suggested. "I'd know if he was lying or not."

"We're not releasing the vampire," Captain Harding said, giving Kit a look that suggested she had perhaps lost her mind.

"Everybody's got enemies," Kit said. "Maybe he's more interested in getting revenge on those who turned him?"

"I've held him in that cellar for... a long time. I'm fairly sure I'm going to be high on his revenge list."

"Okay, okay," Kit said. "But don't you think it would be a good idea to make sure he's well fed and healthy... just in case?"

"He's not a puppy to be cared for," Indie said, the pitch in his voice rising considerably. When Kit's eyes flashed at him in response, he lowered his gaze, knowing the comment went too far.

"He was once a regular person, just like us, before he was turned." Kit planted her fists on her hips and jutted her chin out. "Did either of you even ask him how he became a vampire?"

When everyone stared blankly at Kit, she threw her hands in the air. "Okay, it's a stretch. I get it."

Captain Harding turned to watch his people carrying the first of the dead City Watch members out from the barracks. A woman and a young boy were walking silently alongside. "I'm leaving this with the three of you. Do nothing foolish." And with that, the captain wrung his hands and strode towards the grieving family members.

"We've got the easier job," Indie said, garnering nods from both Kit and Lin.

⌘

Kit padded lightly down the stairs leading to the barracks' dungeons. As she approached the bottom, the air became damp. Everything smelled of mildew and rot and it tasted like mold. Just having to breathe this air seemed like a cruel punishment on its own, let alone having to spend time locked in the rock-walled rooms.

The little priest paused and glanced down the hall. Indie and Lin were still outside helping her father with the next group of mourners, who had come out with their fallen loved ones. They had been arguing over something, perhaps who should have the honor of lighting the funeral pyre. Her father had tried to manage the grieving people, but there were too many of them and the situation was quickly devolving. Kit knew she should have joined in to help, but she wanted to speak with the vampire, alone.

The City Watch had already installed a new door, replacing the mangled one that had been there earlier. The little priest unbolted the entrance to the vampire's cell. The sound of the scraping metal caused the hair on her neck to rise. She took another quick check over her shoulder to ensure nobody had followed her, and with a deep breath, she pulled open the door. She grimaced at the thick waft of death that poured out from the cell. The smell was much worse than she'd remembered. Was the change in smell because he was now healthy? Disregarding the stench, Kit raised her hammer over her head and called upon its power to light the way.

"Helja!" As the light of her hammer penetrated the room's gloomy darkness, it revealed that the cage holding the vampire was now empty. Kit took a step inside, trying to illuminate more of the room.

"Sweet Titan, did they forget to reactivate the wards?"

Kit stepped further inside and took a closer examination of the cage. The door was still locked and none of the bars appeared to have been damaged. Had someone released him? Her father was the only person with the keys to this cell. At least, that's what she thought.

"It was foolish to feed me," a smooth voice said from behind, giving Kit a start. She spun around, her hammer at the ready. The man was filthy and dressed in rags that barely covered his body; his rather beautiful, exquisitely muscular body. His skin was pallid, and it made his dark, penetrating eyes stand out all the more. Kit's heart was slamming into her chest, but she took a step closer to the vampire, anyway. It may have been foolish, but she'd faced vampires before, and she was stronger now than she ever was.

"We needed information." Kit tried to sound calm and confident. She could only hope the man standing before her bought into it. "It was cruel to keep you here."

"Cruel, but necessary," the vampire said, as he slowly glided closer to Kit. His feet barely touched the ground as he neared. Undaunted by his presence, she stood resolute.

"Don't," she warned. "I came here to speak with you, not kill you." A mocking grin pulled at the corner of the man's ruby-red lips.

"You don't fear me," the vampire said, halting his progress. The man's eyes, black as coal, stared deeply into Kit's pools of swirling gold. He inhaled deeply through his nose. "You're not human, but the smell of your blood is intoxicating. A welcome respite from the dank scent of rot that permeates this entire dungeon."

The vampire exposed his elongated canines, letting his tongue run over them.

"Who are you?" Kit asked, ignoring the man's vulgar display. "What is your name?"

"My name?" the vampire laughed. "What does it matter? You won't be alive long enough to speak it to anyone."

Kit smiled brightly at the man. "How badly do I need to hurt you before you'll accept that you're the only person in danger here?"

"Why don't you hand me that lovely hammer?" the vampire asked, pouring his magic into the words.

Kit ignited her hammer. She cocked an eyebrow as red and blue flames danced across its mithril head. When Kit's eyes turned black, the vampire took a few awkward steps away from her. He thrust his clawed hands out to his sides, making himself ready to attack.

"What are you?" the vampire asked, his eyes darting towards the only means of escape.

Kit tossed the hammer beside the exit. "Fury, close the door please."

"Since you asked so nicely." The seven-foot draken appeared in front of the door and slammed it shut. "I like it when you bring me things to play with." The vampire moved to a far wall where he could keep both the girl and the draken in view.

"I asked your name," Kit said as both of her hands became wreathed in flame. "If I wanted to hurt you, you'd already be dead. I came for answers, nothing else."

The vampire's posture became stiff. He straightened his back and puffed out his chest. "I am Ormand Gabryl and to whom am I speaking?"

"You were once the General of the king's Royal Army," Fury said with a tone of approval. "You disappeared over five cycles ago."

Ormand's face soured. "I did not *disappear*. When I was turned, I had no control over my blood lust. I killed many before I was sated. Once I was in control of myself again, I was forced to leave Two Peaks. With few options, I came to Aarall. When I arrived, I handed myself over to the captain of the City Watch. He imprisoned me and starved me. He turned me into a training dummy."

Kit took a step towards the vampire. The fires that had covered her hands died away. "And now you seek revenge on my father for what he did to you?" The vampire cocked his head to the side.

"Your father is King Jordain? I was not aware he had a second daughter."

Kit shook her head at the question, somewhat taken aback. "No. My father is Captain Ray Harding."

"Ah," Ormand said, bobbing his head. "And you think I seek revenge on him for incarcerating me?"

"Are you telling me you don't want retribution for being imprisoned here and starved?"

The vampire stared at Kit, as though trying to judge her. "No," he finally replied. "I'd have likely done the same thing in his place. I was a valuable asset to him. He used me to protect his people. I'd have helped him willingly, but he did not trust me to do so."

"Humans do not understand vampires," Fury said. "They only fear them."

"We should be feared," Ormand scoffed. "We are insidious creatures if we cannot control ourselves. If we are *possessed*, then we have no control at all."

"Possessed?" Kit asked. When she thought back to her encounter with Xin, she remembered the shadow that had been jumping between its hosts. "By a demon?"

"We have no way of keeping the demon out of us," Ormand said. "I'd rather die a thousand deaths than have that happen to me ever again." The vampire shuddered at the thought.

Kit moved nearer to the man. If he attacked, she would be far too close to defend herself effectively. Nothing that the vampire had said had been a lie. There had been no hint of deception.

"If you had been willing to help my father before," Kit said, putting her hand on the vampire's bare arm, "would you help him now? Will you help me?"

Pulling his arm out of Kit's reach, the vampire slowly walked towards Fury, who was steadfastly guarding the door.

"What would you have me do?" Ormand asked, his eyes boring into Fury's.

"I want to unseat the king," Kit said, her voice grave. "He no longer serves the kingdom, only his own self interests."

"Oh, is that all?" Ormand asked, turning back to Kit, showing her a tiny spark of life in his dead, black eyes.

"Would your people still be loyal to you?" Fury asked.

"The soldiers who used to report to me?" Ormand said, half laughing. "It's been many cycles since I was their commander. Who knows what the king has subjected them to? Who knows what he's promised them?"

"Who turned you?" Kit asked. "Why would the king want the general of his royal army turned into a vampire?"

"A woman," Ormand replied, casting his eyes down to his feet. "Her name was Annabella, the natural daughter of King Faol. Turning me was not the king's idea, but when I survived the transformation, he wanted me to turn the rest of his royal army. I refused."

"And for that, he banished you?" Fury asked, clearly intrigued by the man's story.

"For that, he sentenced me to death," Ormand replied. "But I wasn't ready to die just yet. With my newfound powers, my people were ill-equipped to deal with me. Many obedient soldiers died that day. They didn't deserve it. I should have just let them kill me."

The conversation came to an abrupt halt when the door burst open. Indie and Lin came spilling into the room, their blades drawn.

"Kit, what are you doing?" Indie shouted as he bared down on the vampire.

"Indie, stop!" Kit screamed, instantly putting herself in front of Ormand, blocking Indie's attack.

"Princess Aithlin," Ormand exclaimed, taking a knee.

"Stop calling me that," Lin yelled. "I am no princess."

"Sweet Titan." Kit covered her mouth, trying to hide her surprise. "I knew Martelle believed you were the king's child, but I thought—"

"She shares her mother's looks," Ormand said. "When Aithlin was born, I did everything within my power to protect the mother and child."

"You are the bastard child of the king," Fury said, his chuckle now a full-on laugh. "That's why you were banished from the Capital. That's why you were locked away in the Temple."

"It's not true," Lin screamed at Fury, pointing the tip of her flaming long sword at the draken's throat.

"The creature spoke true, Princess." Ormand dipped his head even lower.

Kit furrowed her brow while she tried to puzzle out an answer to the question in her head. "If nobody knew she was the king's daughter, why would they want to kill her?"

Ormand slowly climbed back to his feet. "There are more spies in the king's court than there are flies on a pile of dung. It's rare anything happens without it becoming public knowledge within the court's inner circles. It wasn't until Princess Aithlin's stepfather took ownership of her birth did the rumors stop."

Kit was now grimacing as she tried to understand. There were too many layers and too much politics. "But if everyone believed she was not the king's child, why was she banished?"

"It was against your mother's wishes that you were sent here, but it was a condition of Lord Arthure's agreement with the king. As soon as Princess Aithlin came of age, she was to be sent to the Temple."

"I was an embarrassment, an unwanted, unloved child used as a barter-chip to improve my stepfather's station in the capital." Lin's breaths were coming in fast, shallow bursts.

"That's not true," Ormand said. "Your mother loves you with all her heart. Sending you away to live with your grandmother broke her spirit, but it was a price she willingly paid for your protection."

"I will stick my sword through my father's heart if it's the last thing I do. I will kill my stepfather and then I'll kill the king."

CHAPTER EIGHT

A FAMILY REUNION

Kit squinted as she came out from the dungeons and into the bright afternoon sun. Ormand had willingly put himself back into his cell and Kit reengaged his cage's safety features. Spells had been placed on the room that prevented him from passing through the bars as a cloud of ash. She would speak with her father about releasing the man. He was no threat to the city, and he would make a powerful ally.

"Dragon!" The City Watch guard pointed up to the sky towards the Temple. "Sound the alarm. We're under attack." Panic took hold as the people within earshot of the call snatched up their children, their belongings, and anything that looked like it wasn't being guarded, before seeking refuge. Within seconds, the city center was practically devoid of people, except for the City Watch who were taking up defensive positions.

Kit shielded her eyes and looked up into the expanse of bright blue sky. "Do you see it?"

A moment later Indie responded, pointing north toward the Temple. "There. It looks like it's turning and coming this way."

"It has a rider," Lin called out. "Who in their right mind would ride a dragon?"

Soldiers were running in every direction. Some were heading into the barracks while others were running past the gatehouse, into the city square. From the training grounds came the rumbling of what sounded like enormous wagons.

A group of ten soldiers emerged through a tall set of double doors. They were dragging a wagon with an enormous weapon on it. "They've got ballistas." Indie's mouth was hanging open. "I've never seen one outside of military manuals." Kit's look of confusion prompted him to speak further. "They're like giant bows. They shoot huge arrows, easily capable of downing a dragon."

Fury manifested beside Kit. He surveyed the skies for a moment before a smug look of humor crossed his scaly face. "I'd love to see your people's reaction if they saw an *actual* dragon. That is nothing more than a fire drake." Even though he knew it wasn't an actual dragon, the draken seemed surprised to see a rider straddling its back. Tilting his head back, the draken released a series of screeches and what could only be described as ear-piercing barks. The fire drake's head snapped in his direction before banking hard towards the courtyard, descending at a rapid rate. When the animal was only a hundred feet above the ground, a flurry of arrows sailed towards it. The drake screeched in response, belching out a series of fireballs at those who would dare to attack it.

"What are you doing?" Fury screamed out, blowing a long stream of blue flames over anybody within range. "If anybody hurts that magnificent creature, I will—"

"Cease fire!" The command boomed across the courtyard.

As loud as Fury was, Captain Harding's voice utterly dwarfed it. The command reverberated off the walls, shaking dust and debris from the stonework. Several of the soldiers dropped their weapons to cover their ears. A few guards didn't immediately lower their bows. They released the tension on their bowstrings, but they kept their arrows knocked. The big captain tossed Kit's necklace back to her with a curt nod.

"What is a fire drake doing here?" The question was directed at Fury, but the man's eyes never left the drake and its rider.

"No idea." There was a hint of annoyance in the draken's voice. Perhaps he didn't appreciate that the captain seemed to be blaming him for the unexpected visitor.

Those soldiers who were still in the courtyard immediately scattered to make way for the fire drake as it landed with a whump in their midst. Great clouds of dust swirled around the creature as it continued to flap its leathery red wings. The drake's head was low, and its neck was drawn back. It looked somewhat like a viper ready to strike. It bared its huge, needle-like teeth, daring anyone to come within range of her bite.

The drake's rider, an enormous Gigas with dark skin, heavy muscles, and a remarkably long sword, slipped off the creature's back. He gave her a pat on the neck before striding purposefully toward Fury.

"I assume you are in command of these people," the Gigas bellowed out, his voice as loud and as sure as Captain Harding's ever was. "I am Ulip, Chief of the Fire Drake Clan. I seek my sister, Amara. Take me to her now and there will be no need for violence."

Captain Harding stepped forward, putting himself between Kit and the oncoming Gigas. Indie acted similarly, drawing looks of ire from both Lin and Kit. With practiced grace, the captain pulled his bastard sword from its sheath behind his back. "I am in charge here and you will lower your weapon, or I will remove the hand holding it."

The Gigas tightened his grip on his blade and made no effort to lower his weapon or slow his pace. His heavy brow lowered, obscuring his beady, black eyes. A growl rolled from the big man's chest as a deep scowl contorted his face.

"Ready arms," the captain bellowed out. Besides the dozen soldiers carrying bows, another two dozen soldiers with long spears and heavy shields moved forward. The captain stormed toward Ulip, his body language clearly saying he had no fear of the hulking man closing in on him. When the Gigas' progress slowed, so did the captain's. "If you are indeed Amara's brother, this is no way to introduce yourself. You will either sheath your weapon, or you and your mount will die here and now." The dark-skinned giant paused for a moment and nodded. "I will not give you another warning."

Fury unleashed a high-pitched screech and blew a thick blue flame toward the fire drake. In response, the drake blew a flame into the air that stretched up a hundred feet. Those soldiers who were nearby took a step backwards, shielding themselves from the intense heat. A moment later, the Gigas relented and sheathed his blade.

"Where's my sister?" Ulip's question was somewhat calmer, but his voice dripped venom. "We made no aggressive act towards you, and yet your clan fired upon us. If you seek war, I will bring it to your door." The captain sheathed his sword and lowered his head slightly, perhaps in penance for his people's actions.

"Let the men parlay," Fury said to Kit, motioning with his head toward the fire drake. "I want to have a talk with her."

Kit stole a glance at the Gigas and her father. She had seen no one who could dwarf the captain before. Even so, her father looked to be more than a match for the giant, in both attitude and muscle.

Fury belched out a burst of flames towards the fire drake and emitted a series of quick barks. The fire drake responded in kind, belching another torrent of fire on the ground in front of herself. Indie moved quickly, sprinting towards the drake. He had no weapon drawn, but the creature clearly didn't appreciate his actions. She immediately widened her stance and lowered her chin to the ground. Her lips peeled back, exposing her formidable set of long, pointed teeth.

Indie yelled something that Kit didn't understand, but the fire drake seemed to. She raised her head and took a deep breath. When Indie didn't slow, she blew out a thin stream of fire, bathing the impudent human in flame. Kit's heart exploded at the sight as she immediately engulfed herself in her own celestial blaze.

"Stop this immediately," Fury bellowed out, using his seven-foot frame to knock Kit off course, sending her head over feet across the cobblestones. "Soldier of flame, cease your actions. We will not harm you." The fire drake ceased her attack and barked at Fury.

Kit looked up from the ground and gawped at Indie. He was covered from head to toe in golden scales. She would have sworn he looked even taller than he had before, like he had absorbed the heat of the flames and had become engorged by them. A moment later, his size returned to normal. In a heartbeat, Fury grabbed Kit by the arm and hoisted her from the ground.

"We need to hurry. She will incinerate him with her next attack. That was only a warning." Kit's eyebrows shot up at Fury's comment. She had never really seen dragon fire before. If that was only a warning, her insides liquified at the thought of what a genuine attack would be like, and this was only a drake and not a veritable dragon.

"Is that the best you can do?" Indie asked. His strides towards the creature slowed, but his back straightened, emboldened by his ability to shrug off the drake's attack. Indie suddenly clutched his head and dropped to his knees. He wailed out in agony for several seconds before collapsing on the ground.

A look of terror crossed Kit's face.

"Don't worry, he's okay." Fury's assurances didn't ring true, at least not completely. "It was a psychic attack, meant to incapacitate him." Kit spun her hammer in her hand and tightened her grip. She breathed out a sigh of relief when Indie picked himself up off the ground. His cock-sure attitude had completely melted away.

"Are you Fury?" the draken called out in the common tongue. "Why do you choose to live among these lesser beings?"

"What is your name, soldier of flame?" Fury's posture straightened considerably. "Why would you lower yourself to allow a Gigas to ride you like a common beast of burden?"

"This one named Ulip serves my master, Spur. He requested I bear the rider, and the humiliation that comes with it. You have not answered my question, *draken*. Are you Fury, the venerable dragon lord?"

The question made Fury smile. After his previous encounter with the fire drakes, it was a pleasant surprise to hear one speak to him with a modicum of respect.

"I am but a piece of Fury, trapped within the girl's magnificent hammer. I am the dragon lord, wondrous beyond reckoning, even in my lesser state." The fire drake pulled back a lip in a sneer before shaking her head. She let out something akin to a groan.

"The dragon queen told me of your arrogance, that it is without bounds. You must be the dragon lord if you would risk my fires without fear or forethought." Fury's jaw dropped open as he wrung his clawed hands together.

"You've spoken with Siku? Tell me about her and be quick about it. Is she well?" The tone in Fury's voice made Kit chuckle. There were layers of emotion wrapped in his question that she had never heard from him before. There was a significant connection between Fury and Siku, whoever the dragon was. They were more than friends.

"I have." The fire drake's scaly eyebrows shot up. "She seemed as curious about your wellbeing as you do hers." She bared her teeth in what Kit could only assume was a weird dragon grin. It looked remarkably like Fury's when he smiled. "She was also very curious about you, little human. My nest mates told me about you, too." She looked Kit up and down and scratched her chin with one wickedly long claw. "I have to say, you don't look like much to me. I do like the color of your hair, though. It is such a wonderful shade of red."

"She is much more than she seems." Fury bowed his head respectfully to the little priest standing beside him. "She is so much more."

"Her ability to set herself aflame was interesting. I don't think I've ever witnessed a human do that before. I've known several mages who could cast fire, but I've never met one who could *become* fire."

"It's a part of her celestial heritage, her *daemon* aspect." Fury was sounding like a proud papa, speaking of his child, bragging to anybody who would listen. It made Kit nervous.

"If you two are finished discussing me," she interrupted, twirling her battle hammer in her hands. "Perhaps you can tell me more of the Gigas you brought here. Is he truly Amara's brother?"

"I am," Ulip responded, making Kit yelp. For a big man, he moved with incredible stealth. Kit wished he could teach that to Coldforge. That dwarf couldn't do anything without raising a holy racket. "It seems your chief doesn't know specifically where she is. He told me you were her friend. Does that mean you can tell me her location?" Kit craned her head to look up at the Gigas. He was several inches taller than Fury. His heavy brow covered most of his beady black eyes, but she could still see the concern in them.

"Your sister is seeking an escaped criminal. We left her at the city's cemetery beyond the northwest wall. Even though we could find no trail, she continued the search." Ulip's shoulders slumped somewhat at Kit's words. "I expect she will not be gone for long, though. She will need to report her findings back to Captain Harding before the sun sets." Ulip blew out his cheeks.

"It will be faster if I search for her by myself. If she is outside the city walls, Yuka can bear me there in no time at all."

A low, throaty growl interrupted the conversation. Across the courtyard, Amara was standing next to Silverleaf. Her upper lip was pulled back in a snarl, her hand clenched tightly around the haft of her glaive. With one hand, she pushed Silverleaf away, knocking him onto his backside. The Gigas rolled her shoulders and stalked towards the man who said he was her brother. Kit stared up at Ulip, whose lips were drawn back similarly. With tightly clenched fists, he, too, began striding towards his sister.

"Whoa there," Kit said, grabbing the big man by the wrist. With zero effort, he tossed Kit aside like a rag doll. Indie threw himself in the giant's way, only to meet a similar fate.

"Let him be," Fury said, holding his hand out to both Indie and Kit. "Let this play out."

In a heartbeat, Amara changed from stalking to sprinting. She tossed her glaive aside, its bright silver blade spinning and whirling when it struck the ground. After a few steps, her fists were pumping by her side, her long white priest's robes and straw-yellow hair billowing out behind her. Ulip drew his own sword and tossed it onto the ground in a similar fashion. Like his sister, he broke into a dead run. The two titans barrelled at each other. The collision was imminent and promised to be spectacular.

When they were only feet apart, Ulip dropped his shoulder, catching Amara fully in the chest. There was a resounding thud from the impact, which sent Amara sprawling across the dirt. With remarkable swiftness, she rolled back to her feet. She glanced down at the state of her robes. Ulip raised his fist, ready to unleash it upon his sister. Just as he was about to strike her with his wide arcing swing, Amara threw up her forearm and deflected the blow. With one fluid motion, she stepped inside his guard and delivered an elbow to his chin, staggering the much larger Gigas. He stumbled several steps before the priest swept his legs out from beneath him, knocking the man onto his back.

As quickly as the male Gigas hit the ground, Amara was on him, wrapping her hands around his throat. Ulip tried, ineffectually, to break the girl's grasp on him. After repeated attempts, he switched to a more offensive tactic, striking out with his fist, trying to land a solid punch to her face. With each punch he threw, Amara ducked and wove around them, all the while increasing the pressure on the man's throat. Again, after multiple failed attempts to break his sister's grasp, Ulip changed tactics and with surprising dexterity threw his legs up and wrapped his ankles around Amara's head. With a loud grunt, he yanked her backwards off his chest. As Amara flopped on her back, Ulip pivoted his body and drove his right forearm into her throat. The priest's left arm was pinned under her brother's knee, leaving only her right arm with which to fight back. She threw a solid punch, only to have it caught in the man's left hand. Using his superior size, Ulip used his other knee to pin her right arm. Now, with both of Amara's arms completely trapped, he rained down blows with his right elbow. With each successive strike, blood flowed more and more freely from multiple wounds on the young woman's face.

Silverleaf, fearing his best friend's life was in peril, threw himself at the giant. Before he could lay a hand on Ulip, the Gigas used his free arm to grab the half elf by the throat and slam him to the ground, pinning him next to Amara.

"You would dare to interrupt our greeting?" Ulip bellowed. "What sort of fool are you?"

"Ulip, release him now." Amara struggled to free herself to come to Silverleaf's rescue. "Ulip, release him. He doesn't understand. He's trying to protect me."

The look of fury melted away, transforming into a broad grin. "This tiny man is trying to protect you?" The grin turned into a frightful, toothy smile, followed by raucous laughter. He released Silverleaf and crawled off his sister. "You have the heart of a dragon and the brains of a tiny rock, little man."

After rolling to his feet, Ulip offered a hand up to Amara, who promptly slapped it away. Her white robes were now a mass of brown and red. She ran her finger over her blood-covered teeth to make sure none were missing. With a broad smile, Amara picked herself up off the ground, not bothering to dust herself off. She looked away long enough to hoist Silverleaf to his feet. He was still clasping his throat, gasping from lack of oxygen.

"Welcome, brother," Amara offered. "I didn't know if I would ever see you again. How are mother and father? They are well, I trust." Ulip's face crumpled at the question. His shoulders sagged and his mouth was immediately tied up in a tight bow.

Chapter Nine

The Threat on the Horizon

"Our clan is dead," Ulip blurted out, unable to hold back his grief. His chest heaved and his breath hitched. "Slavers came and massacred them all. All who were left of us were me, you, and Frode." Amara's face turned to stone at the comment. She shuddered when Silverleaf rubbed her arm, trying to comfort his friend.

"Frode has passed." Tears gathered in Amara's eyes as she remembered her friend, the woman who had cared for her and had helped raise her. "We are all who are left of our family?" Ulip nodded slowly. His great shoulders dipped low, and his chin dropped to his massive chest.

"I have disgraced their memory." When he raised his head, his beady black eyes were glassy, his face slack. "I have taken the lives of many people. I... I tried to justify my actions, to say that it was to protect others, but... I'm not sure. I reveled in their deaths. It brought me joy." The last words he spoke came out in a hoarse whisper.

"Brother. I, too, have dishonored our clan's memory. I, too, have broken our laws and have taken lives."

"You saved many," Silverleaf said. His voice was a mix of anger and sympathy. "Had you not acted, I would be dead. So would many of our friends. I'm sure your brother's actions also saved lives. By the look of him, I'll wager he saved many, many lives."

The two Gigas stared at the half elf, holding their gaze for several seconds before nodding and lowering their chins.

"Yuka spoke to me the same words, telling me that my actions were both justified and righteous. I don't think she speaks untrue, but still..."

"But it goes against everything we were taught; all of our beliefs are based on nonaggression." Amara pulled Silverleaf close to her, wrapping her arms tightly around her friend.

"Our clans used to be the fiercest warriors in the north, but it nearly destroyed us. When we had no enemies left to fight, we turned on our own. Our bloodlust knew no boundaries. It was for those reasons that we turned from violence. It was for those reasons that raising our hand against our own became an unforgivable crime."

"You may find that you will need to return to the old ways, at least for now." The voice of Captain Harding was firm, but it seemed he understood the grief the pair was enduring. "The fate of the world teeters on the edge of a blade. We may fall to either side, or we may perish on the blade itself. If we are to survive, we must find a way forward that doesn't end in ruin."

"The behavior of slavers is hardly the end of the world." Ulip straightened and turned his bulk toward the captain.

"The slavers are but one minor aspect of what is coming," Captain Harding replied. "There are gods involved and they seek to bring about Ragnarök."

"And I will do whatever I can to make sure that doesn't happen." Kit stepped forward, straining to look up at the giant. "Maybe you can tell us why you have come here. Your sister has been here most of her life and you have never sought her out. Why now?"

Ulip all but disregarded Kit's question. "What do the gods care about us? Why would they seek to destroy the peoples of these lands, even if some of them deserve it?" Amara took her brother's hand in hers.

"I will explain it to you, brother. It isn't a short tale. You must be hungry and in need of sleep. Why don't I take you to the Temple, to my home, and get you cared for? We have much to discuss." The words seemed to cause the giant to pause. He looked over at Yuka, who was warily eyeing everyone near her.

Fury appeared next to the giant, giving him something of a start. "The soldier of flame will be well cared for here. I will see to it. I wish to speak to her at length. I have heard nothing of my kin in ages."

Ulip turned to the captain. "Is the army that approaches your ally? If they are not, there may be no time for rest or for tales."

"What army?" Kit asked, turning to her father.

"No, they are no ally," Captain Harding replied. "What can you tell me of them?"

"They are many." Ulip showed his first sign of concern. "There are three groups coming. The first has a little over one thousand soldiers. The second group is much larger, at least seven thousand strong. A third group, much further south, has at least ten thousand soldiers, perhaps more. They were at a great distance, and we didn't get a good sense of their numbers."

"We?" Captain Harding was already deep in thought, trying to put together a plan.

"Yuka and myself. She has much better eyesight than I do. It was she who spotted the army to the south."

"Can you estimate their time of arrival? Were they traveling at speed or were their movements slowed by siege engines?"

"The smallest army was traveling at a hurried pace. Many of the soldiers were on horseback. The army that followed them was mostly on foot. They had oxen with them, dragging many enormous weapons. The smaller army will be here before the sun sets on the morrow. The larger army may take five or more days. The army to the south was too far away to be certain; I would rather not guess."

"We need to evacuate the surrounding villages," Indie said. He seemed to stare off to the south as he spoke. "They need to be brought into the city for protection." The captain nodded. His eyes looked unfocused, his body rigid. "Captain? We need to send riders out now."

"Yes." The captain's eyes focused, his jaw set. "I'll send riders out immediately."

"Father, Indie and I would be much faster than your riders. We can get everyone coming here in a few hours." Kit looked to Indie, who was nodding his agreement.

"I can help, too." Lin was ready to go. "Whistler is almost as quick as their horses. You need your fastest riders if you're to have any hope of saving these people."

"Yuka and I would be much faster," Ulip said. The idea of saving people without the use of violence seemed to make him happy. The captain scoffed at his offer, drawing the ire of the giant.

"You'll scare the wits out of the people, my big friend. Your arrival turned seasoned warriors' legs to jelly, caused them to lash out, purely out of fear. How do you think farmers are going to react?" The outrage drained from Ulip's face. His scowl instantly replaced with what looked like a wicked smile.

"I will go to my village," Indie said. "They'll listen to me without question." Lin nodded in agreement.

"And I'll head to Ashcroft. I'll speak with my grandmother. She will ensure everyone leaves without an argument. There are many thousands of people there. It will be difficult to get them to leave their homes."

"I'll notify the villages between here and Two Peaks," Kit said. "I'll leave as soon as Angel gets here."

"I don't think that's a good idea." Captain Harding had that same far off look on his face.

"Don't worry, father. I'll be safe." Kit's reaction was a mixture of outrage and sympathy. She was shocked, after everything they'd been through, that her father would fear for her safety.

"I don't doubt that." The captain chuckled, despite the dire situation. "I want you here to help plan our attack against the lead soldiers. I'm hoping that with you, Fury, and Ulip, we can convince the army that we are not the soft target they think we are. They likely think that the city has already fallen." Kit's back straightened at her father's words. Her chest swelled and her heart raced. She somehow felt more connected to the man. That he saw her as a formidable warrior filled a piece of her soul that she hadn't even realized was missing. She knew she was a capable fighter, but she had never witnessed her father acknowledging her as a peer.

"I think our daughter's idea was on point." The conversation came to an immediate halt at the sound of Aurora's silky-smooth voice. "I will join you in dissuading the oncoming army. I need to discuss with you how we will handle King Faol. He is leading a legion of vampires, and they are force-marching their way here. It's unlikely that your walls can protect you against what is coming. He has far more vampires than I would have ever expected. From what I could gather, he has figured out how to turn his soldiers without the usual bloodlust that drives them insane. I see only one way for Aarall to survive this attack. I will speak with you about it at length."

Kit stood dumbfounded, staring at her birthmother. She barely even noticed when her father pulled Indie aside for a quiet conversation.

***

While the city's fastest riders sped across the barony to warn villages of the impending threat, one young girl took a different approach, whisking the city's unwanted children away from danger in search of safe harbor. If the city fell, they'd likely all be executed simply for being different.

The wagons rumbled across the broken terrain as they headed south-west away from the city walls. The shaggy-haired oxen pulling the precious cargo paused for a moment to drink deeply from the coolness of the fast-flowing stream. They simply refused to accept Iba's urgings to cross until they had drunk their fill. The children, who were now beyond restless, squealed as the wheels kicked up the frigid water, splashing them, soaking their ragged clothing. The mountain Gizmo, or Tahr as she preferred to be called, groaned when one child, a Tahr of only three cycles, leapt from the wagon to splash in the shallow river. She kicked and sprayed the water at the other children who had remained aboard, just as Iba had instructed them. More children immediately followed suit. Even some of the older children, who really should have known better, leapt from the wagon to play in the shallow river. Iba lost control of her tongue and berated them, shaming them for their misbehavior.

"It was not so long ago that you, too, were a child, finding joy in even the smallest of things." Iba jumped at the voice of Akh'lut, the Lupien who led the pack of Hill Gizmos, who lived within the shadows of the Spiderwood forest. "It was my understanding that Aarall was no longer in danger. Why would you bring these children to our domain yet again?" Akh'lut snarled at the sight of a young dwarf sitting quietly aboard one of the three wagons. "Why would you befoul our home with that... dark elf? He is not welcome here."

"It would seem that *she* is not welcome anywhere." Even though the Lupien leader was at least two heads taller than Iba, she bared her teeth at him, ready for any act of aggression he might take towards her. "I would think you, of all people, would understand that. The kingdom shuns our kind. Would you willingly subject others to the same treatment that we had been forced to endure? These children are innocents who have harmed nobody." Akh'lut's surly demeanor didn't change.

"I'll ask you again, Tahr, why did you bring them here?" Iba looked to her left. A substantial group of Lupien had emerged from the treeline.

"The city is not safe. The king seeks to wage war upon Aarall, to enslave the population, to feed them to the Vampire King, Faol."

"What do we care if Aarall gets sacked? You know what they did to my kind. Their soldier, Harding, killed hundreds of us, if not more. I would enjoy seeing him strung up from a tree, his insides splayed open for the local vermin to feast upon." Without warning and with incredible speed, Iba closed the distance on the Lupien leader and slapped him firmly across the muzzle, hard enough to snap his head to the side.

"You know nothing of the man and yet you would speak so harshly of him."

"He killed our kind. He slaughtered them without remorse. I watched as the hulking beast cut down my kin." Akh'lut pulled open his jerkin, exposing a thick scar than ran from his collar bone down to his belly. "He tried to cut me in half with that gods-forsaken steel blade of his."

"He protected his people, just as you would have. He had nothing to do with the raids on our tribes. He fought against the king and his men. He did everything he could to prevent what happened, but he was just one voice. When the leader demands action, a soldier's duty is to obey. He did not. He would not do something he felt was unjust, even if it meant his life. Are you a better leader than that? What more would you have had him do?"

"I didn't know." Akh'lut lowered his head and signaled his people to stand down. "I trust you, young Tahr. Gaia knows why, but I sense goodness in you. I sense you are more than a young girl living in a human dominated world."

"Then fight with us against the king. He is our true enemy. Between him and the Vampire King, they will bring over twenty thousand soldiers to bear. Even with all the priests and acolytes and City Watch recruits in Aarall, they number less than two thousand strong."

"To fight that number would be suicide. We do not wage war like the humans. Our kind stays in the shadows. We defend when we can. We fight when we must. We are less than two hundred. Even if we could convince the spiders to fight with us, we are less than five hundred."

"Then light the fires, signal the others. If all of us come out to fight, we would be at least ten thousand. The girl, Kit, she inspires others to join the cause. She inspired me. She showed me the errors of my ways. Light the fires. Call the others to war."

"We have not lit the fires in over five hundred cycles. They will not come."

"Do you still maintain the signals?" Iba stared up at the Lupien, her eyes hard and accusatory.

"Of course, we do. I would never allow my people to be the weak link in the chain." Akh'lut folded his arms over his chest and cocked an eyebrow. He shook his head and blew out a long breath. "And neither would any of our kin."

Iba smiled warmly. "No. No they wouldn't."

The Lupien was still shaking his head at the girl. "How will we know when it's time to attack?"

"Can you hear the peel of the warning bell this far from the city?" Iba cocked an eyebrow and smirked.

"Yes, we can hear the bells. We can hear when your beloved high priest passes gas."

Iba chuckled at the leader's comment. "Just be glad you don't live within the temple's walls." She quickly cupped her hand over her nose for extra effect.

"We will care for the children. We will come when we are called. Tell your soldier, Harding, and your high priest, Hoarfrost, that they can count on us. They can count on all of us." Iba bowed deeply in reply.

"The city will forever be in your debt."

"If they would give us anything in return for our support, we would ask that they simply let us return home and leave us alone."

CHAPTER TEN

FATHER'S LAST ADVENTURE

Father Hoarfrost stared out his office window and, with a deep sigh, took a seat behind his desk. The man looked exhausted.

"Is everything okay, Father?" Kit asked, stifling a yawn. When Indie did the same, the old priest smiled and shook his head. The pair had been out all day, spreading the word of the impending attack. While many of the villagers refused to believe the king would do such a thing, many more listened and immediately packed their most precious belongings and made haste for the city. A small family had arrived with Indie when he came through the front gate. Apparently, he had passed them on the way back to Aarall and invited them to ride with him. Kit thought little of it at the time. She remembered the man looked much too old for the woman, and the boy, who couldn't have been more than twelve cycles, was much too large for his age. He was at least the size of Indie, if not bigger. Father Hoarfrost cleared his throat, rousing Kit from her sleepy musings.

The old priest gave Kit a wistful look before turning his attention to Indie. "I need to speak with Sister Kit alone. I trust she will share what I have to say later, but for now..."

Kit patted Indie on his lower back and motioned with her head to the door. "Go to our room. I'll be there shortly." Indie blushed at the words. Kit wondered if he was concerned the high priest may take offense to the couple sharing a bed. The young man nodded briefly in acknowledgement, gave Kit a quick kiss on the top of her head, and retreated to the hallway. In seconds, his footsteps receded in the distance.

Father Hoarfrost stepped out from behind his desk and took Kit's arm in his. "Accompany me. I wish to enjoy a bit of fresh air."

The pair walked in silence through the temple's halls until they came upon the door leading into the back gardens. The old priest inhaled deeply, relishing the cool evening air and the heady scent of the night-blooming flowers. He stared longingly up at the bright moon that filled the blue-black sky.

"I think I have one adventure left in me," he said, his voice sounding melancholy. "Before I leave, I plan to retire my post as High Priest and appoint my successor."

"What?" Kit tried to hide another yawn. What the old man had just said made no sense. Her mind swam as she tried to wrap her head around the words. "You want to step down as High Priest?"

Father Hoarfrost closed his eyes and took another slow, deep breath. "Titan saved me. When I brought the Temple down, the falling stones should have crushed me along with the king's people." The old priest's eyes remained closed as he relived his recent brush with death. "And now I will return the kindness."

"Father, you can't go. You're needed here. Especially now."

"I will be of little use against the army that marches upon us," Father Hoarfrost said gently. "I owe Titan my life, and I will honor him by giving it freely to help his people."

"Father," Kit said, her eyebrows knitted tightly together. "If Titan expects you to sacrifice your life, because he came to your aid, well, then... he is not worthy of your love, nor mine." The old priest gave Kit a quizzical look. He tented his fingers in front of himself while he scrutinized her with his dark brown eyes.

"Titan expects nothing but our loyalty," Father Hoarfrost replied, a knowing smile pulling at one corner of his mouth. "My life is my own and mine to offer any way I choose. I believe this is something I learned from you, have I not?"

"Father?" Kit started, her words getting stuck in her throat. She could feel the daemon within bubbling up, along with her anger. Why would this man throw his life away? He was too old for such adventures, and he was too wise to not know that. His wisdom and his knowledge were needed here, at the Temple. It would be foolish of him to throw it away just because he survived the demolition of Titan's statue.

"I need to commune with our god at the Altar of Toka." Kit's jaw dropped open. Her next words came tumbling out without thought or hesitation.

"But you're too old to try something like that!"

The old priest gave her a warm smile and patted her hand. "I am old and that's why this journey will be my last adventure." Kit yanked her arm out of his and shook her head adamantly.

"Let me go, Father. Let me commune with Titan. Even in the summer, that mountain is impassible. Its peaks are forever covered in snow and avalanches can happen without warning."

Father Hoarfrost stood silent as he continued to stare at the mountain. "As you wish."

"What?" Kit said, pulling the old man around so he was facing her. "You didn't need to trick me into going."

"I wasn't trying to trick you," Hoarfrost said as he gazed down at his gnarled, old hands. "I want to make the journey, but you are better suited to the task."

"Could you teleport us?" Kit asked, remembering how Hoarfrost had teleported himself and several others to meet her at the edge of Lake Titan after the enormous ice statue had melted away. "We could visit the altar together. Maybe with the two of us asking for his aid..."

"No, my sweet angel, that's not how this works." The old priest took Kit's hands in his own. "Life is not about the destination. It's the journey that matters. It's the struggles that one must endure and overcome. Like the stairs that lead to the Temple, it's the climb to the altar that will create the connection with our god."

"Father," Kit swallowed hard before speaking further. It wasn't often that she weighed her words, but this was different. She was going to disagree with her mentor's teachings openly and directly. "I don't think that's true. In my limited experience, I have witnessed that Titan listens best when you really need him. Many times, in the past two moons, I have called upon him repeatedly, when things were at their worst, and he always listened."

"And when exactly did you need him?" The old priest's eyes were full of wonder as he looked at the little priest standing at his hip. Kit's face flushed slightly at the question.

"While I was in battle." Kit rubbed the back of her neck. "Usually when I was in trouble, or I felt I was going to be challenged beyond my ability."

"Journeying up the mountain will be a challenge beyond my ability. In my effort to overcome that obstacle, I will be drawn closer to our god. When I stand before his altar and call to him, he will listen."

"And what do you wish to ask of him?" The little priest took the old man's hands in hers. They were as empty vessels. The power that she'd felt in him the first day she arrived at the Temple was gone. All she could feel now was the warmth of his skin against her own.

"I would ask for his strength," Hoarfrost said, staring at Kit. "Strength enough to defeat our enemies and set the world right." Kit's face suddenly hardened. She clenched her teeth while her anger seethed up in a deep, visceral growl.

"Wrong answer," Kit said as she tightened her grip on the old man's hands, causing him to yelp. "Who are you?"

"Sister Kit," Father Hoarfrost said, his voice calm and measured, even though drips of sweat were now rolling down his brow. "I am the same man you've known since you arrived here at the Temple, even if I am but a shadow of my former self."

"Father?" Kit said, relaxing her grip on the old man's hands. "Why did you lie to me?"

"I didn't mean to," the old priest said, flexing his fingers, trying to coax away the pain. "I should have said that I would ask for his strength for *you*, that you might defeat your enemies and set the world right."

"Oh." She grimaced as her mentor continued to work through the pain she had caused him. "Sorry about that." Kit took the old man's hands in hers. They were glowing softly in the pale light of the night sky. A moment later, Kit's eyes were glassy, reflecting the sadness of the old priest.

"You shouldn't have done that," he said, pulling his hands away.

"Father, you're dying."

"I know, child. It's why I would wish to complete one more adventure before my time draws to an end."

"But I healed you." Kit's voice wavered badly. The world was swimming around her. Instinctively, she grabbed onto her mentor's arm for support. How weak she suddenly felt. Even knowing that the old priest was dying, she leaned on him, drawing strength from him.

"You healed my wounds, but my body is failing. I used up the last of my power when I brought Titan's statue down upon the king's soldiers. He is now calling me to his side."

"Father, no," Kit said as her body burst forth in a blinding golden aura. "It's not your time." She wrapped her arms around him, her powers reaching out for illness, or poison, or damage of any sort. When she could find nothing to heal, she buried her face in his chest and began sobbing.

"I'm so proud of you, child," Hoarfrost said, stroking her thick red hair with his free hand. "You have brought so much joy to my life. I am grateful to have known you and to have shared what wisdom I may have with you. I am honored that you would share your love with me, a love you give so freely, expecting nothing in return for it."

"I would gladly give my life to save yours." Her words were muffled as she spoke into the man's robes. She pulled her face away and tried to wipe the tear-stained cloth. "Please, tell me what I should do? I don't care what it is. I'll do anything for you, Father. Let me help you."

"You should stay here," the old priest said, "and let me go on my last adventure. If I know that you're here to lead and to care for the Temple and its followers, then I can meet Titan with peace in my heart."

"You want me to become High Priest?" Kit said, pushing away, her body now covered in a deep red aura. "I will not. I refuse. I will not allow you to die needlessly."

"Be at peace, my child. My death draws nigh, regardless of how I spend my few remaining days. Would you deny me this last wish? Did you not just say that you would do anything for me? Staying here and protecting our people, that is what I am asking you to do."

"Please, Father. Let me come with you." The aura of Kit's anger faded away, leaving only her aching heart.

"They need you here." Father Hoarfrost's tone changed to that of a parent speaking to a young child. "As I said, it's the journey that matters, not the destination, and this journey must be undertaken alone."

"I can't bear the thought of you dying, not again. I just got you back."

"Consider our time together now as a gift from Titan." He drew Kit back into himself, embracing her deeply. "We should both get some rest now. In the morning, I will formally appoint you as High Priest, and then I will begin my journey to the altar."

⸺⸻⸻◈⸻⸻⸺

The morning light had just broken through Kit's window when she entered her cell. Discovering that her mentor was dying, and knowing that the king's army was going to be arriving at the city walls later that day, had eaten at Kit all night. The hope of getting any form of restful sleep was out of the question. However, the sight laid out before her melted her heart and brightened her dismal spirits.

"Well, isn't that cute," she whispered when she saw Indie in bed, snuggled up to Lump, his arm wrapped around the dog, his face buried in the pup's thick, golden-red ruff.

Runt, who had sprawled out across the floor, stretched, and yawned widely, his enormous pink tongue curling out of his mouth. The sleeping man stirred at the sound of Runt's tail thumping out a greeting on the stone floor.

"Good morning, sweetness." Indie buried his face deeper into Lump's fur. "Did you sleep well?"

"Not as well as you." Kit's grin split her face from ear to ear. "Should I leave you two alone?"

"What?" Indie said, as he pulled his face away from the dog. "Holy Helja." His face turned a deep shade of red. Using his hands and feet, he forcefully pushed Lump away. The dog whined, insulted that he had been awakened from his blissful and cozy spot. With a huff, he jumped from the bed and curled up beside Runt, instantly asleep once again.

"I didn't mean to interrupt your cuddle time," Kit said, waggling her eyebrows. The bit of levity did her soul some good. It was a welcomed respite from the pain that had gripped her heart through the darkest hours of the night.

"When did you wake up?" Indie asked as he tried to rub the slumber from his eyes.

"I haven't been to sleep yet," Kit said, her eyes turning glassy. "I was with Lin, brewing potions for Father Hoarfrost and the upcoming battle."

"Why are you crying? What's wrong?" Kit tried to blink the tears away but failed miserably. She struggled to draw a breath. Her hands were now shaking badly.

"Father Hoarfrost is dying." Kit took a seat on the edge of the bed. The boys immediately rushed to her side, placing their heads in her lap.

"He's leaving for the altar atop Mount Toka. I had Lin brew up another batch of her special restoration potions for him." Kit wiped an errant tear from her cheek. "I hope it will help him survive long enough to make it to the mountain top." Indie rubbed his eyes again, perhaps to understand more fully what Kit was saying to him.

"Father Hoarfrost? He's going to climb Mount Toka? It'll kill him."

"It's not the destination that matters," Kit said, parroting her mentor's words. "It's the journey. His life-force is leaving him and he would prefer to die in the service of his god and his people. He believes that his communing with Titan will be our salvation."

"It makes no sense," Indie said, hopping up from the bed, pulling his trousers up over his naked body.

"No," Kit said, watching her man's every movement, his thick muscles flexing and relaxing as he pulled on his clothes. "It actually makes perfect sense that he wants to do this. What makes no sense is that he is going to appoint me as High Priest before he goes."

"High Priest?" Indie's jaw flopped open as he considered what Kit had just said. "That's amazing! Congratulations! You'll make a fantastic High Priest."

"Do you know it means we have to stop..." Kit motioned to the bed, "being *together*."

"What? Why?" When Indie finally got over the shock, he wrapped his arms around Kit, resting his chin on the top of her head. "If you'll be happy, then I'm okay with that."

"Really?" Kit said, wrapping her arms so tightly around Indie that he was struggling to take a breath.

"I will do anything for you."

"I love you," Kit said, releasing her grip on him slightly. "And I was only kidding about that."

Indie blew out a long breath and gripped the girl a little tighter. "Thank Titan!"

Chapter Eleven

The Storm before the Storm

It was late morning, and the sun was shining warm and bright through the windows in Father Hoarfrost's office. A light breeze carrying the scents of summer blossoms filled the room. The old priest pressed his hands onto the weathered windowsill, closed his eyes, and inhaled deeply.

He had summoned a good number of people to join him. There were far more attendants present than the room's limited space could comfortably hold. Kit was standing next to Indie beside the door. Father had said he would announce her as his successor today. Perhaps he wanted to speak to this group privately. Perhaps he wanted to witness their reactions and listen to their comments, something that couldn't be easily done in a large public setting. Perhaps he had changed his mind. Sweet Titan. She desperately hoped he had changed his mind.

"Ragnarök, the end of days, is coming." The old priest slowly opened his eyes. "The Fates will not ensure humanity wins this time. I am stepping down and I am appointing Sister Kit as our new High Priest. I will travel to the altar atop Mount Toka so that I may commune with our god. This is how I will spend my last days before I join with Titan and return to the Great Cycle."

A murmur ran through the room as people tried to come to grips with what the high priest had just said. Kit lowered her eyes, fearful of the reactions they might have to Father appointing her to the role. Then again, she really didn't care what they thought. The anger of Father throwing his life away on a fool's errand gripped her once again.

"Father," Kit said, her voice wavering, unable to quell her still growing rage. "The prophecies are not absolutes. They are written in riddles, posing a likely outcome of what may come to pass. Only we can dictate our future. Prophecies be damned."

"Your mother, Riva, her *far-sight* is very strong," Hoarfrost replied with a warm smile. He turned from the window and took a seat behind his massive dragonwood desk. "She told me of her visions."

"And her visions are difficult to interpret," Kit replied, glaring at the high priest. He carefully regarded the small bits of fire leaking from between her fisted fingers. It took all her effort to quell the flames. A moment later, swirls of molten gold pushed the growing blackness from her eyes. "I have considered your decision all night long. Why don't we revisit this after we get things straightened out here? First, we need to defeat the armies that will soon be knocking on our front door."

Father Hoarfrost clasped his fingers together and drew another deep breath. "Okay, Sister Kit. If I were to stay, what would you see as our next course of action? How should we proceed in the face of an overwhelming force?" Kit's face blanched.

"I am not a tactician," she said, shaking her head. "That is why we need you here. We need your wisdom and your insights. I am a blunt instrument, to be put in harm's way." Kit cocked an eyebrow at Indie when he scoffed at her. "What?"

"You're kidding. Right?" Indie said, his eyebrows raised to comical heights. "You took down four cities in as many weeks. I'm no historian, but I'm going to say that nobody has ever done that before."

"I did no such thing," Kit said, rounding on the young man. "It was Lin and Feigh who took down Silverhawk. It was because of them that Aurora's Guard could..."

"Put your plans into action?" Indie gave her a bright smile. "And it was you who rallied the people of Cormorant. You turned them against the masters. You set Templeton to rights. They were under the control of the king, and Lord

Aster folded under the pressure. You destroyed the vampires and helped the lord regain control of the town. Then you came here and, in less than a day, freed the City Watch from the king's most powerful battle mages. Sure, you had help, lots of help – but if it wasn't for you..."

Kit's heart began pounding heavily in her chest. Even if she didn't believe what Indie was saying, she *knew* he did. Her eyes turned hard as flint, her voice low and threatening. She turned to Father Hoarfrost and shook her head.

"This is how I would deal with overwhelming forces beating down our front door. I would tell you that now is not the time to wander off on an adventure. I would prepare the city for an attack and make sure that everyone is safe behind the city's walls. And then I would gather the smartest people and make them put their heads together until they found a way to defeat a superior army in the field. I would make sure we got all of it done before the second army shows up with their... things that knock down walls."

"Siege engines." Indie said.

"What?" Kit glared at him. She was on a roll, and he interrupted her for no good reason.

"Those things that knock down walls. They're called siege engines. And they don't technically just knock down walls. They can also be used to..."

"Do I look like I care?" Kit's face was turning scarlet. "Father is talking nonsense about leaving, and now you're babbling on about... siege engines. I don't care. War is coming to our door. Father needs to stay put, and we need to figure out a way to destroy an army ten times bigger than our own."

Captain Harding cleared his throat. He had taken up a position at the back of the room, where he leaned uncomfortably against the wall. Sister Amara was at his side, along with Silverleaf. "It will take a miracle for us to stand against King Jordain and King Faol. We don't have enough men to fight either of their armies, let alone both of them at the same time."

Sister Gale, from her seat directly in front of Father's desk, immediately piped up. "And that is why Father will commune with Titan, to ask him to provide us with that miracle."

"While he languishes in his frozen prison, Titan cannot provide any miracles, at least not the kind you're hoping for." Everyone turned and glared at Brother Rimes. He spoke aloud what many of those present were thinking.

"Exactly," Kit said. "Communing with Titan will do us no good. He needs to be free if he is to render aid unto his faithful. Father should stay here and help us defeat the enemy."

"How do you propose we take the fight to the king's army and their vastly superior forces?" Father Hoarfrost asked as he leaned back in his chair, a hint of a grin on his face.

Lin burst into Father Hoarfrost's office, looking more than a bit pleased with herself. "The odds might not be as bad as all that. Grams said we've got allies and that she's called in some favors. She'll be here with everyone from Ashcroft by midday, well before the first of the king's soldiers arrive." Father Hoarfrost's eyes widened, and he quickly smoothed the front of his robes.

"She's coming? Are you sure?" Kit and Lin shared a look, their mouths tied up tight, trying to suppress a smile.

"Who's Grams?" Indie asked. The girls could no longer contain themselves and burst out laughing. "What's so funny?"

The old priest considered Indie's questions before providing him a response. "Grams is Aithlin's grandmother, and a retired priest. She left here many cycles ago to care for a nearby village. As to what's so funny, I have no idea." Father Hoarfrost turned his attention to Kit and Lin, a heavy frown growing on his face. The laughter on the girls' faces died away instantly.

"What sort of army can this Grams person bring?" Ulip's sonorous voice cut through the room. "Tell us of their numbers and their strengths." Lin recoiled slightly from the Gigas' questions.

"She didn't say." Lin shrugged, embarrassed that she hadn't gotten more information from her grandmother. "Not exactly, anyway. She just said that help would come and that we could count on it."

"And what about Ormand?" Kit asked. "We have a powerful vampire languishing in a cell. He's willing to help. He was once a great general, and he knows the king's army. He knows their strategies and their tactics."

The room practically exploded with raised voices. People shouted over each other, trying to ensure they were being heard. Those who did not know of the vampire were quickly learning about his existence. Those who knew of him reacted with fear and loathing. More than once, the phrase *spawn of Faol* was used, identifying him as the enemy; one who should be immediately executed before he caused any harm.

Father Hoarfrost scrubbed his forehead with his gnarled hands. He sighed heavily before finally slamming his fists onto his desk, a wave of deep cold spreading out across the room.

"Enough!" the old priest screamed, causing several of his office's occupants to jump. "Arguing amongst ourselves will solve nothing." He seemed to wobble slightly before collapsing back into his chair.

"Kit," the old priest called out. "If you would be so kind." Father Hoarfrost got up and left his office, with Kit not far behind him, and the boys not far behind her. As the four of them headed down the hall towards the main Temple, they could hear the bickering voices start up again, right where they had left off.

"Do you not see the value in having Ormand helping us?" Kit asked, wringing her hands together. "He willingly submitted himself to my father. He allowed my father to use him as a training dummy. Does that sound like the sort of man who would betray us now?"

"More importantly, little sister, what do you think we should do with General Gabryl? What do you think could be the consequences of freeing him? Do those risks outweigh what you see as potential benefits?"

"It's a risk, Father, I know," Kit said, looking up at the old priest. "But I don't think... Father, I don't know what the right answer is. My heart says that if we free him, he'll help us."

"And what if a demon took possession of his body and his mind?" Father tilted his head slightly. "Ormand said that he cannot stop one from taking control of him. A demon-possessed vampire could lay waste to a good many people, including your father and your friends. Are you so easily willing to risk their lives?"

Kit moved over to a nearby wall. She didn't want to face the question. She didn't want to face Father Hoarfrost. Never had she ever faced such a dilemma. She just wanted to curl up into a small ball and go to sleep. She leaned her back against the wall and let herself slide down until she was sitting on the hallway's cold stone floor. She tucked her knees up to her chest and rested her forehead on them. The boys quickly laid down, pressing their bodies against hers, offering her their strength and comfort. Kit absentmindedly ran her fingers through their fur.

"Father," Kit started, unwilling to look up at her mentor. "I don't want this responsibility. I don't know what to do. I don't want people to die because I've made the wrong choices. I don't want to be the storm. I don't want to cleanse the land with ice and fire."

"Where did you hear that?" Hoarfrost asked, slowly taking a knee in front of Kit, grimacing slightly as he did.

"From a woman in Cormorant," Kit said with a shrug. "She said, *You are the storm. From the ashes, a sword will rise. From the wilds, a child will seek the passive, a mighty roar unleash. From the heavens, a star will fall, to lay waste to the wicked and break the circle.*"

"That was a very specific version of the prophecy," Hoarfrost said, plopping onto his buttocks. "I believe that to be a description of the three who will try."

"Father?"

Hoarfrost closed his eyes and recited the prophecy. "Three will try. Eight Shall Die. Three will go. Two shall grow. One will lose. One shall choose." As he finished, he opened his eyes and stared deeply into Kit's. "I believe the words you just said are a description of the three who will try to free Titan."

Kit's shoulders slumped and her eyes widened. As she slowly exhaled, a smile tugged at the corners of her mouth. "So, I'm not one of the three then. I don't fit any of those descriptions. I changed the prophecy!"

The young priest popped to her feet, suddenly feeling light as a feather, startling the boys with her sudden movement. She quickly helped her mentor to his feet, ignoring his groans as she pulled him up off the cold stone floor. He smiled warmly when Kit gave him a quick kiss on the cheek.

"You may not be *one* of the three," Hoarfrost whispered softly, "but, child, you are definitely the storm. We need to go back to my office and tell the people you have accepted the role as High Priest and that you will enlist the help of General Gabryl in our fight against the kings."

Kit wanted to throw up. "Father, may I be excused? I... need some time alone." The high priest nodded and headed for his office. He patted his thigh, inviting the boys to come join him. Runt was by his side in an instant, but Lump stayed put, sticking as close to Kit as his body would allow.

⟨⟨⟨⟨⟨◊⟩⟩⟩⟩⟩

Lump followed Kit all the way to her cell. His body continued to press against her with every step she took, knocking her off balance several times. She was worried about him. He hadn't been himself for a while now, and his desire to stay with her, rather than enjoy the excitement of the large crowd, had set her teeth on edge. When they got into Kit's room, he hopped up on her bed and hung his face over the edge. His droopy eyes looked so sad.

"Are you okay, Lump? You really haven't been yourself lately."

The wolfdog closed his eyes for a moment before shifting into his human form. He was such a handsome young man with his shaggy golden-red hair and his puppy-dog eyes. All that was missing was his typical disarming smile. He looked on the verge of tears and it was breaking Kit's heart. He stood from the bed and walked to the window that looked out over Mount Toka.

Every other problem troubling Kit's mind instantly melted away. "What is it, my handsome? Why are you so sad?" Unbidden, tears welled up in Kit's eyes. The young man turned away from the window.

Lump stared down at his hands. He had always seemed amazed at the shape and versatility of human hands, but this time, it was to avoid eye contact. Kit invited him to sit beside her on her bed. "I don't know where I belong."

Kit understood what that meant, to not know where you belong, but she didn't understand why Lump might feel that way. Ever since he came to the Temple, he was loved by everyone and welcomed everywhere he went. He was, for lack of a better word, the Temple mascot, but to Kit, he was so much more. He was her soulmate and her best friend. Well, perhaps not her best friend, but among her best friends. Kit had never realized, up until this very moment, that she had many friends. Many close friends with whom she could safely confide in without concern that she'd be laughed at or ridiculed. Her mind flashed back to when she was a child, when her only friend was a straw doll that her mother had made for her. Kit's heart suddenly sank. She feared he had no genuine friends other than her. She had been consumed with so many duties, so many feelings, that she hadn't had as much time to spend with her dog as she used to. A thick lump grew in her throat and her tears flowed freely. When she looked up at the shaggy haired young man, his eyes were glassy.

Lump moved closer and took a seat next to Kit. "You see? You understand me like no one else. I see it in your eyes. I feel it, just being close to you. But you don't need me anymore. It seems like nobody needs me anymore. You have Indie and Runt has Coldforge and..." Kit threw her arms around the young man and squeezed him with all her might. Tears flowed down her face. The thought that she had done something, anything, that might hurt this gentle soul cut her to the bone.

"It's not true. No, it's not true at all. You are a part of me, and me a part of you. You were with me when I felt alone. You gave me strength when I was weak." A flashback broke through to Kit's consciousness. She recalled the time when, in her daemon hysteria, she was going to kill Runt. Lump threw himself between the dire wolf and the frenzied daemon that was going to kill him. "You put yourself in harm's way. You stopped me from doing something unthinkable, unforgivable. You saved Runt. You saved us both. It would take me a lifetime to tell you how many times you saved me, how many times your very presence kept me from losing all hope."

"You needed me when you were very young, but you don't need me anymore. You have many friends. You have a mate. You have mentors. I'm... I'm just a dog." The flow of Kit's tears was renewed and redoubled. She didn't know how to respond, how to tell Lump he was irreplaceable. He provided so many things that she could never repay, not in a thousand lifetimes.

"I love you." It was the only thing she could think of to say. "With all my heart, I love you. I don't know what I would have done without you in my life. I don't know what I would do without you for the rest of my life. You... you are a part of me." The young man had gone back to examining his hands, clenching and unclenching his fingers. "I have an idea."

The tone in Kit's words made Lump raise his eyes expectedly. "What?" His voice sounded hopeful. His doggy expressions shone through in his young man's face. Even as a human, he was unmistakably a golden retriever.

"I can't tell you yet. I have to convince Father to change his mind first. I have to convince him I cannot be High Priest and that he cannot climb Mount Toka. As soon as I do, I'll show you how much I need you."

Lump gave her a broad, toothy smile. Her heart melted and, once again, she wrapped her arms tightly around him. "Never forget that I will love you until the day I pass to the Great Cycle."

"Me, too," Lump said, returning the heart-felt embrace.

CHAPTER TWELVE

THE SPRITES AND THE ELVES

"You're not welcome here, Misty. Crawl back into the hole you came from." The silver-skinned elf lorded her height over the cat-sprite, doing her best to look menacing. Misty shook her head and waved her fur-covered hand at the Elven councilor.

"You need to let it go, Illendielle. It was hundreds of cycles ago and we have done everything we can to make reparations for our actions. Why must you continue to hold a grudge? Galahdes has forgiven us. Why won't you and the rest of the Council?"

"Hundreds of cycles aren't barely more than grains of sand in our lifetimes," Illendielle replied. "Although, if I had my way, you'd have not seen the sunrise after what you did. You nearly destroyed the Tree of Life, you and your cohorts, and your lust for power."

"We did not seek power. We sought only to strengthen the Veil enough that we could stop constantly having to feed it with our magic." The councilor may have understood more about her motivations than she let on. It was actually Feigh, the mouse-sprite, who had desperately wanted to shore up the Veil so that he could spend more time wooing Misty. The cat-sprite knew it, and she liked it. The man was tall and lean, and oh so handsome. She craved his attention, but she didn't see his true nature. Not until after he convinced her to help cast a spell, a spell that would link the Veil to the entire Amberwood Forest, the most sacred of lands to the Elves. Through the magic of the trees, they could feed the Veil for eternity, and they'd be free to live their lives as they saw fit.

"You're a fool if you expect me to believe you." The councilor pointed an accusatory finger at Feigh and Midnight. "The two of you were at the root of this. Don't believe for a moment that we don't all know that. You talk a good game, Feigh, but we know your heart. Tapping into the forest might have made the Veil impenetrable, but it was also going to feed your own magic. You sought to become stronger than Galahdes herself. If it wasn't for your infatuation with Misty, we'd have thought you were trying to—"

"He wanted Galahdes to be his bride," Misty said. "And Midnight here wanted to rule the Council. With the power they'd have gained, none but Galahdes herself could have prevented it."

Illendielle laughed and raised her eyebrows at the sprites. "Instead, you decimated the Amberwood Forest and cursed yourselves, forever forced to live your lives as..." she waved her hands about while a look of contempt etched itself across her face, "these pathetic little creatures."

"We've learned from our mistakes," Midnight said, his head hanging low. "We have repented, and we are doing what we can to set things to rights. Galahdes has forgiven us."

"It is by her order that we are here." Misty did not share Midnight's contrition. Sure, she was as much a part of the colossal catastrophe as the others, but she was duped into helping cast the spell, just as all the others in their cadre.

"Galahdes has been gone since the forest was petrified by your foul magic. I should have you executed for invoking her name just to aid in your miserable deceptions." As Illendielle spoke the words, several dozen Wood Nymphs appeared from the surrounding trees. They were nearly as tall as the Elves, covered in amber-leaf armor, the strongest and lightest armor produced by the Elven smiths. They nary made a sound as they nocked their Elven longbows and leveled their arrows on the sprites. Hobbs drew his sword and leapt at Illendielle. Before she could take a defensive pose, he held the tip of his blade to her throat.

"Lower your weapons or the councilor dies." Before the incident, Hobbs had been the Elven Council's Champion, the most revered, and the most feared warrior in the Elven Kingdom. The councilor sucked in a sharp breath and motioned to the Wood Nymphs to stand down.

"Reformed you say?" Illendielle said. "You would enter this, our Sacred Circle, and threaten to kill the High Councilor, all to save your miserable hides? No longer do you believe in the Hierarchy. No longer do you see fit to follow Galahdes' teachings." It was Misty's turn to laugh.

"I find it interesting that you have placed yourself in Galahdes' chair in her absence. I wonder how easily you'll give it up when the queen returns."

"The queen is dead and gone," Illendielle snapped back. "The council needed a leader, and I was the queen's second."

"Only after you spearheaded the vote to remove me." Misty's head snapped back as soon as she spoke the words. "You will pay for your deception." Misty's blood was boiling. She wanted to challenge Illendielle for leadership, right there on the spot, with the Wood Nymph general there to bear witness to it. "I'll deal with you later, but for now, I need the Guardians of the Wood to join us. The Veil is in dire jeopardy, and they may be enough to hold back Faol long enough to set things right."

"They will do nothing of the sort." Illendielle practically screeched the words out.

"Midnight, if you would," Misty said coolly. "The general needs to see it."

Midnight held his staff in front of himself and closed his eyes. He reached into the aether and withdrew a single bright yellow flower. He held it out for the general to see. "The sun lily. The only person who can grow it is Galahdes. It is proof that she sent us. She calls you to battle."

The general stepped lightly toward Midnight, each footstep barely leaving a print on the soft, loam-covered ground. She took the rabbit-sprite's hand in hers and drew the flower to her nose, inhaling deeply. Any doubt that may have shown on the Wood Nymph's face vanished, replaced with pure serenity.

"Where does our queen wish us to go?" The general bowed slightly to Misty, completely ignoring the screeching protestations of the High Councilor.

"We are to go to Aarall, to the Seat of Titan." The general's face hardened.

"We will be of little use in those open planes. Our magic lies within the forest. It is from the trees that we draw our power."

"Your skills as warriors transcend your magic. Faol and his spawn are marching on Aarall as we speak. Trust in our queen. She will provide." The general took in Misty's words and breathed an inaudible sigh.

"I will send out a scouting party before the sun sets. I will speak to the druids. I don't know how they'll get us there without a body of water, but we will heed our queen's call." The general was about to back away when Midnight cleared his throat.

"There is a large body of water at the foot of Mount Toka. It should suffice."

"There is no lake," the general stated. "There is only the river, Aar, and it is too deep beneath the surface to be of use to us."

"A large lake is now there." It was clear to Misty that Midnight was enjoying knowing something that the Wood Nymph did not. "It was created when that god-awful statue melted. The water is pure, and it is deep. It will serve the druids well." Misty nodded to the general, acknowledging that Midnight was speaking true. The general's eyebrows shot up before she backed away.

"We will heed the call." These were her last words before the general and her cohorts melted back into the forest.

Hobbs continued to hold his blade on Illendielle. "Let me make her pay for what she's done, Misty."

"We need to go, Hobbs. Galahdes will mete out whatever punishment she sees fit. It is not our place to cast judgment."

"To Grams' house?" Midnight asked as he held his staff out.

"No." Misty's gaze bore into the eyes of Illendielle. The woman did not flinch from the intensity of the cat-sprite's eyes. She simply raised her chin and looked down her nose at the impudent sprite who stood before her. "Take us to Father Hoarfrost. We need to tell him help is coming."

Chapter Thirteen

THE KING'S ARMY APPROACHES

Kit had spent the last hour helping Father Hoarfrost get packed and ready for his trip to Mount Toka. He had reluctantly accepted the enhanced healing potions, along with several scrolls that Silverleaf had prepared. He had created scrolls for three ever-burning fires, two domes of protection, and a scroll of silence. The domes of protection would give Father a place to sleep safely in the night. The half elf had gotten the idea from the battle mage, who had created one when they'd fought with Lieutenant Karr. When Father gave him a look of confusion over the scroll of silence, Silverleaf had simply shrugged and told him, "You never know when you might need to be perfectly quiet."

Kit handed Father Hoarfrost a small satchel that contained the potions, the scrolls, and a small batch of wayfarer's muffins. Her chest was heavy, like every breath was passing through a thick pillow. "I wish there was some way I could talk you out of doing this. Please, let me take your place. I hate the idea of you dying, but the thought that you might die cold and alone on that cruel mountain is killing me."

"Would you prefer I feel the pain of knowing that you are putting yourself in danger for me?" The old man cocked an eyebrow. "You would willingly let me suffer like that?"

"Father, you trained me to put myself in harm's way. The last five cycles I've been here were to prepare me for journeys like this. If you have faith in Titan and faith in the Temple's training, you should not be worried about me. You should believe that I will be safe, and I will complete the mission." Father Hoarfrost dipped his head and smiled.

"You will be a magnificent High Priest. There won't be a priest or acolyte who will outwit you."

Kit lowered her gaze, not wanting to look her mentor in the eyes. "Father. I don't want to be the high priest. I am not suited to being a leader. Even if I can be good at it, I will never enjoy it. I would rather be just a regular priest. I have sought nothing more than just being a part of the Temple."

"And that is why you'll be an excellent leader. You do not seek it. You do not want it. You don't want the power, or what little glamor might come with it. You will be fair and honest with everyone under your leadership because that's who you are."

"Please, Father, I beg of you. Don't go. Don't do this. Let me commune with Titan. If I could speak to him at the altar, perhaps he could tell me how to free him. I feel it in every fiber of my being that setting him free is what will bring salvation to the people."

"Excuse me, Father." Kit turned to the voice at the doorway. Indie was standing there dressed in full armor, with the boys by his side. "Kit, you need to get to the city gates. The king's army is here sooner than we expected. There is also a large population out on the planes near Lake Titan. The enemy has cut them off. They won't make it here without intervention."

"Where is this population from?" Father Hoarfrost strode forward, his look deadly. Indie took a step back as the man closed in on him.

"We can't be sure, Father, but we believe it is the people from Ashcroft. We watched a contingent of soldiers break off from the main body of the army and ride their way." Kit's hand went to her mouth, trying to hide the gasp that had escaped.

"Did they attack the people? Was anyone hurt? Does Lin know?" Indie shook his head at Kit's questions.

"Yes, Lin knows. I don't know if anyone was hurt. I came here to get you as soon as we saw what was happening. Char, Angel, and Whistler should already be saddled and ready to go. Lin insisted on coming out to face the enemy. We have no choice, Kit. We either fight or they're going to die."

"Where are the horses?" Father Hoarfrost practically flew to the back of his office and yanked down the huge battle hammer from the wall. Kit had always thought it was just a decoration. The weapon practically ignited the moment his hand touched it. A red flame appeared for a moment before the entire head became encased in ice.

"They'll be at the back door." Indie's eyes went wide as the old man stormed across the room at him. "The door that leads to the stables."

Father Hoarfrost practically bowled the young man over as he blew past him. The boys immediately gave chase, bounding down the hallway, nipping at each other as they vied for position. Kit motioned to Indie with her head, and followed. She broke into a steady jog to keep up with the high priest. A moment later, Indie came up alongside.

"What's happening?" Indie asked, his voice barely louder than a whisper. "Why is he coming?"

"Because Grams is with the people from Ashcroft. I believe there is a *history* between the two of them." Indie gave a nod of appreciation. Kit broke into a full run and Indie did his best to keep up with the tiny priest and the old man.

⚜

Angel, as fast as she was, struggled to keep up with Father Hoarfrost and Whistler. The old man rode like he was in his prime and never had Whistler run faster. A memory flashed back to Kit as she recalled Lin once saying that Angel ran faster than she should, and it was because of her. Perhaps it was the same thing with Father Hoarfrost. Perhaps he had a way of bringing out the best in horses.

When Kit, Indie, and the boys arrived at the front gate, Father Hoarfrost had already dismounted and was in conversation with Captain Harding and Aurora. Coldforge was a few feet away, openly staring at Kit's mother. His mouth seemed to open and close repeatedly, with no sound coming from it.

A contingent of the Watch was handing out longbows and quivers of arrows to a line of people, none of whom looked like soldiers. These were desperate times if her father was enlisting civilians to fight. Many of those who accepted the weapons appeared comfortable with them. Many others looked confused and confounded, unsure of what to do with either piece. Those who knew how to use the weapons immediately set to helping those who didn't. Impromptu lessons were breaking out everywhere across the courtyard. Kit knew these people wouldn't be proficient enough to be effective, but with some magical assistance from the priests, they wouldn't be useless either.

The city gates were still wide open as a steady stream of marketplace vendors were trundling inside. They had as much of their wares with them as they could manage. The more reluctant hawkers were screaming at the guards escorting them inside, insisting that they stay with their stalls.

"What's happening?" Kit asked as Angel skidded to a stop.

"There are at least one thousand soldiers marching towards the city," Kit's father replied. "Ulip's estimation appears to have been extremely accurate."

"And many more are coming through the Forest of Arr," Aurora said. "They're on the main road between here and Two Peaks. The road through the forest is narrow, so it's slowing them down. I don't think they'll be here until tomorrow, at the earliest."

"What of King Faol's army?" Indie asked, sliding down from Char. The boys immediately went to greet Aurora. She gave them both a quick reception before answering Indie's question. A few seconds later, Runt split off to give Coldforge a good face wash. The unruly little man and the giant wolf had become close friends. A small pang of jealousy sprung up in Kit's chest. It was uncalled for, but it appeared just the same. She had to force herself to push it aside and listen to her mother's words.

Aurora regarded the young man who'd shown up asking questions. "Faol's army has stalled. They are across the Arnnor border, but they seem preoccupied. Many have broken off from the main body of the army. They are spreading out, almost like they are forming search parties."

"That makes no sense," Kit said. "If their goal is to take Aarall, why would they be slowing down for anything?"

"It's unknown," Captain Harding said. "Ulip has been flying reconnaissance trying to get a better picture of what their forces are like. Thank Titan that it's buying us some time."

"We need to clear the way for the people of Ashcroft," Father Hoarfrost said. "Nothing else is more important. We must get them behind the safety of the city walls."

"Even their small vanguard has more soldiers than we have," Captain Harding said. "But we have enough volunteers to make them think we are stronger than we are."

"The priests and acolytes will be here shortly," Sister Gale said as she joined the party. She was dressed in light leather armor trimmed with white and silver metal. Across her left breast was the symbol of Titan. She had a longbow slung over her back and a long, pure-black staff. "We will stay with the *new recruits* and offer what magic we can to aid in their aim." She turned to Kit and bowed slightly. "If that suits the plans of our High Priest?"

Kit's face reddened. "I'm not High Priest, Father is." The words came out squeakier than she'd have liked.

"The plan suits me just fine," Father Hoarfrost said. Kit's heart leapt at the man's words. Perhaps the threat of Grams being hurt was enough to make him change his mind. Perhaps the lure of having her within the city was enough to make him stay. "How are we to proceed? Do we meet the main force head on, or do we harry them long enough to let the people get by?"

Captain Harding nodded to the questions. He seemed just as pleased as Kit that Father Hoarfrost was taking a direct role in the city's defense, as well as its people. "The plan is to send the City Watch to deal with those who split off to meet the people heading here for safety. Sister Gale will lead the priests and the recruits to form a wall between the main army and the front gates. With any luck, they'll be able to hold the army back long enough for the people to pass."

A gigantic shadow passed over the courtyard. Cries of terror ripped through the gathered people, including the new recruits. They had already nocked arrows to shoot at the perceived threat.

"Stand down," Captain Harding bellowed. "He's an ally." While many of the recruits listened, way too many loosed arrows, attempting to shoot Ulip and Yuka out of the sky.

"Be at peace," Father Hoarfrost intoned. Even though the high priest's voice lacked her father's volume, it had a chilling effect upon everyone in the entire courtyard. A quiet hush instantly fell over everyone. All weapons were lowered, as were most everyone's heads. Not a single person reacted when Yuka landed in the middle of the courtyard, raising vast clouds of dust from the flapping of her leathery red wings. Ulip gave her a quick pat on the shoulder and sprinted over to join the rest of the group.

"What news do you have?" Captain Harding asked. He had a look of hopeful anticipation on his face. Ulip bit his lip, like he was reluctant to share what he had seen.

"King Faol's army is delayed. Though I could not see them, Yuka told me green shadow creatures were harassing them. These creatures weaved in and out amongst the trees, appearing and disappearing like the ghosts of ancestors long since passed. Each time they appeared, one of the enemy soldiers died." Father Hoarfrost's face brightened at the giant's words.

"What other good news do you bring us?" the high priest said. "What of the forces at our gate?" Ulip seemed to relax after hearing Father's questions. Perhaps he feared he'd be thought a lunatic for speaking of green ghosts.

"The main body of that force has stopped. They are entrenching themselves, taking up defense positions. A smaller group, perhaps forty strong, has split off towards the people." The giant paused and looked towards Yuka, who seemed to shake her head at him. Based on Ulip's body language, they were in the middle of a conversation.

"I would say you're correct," Angel said to Kit through their bond. *"I cannot hear their words, but they are clearly speaking to each other, and I would guess that the one named Yuka is angry with the big man."*

"Enough," Ulip practically screamed at the fire drake. "I will tell them what you saw. They need to know everything."

"What did you see?" Father Hoarfrost roared at the fire drake. He left the group and thundered towards the creature, who took a half-step back as the man bared down on her. "Tell me true, Soldier of Flame. What did your keen perception see that this man did not?"

Yuka raised her head high, her neck coiled like a serpent ready to strike. "You honor me, Father of the Temple." She spoke in the common tongue, loud enough for anyone within a hundred paces to hear her. "I will speak of what I saw, even if it is unbelievable." There was a long pause, like the drake was weighing her words.

"She saw a creature of dust and decay," Ulip blurted out. "She *felt* three creatures that are not of this world; powerful creatures capable of incalculable destruction."

"This creature of dust and decay," Aurora said, stepping past Father Hoarfrost, putting herself easily within the drake's striking distance. "What did she do when she met the people? How did the people react to her?"

"I did not say she was a female," Yuka said. Her body relaxed substantially. "The woman spoke to the people, and they bowed before her. They were like sheep, laying before a dragon, waiting to be slaughtered."

"All?" Father Hoarfrost asked. "Every person bowed to this woman?"

Yuka closed her eyes for several seconds before reopening them. "All but one. An elderly woman stood defiantly against the words."

"Titan's snowballs," Father Hoarfrost said. "We need to move. Now. There is no time to waste."

"That had to be Grams," Lin whispered to Kit. The little priest nodded in agreement, although she didn't fear for the old woman. She instinctively knew there was more to her than Grams had ever let on. Kit had witnessed a taste of her power the day she'd stood at Kit's back, dissuading the village guards from doing something foolish. Grams had been dressed in armor that could only have been described as ethereal. Her battle hammer had also exhibited a remarkably similar appearance.

"Father," Aurora called out as the high priest blew past her. "You cannot go. No one but I can face this woman." The high priest wheeled around, his face filled with fury and determination.

"Do you believe I fear a vampire? Is that what you think?"

A golden aura spilled out from Aurora. Her face became profoundly serene. "She is not a normal vampire, Father. She is Annabella Illum, the daughter of King Faol. Among her people, she is known as Lady Dread."

"I do not fear the spawn of Faol. I fear nothing." Father Hoarfrost turned away from the woman and continued his way to Whistler. Kit cut him off before he could get there, drawing a look of undiluted rage from the old priest, who now looked like he was a much younger, much more virile man. His gray hair was once again black. His skin was smooth and nearly free of wrinkles. His gnarled hands were once again strong and full of power. "Step away, little sister."

"Father, listen to what my mother has to say. Let her finish and then I will go with you to save Grams and her people." The high priest slowed and nodded lightly.

"Father," Aurora said, placing her hand on his shoulder. "She is not just a vampire. She is demon possessed. Unlike other vampires hosting a demon, she controls it. She can bend it to her will, and it has made her unnaturally strong and equally deadly. I have faced her many times. Each time I did, I lost."

"We can fight her together," Kit said. "The two of us can join our strength and defeat this woman."

"She is not the only one you need to be concerned about," Yuka said. "There were two other similar creatures with her. They are not as powerful, but they reek of the same evil. One was a male and the other a female."

"What did they look like?" Captain Harding wore the same look of disgust on his face as Father Hoarfrost. "Tell me, if you can."

"They looked like humans," Yuka said. "The male was large, but not as big as you. He was dressed in armor like yours. The female was much smaller, but not as small as your child, the little priest. Her skin was like honey."

"Helja," Captain Harding said. His look of disgust switched to a look of hate-filled loathing. "Lieutenant Karr is with them. He'll have told them everything that has happened here. Any chance of them being surprised has passed us by."

"The other is likely Xin," Kit said. "She was the head of Templeton's military. She is a formidable warrior on her own, but if she carries a demon-shade within her, she is to be feared."

Chapter Fourteen

LADY DREAD

"You need to stay with the recruits." Father Hoarfrost wasn't giving Sister Gale any room to negotiate. He was arguing to keep the number of people fighting Lady Dread to a bare minimum.

"And outside of yourself, Father, who here can use magic?" Every person, save Captain Harding, raised their hand. The combat teacher groaned. "Who here, besides myself, Father Hoarfrost, and Sister Kit, can cast defensive magic?" Nobody moved. Sister Gale turned to Kit and the high priest. "Do either of you plan on doing anything even remotely defensive?"

"I will." Father Hoarfrost had a look of deep concern etched into his features. "I will protect the people while the others do the fighting." Sister Gale blew out a long breath and clasped her hands in front of herself.

"Father, I cannot remember the last time you were in combat. Is now the right time to test your skills?" The old priest's face grew grim, his deep brown eyes turned so pale they all but turned white. A cloud of frost swirled around his feet. The frost grew thicker and spun faster and faster until he was encased in a spinning cloud of ice shards. With only a glance, one of the ice shards struck out, nicking Sister Gale's cheek. A moment later, a thin red line appeared, and her blood slowly seeped out.

"I remember everything about how to fight, Sister. I may be old, but I am far from feeble."

Kit stared, her mouth agape. It was hardly hours ago when she felt no power in the man. She believed him to be nearing his deathbed. Power was now flowing off him in thick, heavy waves.

Sister Gale placed her finger upon her cheek. She looked down at the blood that now dripped from her hand. A slow smile grew on her face. There was no hint of anger, only joy. "Your powers are as they were when I first met you, old friend, but you cannot protect your warriors and your people at the same time. Protect the people. I will look after your fighters."

"Father," Aurora said. "I will lead my daughter against the three demon-touched fighters. Sister Gale will do what she can to support us. The man who rides the lesser dragon can deal with the regular soldiers. You will protect the people. Once we drive off the enemy, you lead the people behind the city walls. Everyone else will keep the larger army at bay."

Captain Harding shook his head and moved in front of Aurora. He took her by her forearms and stared into her golden eyes. "I am not letting you and our daughter fight Annabella without me. Not when she has so many others there to support her. You have faced her before and have never bested her. I'm coming and that's all there is to it." Aurora smiled up at the man who'd fathered their daughter. "Would you be so kind as to carry me into battle? I find myself without a horse." The captain got a strange, quizzical look on his face.

"Why don't you just..."

"Because I'd rather ride," she said, cutting the captain off before he could finish. The captain glanced over at their daughter and nodded.

Indie rode up to where the captain and Aurora were standing. "I'm coming, too. I've faced vampires and demon-possessed vampires before. I will not let Kit face them without me. Not if I'm still drawing breath at any rate." Aurora's eyes widened.

"You're the man she's in love with." The woman raised her eyebrows and turned to Kit's father. "Is he worthy of her affections?" The big man laughed.

"More than you know. Their bond is as strong as..."

"Ours?" The woman brushed her long blonde hair over her shoulder and beat her eyes lashes at the man, who was now blushing scarlet.

"Captain Harding, if I may have a word with you." When the captain didn't respond to the voice behind him, the man cleared his throat, loudly. "Captain, I must insist you give me your attention."

With a tightly clenched fist, the captain wheeled around at whoever it was bothering him. Before he could speak a word, the captain's face drained of all its color. "General Eagle Claw. Kren. What are you...? Oh, sweet Titan. Beth, what are you doing here?" The captain's eyes continued to widen until they fell upon the general. "Why is my wife here? Where's my son? Is he safe? You were to keep them hidden."

"Hello, Ray," Elizabeth Harding said. Her tone was cool, but her eyes sparkled with mischief. "Is this what happens when you keep me tucked away on a farmstead with only my son and this lovely old man to keep me company?"

"Elizabeth, I... Oh sweet Titan, I'm so happy to see you." The captain swept the woman off her feet and greeted her with a deep, passionate kiss. "Where's Nick? Is he safe? Why did Kren bring you here?"

The captain's wife peered over his massive shoulder at Kit's mother. "Hello, Aurora. I trust you are well."

"Very well, Beth. Thank you for asking. How are you and your son? Has his height eclipsed his father's yet?" Elizabeth laughed gayly at the question.

"No, not as yet, but maybe by the end of the summer. The boy is growing like a weed and he's eating me out of house and home. Never have I seen anybody with such a voracious appetite. I expect he'll be along shortly. He is in the stables fetching his father's horse."

Kit's jaw flopped open. Her heart was racing out of control. Her mind was not far behind. She knew her father had a wife, and that she had a half brother, but never had she really considered them all being together. Their casual, comfortable demeanor was beyond anything she'd have ever expected. She furrowed her brow as she considered the situation further.

I have three mothers; an adopted mother, a birth mother, and a stepmother.

"Father!" a young but deep voice called out from across the city square. The young boy was huge. If it weren't for his baby face, Kit would have thought him to have seen at least twenty summers. The boy was tall and broad shouldered like his father. A braided ponytail hung down his back. It flopped about as the charger he rode jounced him around. It wasn't until the braid fell over his right shoulder that Kit noticed it was flame-red, just like her own. As soon as he approached, he leapt gracefully down from the horse's back and gave his father a deep embrace. The two shared some private words until Father Hoarfrost interrupted the reunion.

"I'm glad your family is here to send you off, Captain, but it's time for us to head out."

Lin wheeled Whistler about and moved next to Indie and Kit.

"Aithlin," Father Hoarfrost called to her. "I will need your mount if it is okay with you. I think it would be best if you joined the priests and other acolytes in ensuring the king's soldiers do not breach our defenses." The woman groaned and rolled her eyes. With an exasperated huff, she reluctantly dismounted and walked her horse over to the high priest. With a nod, the high priest accepted the reins and leapt up into the saddle.

Captain Harding gave his wife and son a quick hug and a kiss before mounting his stallion. He held out his hand to Aurora, lifting her behind him with almost no effort.

"Bring him home safe to us, Aurora. This boy needs his father, and I need my husband. He hasn't warmed my bed in far too long."

With a nod, Aurora bid farewell to the family and tapped the captain on the shoulder to let him know she was ready. In seconds, Kit, Indie, Father Hoarfrost, Sister Gale, Captain Harding, and Aurora were racing through the front gates with Coldforge, Runt and Lump close on their heels. Kit knew they were at the rear because of the dwarf's incessant whooping.

⚜

Angel quickly outpaced the group. Kit's heart was still soaring from having seen the rest of her family, a family she so desperately wanted to get to know better. The rhythmic thumping of her little roan's hoofbeats had changed along the way, turning into something more like the hum of a beetle's wings.

The little priest stole a look to her right, at the main body of the army that had begun their march on the city. They seemed to ignore Kit and her cohorts as they traveled across the fields of green to close in on their quarry. She had to trust that together, the City Watch, the Temple's faithful and the hundreds of volunteer soldiers, they could hold the line long enough for the people of Ashcroft to make it to safety.

"We need to slow down, or we'll face the enemy on our own." Angel's voice carried an air of concern, unlike anything Kit had heard before. Perhaps it was her pregnancy that made her fear for her unborn foal. Perhaps it was Aurora's concerns about Faol's daughter and how powerful she was. *"There are at least thirty soldiers up ahead. You are the most amazing person I've ever met, but even you have your limits."*

Before Kit could respond, Father Hoarfrost moved alongside, along with Aurora and her father.

"There, we're not alone anymore." Kit chided her mount, her emotions swelling when the others joined in beside her. *"We'll head for Xin, the honey skinned woman. Do you see her?"*

"Of course, I see her. What about the others?" Angel replied with a chuff.

"My mother will deal with the woman leading the group. I'm guessing that's Annabella, Lady Dread. I expect my father will deal with Lieutenant Karr, but the truth is, I'd like to skin that man myself."

Father Hoarfrost split off to the left, heading directly to the main body of the town's population. Aurora and her father surged forward, taking a direct path for Annabella.

"Are you slowing down? Why is everyone passing us?"

"I'm running as fast as I can. They're just running faster."

Kit took a quick glance over her shoulder. Indie and the boys were fifty paces behind, and Sister Gale was substantially further back.

"Slow up enough for Indie to catch up." The humming rhythm of Angel's hoofbeats changed slightly, and in seconds Indie and the boys were running alongside. "I'm going to take Xin. You and the boys take out the soldiers."

"I'm staying with you," Indie yelled back. "We'll fight her together." Kit's chest rumbled at the man's words.

"Take out the soldiers. Join me when you're done. We can't have them at our back haranguing us." Indie nodded his agreement, but his expression said he didn't like it. He turned back to Sister Gale and waved his hand for her to follow him.

"Run Xin into the ground," Kit said through their bond. She pulled her hammer from its sheath and let it hang low by her hip. "I hope you're ready for some fun, Fury. You've been awfully quiet lately." The power in the hammer surged into her hand and up her arm. "Nice to know you're still with me, friend."

The feeling in the hammer changed at Kit's words. The surging power turned warm. It felt like she was holding her hands in front of a roaring fire, soaking in the warmth and the comfort of it.

Kit's heart exploded from her chest when her mother leapt from the back of her father's horse and threw herself headlong at Lady Dread. She had a glowing white longsword drawn, ready to strike mid-air. The woman she was attacking leapt up at her, holding a similar looking longsword that glowed with a red, ethereal light of its own. The glow wasn't from flames. It was something different. It seemed to come from within the blade itself. The clash of the two swords rang out with a deafening clang. Xin was trying to move in to assist Lady Dread, while Lieutenant Karr turned to meet the oncoming charge of his captain.

"Don't let Xin make it to my mother." Kit's heart was now racing, fearing that the woman her mother was fighting was too much for her. The daemon within screamed to be set free, to annihilate the enemy, to crush their bones into the ground.

Angel found extra speed, cutting off Xin well before she could join in on Lady Dread's fight. Something in Xin's expression said she was pleased that Kit had chosen to fight with her. With a graceful turn, Xin moved to the side and slashed at Angel with the razor-sharp tip of her long spear. What Xin hadn't calculated for was Kit leaping from her saddle, bringing her hammer down on the woman's head. The mithril hammer landed solidly, knocking Xin to the ground. Kit rolled and spun about, immediately moving into a battle stance. Xin was laying face-first on the ground, her limbs twitching.

From the corner of her eye, Kit saw Angel forty or fifty paces away. She was swaying badly with each step she took. "Sweet Titan, no." Kit stole a glance back at Xin who hadn't moved from where she was laying. *"I'm coming, Angel. Please hold on."*

Kit's feet pumped as hard as they could while she raced to her mount, to her friend. She could see a gaping wound on the horse that ran from her chest all the way to her rear flank. Blood was pouring out at a frightening pace. The ground beneath Kit's feet felt spongy, like she was running through wet sand, slowing her every movement. No matter how hard she tried, she just couldn't seem to close the distance on her horse.

Just as Kit got to Angel, the horse collapsed onto her side. She whinnied softly and shuddered.

"By the will of Titan, you will not die," Kit screamed, throwing herself onto the horse. Her golden aura immediately burst outward, enveloping the roan. The small priest screamed in agony as she accepted the horse's injuries into her body. She didn't care how much it hurt. She didn't care that she was on the verge of passing out. Nothing was going to stop her from rescuing her friend.

The pain in Kit's side was excruciating. Just as it felt like it was about to pass, a new pain exploded in the middle of her back. It was like the agony she'd felt while healing Angel, yet somehow different. It was more confined, more intense. A blood-curdling scream came from somewhere behind. Despite the world swimming in and out of focus, Kit turned to see. She feared it was her mother crying out. What she saw brought a smile to her face. Xin was standing behind Kit, holding a broken long spear dripping with blood. Fury was beside her, his arm buried up to his wrist in her chest. From Xin's body, a black smoke poured out. It coalesced for a moment before Fury's deep blue fiery breath turned it into a cloud of ash. The last thing Kit remembered was Fury giving her a thick, scaly smile.

Chapter Fifteen

Hope is Lost

Kit winced as she rolled over onto her belly. Her aura of healing had dissipated, and she struggled to call upon it again. Dark spots danced in front of her eyes. She tried a second time to call upon her celestial powers, but they wouldn't listen.

"Titan, hear me." She whispered through gritted teeth. A warm yellow glow swam into view, chasing away the dark spots that had been obscuring her vision. Her breathing eased, but the intense pain in her back remained.

"The spear's point snapped off in your back," Fury said, his massive frame hunched over the small girl. "I can remove it, but it will hurt."

"Do it," Kit said. "Just get it out of me." Without another word, Fury reached into the wound with his clawed fingers. He hissed wildly as he yanked the blade from the wound, throwing it to the side as soon as it was out. The yellow aura that had engulfed Kit turned to a deep gold.

"The blade was befouled by evil magic." Fury's hand was severely burned. The scales where he had touched the weapon were now a sickly green. "Are you well?" Kit nodded and hopped up from the ground. Angel was still on her side, but her breathing looked steady and strong.

"Angel, are you okay?" Kit reached out through their bond, desperate to hear her horse's voice.

"I am now. I feared you had died. I heard your screams of agony, and then your mind went silent. I thought you had passed to the Beyond. I... I lost my will to live." Kit kissed the brow of her horse, her fingers pushing her long mane aside.

"Rest, my friend. Regain your strength. I'll be back."

The sounds of the raging battle came crashing in on Kit's ears. She tried to take in the entire scene, struggling to decide what she should do next. Her mother was locked in heated combat with the woman she had referred to as Lady Dread. Her father and Lieutenant Karr were taking vicious attacks at each other, neither gaining nor losing ground to the other. Indie, Coldforge, Sister Gale, and the boys were fighting soldiers who were threatening to surround them. It was difficult to tell the state of the combat with so many people moving about. The entire scene looked like some strange, violent dance. The combat took a quick turn when Lump changed into his dragon form and began flaming the enemy. Screams of terror and agony ripped through the group. It stopped abruptly when a deep red aura surrounded one combatant. She summoned a wall of flame that separated her soldiers from Lump and the others. Two of the enemy soldiers walked through the flames and unleashed a host of nightmarish creatures. As soon as they had, they retreated once more behind their protective barrier.

"We need to help them," Fury said. He was flexing his burned hand, grimacing as he did.

"You're hurt," Kit said, hurrying to his side.

"I'm fine. There is no time to lose. Those creatures cannot be killed and they're already gaining the upper hand on our friends." The draken's words were not lost on Kit. Never before had he referred to them as his friends.

"I will carry you into battle." Angel was up and standing beside Kit. *"Like the dragon said, we must make haste."*

Kit didn't consider whether the little roan was fully healed. She simply leapt to her back and dug her heels into her ribs. In a heartbeat, they were speeding across the grass, Angel's hooves lighting the ground ablaze as she did.

Kit ignored the woman who had cast the wall of fire and took a direct path to the two mages who had summoned the creatures. The sound of roaring flames masked Angel's hoofbeats, allowing Kit to approach undetected. She threw her hammer at the first of the two battle mages, allowing Fury to engage him on his own. When his seven-foot body emerged, he quickly wrapped his clawed hands around the mage's neck and bit his face off. Those soldiers who were within striking distance of the draken immediately fell upon him, beating him with sword and shield.

The remaining woman who had cast the summoning spell threw her hands up in front of herself as she tried to ward off Kit and her rampaging horse. Some form of magic had burst forth from her hands, but she fell under trampling hooves before the spell could fully manifest.

The woman who had created the wall of fire cackled at the sight of Kit. She was young and beautiful, with long, flowing white hair that swirled about her head, making her appear utterly insane.

"Grind her to dust," Kit said, urging Angel to run even faster. *"We cannot fail."*

⁂

Captain Harding's vision was becoming blurred as the sweat from his brow leaked into his eyes. He couldn't take the time to wipe the burning away. He was spending every moment trying to deflect the furious onslaught of blows that Lieutenant Karr was raining down on him. Sweet Titan, the man was powerful, much stronger than he could have ever imagined. The smug look of satisfaction on the traitor's face fueled the captain's fires, allowing him to continue when his muscles screamed for him to stop.

A shriek from his left drew the captain's attention for the briefest of moments. Aurora had just landed a critical blow on Annabella, causing her to drop her longsword. The weapon spun from her hand, landing only a foot away from where the captain stood. That split second of distraction allowed Karr to get in a strike of his own, his blade landing squarely on the captain's left shoulder. Pain erupted in his body. It was like nothing the captain had ever felt. He stole a quick glance, fearing his arm had been cleaved from his body. Relief washed through him when he saw that his pauldron had absorbed most of the damage. It was severely dented. It was likely embedded in his shoulder, but it was a wound the captain could live with.

"Die, Captain," Karr screamed out as he unleashed another devastating over-hand blow. Captain Harding could barely get his sword up in time to deflect the attack. Holding his bastard sword single-handed was not a problem, but the strength of Karr's blow shattered the blade and knocked the hilt from his hand. The traitor laughed like a maniac as he pulled his weapon back and took another mighty swing.

The captain stepped to the side, allowing the blade to swoosh harmlessly past him. With a quick sidekick to Karr's knee, the captain knocked his enemy off balance long enough for him to grab Annabella's fallen sword. A sudden rush of power flowed up the captain's arm. His pain vanished, replaced with a glorious sensation that fueled his spirit.

Again, Karr swung his blade with all his might, looking to cleave the captain in two. Captain Harding stepped back from the first swing, watching as the blade narrowly missed his belly. Karr spun around and followed his first attack with another similar, yet harder, swing. This time, the captain stepped forward and used his new blade to block the attack. It was Karr's blade that shattered this time, its silver pieces scattering about like ice pellets in a blizzard.

The lieutenant's demeanor changed. His eyes became wild and his mouth pulled back in a grotesque smile. "I need no weapon to disembowel you. I cannot wait to feel my hands rip through your innards. I will bathe in your blood as I feast upon your heart. I will...

Karr's expression froze mid sentence. Captain Harding had brought his blade down next to the man's neck, splitting him to his groin. A dark shadow emerged from the lieutenant's body. It stood behind him for a moment, looking like a shadow cast upon a wall. The same gaping wound appeared across the shadow's body. Its red eyes flickered momentarily before its body evaporated into nothingness. Karr continued to stand facing the captain. A look of confusion crossed his face before he toppled to his side.

The captain flinched at the blood-curdling scream that came from his left. Where Annabella had once stood, a gargantuan ram-horned beast now remained. Its skin was a deep crimson mass of bubbling magma. It stood twice as tall as Aurora. Its body seemed to lose integrity before reforming into this horrid shape.

From the captain's right, something approached. It was moving so quickly that its shape could not be determined. Behind it was another equally fast moving being, but the man recognized his daughter and her horse in an instant. As his daughter's quarry neared, the captain's heart skipped a beat. Kit was chasing Aurora. He glanced back to his left, only to find Kit's mother standing before the molten creature. Using his new blade like a shield, the captain held it across his chest, readying himself for the imminent collision.

He must have blinked and missed the woman who wore Aurora's face. Before he could realize it, she had passed him. Kit and Angel followed a breath later with her battle hammer raised over her head, while lightning crackled along its surface.

There was a cataclysmic collision as Aurora's lookalike slammed into Kit's mother. Captain Harding wasted no time throwing himself into the fray. The combat was happening faster than he could fathom, but he seemed to know instinctually when to feint and when to strike. As the power of the sword continued to surge through his body, it seemed to communicate with him on some unconscious level.

There was a moment, frozen in his mind's eye, when the captain's eyes fell upon the three women, locked in deadly combat. Kit had unleashed a lightning strike upon the woman she was chasing. Aurora held her own blade aloft while a golden glow burst from her eyes and powerful white wings exploded from her back. The molten creature bellowed out in rage while Aurora's lookalike bore down on her.

"Hope, stop!" Those were the only words the captain heard before a brilliant light blinded him. The intensity of the flash overloaded his senses, and in what felt like the briefest of moments, he lost consciousness.

"Come back to us, my love." Kit stood dumbfounded at her mother's words as she hovered over her father. Her great white wings wrapped around the man, forming a protective shield. "The danger has passed, and you are safe to return."

Kit's heart skipped a beat when her father's eyes fluttered open. "Hello, my angel." His voice was weak. He blinked rapidly several times before thrashing on the ground.

"Be still," Aurora said, placing her hand on his chest. "We have won the day and we must return to the city. Father Hoarfrost leads the people of Ashcroft to safety. The king's army has retreated for now."

"How?" The man's face was awash with confusion. He looked about frantically, finding the faces of all who had sallied out with him, safe and sound. An exuberant black wolf pushed his way through the bodies and scraped his enormous pink tongue across his face.

"Mother did it." They were the only words Kit could pull together into a coherent sentence. "She did something that drove off the elder demon." Aurora made a noise that sounded like a mixture of a scoff and a chuckle.

"It was not an elder demon, my child. That was merely his shade. Had it been a full demon, we likely would not be alive to talk about it." She reached out to grab Captain Harding's forearm. With the help of Indie, they hoisted the man to his feet.

Kit was more than relieved to see her father up and around, but the image of her mother's wings erupting from her back was still etched in her mind. The sheer magnificence of them was beyond compare. Aurora caught sight of her daughter's expression and smiled.

"Walk with me, child. I will tell you everything you want to know. It is time you understood your heritage."

"Who was that woman?" Captain Harding wobbled slightly as he addressed Kit's mother. "She looked just like you."

"That was my sister, Hope, the now adopted daughter of King Faol." The look of confusion on the captain's face only intensified at the revelation.

"Walk with us," Aurora said to the man, wrapping her arm around his forearm. "I will tell you both the story of Hope and the Vampire King."

"Kitten," Fury whispered. He showed her a sword in his hand as he paced quietly at her side. "After you've spoken with your mother, we need to talk about this sword." Kit cocked an eyebrow at the draken, who was behaving rather oddly. He grinned at her like a kid in a candy shop. "It holds another piece of me."

Chapter Sixteen

Hope and a Prayer

The unconventional family, plus Fury, walked in silence for several minutes. While the draken continued to marvel at the sword in his hands, the other three seemed to soak in the bit of comfort of being together. Kit's heart ached. She desperately wanted to ask her mother a million questions, but she also didn't want to spoil the magical moment she was experiencing.

"I'm very proud of the woman you've become," Aurora whispered. As she spoke, Kit could feel her mother's aura brushing up against her own. They sang together as one, creating a profound connection unlike anything she had ever experienced. The scent of wildflowers and honey permeated her entire being. Kit smiled up, her mind becoming lost in her mother's golden eyes. They were so entrancing. They pulled Kit closer to her, calmed her spirit, and opened her heart. As usual, Kit's mouth opened, and unbidden words fell out.

"Will I have wings like yours?" Kit asked, cringing somewhat at the self-serving nature of her question, but she knew so little about her heritage and what it meant to be a celestial.

"Maybe," Aurora said with a sad smile. "I was about your age when my wings manifested, but I don't have daemon blood in me."

"Daemons don't have wings?"

"Not like mine. Daemon wings are more like dragon wings. They look like leather stretched very thin, but they are extraordinarily strong. Stronger than my angel wings, I would say."

"Is the daemon inside of me evil?" Kit's mind was spinning as she tried to consider all the questions that she had churning in the back of her mind since she'd first discovered her full celestial heritage.

"Daemons are not evil." Aurora glanced over at Captain Harding, a sad smile painted on her lips. Her eyes became unfocused - distant. "Nor are angels good. We are who we choose to be, how we choose to behave. That's what separates good from evil."

"Are vampires evil? Is that why you seek them out to destroy them?"

"That is a more complicated question, my sweetness. Vampires are at a moral disadvantage. They feed on blood. For them, the blood of the still-living tastes the sweetest. The life-force in the blood rejuvenates them, fills them with power, fills them with life. Like anyone else, they can choose their path in life, but the choice of righteousness is difficult because it goes against their very nature. If a vampire can control their bloodlust, they can function as productive members of the community. But the urge to feed, it's always there, gnawing at them, pressing them to satiate their desire for blood."

"Is that why you hunt them?" Kit glanced at her father. He was paying close attention to the conversation, but he was choosing to only be a spectator, to let his daughter have as much time with her mother as she could on their walk back to the city. Even though the aftermath of a battle raged on around them, Kit's full attention was on the here and now, with her family.

"I don't hunt vampires because they are evil. I hunt those who are doing evil. I hunt those who are acting on behalf of Faol and his grotesque desire to rule the entire world. King Faol is a wicked, twisted man. He was the first vampire to walk the lands of Orth. Now, he offers immortality to those who would follow him. He destroys any who break their vows." Aurora took a deep breath and slowly let it out.

"How did Faol become a vampire?" Kit's eyes were wide. Her mind raced, trying to absorb all the information her mother was sharing with her.

"I don't know, not for sure, at any rate." Aurora's face grew dark as she spoke. "The legends suggest he performed a dark ritual. It involved the bloodletting of many *innocents*. He bathed in their blood. He gorged himself on it. The atrocities supposedly opened his soul to the demons of Helja. The power of the ritual, the pure evilness of it, poked a hole in the Veil. It created a portal that allowed a daemon spirit to escape and enter our plane. The spirit possessed Faol and, because the ritual made the king so powerful, he took control of that spirit and bent it to his will." Kit gasped at the tale. Never could she have imagined anything so wicked. "The spirit that King Faol dominated into submission was none other than that of Gorgaraeth, the demon lord himself."

"Gorgaraeth? The chosen one of Bael?" Kit blinked rapidly as she considered her mother's words. Aurora pressed her lips together into a thin line and nodded lightly. "Titan's snowballs."

Laughter broke the tension-filled air, letting it escape with a whoosh. The bit of levity was short lived, however, as Kit dove back into asking her mother questions.

"That must have infuriated Bael? I assume he wants out of the Veil, and this would have ruined his plans." Aurora sneered and shook her head.

"I don't think so. I think it all went precisely as Bael intended. The spirit of his general now walks upon Orth. Faol may have control of him, but the king is likely doing exactly what Bael wants, even if it's unwittingly. Faol is weakening the strongest populations on Orth. When the Veil falls, and it *will* fall, Bael and his demon minions will be poised to sweep over the land and destroy everything. Ragnarök will be upon us, and Bael will win his cruel game."

"If I free Titan," Kit said, her mind reeling from the revelations. "That will change things, won't it?" Aurora shrugged in response.

"Either way, Ragnarök will happen and the world will burn. The god who comes out on top will mean little to the peoples of Orth if they're all returned to the Great Cycle."

"Titan promised me a boon." Kit said, a cheery look suddenly springing up. "If I free him, he promised me a boon. I will ask that Ragnarök not happen. I will ask him to cancel the game."

"It's a nice sentiment, Kitten." Fury finally broke his silence. "But it will not work, not like that. Titan is a willful child, playing a game without concern or remorse for the people he hurts. Let's not forget the other three, Orth, Bael, and

Ollin. They are also likely still playing the game and they won't just quit because one of them tells them to stop." The others openly stared at Fury. He smiled at the attention he was receiving. "The only way to stop the end of days is to not let the gods win their game. We must defeat them and prove to them we are not playthings to be trifled with. Free the dragons and we will drive off the gods."

"And trade death for oppression," Captain Harding said. "I somehow doubt our dragon overlords are going to be magnanimous."

"I do not want to rule the world, nor do any other dragons I know." Fury paused for a moment. "Except, maybe, Ouroboros. He is so full of himself, he may choose to place himself as *Emperor of Everything*. I will not let that happen. We dragons know what it's like to be imprisoned. We want nothing more than to be free." Kit felt the honesty in Fury's words. That he saw Ouroboros as egotistical spoke volumes, considering Fury was the most self-absorbed person she had ever met.

"I think Fury's right," Kit said, giving the draken a coy smile. "At least partially."

"How so?" her mother asked, intrigued by the notion.

"I am going to free Titan. I promised him I would, and I do not go back on my word. For my boon, I will ask him to remain neutral in the coming war." Kit was nodding frantically now as she spoke. The ideas blossoming in her head were clear, and she felt, with certainty, they would work. "If we can, we will free the dragons. I trust Fury's word. I believe the dragons will fight to be free. It doesn't matter if they care what happens to the rest of the world, because I believe they don't care one iota, but they care about themselves. In that one fact, we are united.

"And we have the Fates on our side, as well. Like the dragons, they, too, just want to be free. If we defeat the gods at their own game, it might give the opportunity for the Fates to be unshackled and live their lives as they see fit. Right now, King Faol is the key to this. If we can defeat him, we will break Bael's back. Without his vampires and demons, he cannot win the game."

Nobody in the group argued with Kit's plan. It was unclear if they believed it would work, but no one openly objected to it.

"I just need time to make it all happen." Kit turned to the captain, her expression suddenly deadly serious. "Father, how long do you think the city can stand against King Jordain's and King Faol's armies? How long will our walls hold before they breach the city?"

"I don't know," Captain Harding said, scrubbing the back of his neck. "I've never fought an army of vampires before. I've never seen such magic wielded like we've seen in the past moon."

"What of General Ormand Gabryl? What if he helped? He knows the king's methods, his tactics. Wouldn't that help? He's a vampire, he could fight with us. He might give more insights into how the vampires might be used in an attack on the city."

The big man groaned. "You saw how everyone reacted the last time you brought up this idea. It will cause dissention with the soldiers. An army divided cannot stand." Aurora placed her hand on Captain Harding's.

"He was a good man before he was turned." The celestial exhaled slowly as she considered her words. "If he has enough blood to keep him fed, he will be a powerful ally. Right now, we need everyone we can get."

"You know Ormand?" Kit practically whistled as she spoke. "What about Pental? Do you know of him?"

"That man is insane," Aurora said. "For now, our goals are aligned with his, so he is technically an ally. But his mind is forever in a conflicted rage. It is impossible to know how he'll react in any situation."

Insane was something Kit could work with. After all, she thought herself to be a bit touched in the head as she considered her plan. There was so much potential for it to fail on a global scale that she had to be crazy to think it might work.

"What about Hope?" The words blurted out of Kit. "Why is she with King Faol? How did your sister come to be his daughter? Can she be turned to fight with us?"

"That is a... painful tale," Aurora said, casting her eyes downward. "When we were very young, Faol raided our village, looking for blood slaves for his army. Our parents tried to defend us against Faol himself. He drained them both dry.

The man forced Hope and me to watch. We were helpless against him. When he finished with my parents, he grabbed Hope. When he did, her cries of terror rang out. My mind snapped. The thought of losing my whole family was too much to bear."

As Aurora told the story, her hands convulsed, her golden eyes swirling as a visceral rage took hold of her.

"Mother, if this is too difficult, I don't need to hear it." Kit tried to spare her mother the grief she was feeling, but her words went unheard.

"That was the day I first manifested my celestial powers," Aurora continued. "My attack was instinctual. I clawed at Faol's face. It was like my touch was poison to him. He cried out in pain each time I struck him. I watched as a dark spirit rose from his body. It hissed wildly at me. It tried to possess me. It screamed with rage when my celestial self rejected it. While I watched the shadow-creature rake its claws at the air, Faol struck me, and the world went black. When I awoke, Hope was gone, and I was alone in my hut, lying in the blood of my parents."

"How old were you?" Kit asked, her cheeks wet with tears.

"I was only eleven cycles," Aurora replied, her rage subsiding. "Hope was only seven. I've spent my life trying to get Hope back."

"Is she a celestial as well?" The grief her mother was experiencing at retelling her tale broke Kit's heart, but she needed to the see the complete picture. If her plan was to have any chance of succeeding, there could be no surprises.

"We are born of the same parents," Aurora said. Her golden eyes looked lifeless, vacant. "I have seen no signs that her celestial heritage has manifested, but they may lie dormant. How and when our true nature appears seems to be a mystery."

"I will speak with Father Hoarfrost," Kit said. "I will speak with him and then I will leave for Mount Toka to commune with Titan."

Fury nudged Kit with his scaly hand. "But first, before we go anywhere, you need to get me out of this sword and into your wondrous hammer."

Chapter Seventeen

A Shadow in the Night

No sooner had everyone been brought safely in through the city gates than the skies turned dark and ugly. Lightning ripped through the clouds, illuminating them, casting them in shades of bright green and threatening black shadows. Torrential rains followed, pounding the rooftops, filling the streets with small rivers, instantly soaking anybody who was unfortunate enough to be caught in it. Everyone took advantage of the gloom and retreated to their rooms for a welcome respite.

It was well past midnight when the summer storm had finally subsided. The stars glowed in the night sky, bathing Kit's cell with their cool, white light. The sound of crickets and the occasional sentry walking past her door were the only noises breaking the peaceful silence. She pulled Indie's arm tightly around herself.

"I don't know what to say to Father Hoarfrost," Kit whispered lightly. "I have no idea how I can talk him out of climbing Mount Toka. How do I convince him to let me go in his stead?"

When Indie didn't answer, Kit pushed her back into him and pulled his arm even more tightly around herself.

"Again?" Indie asked, his voice hoarse and distant. "I... I'm so tired."

Kit chuckled quietly to herself and slipped out from under Indie's embrace. She padded silently across the room and pulled one of her priestly robes over her head. The feel of the rough-spun threads scratching at Kit's bare skin made her feel – at home. After giving Indie a soft kiss on his cheek, she crept out the door, quietly pulling it closed behind her.

Despite there being no windows or torches to light the hallway, Kit found she has no difficulty seeing. The cold stone floor felt wonderful on her bare feet as she headed towards the stairwell leading to the acolytes' floor. In moments, she found herself wandering past her old cell, smiling wistfully as she ran her fingers over the oak door's waxy finish. A lot had changed in the brief time since she'd last slept in this room.

In the distance, a set of iron hinges groaned, and a soft red glow lit the end of the hallway. Assuming it was an acolyte out for an evening stroll, Kit headed towards Washout Alley, the row of cells reserved for overage acolytes whom the Temple would never choose to be full priests. As she stepped around the corner, a dim light from the bottom of Lin's cell door drew her attention.

Kit padded down the hallway until she stood in front of Lin's cell. Having no other plan in mind, she rapped lightly on the wooden door, cringing slightly when the sound echoed down the hallway. Lin cracked open the door to see who was knocking. She was wearing skin-tight ebony leathers, with a bow draped over her shoulder, and her twin longswords strapped to her hips. With the dark clothes and her chin-length black hair, her face looked extremely pale, almost white. She had a slight look of disappointment on her face when she saw it was Kit.

"You look disappointed to see me. Are you going somewhere?" Kit kept her voice to barely a whisper.

"I'm leaving for Two Peaks. I am going to kill my father and put an end to this foolishness before his main army gets here. If I do this right, perhaps I can even get them to fight Faol's army when they arrive."

"That's madness." They were the only words Kit could muster. "You can't just waltz into the palace and kill the king." Lin smiled weakly.

"That's pretty much exactly what I plan to do. Ormand is coming with me. He's going to show me how to get inside without being seen."

"Who authorized this?" Again, these were the best words Kit could come up with. The question was cringeworthy. How often had Kit concerned herself with authorization before doing something brash? Pretty much never, that's how often.

"We were lucky in that last battle. We both know it. Had you and your mother not driven off Faol's daughters, the army would not have broken ranks. They'd have annihilated the lot of us. Those battle mages we faced. They were stronger than any we have ever encountered."

"Let me speak with Father. Let me speak with my father, too. This is wrong, Lin. I feel it in my bones. My soul is screaming at me, telling me this is not the right path."

"I've made my decision, Kit. I need to do this."

Kit's first thought was to bind the woman with enough rope that she'd never escape from it. Her second thought was to bonk her over the head with her war hammer. Knock her unconscious and then bind her with enough rope that she'd never get free of it. Her third thought was the winner.

"You can't leave yet. I need you to help transfer Fury's soul from Annabella's sword into the hammer. We need to talk with Coldforge. It will probably take the two of you to perform the spell." This struck a nerve. Lin's eyes widened when she mentioned the soul transfer spell.

Lin fingered the hilt of her sword before giving Kit a brief nod. "Okay. I'll wait until tomorrow before I leave. We can transfer Fury into the hammer and then I'll be on my way."

The sound of heavy footfalls echoed up the stairway. Kit looked briefly in their direction and then back down the hallway. Whoever it was would be at the top of the stairs in just a few moments.

"Someone's coming," Kit said as she stepped into the stairwell, finding a shadow-filled cove to hide in. Lin said something from her room, but she couldn't make out the words. It sounded a lot like she was swearing.

Whoever it was coming up the stairs continued to make a tremendous racket as they climbed. It was difficult to tell now if it was one person or twenty. The way the sounds were echoing off the walls made Kit uneasy. From within the small alcove, she reached for her hammer, finding that she wasn't carrying it. Outside of her priestly robes, she was otherwise naked. She immediately took a battle stance. An image of Sister Gale's combat classes flashed through her mind. The woman seemed to always wear sheer robes and nothing else. Kit thanked the darkness that she would not look like her instructor had.

"Frookin' Helja, girl," Coldforge practically screamed when he spotted Kit as he reached the landing. "Why on Orth would you be skulking like that?" The dwarf's arrival allowed Kit to relax. Had today's battle addled her brain? Why would she have thought it was a group of evildoers climbing the dormitory stairs?

"You have excellent dark vision," Kit chuckled nervously, "but you'll never be a sneak."

"I don't much need to sneak," Coldforge said, adjusting a satchel on his shoulder. When he saw Kit eyeing the bag, he gave her a smile. "Lin traded me," the dwarf stated in his matter-of-fact sort of way. "I forged her some bracers, and she gave me some reagents to enchant me new ax. Someone broke me other one."

"You made her bracers?" Kit asked, trying to not let her face redden too heavily.

"I did," Coldforge said as he beckoned Kit to follow him. "Some of me best work, considering how little time I had to make them. I was on me way to deliver them. Come, I'll show ye."

"What does she need with bracers?" Kit asked, as she followed the dwarf into the hallway.

"They're bracers of defense," Coldforge replied. "She can't be wearing armor all the time when she's traipsing around the castle. The bracers look like jewelry, but they'll give her about the same protection as full plate armor. I've also got a ring of levitation for her. When she showed me the pegasus feathers, I knew just what to do with them." The dwarf's voice was so loud, he would surely wake every acolyte on the entire floor.

"Get in here, both of you." Lin's head was poking out her door. "Now."

"I've got your items," Coldforge practically bellowed out. "Some of me best work."

Kit hissed and pushed him forward. Lin quickly grabbed him by his shoulder and dragged him into her room.

"Why do you need a ring of levitation?" Kit eyed Lin up and down. Lin seemed to ignore the question.

"Did you get the other enchantment on it?" Lin asked. She was practically vibrating.

"I got the death shroud along with a speed enchantment. The reagents you supplied were absolutely top shelf." Lin cringed at Coldforge's words. Her eyes screamed at him to shut his mouth.

"What's a death shroud?" Kit leveled her gaze at Lin, waiting impatiently for a response.

"It's a powerful, very dark enchantment," Coldforge said, again drawing Lin's wrath. "It surrounds the wearer with a cloud of black smoke, obscuring them from view. The cloud smells of rot and decay," Coldforge added. "But it also offers protection from arrows, and it gives the wearer resistance against necrotic attacks."

"Black smoke, levitation, protection from arrows..." Kit practically growled out the words. She thought back to her encounters with Pental and the *masters* in Cormorant. "You're going to pass yourself off as a vampire. You and Ormand? Are you going to pass yourselves off as a couple? A couple of vampires?"

Lin smiled. "It seemed like a good idea at the time."

"And now?" The question fell from Kit's lips, her eyes practically bulging from her head. Who in Helja was this woman?

"Well, truth be told, the way you say it, your plan sounds even better than ours. We hadn't considered passing ourselves off as a couple."

The twinkle in Coldforge's eyes was out of control. "She can even disappear in a puff of smoke. Well, she won't disappear, but if she's quick about it, she can escape before the cloud dissipates. With these enchantments, I'd say she could pass herself off as a vampire before King Faol himself." He started rummaging in the sack he was carrying. He pulled out a small diamond bracelet and a fine gold ring. "Here, try 'em out. Ye got to see how they work before ye go floatin' into the king's chambers."

"Oh, sweet Titan." Kit snatched the two items out of Coldforge's hand before he could close his thick fingers back over them. "You'll do no such thing." Kit pushed them into one of her robe's many pockets. "I forbid it. I'm High Priest now, and I forbid you from going."

"I quit being an acolyte many cycles ago, Mother Kit." Lin's face was filled with fury, but her eyes showed signs of laughter. "You hold no domain over me. I love you with all my heart, and because of that, I'm going to do everything in my power to help you defeat King Faol. This is how I'm going to do it."

"No." Kit folded her arms over her chest and cocked an eyebrow. "I won't let you. I've got your special items and I'm not giving them back."

"Oh, that's very mature." Lin mimicked her movements.

"I don't care what you think of my behavior. It's effective, and that's all that matters." Kit turned to Coldforge and gave him her best smile. "Since you're so willing to help Lin with these magical items, perhaps you could help me with one."

"No." The dwarf's answer was blunt and absolute. "I'll not do it."

"I haven't even asked you yet." Kit feigned innocence and the dwarf's demeanor darkened further.

"Ye don't need to ask. I know what ye want and I won't do it." Coldforge ran his fingers through his unruly orange beard and cleared his throat. "If it's all the same to ye, I'll be on me way now. Me bed summons me and I plan on answering that call. May Gaia watch over ye and keep ye safe." He gave a slight bow before tromping out of the room and down the hall. His footsteps echoed off the walls for a good long while after he left.

"Don't worry." Lin said with a small shrug. "I'll help you transfer Fury from the sword to your hammer. We can do it tomorrow before I leave."

⁓⁓⁓⚬⁓⁓⁓

"I told ya already. I'm not going ta do it." The dwarf's orange beard twitched at Fury's reaction. He had already been put out with Kit for interrupting his breakfast. Judging by how much food and drink were entangled in his beard, it looked like he'd been eating for a while, or he'd really struggled with getting food into his mouth.

"You willingly put dark enchantments on items for Lin, but you won't help me become whole." Fury gave Coldforge his best, most sinister glare. From the way his beard was twitching, it seemed to amuse the dwarf.

Kit stepped between the draken and the dwarf and leveled her absolute best glare onto Coldforge. "We are facing Ragnarök, and you won't help to strengthen our side because of some strange belief that helping to merge his souls is evil?" Coldforge blustered at the comment. His thick orange eyebrows knitted themselves together into a single, fuzzy, giant ginger worm.

"It's not because it's dark or evil, at least not completely. Mergin' his third piece will make him nearly whole. We don't know what he'll be like with this piece. We don't know if it holds some evil aspect of his personality. We don't know if it will bring him powers he doesn't already have. I also don't know if yer hammer is powerful enough to hold three pieces. It could just as easily explode and end the miserable creature's life."

"Miserable creature?" Fury blew a stream of blue flame at the dwarf's feet, causing him to leap out of the way. "I am a magnificent being, a wonder to behold. I am not evil, nor am I a *creature*. I simply wish to be free of the bonds that hold me. I simply wish to be whole once again, free to live my life. Is that so much to ask?"

Kit cocked an eyebrow. Something in the draken's long-winded speech was not a full truth, but it wasn't exactly a lie either.

Coldforge jutted his chin up at Fury, his orange eyebrows further scrunching up, practically swallowing his eyes. "I'll not do it. There is nothin' ye can say or do that will make me change me mind."

"What if I give you the hammer, after Fury is freed from it?" An unmistakable twinkle shot across Coldforge's eyes. A moment later, he shook his head.

"I said, no. End of discussion." Kit shrugged at the declaration.

"Fine, we'll get Lin to do it then. If she botches it, it might mean both their deaths, but at least you won't have to worry about Fury turning into some sort of diabolical, evil monster." She didn't wait to see the dwarf's reaction, nor did she wait for a response. With absolute determination, she strode across the dining hall towards the double-doored exit. When she was too far away, the still glowering manifestation of Fury disappeared.

"I'll not be coerced," Coldforge yelled out from his seat at one of the long trestle tables. Kit ignored the dwarf's parting comment and made her way to find Lin.

CHAPTER EIGHTEEN

FURY AND THE DRAGON SWORD

"You're positive you remember what the Hobgoblins did when they merged my essence from the soul canister? Are you sure you can do this?" Fury, for the first time since Kit had met him, sounded nervous.

"Yes, and no," Lin replied. She was leaning over a table filled with reagents, and what might have been the finest alchemy set she had ever seen, outside of the one the Hobgoblins had set up in Cormorant. "Are you sure Coldforge won't mind us using his equipment?"

Kit quickly peeked over her shoulder at the door into the room. She shrugged and shook her head. "I doubt it." A hint of a nervous grin pulled at the corners of her mouth. With some effort, she tucked it away and gave Lin a straight face. She hated lying. There was a real chance that Coldforge could barge in on them and toss them out of his lab and... Kit didn't want to think what else he might do. The dwarf was pretty damned adamant about not helping Fury get his third piece of himself. She walked over to the door and checked the thick iron bolt that held it shut.

She gave Lin a nervous grin. "But let's hope he doesn't decide to walk in on us. I really don't want to find out the hard way."

"I'm ready," Fury said. "Do you have everything you need?" Lin was slow to nod. Fury took a deep breath and swallowed hard. "I'll return to the hammer and wait patiently for my other piece. Please be careful."

Minutes passed like hours as Lin prepared potions and ointments. She had a small cauldron half filled with herbs and dried animal parts. She gave Kit a questioning look, wondering if she thought if it was time to begin. The young priest's face was stoic, refusing to weigh in on the decision.

"Okay then, let's begin." Lin took the sword that contained another piece of Fury and rubbed the blade down with a purple ointment that smelled of lilacs. Kit inhaled deeply. The taste of copper filled her mouth. She grimaced when she remembered that blood was a major component in the balm.

The bright silver blade immediately turned coal black. Kit looked expectantly at her friend, who nodded lightly and moaned. Lin took one of the potion bottles and poured its contents over the blade. The black color changed again, first to a dull silver and then to a sickly green. The scent that wafted off it smelled of swamp-water and old socks. A satisfied look spread across Lin's face as she reached for a second potion. She drizzled it over the battle hammer. Like the sword, it, too, turned a sickly green. A thick, putrid haze clung to its mithril head. The hammer's pungent aroma wafted out, comingling with the sweaty sock fragrance coming from the sword. Mixed, the smell was unbearable. The haze that surrounded the hammer drifted off, seeming to cling to any bit of exposed skin in the room. It had a warming sensation that wasn't exactly unpleasant, but it made Kit feel dirty, and in desperate need of a bath.

The clinging fog dissipated. A pulsating, deep blue glow emanated from the two weapons. The intensity ebbed and flowed in a rhythmic pattern, like heartbeats. The sword's heartbeat was strong and steady, while the hammer's beat was like the wings of a hummingbird.

Lin picked up the two weapons and closed her eyes. She quietly recited a spell, bringing the weapons closer together as she did. The nearer the weapons got to each other, the more the heartbeat of the hammer slowed. When the sword and the hammer were nearly touching, their rhythmic beating became synchronized. Lin smiled, opened her eyes, and peered into the cauldron. Her expression instantly changed from blissful satisfaction to horrific dismay.

"What is it?" Kit's heart was thumping in her chest in perfect rhythm with the weapons. Lin blinked a few times until the solution became apparent.

"Can you do your fire-thing and light the wood beneath the cauldron?"

Lin hadn't prepared tinder to light the stack of well-oiled wood that she had crammed beneath the iron pot. Kit nodded and shoved a hand into the pile of wood. A moment later, a searing red flame erupted on her skin, igniting the prepared wood. Flames of yellow and green licked up and around the cauldron, growing more intense with each passing moment. In just a few seconds, an acrid, sky-blue smoke billowed out. Kit choked and backed away from the device. While the little priest coughed and sputtered, Lin inhaled the smoke deeply. With each breath she took, she said words that Kit could not understand. Over and over, she repeated the process, blowing the smoke across the surface of both weapons. After what seemed like ages, she took the hammer and jammed its head into the bubbling mixture. She took the sword in both hands and held it over the hammer.

"Cantus. Emotem. Momentous." The sword's blade burst into flames, but Lin maintained her grip on it. "Where there are two, let there be one. Harmony will bind you, for you are of the same spirit." The woman's words were harsh and guttural, her face contorted like she was in the throes of ecstasy. The flame of the sword died out and the head of the hammer burst forth in brilliant blue. The girls had to shield their eyes from the blinding light.

"The hammer cannot hold me," Fury screamed out. "Kit, please, help me." There was nobody in the room, save Lin and Kit and the voice of Fury. "Kit, take the hammer. You'll understand."

The little priest immediately pulled the hammer from the cauldron. She could feel Fury's soul trying to possess her. It was trying to leave the hammer and enter her body. With revulsion, Kit dropped the hammer and stepped away. Fury wailed; his voice filled with unadulterated fear.

"I'm sorry. I didn't mean to do that. My soul is trying to survive. I cannot hold on to the hammer. Its magic is not powerful enough. Its enchantments cannot contain me. Kit, please, I'm leaking out of it."

"I will not let you possess me," Kit screamed at the hammer. "You're a lying sack of crap. This was your plan all along, wasn't it? You had planned to use your new strength to overpower me."

"No, I swear on everything I hold dear," the hammer bellowed. "Listen to me. You know I'm not lying. I didn't know. I didn't do that on purpose. Help me. I cannot hold on much longer."

The door to the room burst open, sending shards of wood in nearly every direction. "What in the name of Gaia are ye doin' in my lab? I ought to skin yer hides and make me a new suit of fool-hardy armor." Kit jumped at the dwarf's untimely arrival, but she quickly regained her composure.

"Lin transferred Fury into the hammer, but he says the hammer can't hold him. It needs more magic or something." Kit didn't back down from the dwarf's threats. "You don't need to transfer him. You just need to make the hammer stronger. Isn't that right, Lin?" Kit turned to her friend, who was on her hands and knees retching on the floor.

"I told ya, didn't I? Didn't I tell ya that this was bad magic? Help yer friend, I'll fix the hammer. Ye foolish little girls playin' with things ye have no business playin' with."

Kit dove next to Lin. The woman was shaking badly, and her skin was deathly pale. She hadn't noticed Lin's reaction to casting the spell until just this moment. She placed her hand on the small of Lin's back and called upon her healing powers. As her aura engulfed her, a buzzing sensation ran over Kit's skin. It didn't hurt, not like when she was healing someone. This was different. It was painful but, at the same time, it was almost pleasurable. She reached out with her aura, seeking any injuries, but found none.

"Lin?" Kit whispered her name, not sure what she was supposed to do. "Lin, are you okay? How can I help?" A crash shocked the two girls. The impact was so loud that it made them both jump. Lin chuckled. It started small and morphed into an insane, maniacal laugh. To Kit's ears, she sounded much too much like one of the crazed Hobgoblins.

"I did it, Kit. I transferred his soul. I know it worked. I felt him pass through me and into the hammer. For a moment, I held Fury's soul. I held his magic. It coursed through me. It spoke to me and I understood it. The hammer can't hold him. His magic is too powerful for the weapon."

"Not anymore," Coldforge said, standing next to the shattered remains of the cauldron. "Ye poisoned that tool. Ya soiled it with your foul magic."

"I'm sorry, Coldforge. We need Fury and... I'm sorry."

"What did you do to the hammer? How is Fury contained?" Lin's hands were practically convulsing, desperate to hold the weapon that contained the soul that had passed through her.

"Nay. I'll not give it to ya." Coldforge held the hammer away from Lin, protecting it like it was his very own child.

"I'll take my hammer, Coldforge." Kit held out her hand. "I will honor that which I proffered. You helped Fury. I will give you the hammer when he is freed."

Coldforge looked at the weapon, slowly turning it in his hand. He blew out a breath, making his mustache flutter. "I put a fortitude enchantment on it. A strong one. This weapon is now nigh unbreakable. It will hold his soul, but only if Fury puts all his effort into not letting himself leak out. If he leaves the hammer, he will die."

"You've trapped him? You tricked me." Kit snatched the hammer from the dwarf and raised it over her head. Her eyes were black as midnight as licks of flame danced over her body.

"I did neither. I made it so the hammer could hold him, but not so strong that he could pop out of it like he did when it only held half his soul. When you get the rest of him, you can transfer him into his body, and all will be as it should be. My enchantment will not be strong enough to hold another piece of him. Only his own living body can do that."

"Kit, can I hold the hammer? Please, let me hold the hammer." Kit rolled her eyes and handed her friend the weapon. That look of ethereal bliss she'd seen in Lin moments ago returned. She was in a state of pure rapture.

Chapter Nineteen

Hoarfrost and Grams

Kit stood motionless outside Father Hoarfrost's office. The sound of softly spoken words barely escaped the ajar door, forcing the little priest to press her ear close to the opening. She barely breathed, hoping to hear what the pair was saying within.

"Sister Kit," Father called out from beyond the door. "It's rude to linger beyond our view. It's much worse that you're trying to eavesdrop on our private conversation." Kit's skin flushed and her ears burned. She slowly eased the door open and poked her head inside.

"Father, I know you're busy, but if it pleases you, I'd like to have a word."

"If it pleases me?" The high priest laughed openly at the comment. This might have been the happiest, most jovial moment she had ever shared with the man. Kit's gaze fell upon Grams who was seated next to him, on a couch that had never before been in the old man's office. Kit smiled awkwardly, wishing she had not come, wishing she had not interrupted what was obviously an intimate moment.

"I am pleased to meet you once again, Sister Kit. You honor me with your presence." There was something about the old woman that was tangibly different, and yet, she looked just as she did the first time they had met in Ashcroft. Well, perhaps not exactly, but it was hard to put her finger on it. Maybe it was because the old woman looked happy, at peace. Kit drew in a deep breath as she struggled to find the right words to say. As she did, the heady scent of old books and peppermint filled her nostrils. It was only at that moment that she realized this was the first time since she'd returned to Aarall that she smelled the familiar fragrance. But like everything else about this moment, it was different. Besides the familiar scents, the room was filled with the smell of grass after a spring shower. The freshness was interlaced with hints of lilies and pansies.

"I'm glad to see you are well, Grams." It was the only thing Kit could think of. Every other thought in her head seemed muddled.

"You are here to convince me to stay and let you take my place." Father Hoarfrost's voice was calm and serene. "You wish to be the one to commune with Titan." Kit's jaw flopped open slightly. How did he always seem to know what she was thinking?

"I do," Kit said. "With the armies on our doorstep, it is much too dangerous for you to make the journey."

"You don't need to convince him you are the right person for the job, little angel." Grams smiled warmly. "I've already done that for you." Kit fidgeted with her fingers for several seconds before clasping her hands together.

"Oh." Kit shifted her weight between her feet, unable to find a comfortable standing position. "Um…"

"Would you like to sit, child?" Grams patted the couch cushion next to where she was seated. "You look ready to topple over." The woman's voice was interlaced with joy and good humor. The tension Kit was feeling drained from her body and a warm smile turned her mouth upwards.

"No, thank you, Grams." Kit shifted her weight once more. "Father, do I have your blessing? Will you stay here and continue to guide the people?" The old man turned to Grams who raised her eyebrows to him, waiting somewhat impatiently for his answer.

"Yes, you have my blessing, and yes, I do plan to remain here as High Priest." Relief flooded Kit's soul. She really did not want to be High Priest and, even more so, she really didn't want Father to make the journey.

"Be mindful of the warning you gave me, Sister. The journey from here to Mount Toka is not safe. You don't know what dangers you might face along the way."

"You will teleport me to the mountain top?" A thrill raced through Kit. The idea of being carried from the Temple to the mountaintop in a single step – it was...

"No, I will not do that. As I have said before, it's the journey that matters."

"You will find your way," Grams said. "I trust you in this."

Kit stood motionless for several seconds. The conversation she'd had with her father about her daemon half, and how he was the source of that aspect of herself, still bothered her. She understood that her father never knew. How could he? But what about Father Hoarfrost? When she'd asked him if the daemon inside of her was evil, he didn't even blink. He wasn't surprised at all that she was part daemon.

"Father?" Kit started. She wasn't sure how to ask the question. She didn't want to sound accusatory. Was he just that trusting of her, that whatever she said he took at face value?

"How did I know you were part daemon?" The old man smiled at her. "Is that what you wanted to ask me?" Kit's shoulders sagged and a small frown pulled the corners of her mouth down.

"You can actually read my mind, can't you. All these years, I wondered how you did it, but now I really need to understand. How? Is it a power you gain as High Priest?"

"No, it has nothing to do with my position in the Temple." Father Hoarfrost straightened himself on the couch. "I can answer your first question with your second question. Your thoughts are very loud. When you don't intentionally keep them private, I can hear them quite clearly."

Kit's mind went blank. She didn't know what to think. How? It was the only word that kept popping into her head.

"Sister Kit," Grams said, her hands knitted together comfortably on her lap. She looked positively radiant sitting next to Father. Come to think of it, they both did. It was as though they were two pieces, finally brought together to form a whole. Kit tilted her head when the old woman paused and smiled brightly at her.

"Sister Kit, as I was about to say, when you get to be our age, you learn a thing or two about how to best work with those around you. Sometimes, we need to be a bit intrusive and listen in on people's thoughts. It's not something we are proud of, but it is often a necessity, for the safety of all."

"You, too? You both?" Kit's head was now swimming, no drowning. She was beyond her depth. These two people, people she knew as her friends, were revealing something beyond her comprehension. None of it made any sense. Grams and Father Hoarfrost both nodded at her question.

"Just how old are you?"

The old couple seated comfortably on a couch in the high priest's office roared with laughter. It continued on and on, much longer than she appreciated. At first, Kit thought she had just said something funny, but now, with the way they were carrying on, it looked more like they were mocking her.

"Sorry, child, we are not mocking you," Grams said, her face still red from her raucous laughter.

"No, not at all," Father Hoarfrost continuing where Grams had left off. "It's just that, well, we've been around long enough to see the start and end of many lives. Never in that time did anyone seem to notice that we lived on."

"What about Tyr?" The words blurted out from Kit's mouth. Had she thought about it, she'd have not pressed the high priest, but she wanted to know. She needed to understand. "He's a god, or a Fate, or whatever he is. Surely, he'd have noticed that you were living well beyond your natural lifetimes."

"Ah, yes, the trickster." Grams pursed her lips and shook her head. "He has played his role well." Father Hoarfrost nodded in agreement. Kit staggered at the words. Her legs lost their ability to hold her upright, forcing Kit to grab the corner of Father's desk lest she fall on her face. The piece of old dragonwood furniture seemed to give her strength. Before she knew it, she was seated in the high priest's chair, her face buried in her hands.

"Oh, dear Nyckolas, I think the poor girl's mind has snapped." The playful tone in the old woman's face grated on Kit. How could she think this was funny? Why were they tormenting her like this?

"Well done, Grams. You've brought her back to us." Kit raised her head to see Father patting Grams' leg in congratulations.

What the Helja?

"Who are you two?" Kit practically screamed the words. Her frustration with their odd behavior was leaking out as fire and brimstone. It suddenly dawned on her. This was likely Tyr and Eris, having fun with her at her expense.

"We are not them," Father Hoarfrost said, his big brown eyes twinkling wildly, "but... it would seem our time together is ending. Seek the altar, commune with your god, free him if you can. That is your path. Don't worry about this city, or your family and friends. All will be well until your return."

"What?" Kit was near ready to explode when Indie came bursting into the room.

"Kit, you need to talk some sense into Lin." The young man's face was red, and his chest was heaving heavily. "She's still planning to go with Ormand to Two Peaks. She wants to assassinate the king." Kit groaned to herself. Lin said she'd wait until they'd had a chance to talk about it. With the army entrenched between Aarall and Two Peaks, the journey would be next to impossible.

"Oh, that won't do." Grams shook her head and stood from her place next to Father. "That is not her place."

"No, that won't do at all." Father Hoarfrost stood next to Grams. "Take us to her. We need to have a talk with Aithlin."

"They're in the stables," Indie said, barely able to manage his breathing. "They're preparing to leave."

⌘

"And where do you think you're going, young lady?" Grams grabbed Whistler's reins as Lin and Ormand came out from the stables. Lin's horse was laden with several saddle bags to prepare for the three-day journey to Two Peaks. Ormand walked comfortably beside her. The pair were dressed in black from head to toe. They both wore cloaks that seemed to make them difficult to focus on. Kit wondered if Coldforge had crafted Lin some more equipment or if these were of her own design.

"I am going to kill the king," she said. The words came out casually, like she was announcing she was going to the market to buy a loaf of bread. "Ormand is going to make sure I get to his quarters undetected, and then I'm going to gut him like a spring pig."

The knuckles on Grams' hands were turning white as she clutched Whistler's leather straps. "Aithlin, you'll do no such thing. We will not let you ruin everything just because you've discovered who your true father is."

"It's the best way for me to help. That's what you both wanted me to do, and this is the way I'm choosing to do it."

"What do you mean by that?" Kit asked. The conversation between Lin and her grandmother made no sense.

"That's not important," Lin and Grams snapped at Kit.

"Aithlin, Kit is traveling to the Altar of Toka. She will commune with Titan, and she will travel to free him. Protecting her is your path. You must help guide her, just as we discussed."

"Wait. What?" Kit stole a glance at Father Hoarfrost, who seemed dismayed by the conversation. Dismayed, but not surprised. "What in Helja is going on? Lin, is this true? Were you *assigned* to protect me?"

Lin looked like an animal caught in a trap, fearing the hunter was about to kill her. Kit knew the answer before the woman uttered a single word.

"Kit." Lin slid down from Whistler and stepped up to her friend. She took her hands in her own and gave them a squeeze. "Listen to my words and hear the truth in them. I beg of you, listen." Kit tried to yank her hands away, but Lin held tight. "With all my heart, I love you. I would kill for you. I would lay down my life for you. Tell me you feel the truth in every word I just said. Tell me you do. I can't stand the thought of you thinking that I have, in some way, betrayed you."

Kit bit her lower lip and nodded.

"Grams is not my grandmother. I was never really an acolyte of the Temple. I mean, I was, but I only went through the ceremonies so that I would fit in."

Kit was about to ask who Grams was, but Lin kept talking before she could get the words out. "When you came to the Temple, Grams sought me out in Two Peaks. My stepfather is the horrible person I said he was. He is a cruel, worthless sack of refuse. He took me and my mother in, just like I told you. What I didn't say, though, was why Grams chose me to come to the Temple. I never told you about her purpose for me."

"And that was?" Kit wiped a bit of blood from her lip where she had been biting it. She turned to Grams and jutted her chin out, waiting for one of the two to finish the story.

"We were certain you were one of the three," Grams said. "Titan called upon you. He specifically called you to come to his aid. He had only ever done that with Ymir and Fenrir. You had to have been the third." She looked over at Father Hoarfrost, who nodded wordlessly in response.

Kit pulled away when Grams drew near. "When the time was right, Lin was to bring you before me so that I could set you upon the path to free Titan. When Titan acknowledged you, that was the sign we were waiting for. We knew who your mother was. We expected you would manifest your celestial heritage. We just assumed that was why Titan had chosen you specifically as one of the three to free him from his prison."

"When you manifested your daemon self," Father Hoarfrost interjected, "we just knew you'd be able to do what everyone else could not." In that moment, it was as though a dark shadow had crossed over Kit's face. Her celestial spirits were rising in her chest in unison, amplifying the anger that was growing within.

"All this time." The little priest's voice was deep and threatening. She could feel the power welling up inside herself, just begging to be freed. "All this time, you've been lying to me. Brother Rimes was right, wasn't he? You were giving me special treatment. You pushed me up through the ranks just so I would become strong enough to free Titan." Kit pulled her hands away from Lin and stormed over to Father Hoarfrost, practically knocking Grams off her feet. "You had no intention of communing with Titan. It was all a part of your sick, twisted plot to manipulate me into doing your bidding."

Kit walked until she was standing toe to toe with the High Priest, her neck tilted back so that she could look up at him. "Why can't I tell if you're lying? How is it you can speak falsehood after falsehood, and I cannot feel the untruth in your words?"

Grams stepped quietly over to Kit, letting her presence be felt without her speaking a word. "We understand why you see things the way you do." Kit practically exploded at the woman's words.

"You understand? You understand? Did you expect I would never find out? Did you hope I would just follow along like a good little priest and do everything you two told me?" Father chuckled slightly at her words. Kit's eyes turned to searing balls of flame at the sound of his laughter.

"We had hoped so," he said, a little too glibly for Kit's liking. "Know this, little angel, even if you can't tell truth from lie when I speak, I have grown to love you as deeply as I love Grams. I do not speak those words lightly. The human tongue cannot express my love in a way that would do it justice."

"I don't understand." It was all Kit could think of saying. "None of this makes any sense to me. How do you expect me to trust anything you're saying?"

"Ormand, Lin, Indigo, begone." Father was about to wave his hand, but Kit caught it before he could finish. "They can all stay. I trust them. I trust them with my life, and you will, too." Father Hoarfrost glanced over at Grams who shrugged her shoulders in response. "Do you three promise to never share what I am abut to tell you, lest you be sent into oblivion?"

Before any of them could answer, Kit did so on their behalf. "No. No they don't. Speak, old man, or I'll leave you and this city to whatever will happen when the kings' armies arrive."

"You would never do that," Father Hoarfrost said with a small smile. "But I understand your sentiment. Fine, I will tell you our secret and you four can do with it as you will. Be aware, though, that outside of only one other person, no one in the universe knows the truth of this." Kit crossed her arms over her chest and raised her eyebrows, feigning interest.

"I am Ollin, son of Titan and Orth. This fine woman is Galahdes, Queen of the Elves. It was we who raised the Veil that trapped my brother and his hordes of demons in Helja. My brother Bael created creatures that none could stand against. I knew in my heart that they would kill everything on Orth as soon as they were set free. I could not allow them to do that. I could not allow my brother's creatures to kill Galahdes and the rest of the Elves. They were too beautiful, too perfect. Everything they touched improved. With every breath they took, they brought new life, new meaning to Orth."

Grams glided next to Father Hoarfrost, her form changing from an old woman to a beautiful, exquisitely tall elf, with hair of green and skin of amber. Galahdes' long, pointed ears poked through her silky silver hair. If this was what all elves looked like, then Kit couldn't disagree that they were the most beautiful people she had ever seen.

"Our magic was strong, but not strong enough to create a barrier that would circumference the entire world. We called upon our magic and bound it with the Tree of Life, the most sacred tree in the Elven Forest. Its roots reached out and commingled with every other root beneath the ground. We were able to contain much of the underworld, but not all. It wasn't until Ollin sacrificed himself and merged with the tree, putting nearly every bit of his essence into the Veil. Only then did it completely encompass the entirety of Orth. We had hoped that it would hold for eternity."

"But you're dying," Kit said, looking at Father Hoarfrost with fresh eyes. Her anger melted away, replaced by something different. She didn't know exactly how she felt, but she wasn't angry. "And if you die, the Veil will fall, and the demons will come and scorch the world." Father Hoarfrost nodded with barely any movement. "Can you not take some of your essence back from the Tree? Could you not heal yourself like that?"

"He can," Grams said. The sadness in her eyes was so profound that it immediately brought Kit to tears. "But he will not. He is trying to buy enough time for you to free Titan. He's hoping you can convince his father to stop the game, to prevent Bael's forces from bringing about Ragnarök."

"Okay," Kit said with a curt nod. "I will free Titan and ask him to stop the game. He promised me a boon, and that is what I will ask of him."

"Just like that?" Lin asked. "You're going to do exactly what they've been manipulating you into doing for the past sixteen cycles?"

"Yes. Just like that." Kit smiled warmly at Indie. "We do a lot of strange things for love. We do things that make sense to nobody but ourselves. I don't care if I can't tell if they're lying to me or not. I believe them. I just need to get to the top of Mount Toka, commune with Titan, and then find a way to free him. And I need to get it done before the two kings' armies show up and kill everyone here."

"You can't be serious." Indie had remained quiet for so long, and now his own concerns were pouring out of him.

"Oh, I am very serious," Kit said with something of an eye waggle. "Lump and I will travel to Mount Toka, while you and Lin travel to Cormorant. You'll bring Runt and Coldforge with you and you'll all wait for me to return. General Gabryl, you know what is at stake. You will tell my father everything you know about King Jordain's tactics and potential strategies, and you will tell him everything about how best to kill vampires in large numbers."

"What's in Cormorant?" Lin asked. "Why do we need to meet you there?" Kit thought about the question. Why had she decided that was where they should meet her?

"I don't know why. Not for certain, at least. I just know that's where my path will take me."

Kit waited for a moment to give everyone a chance to respond. When all mouths remained shut, she smiled brightly. "Let's get to it then. We have no time to waste."

CHAPTER TWENTY

KIT STANDING BEAR, DRAGON RIDER

"Lump, come here, boy." Kit called to the golden retriever from the back gardens behind the Temple. The wolfdog was laying under a large oak, snoozing. He lifted his head at the sound of Kit's voice before laying it back down across a gnarly root that was sticking up from the ground.

"Ah, come on, you old Lump on a Log. I need to talk to you." The dog closed his eyes and feigned sleeping. At least, Kit thought he was faking it. Lump could actually fall asleep in a heartbeat.

"Oh," Kit said, making her voice sound as sad as she could manage. "I was hoping you might fly with me on your back. I was hoping I might convince you to carry me to the top of Mount Toka?" Lump's eyes opened slightly, his ears perking up along with them. "I would be honored to have you with me when I try to commune with Titan." Lump's eyes popped open and brightened noticeably. His familiar golden smile appeared, and his tongue lolled out of his mouth.

Kit took a seat next to where he laid and gave his head a good scratching. "So? Do you think you can do it?" Lump shifted into his human form. Kit still had her hand on his head when he made the shift. She marveled at how silky soft his hair was, even in his human form.

"Father said you could go in his place?" His big brown eyes waited expectantly for her response.

"Well," Kit said, in a non-committal kind of way, "I don't think he ever intended to go. I think he was convincing me to go without asking me. It was all kind of confusing, really." Kit's stomach ached. The news that Father Hoarfrost and Grams had dropped on her was unsettling. They were the gods, Ollin and Galahdes. How could Father, or Ollin, or whoever he was, lie to her all these years? "Father Hoarfrost and Grams are gods. Did you know that?"

Lump stared at Kit and gave one of his shoulders a tiny shrug. "What does it matter? You, too, are a god."

"What?" Kit's head snapped back at Lump's words. He nodded quickly, which only added to her confusion.

"Celestials, like yourself, are not confined to live on this plane. If you can tap into your powers, you can travel away from this world. You could go wherever your heart desires."

"Did you learn that from the secret library?" Lump nodded to Kit's question. She stared up at the blue sky above and then back at her friend. "But I don't want to go anywhere else. Everything I love is here."

"That's nice, but that wasn't my point. Like Ollin and Galahdes, you're also a god. People love you just the same as they did when you were just a human girl. You love everyone in just the same way as before you discovered you were a celestial. What does it matter if they're gods? I'm sure Father loves you because you're you. If he's a god, it doesn't matter. He still loves you."

Kit sighed. She wasn't a god. She was just a girl. What is a god, anyway? Somebody with power? Are kings and queens gods as well? She had heard tales of royalty who were worshipped as deities. She'd even heard tales of cats being worshipped as divinities. The ache in her stomach worsened.

Lump nudged her leg. "Are you sure you want me to come with you to Mount Toka? I would think communing with your god is a very private thing." Kit nodded and smiled.

"Do you think you can do it? Do you think you can fly with me on your back?"

"I don't know, but I will try." His tongue lolled out of the side of his mouth for a moment before pulling it back behind his lips. "Do you think Fury can teach me how to fly? I've only ever jumped. I've never even tried to flap my dragon wings."

"Of course I can teach him." The draken's voice echoed in Kit's mind. He was no longer able to manifest himself as a draken, but he found another way to communicate with her. *"I wondered what had happened to Ollin and Galahdes."* Kit could hear his appreciation in his thoughts. *"Hiding in plain sight was an excellent idea, a dragon-worthy idea."*

⸺⸱⸱⸱⸱⸺

Kit had led Lump from behind the Temple grounds to the combat training fields. There was plenty of room for the dragon-dog to run and spread his wings. Fury was confident that he could teach the basics of take-offs, flight, and landings, even if he had no wings of his own at this point. Flying was as natural to a dragon as flaming and eating. Lump just needed a couple of quick pointers and he'd be soaring the skies in no time.

"Here, Lump. This is a suitable spot." Kit pointed to the far side of the garden. "There is plenty of room for you to get up to speed before you take off." Fury huffed at the girl's words. Kit had been trying to give Lump enough room to get up to a full run before trying to flap his wings. It was how Angel got her best jumps, and she assumed it would work for dragons as well.

"He doesn't need to run. Dragons can take off from a standing position and fly straight up. All he needs to do is kick up with his legs and flap."

Even in dragon form, Lump's doggie enthusiasm shone through. While Fury gave him instructions, he spun on the spot, eager to try out his wings. After Fury became too frustrated by his antics, he simply instructed the dragon-dog to jump in the air and flap his wings. Lump immediately did as he suggested. He leapt up, flapped erratically, and then flopped unceremoniously on his face. He popped up to his feet, wiped the large clod of mud from his muzzle and tried again, and again, and again. Each attempt ending with near identical results.

"Do you think he's ready to try my way now?" Kit said, placing her hands on her hips in an exaggerated fashion. Even though he wasn't physically there to see it, she gave Fury her absolute best condescending look.

"Sure, let's try it the horse *way. I'm sure that will work* just fine *for a dragon."* Fury matched Kit's exaggerated gestures with his own verbal intonations. Kit smiled warmly back at the draken before turning to the wolfdog.

"Try it, Lump." Kit's voice was playful and encouraging. "Just remember, don't fly away. I want you to come back." Without hesitation, Lump raced across the training field. With the enchantments that Lin had put on him, he reached top speed in moments, a golden blur on a field of green. "Jump and flap," Kit called out. "Jump and flap."

Lump followed her instructions, leapt into the air, and flapped furiously. He covered at least fifty paces before crashing hard to the ground, destroying an entire bed of moonflowers.

"That was much better," Kit said with smug satisfaction. "He went a long way before he... fell." Kit got a mental picture of Fury rolling his eyes, his lizard-like tongue flicking at the air. Kit wasn't sure if he was sticking his tongue out at her or not.

"He went a long way because he is extremely fast, and he has muscular legs. Flying has nothing to do with either. It's about channeling his magic." Fury groaned. Kit got another picture of him, draping his clawed hand over his eyes, slowly raking his fingers over his face.

"I take flying for granted. It's natural for me. I don't need to think about it, I just do it. I had no mother to teach me how to fly. I was born as a fully formed dragon. Please get closer so I can speak to Lump. I cannot communicate with him over this distance." Kit jogged across the training grounds, finding Lump in a tangle of leaves and vines. He was uninjured, but his enthusiasm for flying had obviously waned.

Kit ripped out a good number of vines and branches to help extricate the small gold dragon.

"I'm sorry, Lump. I am a poor teacher. If you will forgive me, and trust that my advice is sound, I'll tell you what you need to know to fly." The dragon-dog

bounded from the foliage, his long, reptilian tail wagging slowly behind him. Once again, Kit received an image of Fury. This time, he was hiding his face behind his clawed hand. *"Of course, your tail. I forgot to mention the importance of your tail during flight."* Lump playfully slammed his spiked tail into the ground, his long lizard-like tongue lolling out the side of this toothy maw.

"Don't do that," Fury said, his tone scolding. *"You're a magnificent dragon, not a dog."*

"You are a magnificent dog who also happens to be a dragon," Kit said, running her hand over his scaled head. It was only at that moment that she realized he was much bigger than he was before. He was nearly the size of Angel now. "Listen to the big lizard's flying instructions. Otherwise, just ignore him. He doesn't know how to appreciate the finer things in life."

"I am the finer things in life. I am magnificent. I am flawless. I am... a dragon, and so is Lump. He should not lower himself..." The draken's words were cut off when Lump reared back, his mouth filling with a swirling ball of golden flames. *"That! That right there is the secret to flying."*

Lump's eyes widened, and the fire in his mouth immediately dissipated.

"No, don't let it go out. You need your fire to fly. It is the essence of dragon magic. It is what gives you the power to soar like no other being." Lump's tail wagged slowly behind him again. He took a deep breath in through his scaly nostrils, fueling the fire in his chest with fresh air.

"Very good. Excellent, even. Do you feel that power welling up within you? That is the power of flight. That is your dragon magic. Now, kick up into the air and flap." The draken's voice was filled with exuberance, unadulterated joy. Lump did exactly as instructed, kicking off the ground and flapping. A great wind was unleashed, carrying the dragon-dog up into the sky. The sun reflected off his golden scales, turning the entire area into a kaleidoscope of colors. When Lump was as high as the Temple was tall, he listed badly to the side. His flapping became erratic, and he started into a dive, nose first.

"Your tail," Fury screamed. *"Use your tail to change your direction. Raise it up to climb. Drop it to dive."*

The look on Lump's face was one of pure terror. His tail was spinning randomly, causing him to move in haphazard directions. His descent had slowed, but the crash, likely a life-ending impact, was inevitable.

"Lump, you can do this," Kit called out, her voice calm but powerful. A golden aura had appeared around her, unbidden. "Trust in yourself. Trust me. Raise your tail and look to where you want to go. You know how to fly. It's a part of you. Just trust that you can do it." Lump immediately followed her instructions. His descent slowed momentarily, and then was replaced with ascension. He climbed up into the air at an increasing pace. In moments, he was over three times higher than the Temple. The dragon then banked lightly to his left and then to his right. A bright golden flame blew from his mouth just before he banked again to his left, this time much harder. He went into a tight spiral, descending much faster than he should have. The aura surrounding Kit intensified. "Trust in yourself. You are doing great."

The spiral lessened, but the descent continued. Just as he was about to hit the ground, Lump raised his tail and gave a powerful thrust with his wings. He raised an enormous cloud of dust that obscured his landing. There was no bone crushing whump. There was barely any sound at all. Before the dust settled, Lump, in human form, came running from the cloud. He wrapped his arms around Kit and hugged her deeply.

"Thank you. Thank you for trusting me. Thank you for helping me to trust in myself."

"What about your teacher?" The image of Fury preening his neck scales with his long claws appeared in Kit's mind. *"Where's my love?"*

"You are an excellent dragon teacher. You will be a terrific father some day. Your hatchlings will be the luckiest in all of Orth." Kit couldn't be certain, but she believed that the draken actually blushed at the comment.

"Do you trust him enough to try flying on his back?" Fury said, almost teasing Kit.

"He's ready to carry me," Kit said with absolute certainty. "I don't need him to prove it to me."

⌁⌁⌁

"If you're going to fly to the top of Mount Toka, you will need me to come with you." Ulip towered over Kit. The way her hands were curling into fists at her side quickly caused Indie to intervene.

"My big friend, I don't think you understand to whom you're speaking. This girl needs no help from anyone to do anything." Indie didn't appreciate the way Kit was glaring at him after coming to her defense. He rolled his words over in his mind until he slowly realized why she'd be annoyed. *This girl needs no help from anyone to do anything.* He flashed his love a quick smile and took a step back.

"I have my dragon to carry me to the summit. Once I am there, I will seek the Altar of Toka and commune with my god. When that is complete, I will leave. I have no fear of the wind, or the cold, or any creature that may live upon the mountain." Kit's assertion made the big Gigas laugh.

"And how will you find your altar? The mountaintop is vast, permanently covered with ice and snow. That which you seek may well be buried hundreds of feet beneath its frozen surface." Kit cocked an eyebrow and shifted her weight to one leg.

"Are you suggesting that you know how to find the altar?" Kit raised her eyebrow further, daring the giant to continue pressing her for an invitation to join her.

"No, little girl. No. I do not."

"Then what good are you to me? Why should you accompany me on my quest?"

"Because without us," Yuka interrupted, "you will never make it to the mountain top. You may have the heart of a dragon, but your young friend here will be no match for the flight of protectors that Siku will send out. They will either knock him from the sky and send you both to a horrible, bone-crushing death... or they will simply flame you to a crisp."

Indie cringed. "What sort of protectors? Who is Siku?"

"Siku is the *Queen of Dragons*," Ulip replied. The reverence in his voice made Indie gasp slightly. "Toku is her domain. Only she can grant you passage onto the mountain. Without her blessing, your fate is doomed."

"Kit?" Indie turned to the young woman. "Maybe you need to reconsider?" She gave him a grin as her answer.

"It is but another trial I must pass on my way to freeing Titan," she said brightly.

"It may well be," Indie said. He was struggling to keep the concern from his voice. "But maybe this is about working with others to achieve your goals. Remember earlier how you said it was because of your friends that you were able to take control of four cities? Might this be the same thing?" An odd knot twisted in Indie's stomach. There he was, trying to help Kit achieve her goals and then was stricken with a pathetic case of jealousy.

Kit poked the bare-chested Gigas on his washboard belly. "And how is it you may enter this queen's domain safely when I cannot?"

"It is not he who will get you safe passage," Yuka said, stepping closer to Kit. "It is I. I have served the dragons my entire life. I have met with Siku on many occasions. She knows me and trusts that I will not bring evil into her domain."

"Oh." Kit furrowed her brow as she considered the fire drake's words. "That makes sense, I guess."

Indie chuckled under his breath at Kit's response. She rarely gave in so easily, even to perfectly sound logic.

"When can you be ready to leave?" Kit walked back to Lump and gave him a hug. "We're ready to go now."

"I have already spoken with your chief," Ulip said. "We can leave when you feel you're ready to take flight."

⁐⁓⳼⳼⳼⁓⁐

Runt whined and leaned into Indie's side. The young man couldn't tell if the dire wolf was afraid that Kit and Lump would face troubles, or if he was upset that they were leaving without him. Indie may well have been projecting his own feelings onto the oversized pup.

"Don't worry, boy," Indie said as Kit climbed onto Lump's dragon-dog back. Well before they were ready to leave, Lump had been practicing his flying, but he rarely flew higher than the Temple, and he never seemed particularly comfortable in his practice flights. His wingbeats were often erratic, and he had difficulty maintaining his altitude. Mount Toka was huge, and he had yet to fly with a rider. How would he handle it when the air dropped below freezing and the winds were strong enough to blow him off course or slam him into the mountain side? Indie shuddered at the thought. Runt renewed his whining.

"I'm sure they'll be fine." There wasn't a lot of conviction in Indie's voice and, by the way Runt was looking at him, he knew it. He should have been more confident. He should have trusted Kit and Lump to complete their mission. He should have felt better knowing that Ulip and his fire drake, Yuka, would be with them, to guide them, and to make sure they didn't get into any trouble. It didn't help. Somehow Ulip joining her on this journey only made things worse. That another man was helping her in a time of need gnawed at his soul and left his stomach in knots. He knew it was a childish reaction, but he couldn't help how he felt. Those feelings churned the bile in his belly anytime Kit was near someone else, especially Danny. Runt pressed against him and whined some more.

Even though Indie was only standing a dozen paces from where Kit sat upon Lump, it might as well have been on the other side of Orth. The sensation of being disconnected raced through him and left him feeling hollow and empty.

"I love you." Kit's declaration chased away most of Indie's anxiety, but not all of it. The look of concern on the girl's face got his heart beating faster again. Was she worried about him or was she worried about herself and her mission to seek the Altar of Toka and to commune with her god? "I'll meet you in Cormorant. I will try to be there before sundown, but don't worry if I'm late. I don't want Lump to fly in the dark." Lump roared in response, drawing another whine from Runt.

"You be a good boy and make sure Indie's safe." The look of concern on Kit's face melted away when she spoke to Runt. When the dire wolf barked back a high-pitched reply, the young priest laughed. The sound of it lifted Indie's spirits, making him smile right along with her.

"If we're not there by sundown, we'll meet you when the sun rises. It's a long run from here to Cormorant, but we'll be there." Runt barked in response to Indie's assertion. "I love you, too. Be safe."

Kit patted Lump on his gold dragon neck. A moment later, he kicked off the ground and beat his wings. A cloud of dust obscured the pair as they lifted off. The swirling winds from Yuka's wingbeats practically knocked Indie off his feet. Ulip hadn't said a word before they left. Despite him leaving with Kit, Indie liked the giant.

"Okay, Runt. We've got a long run ahead of us. Let's get the others and head off." Runt barked his agreement and bolted for the stables.

Chapter Twenty-One

To Cormorant

Indie arrived at the stables to find Whistler already saddled and Lin ready to head out. She was dressed in black from head to toe. Her mood was as dark as her clothing. Indie struggled with the woman's personality on the best of days. She could really grind on his nerves, constantly inserting herself in his business, putting herself between him and Kit regularly.

"Where's Coldforge?" Indie was doing his best to ignore Lin's surly behavior. She just glared at him. "Are you angry at me specifically, or are you annoyed at the entire world?" The woman turned away and busied herself with one of her saddle-straps. "Lin, are you okay?"

"I should be heading for Two Peaks." The woman's voice was low, sullen. Indie didn't really know how to react. For once, she was not directing her glib remarks at him. Lin adjusted the swords at her hip and the bow slung over her back.

"I'd have thought you'd be happy to head back to Cormorant. You'll get a chance to see Rusty again." Indie tried to puzzle out why Lin had her forehead pressed against her saddle.

"I'll never get to be with her. The world is against us. You and I have promised to help free Fury. What chance is there for Rusty and me to ever be together? We've spent so much time trying to free slaves and now, we've freely placed ourselves in permanent servitude to a dragon lord for promises that will probably never come to pass."

"We're not slaves. We can do as we please. We just said we'd help." Even as the words escaped his lips, Indie wasn't confident that they were true. Had they just committed themselves to eternal servitude to the dragon? Lin spun around, her face a confused mixture of grief and anger.

"Kit has three pieces of him stuffed into her hammer. Who knows how strong that makes him? Who knows what power he can exert over us now? Sweet Titan, what was I thinking? I was so desperate to cast the spell, to play with the dark magic. I should have listened to Coldforge."

"Ye are quite right." Coldforge came tromping into the stable. "Ye should have listened to me, but ye didn't, and now there may be Helja to pay."

"Leave her alone," Indie said. "We all make mistakes, and we all pay for them, in one way or another."

Runt whined. His head was bouncing from person to person. It seemed the conversation was upsetting him.

⊰⊱

Lin carried Angel's saddle over to Runt. "I'm going to strap this to you, okay, boy? It'll make the ride easier for Coldforge. We've got a long run ahead of us and we can't have him falling off your back every time you change directions."

"I'll not be ridin' that wondrous wolf all the way to Cormorant on a blasted, good-for-nothing saddle. Put that thing away. I haven't fallen from his back a single time." Coldforge called Runt over to him. "I don't want it and he don't want it. Why, in the name of Gaia, would you even suggest it?"

Lin tossed the piece of tack against the wall. "Suit yourself. I was just trying to help."

Indie picked up the saddle and dusted it off. "We should leave Kit's saddle on Angel. The horse won't mind wearing it and Kit will probably want to ride her when she gets to Cormorant."

"You're daft." Coldforge was petting Runt vigorously about his head and neck. "Why would she lower herself to ridin' a horse when she can ride a dragon?" The words had barely left the dwarf's mouth when he was kicked solidly in the head, sending him careening into an empty stall. He had more than a handful of hay and straw stuck in his bright orange hair and beard when he got his senses together. Angel stared down at the little man, perhaps waiting for him to get up so she could kick him again.

"No offense, horse." Coldforge held up his hands in a defensive position. Indie couldn't tell if he was indeed worried or if he was simply trying to appease the animal. "Yer a lovely creature, but ye ain't no dragon."

Indie choked back a laugh when the dwarf rubbed his head. "Her name is Angel. Perhaps you can't understand the bond between a rider and her horse, but it borders on spiritual." Indie's massive black stallion knickered and Angel chuffed.

"If you're all finished doing whatever it is you're doing, maybe we can get going? It's a long ride to Cormorant and if we're to have any hope of getting there before sundown, we need to leave now." Lin finished strapping down Angel's saddle and added two light saddlebags, carefully tying them off. She gave each bag a shake and nodded her approval. Indie could only assume they were filled with potions and scrolls and other such things, but he didn't know for sure. He had no supplies for himself other than what he had strapped to his body, which included his weapons and a small knapsack. Coldforge was similarly equipped, except that he was only wearing a light chain mail shirt for armor, and he had a hefty, double-bladed battle ax strapped to his back. Indie didn't know if the dwarf understood he might need some supplies or if the stout man assumed others would provide what was needed.

As Lin mounted up, so did Indie and Coldforge. Indie checked that his bow was tightly secured to his saddle before nodding his readiness to move out. In mere moments, they were racing from the stables through the Temple's out buildings and through the streets of Aarall.

⤬

Angel lagged as the group galloped along the road that led from Aarall to Cormorant. They were often forced to leave the well-maintained road and run cross-country to avoid areas where merchants traveled with large caravans laden with wares. On several occasions, they had been mistaken for highwaymen intent on robbing caravans. In response, the caravan's guards usually did no more than circle their wagons. But on one particular occasion, the guards had nocked arrows and had tried removing the riders from their mounts. As much as this bothered Indie deeply, that soldiers would willingly kill without provocation, he understood that fear could make people react badly.

The morning sun tracked through the sky, warming the air, raising a lather on the horses. Runt's tongue was lolling out the side of his mouth like a big pink flag. Even Char's breathing was becoming labored. He would run himself into the ground for Indie, but even he needed to rest.

"Slow," Indie called out. "There will be a stream to the east of here. We can take water and rest for a short while."

"Thank Gaia," Coldforge yelled back. "Me arse is aching so bad I can hardly feel me legs."

"If you'd let me put Angel's saddle on Runt, you'd be in a lot less pain." The *I told you so* tone in Lin's voice did not go over well with the dwarf. He made some sort of rude gesture to the woman as soon as she turned away from him.

The group turned east off the road and quickly came upon the stream. They barely stayed long enough to have a deep drink of water and eat some food. Coldforge eyed Lin's and Indie's food supplies with hopeful anticipation.

"Why didn't you pack some food for the trip?" Lin licked her fingers after stuffing the last of her beef rolls into her mouth. "You knew we'd be on the road for an entire day." Runt gave the woman a disappointed whine when she didn't share a bite with him. Coldforge seemed to react similarly. Indie rummaged around in his knapsack and pulled out two leaf-covered bundles.

"Here you go. It's not much, but it should help keep your stomachs from grumbling." He tossed a roll to Coldforge and another to Runt.

Indie turned his gaze back on Lin. "Why must you give him such a hard time?" He shook his head at Lin and went about repacking his knapsack. Lin just shrugged at the question.

"Because you're not as much fun to tease anymore," she said. "And Coldforge doesn't get his small clothes tied in a knot when I ride him."

Coldforge ate the tasty treat Indie had given him almost as fast as Runt had eaten his own. "Girl, you got a lot to learn about jibes if ye think ye can get me goat. Verbal insults are practically a sport where I come from. Ye'd not last a minute with me kind." Lin's mouth flopped open. Some words came out, but they were nonsensical. It made Indie chuckle as he jumped up onto Char's back. Lin's face reddened significantly before her eyes brightened.

"Well, the only reason you don't get my humor is because it's over your head, you soil munching goblin lover. Or maybe it's just the forest of hair growing out of your ears that makes you hard of hearing." Coldforge's beard twitched at the insults being hurled at him. "Maybe if you used a hammer instead of your head when you worked iron, you'd not be quite so damaged between the ears."

At the last remark Coldforge burst out laughing, slapping his thighs for extra effect. His laughter continued on for far too long. The look on Lin's face suggested to Indie that she was now thinking the dwarf was mocking her. When the dwarf's laughter finally died off, he gave his body a shake.

"You know, your jokes would be a lot funnier if your breath didn't smell like you had just sucked the air out of a dead ox." Lin's face went blank.

"I don't think it was dead," Indie said, his voice completely deadpan. "I'm pretty sure I saw the thing moving." Coldforge's bushy orange eyebrows shot up and his eyes twinkled merrily.

"Are ye sure ye don't have some dwarf blood in ye, lad? That was the funniest bit of words I've heard since this lass last opened her mouth."

"We should go," Lin said, climbing up onto Whistler's saddle. The sour look on her face suggested she wasn't sure if Coldforge had just insulted her a second time.

⁂

The group continued to push hard until the midday sun beat down on them, sucking the energy from their bodies. Nobody seemed to care. Runners and riders alike were highly motivated to reach their destination before Kit and Ulip got there.

After another brief break, as the sun hung low in the western sky, they spied a convoy of people on horseback heading along the road from Silverhawk to Cormorant. They were perhaps a league away, too far to get a good idea if they were friend or foe. Indie held up his hand to signal the group to slow.

"What do you think?" Indie was straining to get a good look at the group, but they were too far away to see any details. "We can easily reach the crossroads before they get there, but if they are friends, we might want to talk to them first."

A gust of wind carrying a fetid aroma spun around the group. A cloud of dust swirled, blocking the road in front of them. Runt immediately snarled and barked. Foam poured from his lips. He sprung forward, putting himself between the dust-cloud and his cohorts. In just moments, the cloud coalesced into a Berrat male with bone-white hair, wearing a full-length oilskin cloak. An arrow whizzed at his chest, which the man caught with relative ease. A second arrow followed shortly after, which the Berrat dodged with bored indifference.

"You won't surprise me a second time, young Indigo." The man smiled at Lin. "I do not know your name, young lady, but it is my pleasure to meet you." Runt continued his snarls while Coldforge brandished his oversized double-bladed ax. "And hello to you, too, Runt, carrier of princes."

"Ye know me, wizard?" Coldforge's reaction was hidden behind his mass of facial hair. "I don't recall having met ye before."

"No, I suppose you won't remember me, Coldforge, son of Gimlie. But rarely does the child of a god escape notice."

"What are you doing here, Pental?" Indie had another arrow nocked and at the ready.

"Put away your weapon. I am here to help you." Lin's hands shook when Indie called the Berrat out by name. She had heard Kit's tales of the vampire and how he had coerced her into killing so many innocents. Pental inhaled deeply, using his hand to encourage the air towards his nose. "The smell of fear pouring off you, young lady, is intoxicating."

Lin immediately loosed another arrow at the vampire, drawing a look of annoyed ire from him.

"You know," Pental said, wagging his finger at the woman. "I could have easily continued on to Cormorant without stopping here to share information with you. If you'd rather I leave, I can do so." The vampire drifted higher in the air; his arms outstretched from his side.

"What information do you have?" Indie's tone was flat. He would not give the fiend the benefit of thinking he was welcomed by him.

"You are heading into a war. So, are your friends coming from Silverhawk? I have done what I can to sow chaos within the enemy's ranks. To think that Berrat would turn on their own, it sickens my stomach."

"And what of all the Berrat you've killed?" Char moved forward, his hooves pawing at the ground as he did. Angel moved in beside the big stallion, offering him any support she could. Lin had moved into a flanking position. She had another arrow knocked. Whistler's movements were erratic, but she continued to follow her rider's instructions.

Indie lowered his bow but kept it at the ready. "When the people of Templeton murdered each other and fell to their deaths, where was your outrage at their passing? Why is it that other's ill deeds sicken you, but you somehow find a way to justify your own actions?"

Pental dropped from his lofty perch and landed softly next to Indie.

"I will pay with my life for what I did that day. I took no joy in it, even if it appeared otherwise. I am a monster. I have no delusions that I am anything but. For good or for ill, I am trying to save the people of my kingdom the only way I know how."

"Saving people by sacrificing the innocent is too twisted for words." Lin launched another arrow at Pental. He again evaded the projectile, a bit more slowly this time. It nicked his cheek, drawing a thin crimson line where it had made contact. The vampire snarled in response.

"I came to help you, but if you insist on trying to assassinate me for it, here I am." Pental yanked open his jerkin, revealing his pale bronze skin beneath. "You will need to strike me repeatedly with those arrows if you wish to kill me, or you can let your familiar do it for you. His bite is more than enough to sever my head from my shoulders." Pental spun toward Runt, startling him. "Is that what you want, creature of the north?" Pental leaned his head back, fully exposing his throat. "Kill me now. Rip out my throat and end my miserable existence."

Runt took a tentative step away from the vampire. Beyond the wind lightly blowing through the surrounding grasses, there was nary a sound. Indie's heart was thrumming in his ears. He breathed a little easier when Lin slowly lowered her weapon.

"What information do you want to share with us?" Indie slung his bow over his shoulder. "If war is being waged in Cormorant, we need to get there with haste."

"The Split Crow are descending upon the city. Even now, they sail down the Gaelinora River with thousands of soldiers. To the northeast, slavers from Silverhawk are heading their way. Their numbers are few, but they will force Cormorant into fighting on two fronts. It's unlikely the city gates will keep them out. They have a large flight of hawk riders at their command."

"The slavers in Silverhawk are not our enemies." Lin slung her bow over her shoulder, drawing a look of ire from Coldforge, who had been slowly closing the gap between Pental and himself. His battle ax rested on his lap as he did. "They all work for Sister Kit and if they're heading to Cormorant, then they're on their way to render aid."

"I had wondered about the little priest." Pental looked to Runt and Cold-forge, who were only a dozen paces from him now. "I do hope she is well. I would like to see her again before I meet my end."

Indie shook his head at Coldforge, signaling him to cease whatever it was he was trying to do. "She is communing with her god, and she will be here before the sun sets. She will determine if you are indeed for or against us, and she will end your life if you are speaking false."

"That is good. I think I would like to meet my end under the light of Medeina." Pental buttoned up his jerkin and wrapped his cloak tightly around himself. "Tonight will be a good night to die."

CHAPTER TWENTY-TWO

KIT AND THE DRAGON QUEEN

Yuka banked hard, knocking Lump off balance. He was struggling to carry Kit as it was, so having the fire drake slam into him was no help.

"We are going to be guided in." Yuka said in Kit's mind. *"I am trying to give your dragon instructions, but he's not listening."*

"He's terrified he's going to drop me," Kit yelled out. The pelting snow that was building around them devoured her words before they could travel ten paces.

"Just think the words. No need to scream."

"Oh." Kit blushed. After having had so many conversations with Angel, she should have recognized that Yuka was communicating with her through her thoughts. *"Lump is scared. This is his first time flying, and he's afraid he'll drop me."*

"Can you communicate with him the way we are? Tell him what's going to happen."

"I don't have that type of connection with him, but I can talk to him. I'll try to tell him what to do. I'll try to calm him so that he'll listen to you."

"Then be quick about it. There are eight frost drakes flying directly towards us. When they see a dragon, I don't know how they will react. Make sure your dragon doesn't attack them."

Kit's heart was now racing out of control. She never even had a chance to enjoy the fact that she was flying, soaring through the sky, untethered from the confines of the ground. She leaned forward, resting her body on Lump's neck.

"Lump, can you hear me?" The dragon-dog nodded. His flapping faltered for a moment, causing him to go off balance and tip precariously to the side. Kit used her legs to hold more tightly to his scaled body. She patted him gently on the neck. "I'm okay, Lump. I'm perfectly safe with you. I won't fall. I promise."

Lump's wingbeats settled, and they started gaining altitude again.

"There are eight drakes coming towards us. Do nothing to spook them. Yuka has been trying to talk to you, but she says you're not listening. You need to do what she says. Okay? Don't worry about me. I'm safe and you're doing great." The words had barely left her mouth when Lump banked hard to the right and drifted under Yuka. The swirling vortex created by her wingbeats threatened to knock Kit from Lump's back, but she kept hold, using her thighs to get a tighter grip on her dragon. She held on with one hand, gripping one of the small horns that adorned the side of Lump's neck. She continued to stroke his smooth, golden scales with her free hand, comforting and reassuring her friend that everything was okay.

"When did you get these horns on your neck?" Kit was certain she had never seen them before. Up to this point, the only adornment on his neck was his handsome, glistening scales. Her thoughts were distracted when two pairs of frost drakes appeared on either side of her. They screeched out a call and released a quick burst of flames.

With a quick beat of his wings, Lump surged forward and screeched out a response. It was higher pitched than the drakes' call, but to Kit's ear, it sounded more commanding. The dragon-dog belched out a series of fireballs, each one bigger than the previous.

"What are you doing, Lump?" Kit asked, craning her neck to look behind, searching for the drakes who had been beside her just moments ago.

"Your dog is every bit a dragon. If I didn't know he was only a dog, I'd bow before him myself."

Kit gave Yuka an incredulous look when she took Lump's right flank. *"Did you tell him to do that?"*

The sound of Yuka's laughter echoed inside Kit's head. It was surprisingly sweet, with a hint of a lilt to it. *"Your dog knows more of drakes than I'd have ever imagined. I told him what to do, and he told me he knew how to speak to them."*

The books Lump had read in the secret library. One of them was about the creatures of the north. He must have read about drakes. *"Nothing about Lump surprises me anymore. He is the most amazing friend a person can have."*

"Thank you," Lump said.

"You can speak to me in my head?"

"All dragons can communicate this way. I just needed to believe I was a dragon. When I commanded the drakes, and they listened, I knew that I really was a dragon and not a dog in a dragon costume."

"I love you, Lump, and I was wrong. You just surprised the Helja out of me."

"You two can chat later. The frost drakes are about to guide us into Siku's domain. No shenanigans from either of you. Siku is the queen of dragons, and you will treat her with the utmost respect. If you don't, I will flame you myself."

Yuka followed the frost drakes' instructions, and Lump followed Yuka. In moments, they were in a clearing next to a sizable, snow-covered mound. Lump lowered his tail and began his descent. The first few moments were filled with a series of unsteady movements. His descent slowed, then sped up, and then slowed so drastically Kit feared they'd fall from the sky. Just before they impacted with the ground, Lump beat his wings a single time, halting their fall, allowing him to land softly on a bed of freshly fallen snow.

"You were amazing. Are you ready for this?" Kit slid off her dragon's back and gave his neck a deep hug. His scales were hot, not so much as to hurt Kit, but they felt much warmer than when they were flying.

"I am ready. I am ready for anything, so long as I am with you."

The huge mound suddenly grew; its snow falling off it like an avalanche. Kit braced herself, waiting for the impending impact as the snow raced towards her. Lump blew out a thick flame, melting the snow before it got close. From behind the cloud of ice and fog, a magnificent head appeared, quickly followed by a long slender neck and a thick, powerful body. She shook her tremendous bulk, sending a shower of snow and ice in all directions. Kit looked up in awe at the dragon, who stood nearly as tall as the Temple.

"How is it that a dragon has left its mountain and entered my domain?" Siku's voice rumbled, shaking snow free from the surrounding trees, threatening to start an avalanche that could sheer off the entire mountainside.

"Siku, most venerable dragon queen." Ulip strode through the waist-deep snow like it was nothing more than a thick carpet. "If it pleases you, I would like to introduce Sister Kit Standing Bear and her wolfdog, Lump."

Siku's head turned onerously slowly until she leveled her gaze at Ulip. She lowered her head until her chin rested on the ground. Even then, her snout was still higher than the top of Ulip's pate. Her lips pulled back into a feral grin.

"Ulip, Chief of the Firedrake Clan. I was speaking to the dragon. That you suggest this magnificent creature is a dog is laughable." Without moving her head, Siku's eyes scanned until they fell upon Lump and Kit. "But perhaps you speak true. He is the smallest gold dragon I have ever met. Perhaps that is how he escaped his mountain."

"Queen Siku." Lump lowered his body and spread his wings outward until they were pressed flat on the ground. Seeing how he was behaving, Kit took a knee and lowered her head. "The chief speaks true, for I am but a dog. Through magic, dragon brandy, and chance, I have been graced with the ability to take on this wondrous dragon form. Today was the first day I actually believed myself to be a dragon, but I am a dog, and a loyal companion to my friend, Kit."

Kit ignored the fact that she was bowing before a queen and moved next to Lump. "And I am your loyal companion and friend, too."

"And where may I ask is Fury?" Siku looked to the skies and then back to Kit. "It was my understanding that he would be with you. Why has he not greeted me?"

Kit pulled her battle hammer from its scabbard, drawing the attention of the frost drakes that were surrounding the group. Several of them moved forward while others took deep breaths, ready to unleash a fiery burst if necessary.

"Fury is contained within this vessel. This very day, we merged a third piece of his soul into the weapon. Sadly, my battle hammer is not powerful enough to

hold him and Fury must use all of his will to prevent himself from leaking out."
The dragon queen harrumphed at the comment.

"Bring that hammer to me and lay it at my feet. I sense no dishonesty from
you, but your tale is too tall to take on your word." Kit let the hammer dangle
at her side as she walked forward. She hadn't expected her legs to turn to jelly,
but each step was becoming more and more difficult. "You have nothing to fear
from me, child, unless you are lying to me."

"She speaks true, my queen," Lump interjected. "Whatever this woman says,
you can trust it with your life, just as I do."

Emboldened by Lump's support, Kit strode confidently forward and laid the
battle hammer at the dragon's feet. "For your inspection."

Siku snorted, raising a cloud of snow. When it settled, a good deal of the
powder had landed on the little priest. With her eyes affixed firmly onto Kit, she
placed her thick-clawed foot over the hammer. She raised her chin and craned
her neck back. A deep rumble in her chest shook the ground. "Thank you for
bringing Fury to me."

The dragon bowed her neck and looked down upon Kit. "What now will I
do with you?"

<hr>

"You will show me to the altar of Titan." Kit's voice was firm. It was a statement
and not a question.

"You, Sister Kit Standing Bear, are an impudent child in need of discipline."
The dragon pulled back her scaly lips, exposing teeth that were significantly
longer than Kit was tall. Behind the ivory forest, a bright red fire burned. It roiled
and churned like the flames of a massive forge.

"My queen." Yuka stepped forward. "I have spent little time with this human, but I understand her need. Two armies descend upon her city. She seeks
council with her god. She only wishes to protect the innocent and, if my judgment is correct, she will willingly die to do so."

"Her clan is strong of heart, but few in numbers." Ulip calmly stepped forward. "You asked me to bring her to you, and I have done so. I ask that you not make me regret that decision."

Both Kit and Ulip covered their ears to protect them from the blood-curdling screech that filled the air. Kit turned to see, no, to witness Lump rearing back onto his hind legs, his dragon wings flapping slowly to help maintain his position. He rocked his head back and again unleashed the same deafening call.

"Enough!" The power in Siku's voice knocked everyone back several paces. "You will be silent, or I will incinerate each and every one of you. I will burn you to a crisp and scatter your ashes to the four winds."

"What are you afraid of?" Kit tilted her head back to get a better look at the dragon's face. "You are willing to kill us, but you do not want to. There is something more. I feel it rolling off you in waves of fear."

"I fear nothing." The flames in the dragon's mouth were now pouring from her lips like molten lava. "How dare you?"

"You fear much, but you are too proud to say it." Kit's voice was soft, caring. Her golden aura clung to her, swirling about her as she spoke. There was no hint of malice or deception. "Even the most powerful have fears, things they hope for, or things they dread will come to be."

The flow of flames that fell from the dragon slowed. "You're a celestial." The queen's voice was filled with relief. "It explains much. It explains why Fury would honor you with his presence. It explains why you would willingly stand before me and make demands of me. She flicked the war hammer with her paw, sending it tumbling across the ground, stopping at Kit's feet.

"Take the hammer and call forth Fury. Use your power to help him manifest. It is within you to do so."

Kit stared down at the hammer for several seconds before raising her head to the dragon. "Why would I do so? I am here on a mission. Out of courtesy and respect, I came to you before I did what I must. I came in peace, and you threatened to kill us. If you know I am a celestial, you also know what I am capable of."

Siku rolled her eyes.

"You will do it because I asked you to and because it will answer the questions that you have rolling around in your head. You have not learned how to shield your thoughts, and I can hear each one of them."

Kit raised an eyebrow and held it there for several seconds. After a nearly imperceptible shrug, she reached down and grabbed the bone handle of her battle hammer. She examined its mithril head. The runes were glowing a pale shade of blue.

"Fury? Do you wish to appear?" The dragon bone handle surged in Kit's hand, sending shock waves up her arm. It took all her concentration to not drop the hammer. Her golden aura burst forth, and the pains diminished, but they didn't fully abate. A moment later, Fury appeared in his draken form.

"My queen." Fury bowed low, holding his position for several moments. Kit had never seen Fury bow to anything or anyone. She didn't understand why a dragon lord, second only to Ouroboros himself, would bow to another dragon.

"My love," Siku responded. "Arise. My eyes have not seen such a beautiful sight in far too long. My heart burns for you, even more so now that I am once again basking in your magnificence." Kit clutched her breast, her memories of Indie uncontrollably flooding into her, filling her spirit.

"You're mates?" Kit's gaze flitted between the draken and the dragon. "Fury, why didn't you tell me?" Neither responded. They simply continued to stare longingly into each other's eyes. Finally, after many painfully long minutes, Fury turned back to Kit.

"No, we are not mates, though we would want nothing more."

Siku scratched at the ground with a single claw, rending deep gouges in the mountain's icy surface. "Ouroboros is my mate, but Fury is my love. My forbidden love."

"Why are you not with the one you love?" Kit truly had no idea why they could not be together. It seemed so simple. They loved each other, and that should have been enough.

"Because Ouroboros is a jealous, possessive beast. He created me to be his mate, and in his mind, that is an absolute. I am his for the taking whenever the urge strikes him. I may be bigger than he is, but his magic and his cruelty know no bounds."

"And therein lies my dilemma," Fury said, dipping his forehead against Siku's muzzle. "I need to be free to be with Siku. But if I am free, so will be Ouroboros. He would destroy us both if he discovered our unrequited love for one another."

"Can Titan help you?" Kit didn't know what else to say. "If Titan created the dragons, can he not do something with Ouroboros?"

Siku and Fury both smiled, but they were sad smiles, filled with grief and longing. "It's unlikely," Fury said. "It may be within his power to do so, but it would break the rules of their game and he will not do it." Kit scoffed at the comment.

"The way I hear it from Tyr, the gods break the rules all the time."

"They have never broken the rules of non-interference. They have stretched some rules, allowing themselves to create races that were beyond the norm, but in each case, the other gods could follow suit. To kill his own creation would be a breach he will not do."

"Show me to the altar," Kit said. "I will speak with him. If I free him, he will owe me a boon." Siku was taken aback by the offer.

"You would willingly do such a thing without recompense? You are a strange creature, Sister Kit Standing Bear." Siku's comment made Fury guffaw.

"You don't know the half of it. She is entertaining in so many ways." The draken sighed deeply. "If we can ever be together, I will regale you with tales of surprise and wonder, and this young woman will feature prominently in each story." A look crossed the dragon queen's face that Kit could not understand. It looked like resignation, but all she could feel emanating from her was hope.

"Lump and Yuka," the dragon intoned. "If you would be so kind as to bear your riders away from this place, I have work to do." Kit gave Fury a look of incredulous disapproval. Before she could say a word, he slowly shook his head.

"Climb onto my back," Lump said, urging Kit to do so. *"She is going to help you."*

As soon as Kit was too far away from Fury, his visage winked out. A moment later, the fire drake and the gold dragon were airborne, circling the mountaintop. Hovering several hundred feet in the air, Kit could finally take in the entirety of Siku. Never had she ever seen anything so big, or so beautiful. As the dragon lifted her bulk from the ground, the snow and ice that had accumulated upon her slid off, creating huge piles all around her. In a fashion similar to Lump's display, the dragon raised herself onto her hind legs. She slowly beat her powerful wings, creating a frosty whirlwind. From within the frozen funnel, a bright white flame appeared, turning the blizzard that surrounded her into an impenetrable mist. As her wings continued to beat, the mist subsided, revealing a tiny statue of Titan with an even smaller altar standing before it.

The dragon turned her body from the altar and walked away. Her body and tail left a huge rut in the ground as she did. When she was nearly out of sight, she turned back towards Kit.

"Long have I protected this site. I did not believe I would ever leave here, but today you have brought me hope. I beg of you, do not disappoint me."

⌘

Kit knelt before the altar and laid her hands across its surface and grimaced. The cold that gripped the stone was so intense it burned. The ice that clung to the base of the structure cut into her knees. The memories of when she first communed with Titan flooded back. A flash of excitement ran up her spine, enriching her expectations. The rush turned to a shiver that ran so deep within her, she convulsed.

"You are not yet ready to meet me," a thunderous voice cracked through her mind. "Follow the path I have set out before you. It will not be easy. It will take everything within you to walk it. It may well mean the death of the ones you love. Prove yourself to me and I will bestow upon you whatever boon you desire."

"I wish you to free the dragons and destroy Ouroboros." The thought had barely coalesced in her mind. She hadn't thought it out. It wasn't clear to her it was what she wanted, but it was what Siku and Fury wanted. The shiver that had ensnarled her was nothing compared to the bracing cold that suddenly ripped through her body.

"You would knowingly ask me to break the rules? Perhaps I chose wrong. Perhaps you are no better than Ymir. Perhaps I should rip away that which I have given you. I bestowed my strength and my love upon you, and you would throw it in my face?"

Kit's inner daemon ignited, chasing away the cold that threatened to end her existence. Her flames burned with incredible intensity, warming Kit's body and soul.

"I do not wish you to break your rules, or to cheat. I am but a blunt instrument seeking to fulfilll the path which you have set me upon. I do not understand the bounds of your glory, nor do I understand the moral code that you live by. But my moral code is to help those whom I can, even if it puts me in harm's way. You tell me the path to freeing you may cause the deaths of those I love. Do you understand what you're asking of me? It doesn't seem that you do. You're willing to destroy me because I don't understand you. Maybe I am the one who chose poorly. Maybe I've wasted my life believing in you."

The world around Kit spun and swayed. She pitched and bobbed like she had when she was caught in the currents within the depths of the North Sea. Images flashed before her. They came and went so quickly that she couldn't make out any details. Somehow, they were more like visual feelings. Somehow, the images conveyed a message to her. She felt the pain, the fear, and the outright despair of millions of lives; lives that were shining brightly, only to be snuffed out.

"Thank you," Titan said. The words were honest and sincere. "I did not try to understand your feelings. I did not try to understand the feelings of the peoples I put to death for the sole purpose of my amusement. Your flames have warmed my heart." There was a long pause, leaving Kit unsure what to say or do.

"The path to me is dangerous. You may lose loved ones along the way, and for that, I am truly sorry. It doesn't have to be that way. You can turn away from what you've promised, and I will harbor you no ill will. My time to be free will come, by your hands or not."

Kit's fires burned out and the cold of the mountain top seeped back into her. When she opened her eyes, she was at the altar and the surrounding ground was thawed and covered in small, yellow blossoms.

"What did Titan say to you?" Lump moved up next to Kit. He was in his human form, his long golden-red hair mussy as usual, drooping over his eyes. He pushed his locks back, but they immediately returned to where they'd been.

"He will not destroy Ouroboros." Kit raised her voice loud enough that Siku could hear. Remembering that she needed to hold the hammer for Fury to manifest, she slipped it out of its sheath and gripped it tightly. "Fury, did you hear me?"

"I heard everything," the draken said, materializing next to Kit. "I'm not sure how to react. For once in my life, I don't know what to say."

"Thank you, are the words you are looking for." Siku's voice rumbled across the clearing. It seemed she and Ulip had kept a respectful distance away while Kit was communing with her god. "You willingly tried to help us, without thought for yourself or what your god could have bestowed upon you."

Barely a moment later, Ulip jumped up onto Yuka's back. The pair kicked off and were out of sight in seconds.

"Where is he going?" Kit asked to nobody in particular.

"I have sent him to get you help. I believe you will do what you can to free us, and I will do what I can to help your people survive the oncoming armies. My assistance alone will not save you, but my people will do what they can. Leave now. Make your way to Cormorant; it is where your path lies."

"Do you wish to stay here, Fury?"

Fury turned to face Siku. Her eyes were glassy, tears threatening to fall from them. She slowly closed them and nodded.

"No," Fury said. "I mean, yes, I want to stay, but I need to go with you. We need to get the last piece of my soul so that I can be whole. We will free Ouroboros, and I will kill him myself."

CHAPTER TWENTY-THREE

A FLIGHT OF HAWK RIDERS

Fenrir's voice was unusually panicked as she ordered a pack of gray wolves to search the forests north of Cormorant. It had been two days since Riva had disappeared, and they were no closer to discovering her whereabouts. After an exhaustive search of the new Berrat village outside the city walls, they found some minor clues, but nothing to show where she might be. There was no sign of a struggle in her hut, and it appeared as though she had left her morning meal half-eaten. What Amilta found was a good number of dire wolf tracks at the back of Riva's hut along with the footprints of a large person, possibly Gigas. The ground smelled funny, but she couldn't find the words to describe it. When Amilta reported her discoveries to Fenrir, the wolf god's bronze skin visibly paled.

"Fenrir?" Amilta kept her head low as she approached, her voice tentative. "We might have found something of interest. There were many wolf-prints to the west, along with the same large Gigas-like tracks we found near Riva's hut. The wolves followed the prints for many hours." Amilta hesitated to continue. Fenrir sighed as she waited for the small girl to finish her thought.

"Yes, Amilta? What of the prints?" Before the girl answered, a flight of great hawks and griffins interrupted their conversation. Soldiers, with long colorful banners trailing behind them, rode comfortably on the creatures' backs. At their lead was a large man sporting a bright white streamer. "Griffin riders. What are they doing in Berrathia?" Amilta's expression, a mixture of wonder and confusion, caught her attention.

"I don't know why they're here." Amilta paused for a moment. "Do you want my pack to follow them?"

Fenrir chuckled. "No, sweet child. I was only thinking aloud. I... please, tell me of Ymir's prints you found."

"Ymir? You think the prints belong to Ymir?" The girl's expression changed from confusion to terror. "Do you think we found Ymir and Shade?"

"Helja." Fenrir hadn't intended to speak the ice god's name aloud. She didn't want to worry the girl unnecessarily, but since it was a bit late for that, she acknowledged her thoughts. "I do. I didn't want to say anything until I was certain, but I fear they are. Please, tell me what you found."

"They seemed to meet up with more big footprints, like the one's we found at Riva's hut. There were at least five, maybe more. They crisscrossed over each other and then they just stopped." The small child held her hands up and shrugged. "They just disappeared. There was no trace of the wolves or of the enormous feet. There was a strange smell in the area. It was just like the smell we found around Riva's hut." Fenrir growled at the news.

"Did it smell of stale frost?" Fenrir was still growling as she asked the question. It was a deep, visceral sound. Amilta backed away from the god, her eyes wide, her lower lip trembling. Never had she heard anything like this, especially from the wolf god. She wanted to drop to the ground and prostrate herself.

"Tell me, child." Amilta jumped at the words, a whimper escaping her lips. Fenrir's expression softened. The wolf god turned her body so that her side faced the young girl. This was the body language of wolves. Amilta understood the gesture as being a sign of nonaggression, allowing her to speak to Fenrir as her equal. "Amilta, please tell me. The details are important."

The Berrat girl nodded briefly and dipped her head low. "Yes. The wolves had difficulty describing the scent, but I think saying it smelled like stale frost is an excellent description." Fenrir blew out a bitter breath. She grasped her hands behind her back and began pacing. "Fenrir?"

"I fear Riva is beyond my reach."

"Where is she?" Amilta's eyes were wide and glassy. She had grown remarkably close to Kit's mother in the short time they had known one another.

"I fear she has been taken to Jotunheim, the land of the Ice Giants. I believe they have reconstructed the Bifrost, the rainbow bridge. I thought it was destroyed beyond repair." Amilta stared, dumbfounded. Even though she was only nine and extremely intelligent, there was much she had yet to learn. She could now add the Ice Giants, Jotunheim, and the Bifrost to the list of things she needed to study. She desperately wanted to ask the wolf god what they were, but Fenrir seemed so distraught that Amilta remained silent.

"Fenrir?" Amilta barely squeaked out the word. "What should we do? If Riva has been taken, how do we get her back? Where is Jotunheim?"

"Jotunheim is at the northern most tip of the western continent. It would take too long to get there by boat." The wolf god's ears suddenly perked, and her head snapped around to the south. The high-pitched peel of bells was ringing out. "We need to go. Now. If the Bifrost is functioning, Ymir may well arrive with an army of Ice Giants and decimate Cormorant. I fear they are already there."

Fenrir transformed into her white wolf form. The blue whorls that covered her fur glowed brightly for a moment. Amilta followed suit, changing into her gray wolf form. The great white wolf let out a series of short yips, drawing the entire wolf pack near to her. She barked out orders and took off at a dead run towards the city. Despite her being much larger than the other wolves, the entire pack maintained her pace as she raced through the forested hills.

⟡

"No, no, no. Not like that." Bango bellowed at the group of new recruits, sending them scattering about on the beach like sand crabs running from seagulls. "Mukale, get your group back in formation. Treedale, your recruits are running amok. We need them to simulate an actual attack from seasoned soldiers. Right now, they're behaving like untrained rabble." Truth was, they were untrained rabble, but there was no way the Port Authority Harbourmaster was going to let them be anything other than perfect.

"Red team," Treedale called out. He gave his long, black ponytail a solid tug. "To me. To me."

"White team," Mukale called out, following his friend's lead. "To me. To me."

The two groups, made up of over one hundred of the newest Berrat and Nomad recruits, scurried haphazardly about. Even though they were wearing armbands to identify which team they belonged to, many of them seemed to have trouble remembering it. It wasn't like they were stupid or incompetent, but Bango had been training them hard since well before the sun had come up. They were exhausted but not a single one showed any signs of quit.

Each group huddled together for a few minutes before they broke apart and took up formations.

"Red Team 1, take up a flanking position." Treedale barked out his order, keeping a close eye on the white team. While half of the red team broke away and circled off to their left, the rest of the red team waited impatiently. As soon as the white team started eyeballing the advancing soldiers, Treedale yelled out, "Red Team 2, charge!"

Bango ripped off a strip of salted meat and chewed rapidly. The anticipation of the clash had her heart beating fast in her chest. These new soldiers had enlisted in Kit's army less than a week earlier and they were already showing signs of promise. While the captains all looked after their own seasoned platoons, Bango was given the responsibility of managing the recruits. General Karter, Rusty, was all too happy to have them taken off her hands. She just couldn't seem to get a grasp on working with the Berrat and their *non-standard way of fighting*.

The Port Authority's membership had swelled of late, as well. A good number of the new recruits were brought into their ranks. Besides learning how to be coordinated warriors, they were also being taught how to manage the shipment of goods and how to spot any of the various tricks that smugglers and poachers used to transport illegal commodities.

The clash of blunted steel rang out, drawing Bango back to the training maneuvers she had been overseeing. The Nomad soldiers were larger and stronger than their Berrat counterparts, but the way the Berrat could evade their blows was a thing of beauty. It looked like some elaborate dance. People moved in and out, ebbing and flowing like a relentless cycle of waves crashing upon the shore, only to recede back out to sea before returning yet again. The Harbourmaster cringed when one recruit took a sword to the side of his head, sending him sprawling into the wet sand. It might have been a dance, but it was a very violent one. The young Berrat picked himself up off the sand, wobbled about for a few moments and then plopped himself on the ground. He raised his arm to mark himself as *dead*. The look of shame on his face said it all.

Bango reached for the small pearl necklace around her neck. She smiled at it before gripping it in her hand. "To me." Her voice boomed across the shoreline, grabbing the attention of every recruit. "Red Team, to me. White Team, to me. Yellow Team, to me." While the red and white teams had been practicing close quarters combat, the much larger yellow team of nearly four hundred recruits had been working on their archery skills. Even though they were on the far side of the harbor, they easily heard Bango's magically magnified voice. After having seen Kit's necklace in action, Rusty had commissioned the Hobgoblins to make one for each of her captains, as well as for Bango. These new necklaces were only active when the wearer held them in their hand, allowing them to keep the jewelry on their person at all times.

As she waited for the recruits to assemble, movement in the skies above caught her attention. A flight of hawk riders had flown in over the city. Bango had seen them in the past, but never in such numbers. It was uncommon for them to leave the Silverhawk barony. It was unheard of that they would fly into Berrathia in force, especially with the griffin riders leading the flight.

The Harbourmaster monitored them as they continued to fly past the city. In perfect unison, they all banked to the right and followed the Gaelinora River from where it flowed towards the North Sea. She couldn't help but marvel at the sight. What a wondrous thing it would be to fly untethered, without a care in the world. The moment of serenity turned to ash at the sight of black ships sailing south on the river, on their way to Cormorant. At the distance they were, it was difficult to tell how many ships made up the fleet. The exact number didn't matter. There were way too many of them.

"Bango, what's wrong?" Treedale had moved closer to the harbormaster. Like everyone else on the beach, they were focused on the flight of soldiers as they receded into the distance.

"Look at the river," Bango said. "We're in for a world of hurt." Treedale gasped at the sight.

"I'll sound the alarm." He didn't move from the spot for several more seconds. A bell tower had been erected beside the Port Authority buildings, for just such occasions.

"Go," Bango said, giving the young man a shove. Treedale had to fight through the waves of recruits who had answered the Harbourmaster's call to rally to her.

"What do we do?" Mukale asked. "These recruits aren't ready for this type of fight. Neither am I."

Bango continued to watch the incoming fleet. "Go to the manor. Get the dwarves. Yank them from their forges if you have to. We're going to need every soul here on the beach. Try to get the Hobgoblins as well." Mukale nodded, switched into his horse form, and galloped through the crowd, knocking several of them over as he burst through their ranks.

"Recruits," Bango called out, clutching onto her necklace. "We are under attack. It is time to put your training into action." A wave of panic ripped through the assembled soldiers. Some looked ready to bolt, while others looked ready to soil themselves.

"Remember what we're fighting for," Bango called out. "Remember why you enlisted in Sister Kit's army. Against unfathomable odds, she fought to save you. She fought for your families, your mates, your children. She fought for the very freedom that allows you to stand here on this beach and fight for yourselves."

Her words rallied the recruits. Many brandished their short swords and called out war cries.

"Arm yourselves with bow and arrow. I want to see Red and White teams in five rows of twenty lined up in front of the deep-water docks. Yellow team, assemble into five rows along the beachhead."

It seemed the impending threat of an attack was all these recruits needed. They moved about purposefully, forming into their ranks. Natural leaders emerged from within each team, helping to keep their people organized. They had no genuine sense of what they were about to face, but none showed any fear or hesitation.

When the soldiers had finished getting themselves set, Bango called out more instructions. "The only place they'll be able to land is at the deep-water docks. Most of the ships will have to send soldiers ashore by skiff. Red and white teams, if any ships approach, don't let the soldiers disembark. Those who do will be clustered on the docks. They'll make easy targets. Yellow team, do not let any skiffs make it to shore. Don't waste arrows shooting at them if they are out of reach. Send out a few arrows to gauge your distance. Once they are in range, fire at will."

Bango had barely finished giving out her instructions when the warning bell's peel ripped through the air. *The bell will bring every soldier to the dockyards. I pray to Aurora it will be enough.*

⸎⸎⸎⟨⟩⸎⸎⸎

Indie and the others met up with Selena, Jayne, and the rest of the Auctioneers at the crossroads between Silverhawk and Cormorant. As the unlikely band of heroes approached, the Auctioneers formed up ranks, at least to the best of their abilities. They were solid warriors, but they were not soldiers. They were brawlers, thugs, murderers, and thieves, but now they were fighting for Sister Kit Standing Bear and Aurora's Guard. Selena breathed a sigh of relief when she saw Indie and Lin at the lead. She had to suppress a laugh when she caught sight of the dwarf straddling Runt. The two were as mismatched a pair as she had ever seen. One was a silly furball, and the other was Runt. She was about to enthusiastically greet the trio when her heart sank. She struggled to maintain control of her emotions at the sight of the riderless horse. Where was its rider? She prayed to Titan that Kit was safe. How would she explain it to her mother, Aurora, if she had not survived the journey here?

"Where's Sister Kit?" Selena's eyes shifted between Indie and Lin. Her chest tightened, making it difficult to breathe. Tears threatened to sting her eyes when Indie's gaze fell upon the riderless, yet still saddled, horse.

"I expect she will fly here shortly." Indie gave the woman a shrug. His nonchalance bothered Selena deeply. How could he toy with her emotions in such a callous way?

"You scared the life out of me," Selena said. The look on Jayne's face was almost a perfect mirror to her friend's. The pair had been managing the Scarlet Tavern since Kit had left for Cormorant. It was the last time they had seen either the priest or her mother, Aurora.

"Why are you here?" Jayne asked, nodding a quick greeting to the pair. "Did you say Sister Kit is flying here? Does that mean she got her wings?" When Selena saw the dumbfounded expression on the faces of the new arrivals, she quickly changed the question.

"How is Sister Kit flying here?"

"She's riding dragon-back," Coldforge said. He had slidden off Runt and was busy making his way to the two women. His gait was unnatural, making Selena think he might, in some way, be disabled. "Ye are two fine looking women, if ye don't mind me sayin' it. Me name is Coldforge, and to whom do I have the pleasure of meeting?"

"I'm Selena and this woman is Jayne. Did I just hear you correctly or did your thick accent fool my ears?"

"Ah no, lass, ye heard me just fine. Kit is riding a gold dragon by the name of Lump." Selena's gaze fell on Indie, her eyebrows raised, and her head tilted somewhat. Her mouth opened and closed without saying a word.

"It's a bit of a long story," Indie said with a chuckle, "but what my friend here is saying is the honest truth. Lump can change into a dragon, and he's carrying her to the top of Mount Toka so she can commune with Titan."

"We need to cut this short," Lin interrupted. "A lot has happened and a lot more is happening right now. Cormorant is under attack by the Split Crow and they're going to need our help. We need to get moving."

No sooner had Lin finished speaking than the city's warning bells peeled. Selena didn't waste a second to question Lin's words.

She immediate addressed her people. "We came to render aid. We will heed the call. To Cormorant! Fly!" The Auctioneers immediately broke into a gallop, raising a heavy cloud of dust as they thundered towards the fortified city.

"We'll meet you there," Indie said. Without a word, his big stallion wheeled around and broke into a gallop. Angel, the riderless roan, caught up with him quickly. Lin gave Selena a quick nod and motioned to Coldforge for him to follow. The dwarf clambered up onto Runt's back.

"Ye best get going, big guy, or there won't be no Crows left for you to eat." The dire wolf bolted forward, covering the ground at an incredible pace.

Jayne and Selena, who were holding back, looked at each other with wide eyes. "A lot has happened indeed," Jayne said, moving closer to Selena. "When they said she was flying here, I was sure Kit had gotten her wings."

"Me, too," Selena replied.

⟨⟩

Lady Kandyce watched from the quarter deck of *The Black Witch* as a flight of hawk riders passed soundlessly overhead. She had only ever heard tales of griffins and their riders. Her mouth and eyes were wide open as they soared above on their way north. The stories had not done them justice. They were much more noble and majestic in real life. She gathered her wavy black hair that was whipping about her face and clasped onto it. She let out something of a moan as the riders continued into the distance.

"Hawk Riders this far north?" Admiral Robyrts scowled at the sky, the pony-tail of his powdered wig blowing out behind him. He turned up his hawknose and squished his razor-thin lips together. He gave a solid tug on the lapels of his crimson cloak and stated with his painfully shrill voice, "I don't like it. They've never come into Berrathia, at least not in these numbers. Something's up." Lieutenant Barclay nodded in agreement.

"I know little about them, except that they are both feared and respected as the most elite soldiers in all of Arnnor."

Admiral Robyrts harrumphed at the lieutenant's assertion. "We will be the most feared and respected fighting fleet in the four kingdoms. Nobody will sail the seas of Gaelinora once I take hold of Ravenlord and seize control of Berrathia."

It seemed to Lady Kandyce his nasal drone got worse every time the man felt the need to thump his sizeable, well-muscled chest. She had had the unfortunate chance to see him in his small clothes as he was changing. The man had the body of a god, but there was little else of benefit to speak of. He was an arrogant man who'd risen from the gutters. He spent his whole life desperately searching for power and recognition. He wasn't a wicked man, but his goals were entirely self-serving.

With two Hobgoblin air elementals on board *The Black Witch*, the giant vessel could navigate the Gaelinora River and move as fast or faster than the smaller ships in the fleet. Having elementals on the biggest ships really made the fleet a force to be reckoned with. There were nearly fifty ships ranging from the nimble cutters to the large tubs the admiral liked to refer to as *Dragon Ships*. Considering the firepower they carried, it was an apt name.

"Admiral!" a voice loud enough to cut through the thickest fog called out. The man was perched in a crow's nest at the top of the tallest of the ship's three main masts. "Black ships in the Cormorant harbor. The beach is crawling with soldiers."

"What?" The admiral's mouth turned into a sour-pickled frown. "There should be no black ships there. They were all to have sailed south days ago." Kandyce had to jump out of the man's way as he made for one of the rope ladders that led up to the ship's rigging. He climbed the ladder as easily as a cat climbs a tree. When he got to the boom, he scampered from the ladder and stood upon the thick wooden beam that held the mast. He shielded his eyes from the sun to get a better look at the harbor.

"Ready the ballistas," he called out. Much of his voice was swept away with the wind, but the ship's hands knew exactly what he had said. While the dragon ship's principal weapons were being brought to the ready, flags were employed to pass the orders along to the other ships.

From her position on the quarterdeck, Kandyce watched in wonder as the ship's crew flew into action. Everyone had a job, and they knew exactly what to do. Hardly anybody issued orders as hundreds of soldiers made ready for war. Once the ship was in full preparedness, most of the soldiers equipped themselves with longbows.

"What do you think?" Lieutenant Barclay asked, nudging Lady Kandyce with her elbow.

"Of the admiral?" She gave the lieutenant an odd glare. "He's a buffoon, but he's an excellent commander." The lieutenant sniggered and shook his head.

"No, not Admiral Fancy Pants. What do you think of the ships and soldiers waiting for us at Cormorant?"

Kandyce blushed lightly and clasped her lips tightly together. "It's got to be the Split Crow. I'm guessing they've brought everyone from Wantage here and those are their soldiers." She looked to the ship's aft. "I'd say we have more than enough ships and soldiers to overrun the beach. We can scuttle their ships and send our soldiers ashore to slaughter the lot of them."

"A bold plan," Admiral Robyrts said, startling Lady Kandyce with his unexpected appearance. "The entire army is only five hundred soldiers, all armed with longbows. I suggest we let the elementals drive them back with tidal waves while we send in our landing parties. The waves will either sink their ships or make it impossible for the ship's hands to be functional. The rest of the soldiers will be forced back out of missile range."

"Let's do it, Admiral." Lady Kandyce turned to face the port city. "We don't want the Crows at our back when we sail on to Ravenlord."

CHAPTER TWENTY-FOUR

FIRE ON THE WATER

The high-pitched peel of the warning bells rang through the manor. Danny leapt from a couch in the war room with a startled cry. He took a quick glance around to see if he was alone. Fortunately, nobody had heard him. Surely, had Rusty been there to witness his startled yelp, she'd have ridden him for a moon.

"Need me to hold your hand while we investigate?"

Helja! Danny turned to look over the couch to find Rusty standing behind one of the many tables. She had already strapped blades to her waist and was reaching for one of the small shields that adorned the wall.

"Who's ringing the bells?" Danny scrubbed his face to wake himself. "What hour is it?" His second question was answered by a quiver of arrows that hit him in the head. "Hey!" He rubbed the tender skin of his scalp and turned just in time to see a heavy hunting bow flying at him. With a deft hand, he snatched it from the air and followed it up with a surly frown.

"Let's go. Whoever is ringing that infernal bell is likely doing it for a reason. Stop asking questions and get moving." Adjusting her belt one last time, Rusty made for the door.

"Rally the soldiers," Danny said as he passed Rusty on the sweeping staircase down to the manor's main floor. "I'll fly on ahead." It wasn't clear what the robust general had said to him, but it sounded like a suggestion of where to put her foot. The red-haired Berrat spun around, blew Rusty a kiss, and literally flew out the front door.

In moments, the phoenix was hundreds of feet in the air. He turned to the west and made his way towards the harbor front. It didn't take long to see why the alarm had been sounded. Two dozen black ships were sailing down the Gaelinora River toward the city. A huge three-masted vessel was at their lead, and it looked to be heading towards the deep-water docks.

I wonder how many of them I can set on fire at once.

The crackle of his flames resounded in Danny's ears as he increased his wing-speed. He maintained his altitude so he could take in as much of the scene as possible. Four enemy ships were in the harbor, and over a dozen more were exiting the mouth of the river. They'd be joining the lead ships in the harbor in mere minutes. On shore were hundreds of soldiers. Because they were showing up as bright yellow, the phoenix recognized them as allies.

Helja. Bango had said she was going to take the newest group of recruits to the beachhead for training exercises. I'll bet facing an armada wasn't what she had in mind.

Danny unleashed a war cry that easily drowned out the peel of the bells. He had surprised himself with the power of his call. It was exhilarating. He put himself into a power-dive, increasing his speed until the ground below was turning into a hazy orange blur. At the last moment, he pulled out of the dive, leveling off only a few feet from the ground. The phoenix ripped across the shoreline and passed the recruits.

Steam rose around him as he flew over the water. He headed toward the nearest of the four ships that had entered the harbor. With all the sails billowing out on that three-masted tub, it would make an excellent test to see what his phoenix flames could do against a sailing ship.

He beat his wings again, turning himself into a fiery missile.

A great gust of wind blew across the water, knocking the phoenix slightly off course. Danny missed the largest of the ships, but with a minor course adjustment, flew through the mainsail of a smaller vessel. As expected, he passed through the fabric as easily as he sliced through the air. Almost immediately, the ship's sail burst into flames.

Again, Danny unleashed an ear-piercing war cry before soaring back up into the sky, readying himself for another assault, this time on the lead ship.

The phoenix rose high in the sky. He banked toward the south to get a quick view of the recruits. Danny was impressed by how organized they were. They had taken up positions along the deep-water docks and the beachhead itself. To the phoenix, they appeared as neat rows of yellow dots. Farther to the east, toward the city center, lines of yellow dots were headed toward the harbor.

Rusty has already mustered the army. I wonder if there will be anything left for them to fight by the time I'm finished with these ships.

The phoenix turned back towards the largest of the vessels and went into a steep dive. Like the last time, heavy winds buffeted against the firebird, trying to push him off course. They were vicious, hurricane-force winds that were focused directly on him. Fear ripped through Danny. Did the Split Crow somehow retake control of the East Wind? He had been freed during his encounter with The Wing. Perhaps the elemental was in league with them all along.

Boreas holds no domain over the phoenix.

Those were Old Sky Eyes' words to Danny when he was fighting with the North Wind. The phoenix had easily penetrated the vortex the elemental had created. The power he was feeling from these winds was different, but the phoenix within Danny didn't care. She was going to help him light each one of these ships ablaze.

The phoenix turned directly into the buffeting winds. Danny's speed was reduced by the heavy gusts, but he continued to make progress. He beat his wings harder, intent on hitting the vessel's sails with as much force as he could muster.

The ship was enormous. It was covered in hundreds of red dots. Each of them was his enemy, looking to end his life. With renewed vigor, he flapped his flaming wings harder, fighting the winds, increasing his speed. He paused when he caught sight of two yellow dots on the ship's quarter deck.

How are there allies aboard that ship?

Danny broke off his attack and soared high into the clear, early evening sky. He banked hard to the north and flew over the fleet. While most of the ships were teaming with enemies, there were eight heavy warships that were entirely crewed by allies. Lady Kandyce had left port from Lilloet with eight heavy warships. Had she joined forces with the Split Crow? That made no sense at all. If she had, she'd be an enemy and...

What if the other ships see me as an enemy because I attacked them? That has to be Lady Kandyce on the large ship. Maybe Lieutenant Barclay is the ally that's with her. Oh, sweet Titan, I sure hope this plan works.

Danny flew back toward the lead ship. The cutter he had set ablaze had moved away from the rest of the fleet; its flames already extinguished. It was no surprise that every member aboard saw Danny as an enemy. He'd have been upset as well had someone set his home on fire.

The phoenix turned for the lead ship and hovered in the air to get a better look at what he was seeing. The quarterdeck was covered in yellow dots. The notice that Danny was an ally was spreading through the crew, but not every one of them seemed willing to accept that the phoenix was not their enemy. Danny flew to the rear of the ship. There were no winds preventing his approach. With practiced grace, he morphed from phoenix to Berrat form and landed easily next to where Lady Kandyce stood.

Danny strode towards the elegantly dressed woman. Lieutenant Barclay, in his formal military attire, was standing at her side, along with a pompous-looking gentleman wearing a powdered wig and a fancy red cloak. "What are you doing here?"

⚭⚭⚭

Back on the shore, amidst thousands of soldiers and hundreds of raw recruits, Danny tried his best to explain the situation Cormorant was facing. It took repeated attempts before he could tell his story.

"The soldiers can stand down," Danny said. He was completely exasperated at this point. "The ships and their crew are allies." Even though he had explained how the phoenix could tell friend from foe, Rusty and Bango struggled to accept what they were being told.

"If the phoenix recognized them as friends, then they're friends. I have met Lady Kandyce and Lieutenant Barclay myself, and I know their hearts to be true." Breayn's voice was strong and sure. Like the other women, she didn't fully understand the powers of the phoenix, but she knew some of these people and trusted Danny well enough to take him at his word.

"Why would the Split Crow navy switch sides?" Bango crossed her arms over her chest, tilting her head slightly to the side. "It makes no sense."

"It makes sense," Captain Maidsson interjected. He was the lieutenant who had been given his captaincy after Lord Buttsworth's previous captain had been unceremoniously removed from his post. "We didn't want to fight for slavers, either. When Sister Standing Bear came and removed the masters, we had no reason to continue doing the despicable acts those vampires had forced us to commit. With the masters destroyed, the lords who owned us were effectively neutered. Perhaps these sailors have done the same thing? Perhaps they've overthrown their oppressors and are now trying to make amends for their actions."

The other captains who had gathered on the beach spoke of their agreement. While some chalked up their actions to, *we just followed orders*, the majority followed the orders because the consequences of failing the masters were unbearable.

"Let's wait for Lady Kandyce and Admiral Robyrts to arrive, and then you can talk to them. They trusted me enough to come ashore and ask for a parlay. Surely you can put aside your fears and listen to what they have to say."

The group waited impatiently as two skiffs rowed towards the shore. They each had a Hobgoblin aboard, brought along to help propel the row boats at a faster pace. Their presence had been a bit of a sticking point with Danny when he had negotiated with Lady Kandyce and Admiral Robyrts the terms of their coming ashore. The pure arrogance of the admiral had grated on Danny's nerves. He'd desperately wanted to break the man's hawk nose before strangling him with his infernal powdered wig.

The delegation of senior officers stepped into the surf, along with several dozen soldiers who helped pull the skiffs ashore. The admiral practically knocked Danny over as he leapt dramatically from his boat and quickly offered a helping hand to Lady Kandyce.

"Step to the front of the boat, my lady," he said with sickening poise. "No need to soak your lovely boots in the brine." Danny saw the look of derision that appeared for the briefest of moments on her face.

"Thank you, Admiral. You are a true gentleman's gentleman." The woman stepped lightly across the seats and up to the boat's prow. After a slight jump to clear the bow's railing, she landed lightly on the sandy shore.

"Lady Kandyce," Danny said. "I'd like you to meet my friends, General Rustnig Karter, and Harbourmaster Bandolion Goggler. You already know my cousin, Breayn."

"I know this man," Aput said, stepping through the crowd of officers until he was nose to nose with the admiral. The leader of the dog soldiers, the Lycosian shapeshifters that Danny had met near Lilloet, was as surly a man as the Berrat had ever met. Ever since Danny and Calian had become *close*, her big brother's demeanor had only gotten worse.

"Brother, enough." Calian moved quickly to the dog soldier's side, grasping his wrist. "If Danny says he's an ally, then he's an ally."

"Dog soldiers, here in Cormorant?" Admiral Robyrts gave Danny a questioning look. "You knowingly work with these pirates?" Aput's fist caught the admiral flush in the jaw, knocking him back several paces. The admiral rubbed the skin where Aput had struck him. He ineffectually tried to hide his wince. A deep purple bruise had already appeared. "Boorish brutes, the lot of them."

"*Pirates* is a funny word coming from the mouth of a slaver." Calian had the man by his ruffled shirt before he could raise his defenses. Slipping her foot in behind his, she neatly tripped him onto his back and dropped her knee to his throat. "The only ships we've ever raided belong to the accursed captains who sail under the banners of hate and oppression." She raised her clawed hand over her shoulder, ready to rip the admiral's throat out.

"Be still, Calian." Danny lightly grabbed the woman's wrist. Her head snapped around, seeking whoever had the audacity to interfere with her and her prey. She glowered up at Danny, her yellow eyes hungry for blood.

"He is no longer our enemy." Danny released his grip and held his hands up defensively. "He will atone for his crimes, or he will be hung for them." The admiral sputtered under the woman's knee, his face becoming redder with each passing second.

Calian took her weight off the man's throat and stood. Despite her clawed hands returning to normal, the yellow in her eyes remained. "We shall see," she said. "We shall see."

⌒⌒⌒◇⌒⌒⌒

There were nearly as many soldiers aboard the black ships as there were soldiers stationed in Cormorant. There were also over sixteen thousand slaves aboard. The new Berrat village that had been built outside the city walls was too small to accommodate the entire lot of them, and there was insufficient housing within the city itself to hold the freed Berrat or the soldiers.

Cormorant was literally busting at the seams trying to hold the massive influx of people. The Port Authority warehouses had to be used as temporary residences, much to the dismay of everyone who was left with no other alternative but to stay in the smelly buildings.

The respective leaders from Cormorant and the newly arrived black ships met in General Karter's war room. Rusty was getting a better appreciation for why her father used this room to host dignitaries. The space was massive, with enough tables, chairs, and couches to comfortably accommodate everyone.

Danny and Breayn sat on either side of Fenrir on one of the many overstuffed sofas. Amilta had curled herself up on the wolf god's lap while three gray wolves slept peacefully at her feet. Lady Kandyce and Admiral Robyrts had strenuously objected to the presence of the child and of the wolves, but when Fenrir said their presence was non-optional, they immediately stopped complaining. It seemed like all the guests were struggling with the fact they were meeting with a god.

"If we don't have space for the new Berrat slaves, why not just release them back into the wilds? It's where they're happiest anyway, isn't it?" Rusty's suggestion did not go over well. She tried to reform her words, so they didn't sound so... uncaring, but there was no undoing what she had said.

"You cannot simply release them," Admiral Robyrts said. His nasally, high-pitched voice was grating on Rusty to no end. "These are people, no different from us. They are far from home. They are tired, hungry, and disoriented. They need to be carefully cared for. I will send my people to their makeshift quarters to ensure they have everything they need until I can return them safely home."

Weasel. Rusty was certain the man was now playing the room. He didn't care about these people. All he cared about was how everyone would see him. He was looking to make his bones off the Berrat's misfortune. He saw this as an opportunity to raise his station.

"No." Rusty glared at the pompous, pretentious peacock and his ridiculous powdered wig. This was her house, and her city, and these were now her people. "No admiral, you will do none of those things. You would be wise to mind your place and keep your tongue in check while you breathe under my roof."

The admiral's eyes darted about. He was looking to see who was supporting him. When his face twisted, Rusty knew he found no one willing to stand behind him. At least, not on this point.

Fenrir sighed and gave the admiral a withered look. "I will lead the new Berrat arrivals to the village. There will not be room for them, but the people will welcome them just the same. It is a lesson that others would do well to learn." The little god's face suddenly changed from sad to grave. "I have to say, though, the arrival of the additional soldiers is timely. We are at a crossroads. I fear Ymir will arrive soon, and I expect he'll be coming with an army of Ice Giants."

"Ymir? Ice Giants?" The admiral blustered. His powder wig practically fell from his head when it snapped backwards. "What sort of fairy tales are these? This is preposterous. We have no intention of staying to fight your wars, especially against gods and imaginary creatures. Once my people are rested and we restock our supplies, we'll be on our way to Ravenlord."

"You are a coward and a cad," Aput said from a nearby table. Calian held up her hand to stay her brother's outburst, but it did nothing to slow him down.

"It doesn't surprise me you would turn tail and run at the first sign of a proper fight." The leader of the dog soldiers stood from his place and thundered across the room. "You act all high and mighty when you sail aboard a massive vessel, and you outnumber your enemy a hundred to one. But now, faced with an actual threat, you show your true colors."

"And you expect me to feed and house your soldiers out of the goodness of my heart?" Rusty shared Aput's indignation. "Your station within the Split Crow means nothing here among the free peoples of Cormorant. I only allowed you to land on my shores because of the company you keep. Had it not been for Lady Kandyce, you and your crew would be food for the Makara."

The admiral's eyes went wide as saucers. His lower lip quivered, and his already weak chin seemed to recede even further. "This is outrageous." Spittle flew from his lips. He jumped to his feet and reached for the saber that hung at his waist. "I... I will command my soldiers to wipe out every one of you. I... Never have I been so humiliated."

Aput promptly smashed his fist into the man's face, shattering his oversized nose, knocking him unconscious to the ground. The room fell deathly silent.

"The man is an outstanding commander, but his ego is far larger than his worth." Lady Kandyce sniggered at the man and his ruined nose. "I am grateful for the hospitality you have shown us, General Karter. Most holy Fenrir, in what way can we be of help? Do you truly expect an army of *Ice Giants* to attack?"

CHAPTER TWENTY-FIVE

THE HEART OF THE SLAVERS

"Are you planning to throw the admiral in prison?"

Rusty couldn't tell from Lady Kandyce's body language what answer she was hoping to hear. The only thing the general knew for sure was this man had come into their inner sanctum and threatened to kill each one of them. From all accounts, the admiral was a nobody who'd risen through the ranks at an unprecedented pace. His meteoric rise came to an abrupt halt when the ruling bodies refused to accept him into the royal cadre because he was low born. That stone ceiling ended when he joined the Split Crow. It was they who afforded him title and power. It was they who promoted him to admiral and put him in charge of their fleet.

And at his first opportunity, he took what they gave him and used it to serve his own purposes. Rusty had only met the man a few hours ago, and she already despised him.

"That's exactly what I plan to do. Admiral Robyrts cannot be trusted. He is too smart, too ambitious, and too egocentric to be left to his own devices." Rusty chuckled. "It's too bad, really. He's such a pleasure to be around." The general's attempt at humor was lost on the crowd. While some of the war room's attendants smiled politely, the majority remained stoic.

If Danny had made that joke, they'd have laughed their butts off. A low growl rumbled in Rusty's chest as she glared at the red headed Berrat. He caught sight of her annoyance and gave her a questioning look.

"Okay," Danny said brightly, assuming that Rusty was prompting him to speak. "Now that we've decided to toss the egomaniac into the dungeons, what are we to do about Ymir and the Ice Giants?" All eyes fell on Fenrir.

The wolf god paused for a moment to consider her words before speaking. Rusty appreciated that about her. She was always so calm and measured in her approach to problems. Unlike Lin, who was brash and forthright. She was as quick with her tongue as she was with her sword. The woman never backed down from anything. Several moments continued to pass while Rusty continued to contemplate the many virtues of Aithlin. It was only then she realized Fenrir had been talking, and she'd missed everything the woman had said.

"Sorry, Fenrir," the general interrupted. "Can you repeat that? I was... distracted." The wolf god raised her eyebrows slightly and smiled.

"Certainly, General." Fenrir inclined her head to Rusty and then continued. "As I said, I can't say with any certainty that Ymir will attack with the Ice Giants, but we cannot rule out the possibility. The Bifrost has been repaired and my pack has found evidence of the Ice Giants' presence less than a league from here. It is our belief that Ymir is responsible for Riva's disappearance. Based on what we have found, he stole into the Berrat's village and whisked the woman away. I expect she is in Jotunheim as we speak."

A collective gasp rolled through the room. The leaders stared blankly at one another, unsure what to say or do in response to this news.

"Why was I not informed sooner?" Rusty's face was turning bright red. She might have enjoyed the idea of running Cormorant, but when faced with this level of trouble, she would be more than happy to have her father take control. She looked down at the little gold ring on her finger, the one that kept her father's spirit at bay. She considered removing it, to let him have a say in the proceedings, but thought better of it.

I'm sorry, father. We can discuss this meeting later, but for now, I need to remain in control of my voice.

"Amilta and I had only just discovered this information when the warning bells rang out." Even if the wolf god's voice was serene, the look that Fenrir was giving Rusty was not. With her peaceful personality, it was easy to forget the tiny Berrat was a god. The general's legs became unsteady.

"My apologies, Fenrir." Rusty bowed her head and clasped onto a table to avoid stumbling. "I am under more stress than I can comfortably handle. I forgot my place."

"My apologies as well, General. With Riva missing and the threat of Ice Giants invading our lands, I'm not quite myself, either." The little god took a deep breath and slowly blew it out. "As I was saying, I have no evidence the Ice Giants will come to attack, but if they are working for Ymir, I fear it is a possibility."

"What exactly is the Bifrost?" Danny asked.

"It's a portal device," Fenrir replied. She suddenly looked smaller than normal, like she was carrying the weight of the world on her shoulders. "Anybody carrying a key can activate it and transport themselves, and anyone around them, anyplace on Orth. Maybe even beyond Orth's boundaries."

Danny ran his fingers through his hair. "Could it be used to transport somebody through the Veil?"

Fenrir slowly closed her eyes and shuddered. It wasn't clear if she was considering the question or if she knew the answer and didn't like it.

"I don't know." The tiny woman looked tired, completely worn out. "With the Veil getting weaker, we have to assume it's a possibility. If they can do that, if they can release those beyond the Veil, we are doomed."

"Why would they want to break through the Veil?" Aput asked. "Are they not children of Titan? Wouldn't they be more interested in freeing him than tearing down the wall that keeps their enemy at bay?"

"So, what are we to do, then?" Lady Kandyce said. She threw her hands in the air and grunted. "Are we to stay here, cowering in fear of what might come? The slavers are actively destroying the north. They are uprooting the peoples, chaining them like animals, and using them for whatever sick purposes they choose. The Split Crow are turning against their own. They harvest the people of the north like farmers reaping their crops. Many are sold to Faol as blood slaves to feed the vampire king's army. We cannot live in fear of what *might* happen.

We need to help those we can, while we can. If the world ends because these frozen fools release demons or whatever else is beyond the Veil, do we want to meet oblivion sitting on our hands?"

The woman's speech got Rusty's blood up. She was right. If Armageddon was coming, there was very little they could do to stop it. But, if there was still good left to do, she would not let fear of the unknown stop her from doing what she could. She would fight the slavers and she would free her father from the prison in which she kept him.

"Fenrir, what chance do we have standing against an army of Ice Giants?" Rusty's breathing was now quick and shallow. She had a rough plan in her head, and she wanted more details before speaking it aloud. The look of defeat on the wolf god's face gave her the answer. It might have even been the answer she wanted.

"Lady Kandyce," the general's voice thundered. She was filled with renewed vigor. "How many soldiers arrived with you in the fleet? By my accounts, it was over twelve thousand." The woman nodded her agreement. "Excellent. We offloaded over sixteen thousand Berrat slaves as well. That would mean we could replace them with at least six thousand more soldiers. Plus, with our own five black ships, we could put together a fleet with over twenty thousand soldiers."

The assembled people mumbled and grumbled amongst themselves. None spoke against the general, but many didn't understand where she was going with this train of thought.

Captain Ruckham, the captain of the black ship *Narwhal,* spoke up. "If you've got more soldiers, we can outfit the ships to carry even more than you suggested. If I read you right, you plan on sailing on Ravenlord. You plan on taking the war to the heart of the Berrathian slave houses. The ships will run low, but we can likely carry near thirty thousand soldiers in all. I know every captain in... your navy... and I tell you they're the best damned sailors you have ever set your eyes on."

"It is not my navy," Rusty said, quickly correcting the sea-captain's choice of words. "We fight for Sister Kit Standing Bear. If you and the others fight with us, then you're fighting for her, too."

"I do not know this person you speak of, but if you believe her worthy of your loyalty, then so do I." There were several other black ship captains in the room. Each of them voiced their agreement with Captain Ruckham.

"I am Captain Nelsyn of the Sea Wind. I would be remiss to not speak my mind, so if you will indulge me." The man waited a few moments before continuing. "It was Admiral Robyrts' plan to sack Ravenlord. He had intended to free the people and seat himself as the ruler of Berrathia. I cannot speak to his ability to rule, but I can say that his plans to seize control of the city were thorough and well conceived. His plans only required eight thousand soldiers, which is all he had at his disposal. If we can float an army of thirty thousand, I expect we can do more than just take Ravenlord. I expect we can sack every slave house from here to Lycos."

Rusty's face grew dark. "Are you suggesting we free your admiral and let him lead the fleet into battle?"

"Holy Helja, no." Captain Nelsyn looked over at Captain Ruckham and smiled. "We have neither need nor desire to free the admiral. The man, for all his failures, kept meticulous notes. He drew out detailed plans from bow to stern about how he would achieve his goal. These plans are all aboard the dragon ship."

"What is a dragon ship?" Danny asked. "You have a dragon with you?" The red-haired Berrat shot a glance over at the twins, Ashlay and Cilya. At one point, they had said their father had a pet dragon. Rusty had never believed them. The girls were dim. They were also extremely pretty and equally vain, but they seemed to have good hearts and they put their energies into doing good things. Maybe going through life somewhat oblivious wasn't the worse thing in the world. It would certainly be easier than having to carry the weight of command.

Captain Nelsyn shrugged a shoulder and smirked. "That's what the admiral called, *The Black Witch*. The ship is so big, and so laden with firepower, he liked to refer to it as a dragon."

"Well then, Captain," Rusty said. "Unless anybody has any objections, why don't we review the admiral's master plan and see if we can't put it into action?"

"We're coming, and that's all there is to it." Lady Kandyce took a big step backwards as the general bared down on her. Rusty had her fists planted firmly on her ample hips as she thundered toward the woman.

"You don't know if your father's husk is even in the city. If his body is there, we will return him to you. You should be with your people. You are their leader and if the Ice Giants do attack, they're going to need you." Lady Kandyce was trying her level best to remain calm, but the general's insistence on joining the fleet was going to cause problems. None of the admiral's complex and intricate plans included looking for the husk of a man, and if the general took their mission off course, all could be lost.

"If my body is there, I will ensure I am returned to it. I do not know you, *Lady Kandyce*. Since I don't know you, I cannot trust you."

"I assume I'm now speaking with Lord Karter?" Lady Kandyce cocked at eyebrow at Rusty. "If you're going to seize control of your daughter's body, you could at least do me the courtesy of letting me know."

"I am not accustomed to answering to anybody." Rusty's face was a deep purple. A thick vein at her temple was standing out. Every heartbeat could easily be counted as the deep red line throbbed.

"Yet another reason you should not be going. These sailors do not know you and they do not report to you. Your inability to maintain control of your emotions will be the death of them." Any semblance of Kandyce being a *lady* disappeared. She was ready to confront Rusty or her father or the two of them together, head on.

Rusty slid on her gold ring and her face slackened. "I will keep my father quiet. We will cause you no delays. If we do, throw us from the ship and leave us behind. I need to go with you."

"And if she doesn't go," Breayn interjected, "neither do I. With your ships overburdened the way they are, without my help, it will take them a moon to reach their destination. The Hobgoblins have joined their kin beneath the manor, and they will no longer assist you."

Captain Ruckham nodded lightly. How the admiral got the Hobgoblins to assist the fleet in the first place was a complete mystery, anyway. Never had

Lady Kandyce met such individuals. They were powerful elementals, but they behaved like they were utterly insane, like they had no connection to reality. And their crazed laugh was enough to make her skin crawl.

"Fine," Lady Kandyce finally relented. "You and Breayn will join me on *The Black Witch*. Captain Ruckham, will you captain the vessel? Do you have someone who can take the helm of *The Narwhal*?" The captain nodded curtly at the question. "Excellent. Let's make ready to sail then."

<hr/>

While the ships made ready to set sail for Ravenlord, Danny sought out some alone time in his room. Calian had followed him. It seemed she was able to sense his concern. His stomach churned when Breayn insisted she board the admiral's vessel along with Rusty. His cousin wouldn't say it specifically, but Danny believed she hoped her mother or father might be in Ravenlord. Based on King Karter's ledger, Danny was certain they were being kept at King Faol's castle, but Breayn would not miss an opportunity to search for them.

"She'll be okay," Calian said, squeezing Danny's hand tightly. "You two come from excellent stock, and she has the spirit of her mother to help. Never underestimate the resolve of a woman." The Berrat squeezed the dog soldier's hand. They rarely had anything close to physical contact, but whenever Calian's skin brushed against Danny's, his legs turned to jelly. The fact that she was actively holding his hand left him nearly incapacitated. He smiled warmly at the young woman.

"I know, but the admiral's plans could just as easily fail. If the enemy catches them on the open sea, there is no way our fleet will be able to defend itself. They're so overburdened. They'll be like ducks on a pond."

"Sometimes we just have to trust things will work out for the best." Calian stroked the young man's arm. "We cannot live in fear of what might come to be." The woman's touch sent shivers up Danny's back.

"What about your brother?"

"Aput will be fine. When the fighting starts, he and the other dog soldiers will be a force to be reckoned with, all on their own. They can be very intimidating."

"I know," he said, his eyes wide. "I've met the man. But I wasn't referring to him fighting the enemy." Danny lifted Calian's hand putting their connection on display. "I'm talking about us. What is he going to do if he sees *us* being together?" The girl's eyes also went very wide.

"Oh, he'll kill you. He will change into a dire wolf, and he will rend you limb from limb. I'm quite certain that even the phoenix cannot protect you." Danny's brow furrowed, and he swallowed hard. "Oh, lighten up, would you? Aput will howl and growl and put up a fuss, but my life is mine to live. I will choose whom I mate with, and he has no say in the matter."

Danny's heart beat frantically in his chest and his mouth went bone dry. Had she just said what he thought she'd said? What if he had misheard Calian's words? He had no idea what else it could have been, but still, if he'd heard her wrong...

"You want to mate with me?" *Bloody Helja.* The words came out of his mouth before he could consider the outcome if he had misheard her. His thoughts jumped to Kit. Not romantically. No, not at all. It was like her to speak without thinking it through; to just let whatever was in her heart or in her mind come flowing out of her mouth with no concern for the consequences.

"I could do worse than to take you as a mate," Calian said, a coy smile tugging at the corner of her mouth. "That is, if your heart has gotten over the little priest."

Had he gotten over Kit? He must have. Danny was happy for her and Indie. In his heart, he knew they were good for each other. He knew Indie would do everything to keep Kit safe and make her happy. With only having known each other for such a brief period, Calian's consideration of having him for a mate filled his stomach with butterflies. Even the phoenix within burned with joy. Did he have true feelings for this woman or was it only lust? Was that all it was? Calian was beautiful. In so many ways, she was everything he could have ever hoped for. And now she said she wanted him for her mate.

"Without a doubt," Danny finally said. "I am over Kit." He gave the woman his best smile and ran his fingers through his hair. "When you say mate, you mean being a couple and not just, you know..."

"I was hoping it would be both." There was a hint of a growl in Calian's voice. A sexy, playful growl that made Danny's insides squirm in a most delightful way.

"And, just to be clear," Danny said, turning to face the woman, putting his hands on her hips. "When your kind mate, they do it for life, right? Not just for a season?" Calian nodded, her eyes growing wider as she did.

"Does that appeal to you?" The woman moved closer until her nose was practically brushing his. "Would you like to lie with me when the moon is high? Would you like to wake up next to me, our bodies wrapped in each other's arms?" Her voice stole Danny's breath. All he could do was nod like an idiot.

Calian patted him on his chest and cleared her throat. "You best go see Aput then, before they set sail. You'll need his permission before you can have me as a mate. It requires a pack leader's approval before we can mate outside our kind."

Danny's legs failed him. He practically had to grab the woman to stop his knees from buckling. Calian laughed and took his chin in her hand.

"I'm just kidding. I don't need his permission, but I suggest you tell him, anyway. He will respect you for it, and it might give him a bit more incentive to rip the throats from the enemy."

"Okay." The word came out of Danny's mouth like a croak. Unwilling to waste a moment, Danny dashed for his window and leapt out and burst into flames.

⟨⟨⟨◆⟩⟩⟩

The phoenix flew over the docks, searching for Aput's ship. After several passes, and not finding the dog-soldier's ship, he flew out to sea. They had to have already left. The pack leader was excited to get the modified silvered weapons to Lycos. Where they had originally been designed to be devastating to lycanthropes, were-creatures, the Hobgoblins, and the dwarves had modified their enchantments to make them powerful in the hands of the Lycosian soldiers. There were enough weapons here to outfit a significant army.

It didn't take Danny long to find the narrow, single-masted ship as it sailed south. The dog soldiers' ships were designed for speed. They looked like over-sized canoes with sails. Regardless, they were excellent ships and the sailors on board knew how to get the most out of them. The trick for the phoenix would be landing on one that was traveling at full speed.

Danny dropped low and pumped his wings. With some effort, and several failed tries, he managed to keep himself directly over the ship long enough to change into his Berrat form and drop onto the boat's narrow deck.

"What is the meaning of this?" Aput said as he quickly closed in on Danny. Sweet Titan, the man was intimidating. "Is there a problem? Is Calian okay?"

I'd say she's better than okay. The dog-soldier glowered at Danny and the smirk that had accidentally appeared on his face.

"Calian is fine. There is no problem." Danny held his hands up defensively. He didn't know why he was doing that, but the man was truly terrifying and there was little room on board for the Berrat to maneuver.

"Then why have you come?"

Danny swallowed hard and looked around the boat. "Is there any place on this boat for us to have a private conversation?" The question made Aput laugh. He spread his arms out and gestured to the prow and stern.

"We are all family," Aput said, drawing cheers from everyone within earshot. "We have no need for a place for private conversations." The man's face suddenly darkened, even more than it already was. "Why are you here?" Danny suddenly wished he hadn't come.

"I seek your permission," he croaked out. The dog-soldier's eyes changed from black to jade green and a low, menacing growl rumbled in his throat. Danny wanted to run. He wanted to let his phoenix take him away. Immediately. "Calian and I wish to..."

"Wish to what?" Aput's asked. His fingers elongated into wicked claws and terrible fangs emerged. Danny could feel his bowels loosening. Mustering as much nerve as he could, he tightened his cheeks and set his jaw.

"We wish to... be a couple." He didn't want to use the word mate, for fear it might be misconstrued for something other than joining as a pair. Oh, sweet Titan, even in his head, the word sounded bad. Danny stood up straighter and clenched his cheeks tighter still. "I would like to wed your sister."

Aput threw his head back and howled. The entire crew did the same, but Calian's older brother was the only one who actually sounded like a wolf. A big, scary, black wolf. The dog-soldier thrust out his hand towards Danny's chest. The Berrat recoiled, fearing Aput was trying to snatch his heart out of his chest. When he looked down, the big man's hand was back to normal. There was no sign of wolf, or claws, or any sort of threat whatsoever. Danny raised his eyes to see Aput's smile.

"Calian has already warned me of your arrival," he said. "I didn't think you'd have the nerve to speak to me yourself."

"So, we have your blessing?" Danny grasped the man's forearm. He hoped he had done it with sufficient force as to not appear frightened.

Aput looked around the ship. All eyes were on him. "He wants to know if he has my blessing," he called out. The dog soldier tightened his grip on Danny's forearm. "What say you, brothers in arms? Does he have my blessing?"

There was a prolonged silence. The only sound was the waves lapping against the prow of the ship and the wind filling the sail. In the distance, the call of a gull sounded like a cruel laugh. Just when Danny's heart couldn't take another moment, the entire crew burst out with cheers.

"It seems you do, Dannith Fox-Dancing. You would be a welcomed addition to the pack." Aput yanked Danny into himself, giving the young Berrat an overly tight embrace. "But know this," he whispered in his ear. "If you hurt her, there won't be any place for you to hide."

CHAPTER TWENTY-SIX

BOREAS

With Breayn's assistance, the fleet made exceptionally good time on their way to Ravenlord. Before summoning the powers of Boreas, the sea had been dead calm. With the North Wind at their back and still waters at their prow, the ships could sail at maximum speed. Breayn and her mother could now work in concert to control Boreas without nearly as much individual effort on their part.

"When we near the port, we'll move the warships to the front." Captain Ruckham practically had to scream in order to be heard, even though they were in his private cabin. In the past few minutes, the sound of the ship cutting through water and the wind that was urging them forward had become nearly deafening. Captains from several other vessels had come aboard for a final meeting before they reached Ravenlord. Rusty had had an idea about how they might improve on the admiral's plan. Lady Kandyce thought her ideas had merit and wanted to discuss them with the others. The wind was now howling so loudly that any sort of conversation was becoming impossible. Captain Ruckham whirled around, leveling his ire at Breayn.

"Oh, bloody Helja. Can you pull the reins in a bit? We can't hear anything but the blasted winds."

"It's not me." The woman's eyes were wide, almost wild. "We have company, and not the kind you want to have around." Breayn's eyes had turned a dark, swirling gray, closely resembling the skies of an impending storm. "Yes, maintain control and I'll go topside." Before anybody could say anything more, she had already disappeared from the room, climbing the cabin's circular staircase that led to the upper floor of the captain's stateroom.

"Who was she talking to?" Captain Ruckham seemed torn, his expression vacillating somewhere between concern and annoyance.

"She was speaking with her mother," Rusty said. "Continue discussing the plans if you can. I'm going to go topside and see what's going on." The captains all started shouting over each other as the general made her way to the staircase. They all seemed annoyed with Rusty when she walked out in the middle of their strategy session.

When Rusty got to the upper stateroom, Breayn was not there. The cabin's door was wide open, allowing the winds to thrash its contents, sending anything not nailed down in every direction. The sound of the howling winds was near deafening. The raging tempest forced Rusty to use the room's heaviest pieces of furniture as anchors as she worked her way to the exit. Through the doorway, churning black clouds became visible. The great, square sails were snapping wildly while sailors clambered about, trying to stop the winds from ripping them free of the masts.

Rusty gasped as she stepped out onto the ship's deck. A water funnel stretched up into the roiling black sky, barely a hundred paces off the stern of the ship. It had a warship in its grasp, ripping its sails to shreds, snapping off its masts like they were twigs. Beside the railing, Breayn held her hands aloft, looking like she was pleading for the wind to stop. Another gust of wind carried sub-zero temperatures, turning the deck into a thick slick of ice. When the boat pitched, Rusty fought to keep her footing; forced to clutch onto a port-side railing to prevent herself from sliding overboard. Beyond her view, she could hear the cries of Breayn. Rusty couldn't make out anything she was saying, but the panic in the woman's voice was palpable.

A moment later, the boat pitched again. Rusty released her grip on the railing and allowed the boat to send her careening toward the aft of the ship, to where she had last seen Breayn. It seemed like it was the only way she was going to reach her. She hadn't counted on just how slick the deck boards were. Her feet flew out from beneath her. As she watched her feet soar over her head, her last thought before blacking out was *Oh, this can't be good.*

⟨⟨⟨⟨⟨◇⟩⟩⟩⟩⟩

Breayn watched in horror as Rusty lost her footing and slammed hard on the deck. The woman's head and neck moved into unnatural angles when they impacted with the floor's frozen slats.

The wailing squalls and the sound of Boreas' insane laughter were pushing Breayn to the brink. Aided by winds of her own making, she slid across the frost-covered boards until she was near enough to the general to latch on to her. Rusty had moved precariously close to the edge of the deck and could have easily slid overboard and been swallowed by the sea. Breayn motioned to a deckhand who had just finished lashing a dinghy to the main mast. The man was over in an instant and swept Rusty up into his arms.

"Get her inside. If the ship's healer is available, have him look at her." Breayn feared her words were lost in the tempest, but the ship's hand nodded briskly and quickly made his way to the captain's quarters. Despite the slick wooden surface and the freezing temperatures, the sailor moved across the deck as easily as one might walk across a carpeted room.

"What do you expect me to do?" Breayn screamed at the sky, thrusting her fists at the winds.

"Free my brother," screeched the frost-laden gale. "Free my brother and we will cease our attacks."

"Cease your attacks and we can discuss the matter. I will not parlay while we are under siege." The words had barely left her mouth when the waterspout changed directions and headed directly for the dragon ship. "Destroy this vessel, and your brother dies with me. I will not let him be free of me in death. Mark my words."

The waterspout swung wide of the ship, but its gale force winds still ripped the main mast from the deck, sending it toppling over the edge. A moment later, the winds ceased entirely. Breayn tried half heartedly to straighten her hair but gave up almost instantly.

A light wind, a breeze really, swirled around her legs, whipping her cloak about her ankles. "Free my brother and we will leave."

"Where will your spirit go?" Breayn asked Boreas. She had pulled the North Wind from his corporeal form many moons ago in order to save her mate, Ryn. Without a body to return to, the North Wind's spirit would simply float aimlessly about.

"Do not free him. It's a trap." Breayn's mother's spirit spoke to her in her mind. It hadn't taken long for Breayn and her mother's essence to find comfortable living arrangements. Unlike Rusty and her father, who couldn't comfortably coexist in the same body, Breayn's mother was both helpful and respectful of Breayn's privacy.

the mother and daughter combination had no such difficulties.

"Mother, we have little choice. We may defeat the winds, kill them or drive them off, but at what cost?"

"Do not believe his words, I beg of you."

"Trust me, mother. Trust that I will do the right thing." Breayn waited for several seconds, expecting a retort of some sort. When none came, she returned to conversing with Boreas.

"Tell me, Boreas, where will your spirit go if I released you?"

"You were talking with your mother again, weren't you? She doesn't trust me. I don't know why, though. And, to answer your question, my brother has my body with him. If you release me, I can return to it."

"How? It takes special magic to transfer a soul." It was Breayn's turn to not trust him. She witnessed the magical process firsthand when her mother was transferred into her body.

"We are immortal. We are magic. We are..."

"Okay." Breayn cut him off. She had had his thoughts in her head for far too long. She knew he was going to go into a long-winded diatribe about who he and his family were. She couldn't listen to it again. *"I will consider freeing you under certain conditions."*

"And they are?" Boreas' words were thick with skepticism.

"You will hold no ill will against either me or Ryn."

"Why would you choose him as a mate? He is beneath you. If I destroyed him, you'd be better off. Even your mother agrees with me." Breayn growled at the comment. *"Oh, don't be so surprised. I've been in your head a long time, and I've had to listen to your incessant nattering. When you and your mother have your private conversations, they're not private. I am forced to listen in on every single word, no matter how hard I try to ignore you."*

A deafening silence filled Breayn's mind.

Boreas sighed. *"Fine. I promise to harbor no ill will against either of you, nor will I, or any of my family, take hostile actions against you. Does that satisfy your concerns as well as your mother's?"* There was another silent pause as Breayn considered the wording the elemental had used. She could find no trick or trap woven into the clauses of the accord.

"What's your second condition?" Boreas' voice inside Breayn's head sounded annoyed. She was struggling with the revelation that he could hear every word she had spoken with her mother. They had enjoyed many private, personal conversations. The sort of exchanges that could only be shared between a mother and daughter.

Finally, Breayn pushed her embarrassment aside and continued her negotiations with the elemental. *"I want you to remain neutral in this war. You cannot join King Faol or fight against us in any way."*

Boreas didn't answer. The time he was taking to reply made Breayn nervous. She thought that this may have been his plan. Once he was free, he and his family would sink every ship in their armada except for the *Black Witch*. He would not have gone against his word, but he would have had his retribution.

"Neither I, nor any member of my family, will join with King Faol. But I cannot say that we will remain neutral."

"Remain neutral or you will remain with me and die with me. I will not leave you to fight against our cause."

"I cannot and will not remain neutral." There was a tone in Boreas' voice that gave Breayn cause for concern. It sounded like he was, in some way, being

deceitful. *"As I said, I will not fight against you, nor will my family. However, I cannot remain neutral. I will choose to fight with you, to defeat the slavers. I cannot say if my brother and my sisters will do the same."*

"What?" Breayn heard the words, but they made little sense.

"I don't think he's lying." Hearing her mother say this was even more confusing than Boreas' declaration that he wanted to be her ally.

"Don't be so surprised. I have been a prisoner for a relatively short while and it is unbearable. I cannot imagine the pain one must endure being kept as a slave, a prisoner for their entire natural life. I cannot abide by it. I will not abide by it."

"Mother? What do you think?" There was another moment of silence.

"I believe him."

Something of a maniacal laugh echoed in Breayn's head.

"Do you have any more conditions? My brother and sisters are growing impatient. I expect they'll attack again at any moment for fear they are being tricked." Boreas' words were again met with prolonged silence.

"I don't have any further conditions." Breayn paused and looked out over the open sea. The crew of the ship who had been ravaged by the waterspout was busy trying to make repairs. Another ship had been capsized and its occupants were clinging to the hull, waiting for help before it fully submerged.

"Do we have an accord?" The desperation in Boreas' voice was tangible. *"Will you set me free?"*

"How am I to return you to your body?" Breayn's stomach was knotting. She couldn't tell if Boreas was lying or not. If he was, and she released him, the four winds would systematically destroy every vessel in their fleet and kill every soul aboard.

"You have my word," Boreas said. *"I am on your side. When you free me, I'll speak with my family. I will do everything in my power to persuade them to join me in helping to fight your cause. All you need to do is let me go."*

Breayn continued to cast her gaze out over the sea, her eyes falling to a skiff that had moved close to the capsized ship. The poor souls who had been tossed into the drink were swimming hard to reach the small vessel. Those who were too injured to swim were being assisted. Lifelines and preservers had been tossed to them. Many sailors were diving into the water to render aid to their cohorts.

"For good or for ill, Boreas, I release you." A sudden hollowness wracked Breayn's body as the soul of Boreas rushed from her. The winds shrieked and cried out, perhaps in celebration, perhaps as a war cry. Breayn thrust her chin into the air, ready to accept the consequences of her actions. Her heart raced as she thought of the souls whose fate she may have just sealed. Her bright red hair whipped about her head as a swirling wind wrapped itself around her. She slowly skidded across the deck until she was at the railing. A large Makara broke the water's surface, its great blue-black skin glistening for a moment before it fully submerged beneath the waves.

"Thank you." A translucent shape appeared next to Breayn. It was tall enough that she was forced to tilt her head back to see its top. "My brother will stay with me to assist in your quest. He, too, remembers the sting of being held captive. He, too, believes all should be free. My sisters have returned to their realms. They will remain neutral in your war. They want only to return to their lands and care for their peoples."

"Care for their peoples? What does that mean?"

"We winds are free spirits, but our existence is beneficial to all. We fill your sales, we cool your skin on hot, humid days. We dry the grounds after a heavy rain. I could literally bore you to death with what we do for you, but rarely are we thanked for our efforts."

"Thank you," Breayn said with something of a chuckle. "Now, will you help us make our way to Ravenlord so that we may defeat our enemy?"

"No, I will not." Boreas' tone was absolute, drawing the immediate ire of Breayn. "You do not need our help to defeat the people of Ravenlord. King Faol's army has already left. They are heading south, following a thin ribbon of dirt. They are too far inland for us to provide any benefit to your sailing vessels. Would you like us to destroy them?"

Breayn hadn't considered that their cooperation could be so significant. She hadn't really considered at all what sort of help they might provide. The only thing she was thinking about was saving the people in the fleet.

"No," she finally said after much consideration. "We need to fight this battle ourselves. We need to earn our freedom and teach those who would imprison us that we will fight back, at all costs." Boreas swirled around Breayn, once again tussling her hair until it was a red, unruly mass of curls.

"If you decide you need us, all you need to do is whisper into the wind. We will hear you, and we will come." A heavy gust lifted Breayn off her feet and twirled her. It was like she and the North Wind were dancing. She laughed, an actual joyous laugh, at the elemental's playfulness.

Breayn turned her face into the warm breeze that now blew at their backs. "I'm sorry for having held you prisoner. I hope you understand why, and I hope you will forgive me for it." Breayn suddenly felt shame for what the Berrat had done to the spirits of animals they'd bonded with, especially those who were killed so that the Berrat could subsume their essence. Those animal spirits she held within her joined freely, but she didn't know about the spirits of those who were taken forcibly.

Captain Ruckham came up from his lower cabin along with the other captains who had joined them. "Have you captured the winds? Are we safe from them?"

"No, the winds are free, but they will no longer interfere in our matters." Breayn considered telling the captain of their offer to assist, but she thought better of it. She couldn't explain why, but she was concerned that having the power of the North and East Winds at their command might be too much for any person to manage.

"Can we continue on to Ravenlord now?" Lady Kandyce asked. "We have a city to conquer."

Breayn nodded in response before addressing the ship's captain. "According to the winds, there will be little resistance at Ravenlord. King Faol's army has left. They are headed south along the main roads. They are moving towards Ashenburg, likely to crush it and every other city on their way to the Crystalline Palace in Lycos."

"That's good news," Lady Kandyce said, her eyes brightening. "If Ravenlord has minimal defenses, we can secure the city, and commandeer the fleet they'll have left behind. We can then take the ships, along with every soldier who willingly volunteers, and head south to Ashenburg. If the city has not yet fallen, we can reinforce their numbers and force Faol's army to pass them by and continue heading south. If Aput's ship did not meet the fury of the four winds, he will be well on his way to delivering the shipment of silvered weapons to Lycos' dog soldiers. We can then harry Faol's soldiers and drive them right into the Lycosian army. King Faol's people will be overwhelmed and decimated."

This was Rusty's modified version of the admiral's plans. A much more effective version that would ensure King Faol's army would be utterly destroyed.

Breayn hadn't even considered the fate of Aput's ship. Fear gripped her heart. Like many of the vessels in the armada, the dog soldier's ship was heavily laden. She stepped away from the others and turned to face the southerly breeze blowing across the sea.

"Boreas? If you were listening, can you tell me if our comrade's ship is safe?"

A cool breath whispered in her ear. "My family did not accost the ship. It is safe and heading south at a steady pace." The whisper paused for a moment. "It is now heading south at a much faster pace. It should reach its destination before Pele has set and Medeina once again graces the night skies."

"Thank you," Breayn said, inclining her head slightly. She spun about and headed back to the group, ready to share the news.

"I will remain at Ravenlord," Rusty said. "I will search for my father's body and provide what support I can to the city during its transition of leadership."

"As will I," Lady Kandyce added. "Once the city is stable, I will return north to my home in Wantage. If my people accept me as their leader, I will see that the city is rebuilt."

"Will you be joining us, Breayn?" Rusty asked. "Will you search the city for your parents' bodies?"

"No, I don't think so." Her mother's presence filled her mind with sadness. "I don't expect them to be there. I expect they are in Faol, as Danny had suggested. But, while you're there, please search for them. Question the departing leadership. Perhaps the members of House Nobilis know something more."

While she had been speaking, Breayn noticed Rusty had been playing with her ring, the one that suppressed her father's spirit. With something of a huff, she pulled it from her finger and handed it to Breayn. "I won't be needing this anymore. We will find my father's body and I will return him to it. If not, I will find a way to live with him. I will not hold him captive." Breayn gave her a questioning look. "I heard your conversation with Boreas. I will not hold my father hostage."

A hint of a smile pulled at the corner of Breayn's mouth. "Do you plan to live in Ravenlord? What of Lin?" A sadness crept across Rusty's face.

"If she wants me, she'll know where to find me."

CHAPTER TWENTY-SEVEN

CROWS ON THE HORIZON

The shadows were growing long, and the recruits were beyond tired. With Fenrir's concern that an Ice Giant attack may be imminent, Bango felt compelled to drill the recruits on how to keep an enemy at a distance and use tactics to whittle down their numbers. This was more than just using their bows and arrows. It was about running through exercises designed to draw the enemy into kill zones, areas where many archers could lie in wait. One group of archers would harry the enemy before leading them into the mouth of the trap. While the second group engaged the enemy, the first would move deeper into the city and set the next trap. Once the second group had taken their shots, they, too, would immediately retreat and lead the enemy into the next zone.

"Do you think they'll be able to fight the Ice Giants?" Treedale asked.

Bango's jaw tightened. The recruits were doing well, better than expected, in fact, but in the face of a twelve-foot, ice-armored enemy, it was difficult to know if they could maintain their resolve. The harbormaster had fought in many skirmishes, but the fight on the beach against King Karter's armies was the only true battle she had ever experienced. The conflict had appeared brutal and haphazard with the selection of combatants seeming to be almost at random. How ally hadn't attacked ally was beyond her. With so much blood and violence, the scene had become overwhelming.

Running the recruits through these exercises was as much for her benefit as it was for the soldiers'. Each time they ran through a simulation, Bango's confidence grew. She was learning how to anticipate what would happen as each scenario was played out. She was feeling like their situation was not entirely hopeless.

"Bango?" Treedale gave her a nudge.

"Yes," she replied with a nod of approval. "The dwarves forged thousands of cold-iron arrow-heads. The fletchers have them and are affixing them to arrows as we speak. If we have time, we will have enough to equip our entire army.

"We don't have much of an army anymore." Mukale stretched and tried to suppress a yawn. "General Karter took the vast majority of the soldiers with her to Ravenlord. I don't think we even have five thousand left to garrison the city."

"We're well short of five thousand," Bango said, her eyes still locked on the recruits as they continued to practice. "But we've also got a phoenix and four yetis. I don't know about you, but I wouldn't want to fight any of them, let alone all of them, at the same time."

"I wouldn't want to face the dwarves, either." Treedale's eyes were wide as he slowly shook his head. "Never have I seen people who enjoy fighting like they do. I went down into the cellars to check on the progress of the new arrow-heads. There was a group of them beating the snot out of each other. They seemed to fight for several minutes, stop to get their breath, and then go right back at it. It made it impossible to get into their forge, or laboratory, or whatever it is they call their workspace."

Bango blew out a breath. "Ever since Coldforge left and put Garragh in charge, they have let nobody into the rooms. If I didn't know Coldforge was an honorable man, I'd swear they were up to no good down there. But they removed the magic from the silvered weapons designed to kill the dog soldiers. Apparently, they twisted the enchantments on the blades so that they would be deadlier when wielded by any lycans. It's why Aput set sail for Lycos. With those weapons in the hands of the dog soldiers, they're going to be truly frightful."

The harbormaster paused. Activity in the forest north of the harbor drew her attention. "Oh, sweet Titan, what's happening now?"

A band of Berrat had come bursting through the treeline and was running full out towards the beach. Bango quickly wrapped her fingers around her necklace. "Archers, form lines, three rows deep. The enemy approaches from the north." While the recruits fell into position, the harbormaster kept her eyes on the approaching Berrat.

"Hold your fire until I say otherwise." Several arrows immediately sailed over her head, landing hundreds of paces short of the oncoming attackers. She spun towards her people. "I said hold until I give the word." Several red-face recruits caught sight of her ire and decided it was time to carefully examine their boots.

They are not ready. We are in so much trouble.

⊷⊶⊷⊶

Ryn, Breayn's mate, ran out from the forest just north of Cormorant. He had a group of over five hundred Berrat with him. Some were warriors, but most were children or elderly. The Split Crow were hot on their heels. If he couldn't get his people inside the city, the Crows would slaughter them all.

Ryn's heart leapt into his throat at the sight of hundreds of soldiers taking up battle formations on the beach. From what he could see, they were not dressed in Split Crow uniforms, but that didn't mean the city hadn't fallen. Panic ripped through his chest. If Cormorant had fallen, was Breayn okay? Had he just led his people into the heart of those he had been fighting against? Doubt crippled the man. If Ulip were here, he would never have made such a mistake. He'd have planned for all contingencies. Ulip was a true leader.

"Hold!" Ryn stopped running and held his hands wide to his side. His command rippled through the people and the entire group came to a halt.

"Elder Ryn, why are we stopping?" A young warrior approached. He kept his voice low, perhaps fearful that his words might panic the children who were only a dozen paces behind them.

"I am no Elder," Ryn replied, his eyes locked on the warriors still moving into formation on the beach.

"You are older than me, and you're in charge," the young warrior said with a shrug. "That makes you our elder." He motioned to the beach with his chin. "Do you fear they are the enemy? I thought this city was safe."

"I don't know," Ryn said. "I watched allies conquer the slavers that held this city less than a moon ago. Breayn is here. If it's not safe, all hope for us is lost." The bronze skinned warrior's face paled. The fear in the young warrior's eyes crushed Ryn's soul. "I will find out if they are friend or foe. Have the people follow me but stay well back. Tell the warriors to stow their weapons. Under no circumstances, save my death, will there be any sign of hostility shown towards these people." The warrior's eyes were wide. "Do you understand?"

"I do, Elder Ryn. I will spread the word immediately."

Ryn cringed at the title the young man had given him. It did, however, spur him on to be the best leader he could be. If that meant risking his life by stepping into the bear's den, then that's exactly what he'd do. He gave the warrior a quick nod and broke into a run, heading straight for the awaiting teeth.

As he closed the distance, three people moved forward to intercept him. It appeared to be a Nomad woman with short black hair, a young Nomad male with a long single ponytail, and a Berrat male with bone-white braids. All three were dressed in light leather gear, and they all carried weapons. The young males both had arrows nocked, but neither had raised their bows to shoot.

"Hail," Ryn called out in his race's native language, his hands held wide, away from his sides. In Berrathia, it was the universal sign for *I come in peace*.

The Berrat male in the group replied. Even though he had spoken in Berrat, the young man's words were barely comprehensible. His language was unlike Ryn's northern dialect, but there were enough words to get the gist of what he was saying. At the heart of it all, he was asking if Ryn could speak in the common tongue.

"I am Ryn, mate of Breayn. My people are under attack by the Split Crow, and we seek shelter within your city." Ryn could only hope that he spoke it well enough that all three understood his meaning. Judging by the look twisting the woman's face, he wasn't certain.

⸎⸎⸎⸎◇⸎⸎⸎⸎

Bango practically hissed at the Berrat's words. If he'd brought the Split Crow down on the city, their problems had just become much, much worse. Fighting giants was bad enough, but the thought of having to confront them, as well as the most notorious group of slavers in Berrathia, well, it made the harbormaster's blood run cold.

"I am Bango. My two cohorts here are Treedale and Mukale. How can I be sure you are Breayn's mate?" Bango had to ensure he was who he said he was before she would admit this large group of potential enemies within the city's walls.

"Is she well? Is she safe?" the man responded. He didn't answer her question, but his concern for the woman was obvious in his facial expression.

"You appear anxious for her, but you're not giving me any proof that you are her mate." Bango motioned to Treedale and Mukale. They both immediately raised their bows and made ready to shoot.

"Do you know the spirit she carries within her?" Ryn asked. Bango immediately became suspicious. How could he know she carried the spirit of her mother? It wasn't something she shared with anybody outside their most inner circle.

"I do," Bango replied. "Do you?"

"I do," Ryn said. "She carries the spirit of Boreas, the North Wind."

The woman's muscles loosened at the man's declaration. Breayn carried the soul of Boreas, but that may or may not be common knowledge in the north. Her test wasn't as well thought out as she had hoped. She remembered Breayn's tales of fighting the northern slavers. Danny was with her, along with a Gigas warrior named Ulip.

"What were the names of her cohorts, and why were they special?" Bango was pleased with this question, hoping that it would be enough to prove the man was her mate or an imposter.

"Breayn and I used to be led by a Gigas named Ulip. He was special because he was the best leader I had ever met, and he was the only Gigas I've ever heard of who willingly sought to bring violence upon his enemy." Bango nodded, prodding the man for more details. He seemed perturbed by the request, perhaps because he didn't have any additional information.

"Is that it? Is that all you can tell me?" Bango placed her hand on the hilt of her sword, causing Treedale and Mukale to draw their bowstrings even tighter.

"No, there was another." The man's eyes became hard. His mouth screwed up like he had just bitten into a lemon. "Dannith Fox-Dancing, Breayn's cousin was among us. The man is completely insufferable, but he also carries the soul of the Phoenix within him." Bango burst out with a harsh laugh at this man's description of Danny.

"Lower your weapons," she said to Treedale and Mukale. "I believe he is who he says. He obviously knows Danny." The tension melted away, but Ryn still had a look of concern etched into his face.

"Breayn is fine," Bango said, trying to ease the man's worries. "She left this morning with our armada. They are sailing south for Ravenlord." The look of concern on his face morphed into abject terror.

"They are attacking Ravenlord? The word is there are thousands of King Faol's soldiers there. Many of them may be vampires."

"There are no vampires among Faol's army, at least not in Ravenlord. Our army outnumbers them, and we are prepared to lay waste to the city if we have to." Bango looked past the Berrat to the people walking across the field, heading towards them. "Let's get your people to safety, and then we can discuss Breayn in more detail."

"How many soldiers do you have here?" Ryn asked. "There are thousands of Split Crow coming. If this is the entirety of your army, this city is doomed."

"How many thousands?" Treedale asked. "What numbers are we facing?"

"At least five, but perhaps as many as fifteen. We could never get a clear number of the warriors under their command. The Split Crow have apparently mobilized their entire army and they're headed this way. I can't say for sure how many were directly behind us. I was too busy keeping my people out of their range. The forests north of this city are very dense and difficult to move quickly through. If the main body is not with them, they'll likely come in by the main road from Owl's Dell."

Ryn surveyed the soldiers who were present. "We need to get these warriors and my people behind cover. There will be too many Crows to fight them here in the open."

"My soldiers are well trained to fight on an open field." Bango sounded both annoyed with the Berrat standing before her and proud of her soldiers, knowing that, even though they were totally green, they were well trained and ready for combat.

"They may be well trained," Ryn said, "but there may be thousands of Crows coming. No matter how good your warriors are, they will all die."

"We can fall back to the Port Authority Buildings," Mukale said. "We can lead these Crow soldiers into the city streets. We can use the same tactics we had planned for the giants. We'll use the buildings for cover while we draw the enemy into kill zones."

"I couldn't have said it better myself," Ryn said, giving the young Berrat a nod of approval. "What's this about giants?"

Bango completely ignored the last question. "Get your people here and we'll take them into the city. Can we use your warriors to lead the enemy into our trap? Are they up for the task?"

"My warriors will fight to the death if they have to." Ryn was practically thumping his chest as he spoke of his people.

"Good," Bango said. "Get your people and we'll get ourselves set." Ryn nodded and ran off towards the crowd of Berrat, who were slowly nearing the beach.

"Treedale, ring the alarm bells. Mukale, get to the manor and fetch the dwarves. They didn't come the last time they were called to battle. Make sure they do this time. It sounds like we're going to need our full army to face this foe."

CHAPTER TWENTY-EIGHT

THE KILL ZONE

The peel of the warning bells was deafening. As the sun lowered in the western sky, Bango hoped the sound would be even more disconcerting to the enemy than it was to her own people. Her soldiers were visibly shaken by the rhythmic, high-pitched clang, clang, clang, that repeated over and over. The Split Crow's insidious reputation was established across northern Berrathia. Knowing they were about to face such a vicious enemy, up close and personal, did nothing to soothe the recruit's jangled nerves.

While waiting for Ryn's warriors to draw the enemy into their trap, the recruits took positions behind the Port Authority buildings. The alleyways between the structures were narrow, and they'd force the enemy to trickle through, rather than storm the area in a large group. Bango and Ryn put themselves between the recruits and the kill zone entrances. From their vantage point, they'd be able to survey the situation and still command the soldiers, telling them when to attack and when to retreat.

"How long will your man keep ringing those infernal bells?" Ryn grimaced at each ring. "Surly your people know to come now."

"Treedale will keep ringing them until a commander tells him to stop." Bango was trying to not let the bells get to her, but they were grating on her nerves as well. All she could hope was that they'd affect the enemy even more when they neared.

"How many of your soldiers can we expect to come?" Ryn asked. Bango wondered if his chatter was to take his mind off the incessant peels. "If the Crows show up in full force, do we have any hope of defeating them? These tactics will kill many, but their superior numbers will eventually win the day. If the Beak and the Claw are among their ranks, there will be little chance that we'll survive to see another sunrise.

"We are at least five thousand strong, including dwarves and four yetis. We've also got the phoenix." Ryn's eyebrows shot up when Bango mentioned Danny and the yetis.

"Danny Fox-Dancing is here?" Bango nodded at the question. A confusing expression washed across Ryn's face. It looked to be a combination of relief mixed with loathing. It was clear that he couldn't stand Danny, but he recognized the phoenix was a powerful warrior.

"Where are our soldiers?" Bango's voice came out as a harsh whisper. "They should be here already."

"The Crow are coming." Ryn pointed to the woodland off to the left, near to where the Gaelinora River flowed. "A large group has just emerged from the forest."

Bango strained her eyes to get a better look, but with the day's light failing, all she could see were dark shadows. "How many can you see? All I see are silhouettes against the forest."

Ryn craned his neck and narrowed his eyes. "It's difficult to tell, even with my night vision. It looks to be only about a hundred."

"That's not as many as I feared," Bango said, blowing out a breath, "but if they are as fearsome as you describe, they're likely still going to be more than my recruits can deal with. I can only hope our plan works."

"My warriors have seen them, too," Ryn said, pointing to his two-dozen people out on the beach. They were each equipped with short bows and as many arrows as they could carry. They had already started firing at the enemy. The sight made Bango groan.

"The Crows are too far away. Why are they wasting their arrows like that?"

"They're checking their range. Now that they have it, they'll wait for the enemy to come to them." As Ryn had predicted, his warriors ceased firing their weapons, and they all took a knee.

The next few minutes passed like hours. The Crow soldiers were making their way across the open grassland. Bango could hear them screaming, but she couldn't see anything more than a great shadow moving across the open expanse.

Ryn's warriors popped up to their feet and began loosing arrows. The steady twangs of their bows and a light breeze blowing in off the water were all Bango could hear.

"Something's wrong," she said. "The Crows have stopped their yelling."

"It makes no sense," Ryn said, moving from his place of cover, striding towards the beach where his warriors stood. "The Crows are scattering. They're running in every direction except towards us."

"That's a good thing, isn't it?" Bango didn't really understand the concern. She thought the archers were being effective. How was that not a good thing?

"The Crow do not run from their prey. Loss of life is an acceptable and expected outcome during a charge. They are too disciplined to break ranks." Ryn broke into a run. He was shouting something to his warriors that Bango couldn't understand. He was likely speaking in Berrat.

In no time, Ryn and his warriors were running headlong toward the enemy. Unsure what to do, Bango held back, cursed loudly, and waited for the outcome.

⁓⁓⁓◇⁓⁓⁓

Bango was growing impatient. The sun had set, and with the heavy cloud cover, the area around the beachhead was nearly pitch black. She could no longer discern the forest from the grassland. Everything was a solid mass of darkness. Chills ran up her spine. She felt like she was standing out in the open, just begging some unseen assailant to attack her. What of her recruits? Many minutes had passed, and they had been left waiting in the kill zone.

This was not going the way she'd expected. Not at all.

She was just about to make her way back to her people when the sound of many feet crossing the rough-sand beach reached her ears. Her heart pounded in her chest as the darkness seemed to crush in on her. Not wanting to stand by herself in the oppressive blackness, Bango bolted to the Port Authority buildings and the relative cover they provided.

She didn't stop running until she had made it to the alleyway that led to the kill zone. Her heart was now pounding out of control. Her breathing was so erratic that she feared she'd pass out.

More footsteps, except these were coming up behind her. Bango glanced over her shoulder. All she could see was darkness. She tried desperately to control her breathing, but that only made matters worse. She had to risk announcing herself. She could only hope that she had allies at her back.

"It's me, Bango. Hold your positions." She hissed out the words, hoping it would be loud enough for whoever was behind her to hear.

Thump. Thump. Whiz.

Two arrows struck the wall right beside her while a third flew past, close enough to her ear that she felt the breath of wind from it.

"Stand down," she ordered again. This time, much more forcefully.

Thump. Whiz.

Another arrow landed against the wall near her. The second arrow missed the mark by a good deal.

"Stand down, fools." Bango practically bellowed out the words.

"Harbourmaster?" A squeaky voice called out from the darkness. "Is that you?"

"Of course, it's me," she replied, her voice filled with fury. "Why did you break position?"

"It sure sounds like her. What do we do?"

The not so quiet whispers reaching Bango's ears made her growl. She was going to send them back to the others, but she feared they'd be fired upon in a similar fashion. The sound of foot falls upon the sand was getting louder. There were too many of them. If a fight was going to break out, her people were done for. They were too green to manage such a battle.

Bango took a solid hold of her fear and gripped her necklace. "Who goes there!" Her words blasted out towards the open sea.

"We're your recruits," said the voices from behind her.

Sweet Titan, are they truly that dim?

"Hold," a voice from the darkness called out. "Bango, there is no need for alarm."

"Ryn?"

"Don't shoot," the voice called out again. "Can you not see me?"

Bango couldn't see squat. She could see less than squat. Whether it was the sheer darkness or the blood pounding in her ears, she felt utterly helpless. "I pray to Titan that's you, Ryn. I'm stepping out."

The peeling bells finally fell silent.

⸺⸺◆⸺⸺

The captains had heeded the call of the warning bell. Nearly five thousand soldiers stood in formation on the beach while Bango, Danny, Calian, and Ryn met with the battle commanders.

"For the last time, I am not delusional." A deep growl rumbled in Ryn's throat. Danny recognized that sound to be the grizzly bear spirit he held within his body. "Escaped prisoners did not spook me into a panic. A Split Crow army was chasing us."

"How many were there?" Danny asked. "I know you said you didn't know, but can you give us a guess?"

"No, I cannot give you a guess. We never learned the actual size of the Crow army. But if what you said is true, that they have abandoned Wantage and are heading south, they are going to have many more warriors than you have here."

"Can we not use the same tactics we've been practicing? We draw them into the city, force them into smaller groups, and kill them at a distance." Bango let the words hang there.

"The Berrat fighting style does not work in such great numbers," Danny said. "In a large-scale battle, the human's way of fighting is far superior. The Split Crow are well versed in both forms of combat. We cannot easily trick them."

Calian moved closer to Danny. "How are we to know how many soldiers they have? It's too dark to see, even for the Berrat."

"There are no enemies across the fields. If they're there, they're hidin' deep within the trees," Garragh said in his gravelly baritone voice. "We can set some fires to light the field. That way, ye can see if anyone's comin'."

"Lighting fires is a good idea," Danny said. "I'll be right back." The Berrat sprinted towards the forest and burst into flames as soon as he was clear of the people. Everyone standing nearby had to shield their eyes from the sudden brightness.

"He's somethin' to look at," Garragh said. The black-haired dwarf had taken over the leadership of the dwarves after Coldforge had left for Templeton. "But unless he's going to gather some firewood, any fires he starts won't last very long."

"You'd be surprised at the fires he can start," Calian said, thankful that the darkness hid her blushing skin.

⟋⟋⟋⟋⟨◇⟩⟋⟋⟋⟋

While Danny flew about, lighting up sections of the grasslands, Bango had a chat with Garragh. The flames in the distance were dancing off the stout man's heavy, highly polished armor. She lightly rapped her gloved fist on a pauldron. "Where are the rest of the dwarves? When we rang the warning bells, all soldiers were called to battle. That included you dwarves."

"Me kin were too deep to answer the call."

"They're drunk?" Bango knew the dwarves to be heavy drinkers, but the idea they'd gotten so drunk as to not show up for battle was unheard of.

"Nay, they're not drunk. They're diggin'. When we get to diggin', we don't drink."

"Why are they deep? Are you digging new tunnels?" Bango urged Garragh away from the group to have a quiet conversation with him.

"Nay, not new tunnels. We're doin' what we came here ta do. We have done what ye needed of us, and now we're lookin' after our own." Bango's face darkened at the dwarf's words.

"What do you mean by that? What are you digging for?"

"We're working to free our god, Gimlie. Why else did ya think we came? We'd have never boarded those ships just because that god-cursed woman and them long-toothed maniacs told us to." The dwarf lowered his head, exposing a rather large bald dome that Bango had never noticed before. "We didn't expect them to double-cross us. We were coming willingly. They didn't need to put us in chains."

"What god-cursed woman are you talking about?" Bango peered over her shoulder to see if anyone was trying to listen in on the conversation. Ryn and the other soldiers were too deep in their own worries to care about the dwarves.

"That thing they call Arachnielle. I hate spiders. The only good spider is the one squashed beneath yer boot."

"Arachnielle, the god? She was with you?"

The dwarf nodded. His expression was one of complete disinterest in whatever Bango thought of the woman. "She told us the Veil that keeps Gimlie from rejoining his kin is weakest here, that with the help of the Hobgoblins' magic, we should be able to breach it. As far as we can tell, she spoke true. But even if it's weak, it's still exceedingly difficult to penetrate. We're getting closer, though."

Bango didn't know how to process this revelation. She didn't understand the full ramifications of what it meant to breach the Veil, but she feared the worst. She feared it would bring about Ragnarök, the end of days. Her preoccupation with the conversation blinded her to Danny's return.

"We've got troubles," he said, loud enough for everyone nearby to hear. "The forest is full of people. Many of them are enemies, but most of them are not."

Chapter Twenty-Nine

The Darkest Night

Danny shook his head, his normally green eyes taking on a smoldering red. "There are more people coming than I could estimate. The Crows are traveling in small groups, surrounded by what I can only guess are Berrat civilians, likely from Taseko. Lady Kandyce had said they emptied the city. I was thinking I might set the forests on fire, burn up the lot of them. If I had, I'd likely have killed innocents by the thousands. These people have no moral code."

Ryn's shoulders slumped. "How many Crow do you think there are?"

"It was difficult to tell, but I'm going to guess there were fewer than one hundred. I would say the entire group is going to come through the treeline in the next ten minutes. We'll have a better idea once they are in the open."

"Less than one hundred?" Ryn asked. "That makes no sense. Why would they have so few soldiers managing so many people?"

"Is there any way to pick out these Crows from the civilians in the group?" Garragh asked. "If we can, we should have no difficulty crushing their skulls."

"The Crows will be dressed in black uniforms," Ryn said. "They wear feathered black capes."

Danny shook his head. "Even if they were carrying signs telling us which of them were the Crow, it would be impossible to get to them without catastrophic loss of life. They're using the people as shields. When I'm in my phoenix form, I can tell friend from foe, but I have no way of telling you who's who."

"How can we possibly fight them, then? If we can't tell friend from foe," one yeti asked. The others nodded, hoping to hear an answer that would allow them to engage the enemy sooner rather than later.

Garragh groaned loudly. "By Gimlie's beard, yer all too weak for words. If they're wearin' them feathered cloaks like you say, me and mine will just walk up to 'em and give 'em a good beatin'."

"Maybe if all of you had come," Bango said, not trying to hide her annoyance with the dwarves. "That plan might have worked. There are only seven of you. You expect to kill a hundred trained soldiers while they shield themselves with civilians?"

"I could probably do it on me own," Garragh said, "but we're in a hurry. I want to get back to me diggin'." The dwarf obviously caught the look of disbelief on Bango's face. "In the forest, it's gonna be pitch black. Them Berrat folk don't have dark vision like we do. We can see as clear as day out here. We're just gonna walk right up to 'em and crush their skulls. It hardly gets any easier than this." And with that, Garragh hoisted his double-headed battle hammer over his shoulder and beckoned his kin to follow him. They chugged forward toward the forest at a steady pace.

"It will not be dark," Danny said. "I lit enough fires that the Crows are going to see them coming the whole way. A moment later, the flames in the grassland died out and the entire field fell into darkness.

Perhaps an hour had passed. Standing in the blackness made it difficult to gage the passage of time. The soldiers had broken ranks and were milling about, chatting with each other. There was an almost jovial mood as people started joking about how the seven dwarves were going to attack nearly one hundred soldiers. Bango didn't appreciate that they were taking bets on how many of them would survive and how many would come running back looking for their help.

Shouts from the forest carried across the night air. At first, it was difficult to discern what the screams were about, but it quickly became apparent they were cries of joy and excitement.

"I'm going to guess that a few soldiers are going to make a lot of silver on their wagers." Ryn was practically dancing on the spot. "It sounds like they freed the slaves. Against all odds, it sounds like they did it."

"Only one way to know for sure," Danny said. He stepped away from the group, lit himself ablaze, and launched into the sky. He flew out towards the forest, circled twice, and then returned.

"And now we know," he said brightly. "Those damned dwarves did it. There are several thousand people coming, and not a single one of them is an enemy."

"We're going to have to find a place to put them all." A small voice called up to Bango. "Their village cannot house another soul. A good many of the people are already sleeping in the forest."

Bango spun around to find Amilta standing behind her. Several pairs of yellow-green eyes were barely visible in the darkness.

"Fenrir sent me here to tell you she is patrolling the area. When we saw the people being led this way, she suggested I come find you."

"Hello, Amilta." Bango had wondered why Fenrir and her wolves hadn't come when the bell tolled, but it seemed they had. "Did Fenrir find any other signs that the enemy is nearby?" The sound of beads and shells rattling was the small girl's reply. "I can't see in the darkness," Bango said, a smile in her words. "You're going to need to speak up."

"Yes," Amilta said. "There are many enemies. Some lay in wait while others travel towards this place."

"Where?" Danny asked. "How many?"

"Too many," Amilta replied. "There is a large number waiting on the road to Owl's Dell."

"Waiting?" Bango asked. "Waiting for what?"

"Waiting for the others. There is another group marching up the road. They will meet before the moon is high. If they come directly here, Fenrir believes they will be here well before sunrise."

"How many?" Danny asked again. "How many did Fenrir say were coming?"

"The wolf god did not say a number. She only said there were too many, and I was to tell you."

"I'll go see," Danny said. "I'll try to get a good count of what we're facing." Bango grabbed him by the arm before he moved away.

"No, the number isn't important. Fenrir said there were too many soldiers coming. You need to stay here, and we need to make a plan for how we're going to deal with them.

The muted sound of hoofbeats rushing through the surf got everyone's attention. Excited shouts rippled throughout the assembled soldiers. The echo of steel being drawn rang out.

"Hold!" a deep male voice called out. "Hold! We are friends." Bango recognized that voice, but she couldn't say who it was.

"Runt is here," Amilta squealed. The joyful excitement in her voice was infectious. "Runt has come. He's bringing friends." The little girl's feet beat on the sand as she ran squealing towards the sea.

"Stand down," Bango called out. She quickly wrapped her fingers around her necklace and called out again. "Stand down. There is no cause for alarm."

"It looks like Indie is back," Danny said. Bango wasn't sure if she'd picked up a bit of anger in the man's voice, but she let it go.

"We need every ally we can get," Calian said. Bango didn't even know the woman was nearby. Although, it shouldn't have surprised her that a dog soldier would be comfortable under the darkness of the night sky.

"Danny," Bango said, "can you give me some light? I need to speak with the captains." Danny lit his hand aflame and held it aloft. A moment later, the flame grew taller and brighter. The harbormaster gave him a quick nod before clutching her necklace. "Captains, to me. Captains, to me."

⚭⚭⚭◇⚭⚭⚭

Torches flared to life, lighting the inside of the Port Authority office building. Bango had moved inside to speak with the senior officers. She had ordered the Berrat peoples to be taken to a warehouse where they could rest and eat. Their disposition could be dealt with in the light of day.

Indie had introduced Sellina and Jayne, the two members of Aurora's Guard from Silverhawk, to the assembled group. When they said they had brought three thousand more fighters with them, a quiet cheer ran through the group.

While Indie was busy speaking, Lin had pulled Bango aside. "Where's Rusty? Why isn't she here?" The concern in Lin's voice practically broke the harbormaster's heart.

"She has left for Ravenlord. We sent an armada south to conquer the city."

"An armada?" Lin blinked at her. "Rusty has an armada?"

"Sister Kit does," Bango corrected, "but that's not important right now. Rusty went with them in search of her father's body. She was hoping he would be there and that she could return his soul to him." Lin nodded weakly. She looked shattered.

"What of Commander Bishop?" Sellina asked. "He and the other Hawk Riders flew ahead. Where are they?"

"We saw them fly overhead, but they didn't stop," Bango said. "They flew north along the Gaelinora River before disappearing in the distance."

"And there has been no sign of Kit?" Indie's eyes raked over the assembled group, waiting for someone to say they had seen her. All he saw were people shaking their heads.

"I'm sure she's fine," Danny said. "That girl would walk through the fires of Helja to be at your side."

The sound of Coldforge's thick hands clapping together put an end to the dialog. He and Garragh were off to the side, having their own conversation. It had been relatively quiet until this point. When all eyes turned to him, the dwarf clapped all the harder.

"Our worries are over," he said. He was practically doing a jig as he spoke. "Me father will soon be here. When he is, me and me kin will set things to rights." He seemed to be confused that nobody was cheering. "Garragh has informed me they have nearly broken through the Veil. Me kin are beyond and soon they will be freed."

"How long?" Bango asked, a thrill of relief welling up in her chest. "How long until they breach the Veil?"

"Breach the Veil?" Indie's voice was incredulous. "What are you talking about?"

Garragh mumbled something to Coldforge. "Two days. Three at most." Bango's spirit instantly deflated.

"The enemy will be upon us in an hour or two," she said. Bango couldn't help but wonder if the dwarves didn't understand time or if they simply didn't understand the magnitude of the problem. She also didn't know why Indie was so upset at the news.

"And who else will be released from beyond the Veil?" There was an unexpected rage in Indie's voice. "There was a reason the Veil was created. If you break through, you'll also be releasing Bael, Gorgaraeth, and their horde of demons upon the land." Indie pushed his way through the stunned crowd. "Did you even consider that? Did you think beyond your own personal interests?"

Oh, Helja. Bango had considered none of that. She only saw the enemy on her doorstep. She was only thinking about how to save her people.

"Ya listen ta me, boy," Coldforge bellowed. His hands were clenched into tight fists. They looked to be carved from blocks of heavy white granite. "Me kin are the first thing I think of when I wake up. They are the last thing before I lay me head down to sleep. Tell me you wouldn't risk everything to save your lady love. Me and mine are looking after our own. When me father and me kin are freed, we will defeat the demons, and all will be as it should be. Do ye truly want to live with the specter of those creatures clawing at the ground beneath you, bubbling up from below on the day you least expect? Use the brains that Gaia gave ye, boy. Ye never want to be taken unawares, just like ye all have this very night."

Bango watched as a multitude of expressions crossed Indie's face in a matter of moments. She could understand why Indie was so upset, but she could also hear the logic in the dwarven prince's words.

There was an awkward, prolonged silence.

"If you are all finished warring amongst yourselves," Fenrir said as she quietly entered the room, "maybe we can address the monsters at the door."

"Monsters?" Bango narrowed her eyes at the comment. "There are more than one?"

"Yes," Fenrir gazed over the assembled group. "There are four, as best as I can tell."

"What do you mean, four?" Indie asked. The wolf god's words seemed to have distracted him from his ire with Coldforge.

"There are four armies coming. At their lead are the Beak and the Claw, plus the banners of three other slave houses. As strange as it sounds, it would seem the Split Crow has made several allies."

"This is good news," Coldforge declared. He renewed his clapping, his furry orange face bobbing emphatically. "If Rusty has led an armada south to crush Ravenlord, these soldiers coming our way represent the rest of the Auctioneer slave houses. When we defeat them, we'll have broken the slavers' backs."

CHAPTER THIRTY

A FIRE TO LIGHT THE WAY

Breayn arrived about an hour before the enemy's expected arrival time. Ryn practically broke into tears at the sight of her. It had been too long since they'd been together. She was explaining to him how she held her mother's spirit within her, and how she had freed Boreas. Indie couldn't tell if he was happy or upset at the news. Ryn mostly appeared stunned at the revelation.

Danny quickly started explaining the situation to Breayn. He told her how he had flown over the enemy's army several times to get an idea of how close they were and how much time would pass before their arrival. Indie had struggled to believe him when he had said over thirty thousand warriors were coming. That was a lot of soldiers, and those numbers would be difficult to reckon with any sort of accuracy. Danny hadn't really cared if Indie had believed him or not, and suggested that, if he wanted, he could go count them himself.

Indie watched with amusement as Calian wrapped her arms around Danny's neck and gave him a kiss. It seemed she was trying to send Indie a message, but whatever it was, it was lost on him.

Bango stepped between Danny and Indie, breaking up the two men and their foolishness. "We are eight thousand standing against thirty. We have defensive advantage, but that won't be enough to hold back the flood of soldiers that is going to wash over our lands."

"I don't know how long I could keep it up," Danny said, still glaring at Indie. "But I could see how many I can set on fire. When I flew over them, a good deal of the soldiers appeared orange rather than red. Maybe they'd switched sides like

Lilloet's soldiers did. Not everyone wants to follow the orders they're given. If I can light up the reds and leave the oranges, maybe they'll lose their will and go home."

"Ye don't want them goin' home," Coldforge said. "Ye want them dead. If they go home, they'll just come back, but in greater numbers. Ye can't let these sorts of broken minds fester on."

"I don't disagree with Coldforge," Bango said, "but if they show up here, we're all going to die, and they'll still continue to fester on. We can't tell the difference between red and orange soldiers. If they're willing to attack us, we need to be ready to kill them."

"Danny?" Indie gave his black ponytail a tug. The thought of collaborating on a plan with the man grated on him. The trouble was, the phoenix was far and away, the most powerful person in their group. If Kit were here, he'd think differently, but he had no idea how long it would be before she might arrive.

"Yes?" Danny replied, cocking an eyebrow.

"What if, instead of trying to drive them away, you drove them forward? If you set fires at their back, they'd have no place to retreat to." Indie knew what he wanted to say, but he simply couldn't find the words to fully express his idea.

"How is forcing them to attack going to make things better?" Bango's voice was incredulous. Indie wanted to back down, but he thought he had a plan worth talking about.

"Give me a minute," he said, holding up his hand to stop Bango from continuing. "Danny said that if he set them on fire, they might run away. But if he gives them no place to run to, they will break into a panic when he lights them up. Panicked soldiers do not fight well."

"We can help," Breayn said. Ryn nodded slowly. The two had been locked together since the moment Breayn returned. "If we can get two riders, we can turn into great hawks and carry them over the armies. The riders can carry bottles of oil to throw at the enemy. We throw the oil and Danny can light them up."

"We can do better than oil," Lin said. "There is a potion called *liquid fire*."

"Ah, lass, that's not what it's called." Coldforge's eyes were bright and wicked. "It's called *dwarven flame*. We use it when we need to forge mithril. Regular forges don't get hot enough to work the wondrous metal. This potion, when added to any flame, burns hot enough to melt mithril and anything else, for that matter. We've got cases of it below the manor. We're planning to use it to cut through the Veil, but we can spare some to beat back this lot."

"It's a shame Commander Bishop and his hawk riders aren't here," Sellina said. "They are some of the best fliers in all the lands."

"We only need people brave enough to ride our backs," Ryn said. "We'll do all the work getting you over the enemy. You'll just need to drop the fire potions."

"We'll do it," Treedale piped up. "Mukale and I will fly with you."

"I see you didn't volunteer." Danny raised his eyebrows at Indie, daring him to offer to ride a hawk in the dead of night.

"He's a bit... big," Breayn said. "Bigger than I remember."

"A bigger coward." Danny's voice sounded like he was teasing, but Indie knew he was simply trying to get a rise out of him.

"I'm better suited on the ground," Indie said. "I'd rather be in the thick of a battle than fly safely over it."

"And how much damage do you think you can do in the thick of it?" Danny's playful tone vanished, replaced with an outright challenge. Indie smiled and closed his eyes. Like a molten ripple, golden scales flowed down his head. His long black hair turned into long spikes that ran from his crown down below his obsidian plated armor. His arms and hands, too, became encased in the same slick draconic hide.

"I can do enough, I think." Danny blew out a long, low whistle.

"A lot has changed since you left. It's hard to keep up with things." Danny's eyes brightened. "How much heat can those scales withstand?"

"Danny, enough!" Calian stepped between the two men. "I've had enough of this nonsense. If you want to be with me, you need to let this rivalry go. It's over, or we are."

"Calian." Danny took a step back from the woman. Her hands were mid change. Long, black claws hung from the tips of her fingers. "I didn't mean it like that. I was going to ask if he'd be willing to ride with me into combat. I wanted to know if he could withstand my flames."

Calian's claws withdrew, returning her hands to normal. Indie watched intently as the two of them stared each other down.

Danny's got a new love. A flood of relief washed over Indie. The red-headed man had finally given up on Kit and he could stop worrying about the Berrat making advances on her. Indie suddenly wanted to hurl. Why was he jealous? Why was he reacting this way? He knew Kit loved him. He knew it down to his very soul.

"I don't know if my scales would protect me from your fires," Indie said. "As much as I would like to test them out, I don't see how I would be of much use on your back. I also don't think I would want to be carrying flammable potions while sitting atop a flaming bird."

Indie's words made Danny chuckle. "It would have been an interesting site, though. A dragon-man riding a phoenix. The bards would sing of it for centuries."

"Maybe when the fate of the people isn't depending on us," Indie said with a shrug. "I'd like that very much."

It was in that moment that Indie's feelings of jealousy for the man vanished. It was like a tremendous weight had been lifted off his shoulders.

"Okay then," Bango said. "Now that we have that settled, how long will it take to get those potion bottles here?"

"I can take him to the manor," Mukale offered. "If Coldforge doesn't mind riding bareback." Coldforge gave the Berrat a sideways look.

"I can turn into a horse," Mukale said with a laugh. "You'd be riding a horse, if that's okay with you."

"I have little use for horses," Coldforge said. Even behind his bushy facial hair, it wasn't difficult to see the dwarf smiling as Runt came trotting up to him. "But I can ride the big lad here. If ye can carry a crate, it'll go much faster." Runt quickly barked out his agreement and gave the dwarf a few slobbery licks to make sure his point was made.

"Coldforge, can you spare more of your *dwarven fire?*" Bango tucked some loose hairs behind her ear. "I don't see why we need to drop it from the sky. Can't we throw it at the enemy when they draw near?"

"Ye can do that," Coldforge shrugged, "but if one of ye drops a bottle when ye are trying to toss it, it won't go well for anyone within thirty paces."

Lin piped up. She had been standing silently away from everyone while the discussion was going on. Indie could only assume her thoughts were with Rusty and not on the here and now.

"Coldforge, did you put the potion in ampules or in large vials?"

"Ampules, Lady Lin," the dwarf replied. "They burn hot enough in small quantities to burn through anything. If the bottles are too large, they're too dangerous to use."

"Do you think we can affix them to arrows?" The excitement in Lin's voice was contagious. "I can launch an arrow over two hundred paces with my bow. We can reach a lot more of the enemy that way."

Coldforge scratched at his matted orange hair. He seemed dismayed by the suggestion. Finally, with a loud harrumph, he nodded his head. "Sure. It would work, but it's not the dwarven way. Fighting at a distance is not honorable."

"I'd rather stay alive than try to fight the *dwarven way,*" Lin said.

⟡⟡⟡⟡⟡⟡

Indie, Danny, and Ryn stood out in the chilly night air. They stood in front of a long line of fires that had been set across the beach. The dancing flames lit their dark, brooding faces.

It was a few hours before sunrise when the first of the torchbearers came into view. The approaching army showed no concern about being seen. They had overwhelming numbers, and they were using them to their advantage. Surely, they were counting on this obscene show of force to break the heart of the city. Based on every bit of tactical knowledge from Cormorant's military leaders, they predicted the Crows would march up the road from Owl's Dell and congregate on the grasslands to the north of the harbor. The area wouldn't be big enough to hold the entire army. The rest of the attacking soldiers would have to wait on the road and couldn't be a part of the initial charge.

"Do the captains really expect the Beak and the Claw to be at the head of the army?" Danny asked. "Every text I've read on military combat suggests that the leadership stays safely at the rear. That gives them a simple escape route if things go badly for their soldiers."

Ryn blew out a breath. "The Beak and the Claw are notoriously confident in themselves. They may not a part of the vanguard when the army moves on the city, but they'll be at the lead until they do. They're going to want a front row view to witness the carnage."

"If you killed them right off, might the army lose faith and bolt?" Indie's nerve wavered as the pinpoints of torchlight gathered in the fields. There were so many soldiers. There were so many more snaking their way towards the field.

"Maybe," Ryn said, but it's unlikely. "I've seen the Crow in combat. Most of them revel in the killing. Their cruelty to their prisoners suggests they're just as sick and twisted as their masters."

Bango and Breayn joined the trio of men. Their greetings were somber.

"That's a lot of soldiers," Bango commented after several minutes of silence. "If this plan fails, I just want to say, I've really…"

"The plan won't fail," Indie said. "We can't let it."

"When will you take flight?" Bango asked.

"Are our soldiers ready?" Danny asked. "Have they all been given fire arrows?" Bango shook her head, but her gaze never left the gathering mass of enemies.

"There were not nearly enough to equip everyone, but we have more than I would have expected. I don't know what the dwarves were planning, but they created more crates of potions than I could count."

"We should go as soon as Treedale and Mukale show up," Breayn said. "We don't want the enemy to get too organized out there. We need to hit them while they're still filling their ranks."

"Okay then." A nervous laugh escaped Bango's lips. "You all know what to do. I'll get our army set up on the beach as soon as you take flight."

"We're ready," Treedale said. The two young men jingled with every step they took. "We've each got nearly a hundred potions with us."

They were both wearing crossing bandoliers. Each bandolier held two rows of ampules. Around their waists were similarly shaped belts, also holding two rows of ampules. Mukale brandished a large leather sack and gave it a small shake, causing the vials within to tinkle. The assembled group gasped and took a step back.

"They won't break," the young Berrat said. "The Hobgoblins said they were safe to carry like this."

"Didn't their crazy laugh make you nervous?" Treedale said. "The way they cackled when they handed you the bag. It ran chills up my spine." Mukale just shrugged.

"If you're going to ride on my back," Ryn said. "You will not be shaking that bag ever again. Got it?" Mukale shrugged yet again and hoisted the bag over his shoulder.

"I'll take a pass over the forest," Danny said. "If there is anyone in it, I'll light it up. Otherwise, I'll head to the back of the column and start lighting fires behind them."

Chapter Thirty-One

Night Fliers

Danny took flight and made his way to the enemy. He smiled to himself when several hundred arrows sailed his way. Very few came close to him, and none found their mark. He wondered how many of the soldiers might have inadvertently dropped arrows on their own people.

The enemies, who had initially appeared as red dots, were changing to orange as he passed over. He sped low over their heads as he continued on toward the forest. The woods were completely devoid of the enemy, which was exactly what they were hoping for. They were in the open, ripe for the picking.

The phoenix screeched out a battle cry before following the road northwest, to where the end of the army would be. The farther back he went, the less red he saw in the soldiers. It wasn't until he got to the very end of the procession that he saw any significant mass of enemies. It made sense the Split Crows would want their true believers at the back of the column, making sure nobody broke ranks and ran away. Danny issued another war cry and banked towards those at the rear and went into a steep dive.

His flaming form burst through the bodies of a half dozen soldiers, instantly setting them ablaze. Many of the soldiers shot arrows at him, while many more scattered, trying to avoid the firebird. Danny focused on those who were the brightest red. One after another fell to his fiery form. When the last of the red-dot lives were extinguished, Danny started setting the countryside on fire. As planned, the soldiers surged forward, trying to stay away from the flames. With a few quick beats of his wings, Danny launched himself skyward and turned back towards the bulk of the army.

The number of red dots in the column had significantly reduced. The vast majority of them were bright orange, bordering on yellow. They definitely weren't allies, but they were losing heart. Many looked ready to rout from the field.

The closer the phoenix got to the head of the line, the redder the soldiers looked. These were the hardcore fanatics, the soldiers who enjoyed being slavers. They reveled in what they did. Danny filled his lungs with air and let out another battle cry. Seconds later, the first of two fireballs erupted in the middle of the gathered army. A moment later, two more erupted, and then two more.

Soldiers on the road surged forward, running headlong towards the fires. Danny hadn't expected this behavior. Perhaps they thought the bursts of flames were a signal for them to attack. Perhaps they were curious. Perhaps they were all homicidal maniacs desperately seeking carnage. Whatever their reasoning, this was not a part of Danny's plans.

The phoenix surged forward, flying low over the enemy convoy. When he neared the location where the road met the main body of soldiers on the open field, Danny swooped and again used his flaming form as a missile, flying through the bodies of the enemy. He flew high again and circled for another pass. This time, instead of flying directly at the procession of soldiers, he flew low enough to the ground that he was igniting the grasses, the bushes, and the trees. He kept repeating this until he had built up an impenetrable wall of fire. This time, the plan worked perfectly. The soldiers backed away from the flames and tried to go around them. They were left with two choices. Head for the river or head for the forest. Unless they were planning on swimming, the forest was their only viable option.

With a few quick wingbeats, the phoenix rose again into the night and turned towards the main army.

What the Helja?

There were over two dozen red dots streaking across the sky. They were closing hard on Ryn and Breayn. Who were they? The phoenix's flames brightened when the realization washed over him. They were the Griffin Riders from Silverhawk. They had to be.

⁂

Breayn swore under her breath as a griffin swooped at her. Treedale struggled to maintain his position on Breayn in her great hawk form. He tried to throw a potion at the griffin's rider, but it flew harmlessly past, exploding on the ground below. She wanted to tell him to stop and just hold on, but she had no way of communicating with the young man. He had yelped whenever she had changed directions too quickly, obviously fearful that he'd fall from his perch. She just wished he'd take a tight hold of her neck and let her fly.

Treedale yelped again as his mount was forced into a steep dive to avoid two hawk riders. He threw his sack of potions and grasped onto Breayn's neck. The sack hit the ground and erupted into a huge fireball. The rising heat blew Breayn upwards, singeing her feathers. She banked hard to clear herself of the flames. Her rider's grip on her neck tightened. He had finally caught on.

The fires flared in the field below, lighting up the undersides of the fliers. It was the only way that Breayn could see the enemy. Her hawk vision was unparalleled in the daylight, but at night, she was practically blind. Her heart was beating out of control from the exertion, but it nearly stopped dead when a trio of enemies converged on Ryn and Mukale. Two great hawks seemed to corral her mate while a griffin was moving in for the kill. She beat her wings with all her might while her muscles screamed in protest. Her mate would not survive.

From above, a bright flame descended so quickly it looked to be nothing more than a streak in the sky. It left behind a one-hundred-foot trail of sparks in its wake. It was heading directly for the griffin in what would be a catastrophic collision.

Ryn banked to his right, nearly careening into one of the riders harassing him. The griffin followed his movements and flew directly into the phoenix's path. Danny didn't even slow as griffin and rider burst into flames. He continued his descent until he was only a dozen paces above the ground. The people below scattered as he leveled off and skimmed over the enemy's heads. He had just started to ascend when a brilliant white light arced up from the ground, striking the phoenix's flaming body. The bird's fires immediately extinguished. Breayn's heart sank as Danny switched back into his Berrat form and fell from the sky. He landed in the middle of a raging inferno that was spreading out across the grassland.

Treedale screamed out. Breayn thought it was at the sight of Danny's fall, but the sound of wingbeats told her she was being attacked from above. She had been so entranced by Ryn and Danny's problems that she completely neglected her own. Treedale screamed out again. Not knowing what was going on above her, Breayn tucked her wings to her side and dropped altitude. As best as she could, she craned her neck around and peered up into the night sky.

A blast of flame ignited a pair of great hawks. Breayn's mind reeled at the sight. She had seen Danny fall. It couldn't be him. Another series of bright red bursts lit up the sky, along with the face of Ulip, sitting astride a fire drake.

He did it. He actually did it. He got the fire drakes to bear him into battle.

⸎

"Sweet Titan," Kit exclaimed as she took in the sight. The night sky was filled with griffin riders, hawk riders, and fire drakes. She watched as a griffin rider, with his long, trailing white banner, swooped towards a hawk and its rider. Three hawk riders, all sporting long red banners, joined in the pursuit.

"Do you have enough strength to fight?" Kit asked Lump through their bond. *"If you don't, we need to stay clear."*

"I don't know," Lump replied.

Kit could feel the trepidation in his words. It was possible that he had enough strength to continue flying, but he was fearful of engaging in aerial combat.

"Lump, if you're afraid, please tell me." There was a prolonged silence.

"Lump," Fury said, *"Fighting in the sky is a part of you. You can do this, but if you are afraid to fight, you will fail."*

"I am afraid," the dragon-dog said, *"but I will not let our friends die for it."*

"Okay then," Kit's heart surged, *"let's go help the griffin riders."*

"The riders with banners are not our friends," Lump said with absolute certainty. *"They are attacking Mukale and Treedale. Yuka and her nest mates are attacking the right people. We need to keep the enemy off our friends."*

"We dragons have excellent vision and even better insights," Fury said. He really sounded like a proud pappa when he spoke of Lump.

"I trust you, Lump. Flame on."

Lump filled his chest with air, stoking the fires within. He pumped his wings several times and rushed forward. The fire drakes screeched out a greeting to the approaching dragon. At least, that's what Kit believed it was. They all blew out a quick series of fireballs before continuing their attacks on the enemy.

In moments, Lump was in the fray. The frenetic flight of the great hawks made them difficult to follow. Kit strained to pick out Treedale and Mukale in the mix. Even though her dark vision was excellent, everything was happening too quickly for her brain to process. Griffins were swooping in and out between the fire drakes. They were far more agile. They flew in over the fire drakes and raked their eagle claws across their thin, leathery wings. While the drakes could flame any enemy in front of them, their clumsy maneuvering made them mostly ineffective against their smaller, faster opponents.

"Hold tight," Lump said just before rolling over onto his back. He unleashed a steady stream of golden flames into the sky, igniting two hawk riders who were above him. A moment later, he righted himself and made his way back into the fray. *"Mukale and Treedale are directly ahead of us."*

The pair of young men were flying in concert, dipping and weaving, drawing enemies toward themselves before changing direction at the last moment. Three great hawks collided, sending their riders tumbling to the ground below. With nobody on their backs to guide them, the enormous birds broke off and flew east, likely returning to Silverhawk.

Kit's back suddenly exploded in pain. The screech of an eagle told her a griffin had just raked its claws across her back. She struggled to maintain her hold on Lump as her vision blurred.

"You're hurt," Lump called out into her mind. *"I'll take you to the city for healing."*

"No," Kit screamed at him. *"I just need a moment. Help our friends."* She could feel the indecision in Lump, but he followed Kit's orders and pressed forward, quickly flaming two more hawks and their riders.

"Titan, hear me." Kit struggled to get the words out. She could feel her consciousness slipping away. She couldn't finish her prayer. She just wanted to close her eyes.

"Your strength is my strength. Your journey is nearing its end. Now is not the time to give in to pain."

With the strength of Amaruq aiding her, Kit fought through the agony. "Titan, hear me." She grated out the words, fighting to remain conscious. "I need your healing." A faint yellow glow appeared on her hands. With each beat of her heart, the glow increased in intensity until it became blinding. An intense cold ripped through her, causing her muscles to spasm. Lump's body suddenly radiated intense heat. She felt like she had just stepped out of a blizzard and parked herself in front of a roaring fire. The deep cold continued to chill her body until she felt she could take no more. Lump continued warming his rider, sucking in deep gulps of air, stoking the inferno within his chest.

The intense cold vanished as quickly as it had appeared, releasing its grip on Kit. Lump's body cooled in response. "Thank you," she said, giving the dragon-dog a pat on the neck. "You saved me, again."

Just as Lump was about to engage in another combat, a powerful voice ripped through Kit's mind. *"Your end draws near, little priest. We will crush you and your pitiful force. Before the sun rises, you will all be dead and forgotten."*

CHAPTER THIRTY-TWO

THE VOICE AND THE CLAW

"That which happens in the sky doesn't matter." The voice rolled across the open grasslands, smashing into Indie with the force of a war hammer. The power staggered him. The words pounded into his brain, muddling his mind.

"You will learn to bow before your betters, or you will be crushed into the ground. Your blood will feed the worms and the beetles. Your bones will be gnawed on by the ravens." Again, the words slammed into Indie, and again their effect was profound. His legs wobbled and his resolve wavered.

Indie closed his eyes tight, hoping it might help to shut out the voice. He had felt this before, but this time it was different. *It was compulsion. A vampire was casting her voice directly into his mind.*

"You will lay down your arms. You will welcome us as friends. You will willingly die for us."

The power in the words was even stronger this time. Indie's mind churned while his resolve crumbled. Those who stood near him obeyed the commands and threw their weapons to the ground. Their eyes were vacant, their faces were slack. A soft whine and a nudge drew Indie's attention. Runt had moved in beside him and jabbed his muzzle against the young man's arm. The dire wolf's rough tongue rubbed against the back of his hand.

Indie blinked at the oversized pup. What was he doing? His bright, jade green eyes were speaking to him, but he didn't understand. Their intensity screamed a message that Indie couldn't hear. The wolf nudged him with his muzzle again and turned his nose skyward, toward the battle that raged overhead. There were hawks, and griffins, and drakes, and a dragon. There was a gold dragon flying through the sky above. It was carrying a girl. A beautiful girl with long red hair. A griffin nearly snatched her off the back of the dragon. Indie's breath hitched and his heart swelled.

In an instant, his mind cleared. Indie quickly surveyed the people with whom he stood shoulder to shoulder. All but Runt were mesmerized, enthraled by the voice ringing through their minds. Runt stared up at Indie, waiting patiently for something.

"Thank you, boy." Indie's voice was barely a whisper. Runt's lips parted, allowing his huge pink tongue to loll out the side. "I'm back."

⌖

The griffin that had attacked Kit circled around to come in for another pass. Lump was doing his best to maneuver himself into battle, but he had barely just learned to fly. He was not ready for such aerial acrobatics.

In the chaos, it was difficult to tell friend from foe. Kit was thankful the griffin riders from Silverhawk were all wearing their colored scarves. It was the only way she could easily tell them apart from Mukale and Treedale.

Why were the griffin riders attacking their allies?

Jayne and Sellina had assured Kit that the riders had all been bought and paid for. And several of these riders were trailing white banners. They were the healers. They were already supposed to be on their side. Had something changed?

Lump pumped his wings to gain altitude. Flames were leaking out the corners of his mouth with each beat. His dragon magic surged within his chest, giving him the strength to climb. The griffin giving chase followed. The griffin was swift and nimble, easily able to match Lump's maneuvers. The gold dragon suddenly dipped. A deafening screech drew Kit's attention just before a dark red blur raced past. She watched in horror as Yuka snatched the rider off the back of the griffin. The fire drake bit the person in two before releasing his remains, letting them fall from the sky.

"Hold on," Lump called out, just before rolling onto his back. He blew a thick column of flame into the sky, lighting up two hawk riders that were directly overhead. The pair screamed out as the firestorm engulfed them, sending them tumbling into the darkness below.

"Can you get me closer to Treedale and Mukale? We need to keep the enemy off them." Kit's neck craned about, looking for other attackers while Lump increased his speed. The wind whipped her flaming red hair about her head. Even if the sky smelled of smoke and tasted of ash, the exhilaration of the flight and the fight was intoxicating. Perhaps she was enjoying it a little too much.

The same voice Kit had heard earlier rang in her ears. *"Cease hostilities. Come to me."*

The magic in the words washed over Kit. They were compelling. Their siren's song pulled at her, commanding her to listen and obey. Her body suddenly felt cold, like a chill had crept into her and clutched her heart. Lump dropped abruptly, leaving Kit's stomach hundreds of feet above her. The dragon-dog's body became an inferno. It was pleasantly hot, warming Kit from head to toe, forcing away the chill, clearing her mind.

"Thank you, Lump." All the fliers who had been in combat were now earth-bound, heading for a trio that stood at the lead of the army. Ulip sat limp on Yuka's back as she slowly circled, her altitude dropping at a controlled pace. The other fire drakes followed her in a similar fashion. It took Kit several seconds to realize they were all under the influence of compulsion, a magic that was infinitely stronger than anything she had previously felt.

"Follow the other drakes," Kit said, patting the dragon's scaly neck. *"Mimic what they're doing."*

Lump spread his wings and drifted lower and lower. The mounted hawks and griffins had already landed. Their riders slid off their backs and bowed to the leaders. Mukale and the hawk he was riding landed shortly thereafter. When the bird's feet hit the ground, the young man slipped off its back and took a knee. The hawk he was riding shifted into Berrat form. It was Breayn. Lump continued to circle. The hawk Treedale was riding landed beside Breayn. The bird shifted into a Berrat male Kit didn't recognize. Rider and mount immediately took a knee, lowering their heads in respect to the leader, the woman who had called for them to land.

Where's Danny? She had seen the phoenix in the skies when she'd arrived, but she had lost him in the heat of the battle. Her eyes scanned the area, but she couldn't see him.

One by one, the drakes landed. Like the other riders, Ulip slid down and took a knee. The drakes circled the trio, spread out their wings, and rested their chins on the ground. When Lump touched down, Kit slid from his back and kneeled. Lump looked at the drakes, saw their posture, and mimicked it.

"Excellent," a different voice called out. It was smooth and practiced. It was accustomed to being in command. There was no magic in it, but there was power. The man was dressed in gold armor and had a plumbed helm. A low growl gurgled in the back of Kit's throat. It was King Karter, or his body at least, and whoever had possessed him. Rusty's father walked up to Ulip and Yuka and practically cooed. "I hadn't expected to garner the support of such wondrous creatures. A fire drake willing to bear a rider, and a Gigas warrior, no less. It's unheard of. I look forward to hearing your story."

King Karter's gaze shifted from Yuka to the gold dragon who was laying prostrate next to the drake. He clapped his hands together, looking like a small child who had just been given an extra helping of sweets. He was giggling as he continued his childish display.

"The universe is with me," he said, his eyes wide. "The universe has given me a dragon, a wondrous, spectacular gold dragon." With those words, his clapping stopped, and his lips pressed together into a thin red line, dragged down at the corners by a frown. "And how has a dragon escaped the mountains? I don't know what creature you are, but you are not a dragon."

The look of disillusionment melted away when King Karter's eyes drifted over to where Kit was. It was the first time he noticed her or recognized her. His giggles were renewed. "What have you caught in your web, Lady Voice? What treasure have you pulled from the heavens and delivered unto me?"

Kit lowered her head, trying to appear reverent, or at least fearful. She could no longer see the man, but she could hear his giggles and his silly clapping.

"Lady Voice, tell her to stand before me. No, no. Tell her to stand and to *bow* before me. I want to watch her grovel, like the dog she is."

⁓⦿⁓

Indie and Runt moved forward with the rest of the throng. Coldforge kept pace with Indie, stepping mindlessly forward. The sparkle in his eyes was completely absent. Lin was walking next to Whistler, with Char and Angel just a few steps behind them. Char glanced over at Indie and shook out his mane. Angel mimicked the action. Indie couldn't tell if Lin was acting entranced or not. If she wasn't, she was an excellent actor, and that bothered Indie more than he'd have liked. This girl just seemed to be good at everything that involved deception.

The sight of the drakes and the gold dragon lying prostrate before the enemy made Indie's stomach turn. If the voice in his head was a standard compulsion, he knew Kit could easily withstand it. But if it wasn't, he wasn't so sure. He and Runt had been trained on how to steel their minds to such events, and even so, the commands had taken hold of him. If it wasn't for Runt... his worries lessened. Lump had also undergone the same training. Runt had withstood it, so surely, Lump could have as well. He and Kit had to be faking. They just had to be.

The man in the plumbed helm came into clear view. Indie remembered him from their last encounter on the beachhead. Kit had bested him, then. She would best him again, now. It was Rusty's father, King Karter, and whoever had taken up residence within his body. He had just said something to the Berrat woman standing next to him. She was strikingly beautiful. Her skin was a pale bronze, and her hair was long and straight, hanging well past her waist. She had smiled warmly to King Karter and nodded. She glided over to Kit and whispered something. Indie's heart stopped when Kit slowly rose to her feet and bowed to King Karter.

Sweet Titan, she wasn't able to resist. Runt whined and rubbed his body against Indie's waist. Angel knickered and shook her head.

"What am I to do with you, little priest?" King Karter's words were loud and clear. "You and your pet are wondrous creatures. How best can I use you to achieve my ends?"

"I am but a blunt instrument at your command," Kit replied, bowing again before the king. "Wield us as you will." The King's eyes widened at her words. He slipped his helm from his head and leaned in close. He was much too close. Indie's blood boiled. The vile man bent himself low and kissed Kit full on the lips. Kit kissed him back. The desire to rip the man to pieces coursed through Indie's veins. His heart pounded in his ears like a kettle drum. The dragon in Indie reared up, ready to unleash its fury upon the man who would force himself upon his love.

Runt whined and bumped into Indie. He shook like he was trying to rid his body of unwanted fleas.

"Excellent," the king said as he stepped back. His fingers went to his lips. He closed his eyes as though savoring the taste of the girl. A slight hint of derision followed before he wiped his mouth with the back of his hand. "And what else do we have here?"

He moved past Kit and stood next to the gold dragon. "You cannot be what you appear to be." King Karter rubbed his chin thoughtfully. "If you are not a dragon, then what are you?" Lump immediately changed from his dragon form to his human self.

"I am known as Lump." The young man's voice was reverent. He bowed deeply. "I was touched by dragon magic, and this was the result. I hope it pleases you." The king giggled, the glee in him overflowing.

"It does please me. It pleases me very much. I would ask how you came upon this dragon magic." Lump was just about to answer when King Karter spotted Danny. He was a few dozen paces away on one knee. He was breathing heavily. Before Lump could answer the king's question, the man waved his hand, dismissing whatever tale the dragon-man might tell.

"The phoenix. I have the phoenix at my command." King Karter motioned to the Voice to follow him. The other Berrat man who was standing beside them stayed in close lockstep as he strode towards Danny. "Stand before me, young man. Why are you breathing so hard?"

Indie was relieved to see King Karter move away from Kit and Lump. His relief was swept away when he saw Danny. Like Kit, he, too, had been caught in the vampire's snare. If both he and Kit had fallen, all hope was lost. Dread welled up in his belly as he watched Danny fold to the pressure of the woman's voice.

⊂⊂⊃⊙⊙⊙⊙⊂⊃

Danny stood and bowed deeply. "Changing into the phoenix is difficult. Fighting the griffins and great hawks used up much of my energy. Forgive my weakness."

The Berrat who had stood with the Voice and King Karter stepped forward. It had to be the Claw. It was the only thing that made any sense to Danny.

"You are untrained." The Claw's voice was that of a seasoned commander. "Under my tutelage, you will achieve your maximum potential. You will be the most devastating force to have ever graced the skies."

"Do you think he can kill a dragon?" King Karter asked of the man. When the Berrat didn't answer, the king's voice raised. "Lord Claw. I asked you a question." The Berrat sneered at the king.

"Your impatience is your weakness, King Karter. You would do well to remain calm when things appear to not be going your way." The King's hands curled up into tight fists. His neck and cheeks flushed, and a heavy sneer twisted his face. "In your current state, dear king, you would do well to not engage in martial combat. It would not go well for you."

King Karter swallowed hard and looked around. The confidence in his stance vanished.

"And, to answer your question, yes." The Claw smiled and cocked an eyebrow. "After watching what the phoenix can do, and how he will grow with proper training, I believe he could kill a dragon with little effort. Although, I'm not sure how hot his fire burns. It may not be enough to surpass the resistance of a true dragon. But dragons have weaknesses if one knows how to exploit them."

Danny struggled to maintain the phoenix within. She wanted to burst forward, to incinerate the enemy who stood so dangerously close to her. She wanted to burn everything and everyone who associated with these heinous people. Danny wanted to let her. He wanted to revel in her righteous flames. He let his eyes drift to Kit. She was standing so still. She didn't react at all when the vile creature kissed her. It took every ounce of his self control to not let the phoenix out when that happened. It was not the time to react. He had to keep control of himself, and the firebird who was begging for him to release her.

"I think it might be fun to see just how much damage this phoenix boy can do." King Karter wrung his hands together. His eyes were wild. The grin on his lips was nothing short of pure insanity. "I want to see him fight the little priest and the dragon-boy. Let's see how the firebird will fare against such a dangerous opponent."

"Why would you pit me against a little girl?" Danny's brows furrowed while the phoenix blazed behind his eyes. "If you wish to test me in combat, let me fight the big man and his drake. That would be a worthy opponent."

"Is that fear I see in your eyes, oh mighty phoenix?" King Karter pushed his face towards Danny. The young Berrat stepped closer, allowing his nose to brush lightly against the king's.

"If you would prefer, I can fight them both. I will prove my strength. I will prove my loyalty. In fact, I will fight this one." Danny turned to Lord Claw. "The bards sing epic songs, describing him as the most powerful, the most skilled fighter to have ever walked the lands. He thinks he is my better. Let me prove to you he is not."

King Karter's head snapped back. His grin widened into a broad smile. "Oh, that sounds wonderful."

"No, he will not fight my brother," the Voice said. "How dare you? The spider god will hear of your treachery. You will rescind that statement. Now!"

Even though the Voice had not directed her magic at Danny, he felt it wash over him. His will practically crumbled. He wanted to fall at the woman's feet and beg for her acceptance.

Sweet Titan. Her words are pure power. They are compelling even when they're not directed at me. The phoenix must have protected me from her.

King Karter lost control. Even in the gathering darkness, the rising purple in his face was visible. "You would dare to use your powers on me, vessel. It was because of me you have your powers. I gave them to you. I gave you both the powers you possess. I can just as easily withdraw them and grind you into paste."

"You will bow before me, deceiver. I do not take orders from you. The gifts we were given are ours to do with as we please. You cannot order me to do anything for you. I will not allow you to put my brother in harm's way." The Voice was screeching the words out. Her eyes took on an intensity that Danny had never seen before. With every word she spoke, his will crumbled further. He wanted to kill the man standing before her. He wanted to wrap his flames around him and burn him to a crisp. She was just about to continue her tirade when her head snapped to the side, her voice permanently silenced.

"I didn't think she'd ever stop talking." Pental shrugged as the woman crumpled and dropped to the ground, her head and neck in an unnatural position.

Indie launched himself at Pental. He had about fifteen paces to cover to reach the vampire. The man had just done them a service, but without the woman's control over the people, all Helja was about to break loose. Was that his intent? To sow discord and watch the people rip themselves apart? This was exactly what he had done to Kit at Templeton. He wasn't sure Kit had ever recovered from the deaths she'd caused, the deaths of dozens of innocents.

Well before he had reached the vampire, Pental swept in at the Claw. With inhuman reflexes, the Claw reached out and grabbed Pental by the throat and slammed him to the ground. Indie stumbled as he tried to close the gap. He watched in hopeful fascination as the Claw closed his grip on Pental's neck, only to see the vampire turn into a puff of ash before reassembling once again behind the Claw. He thrust his dagger-like fingers forward, burying them into the small of the Berrat's back. The Claw bellowed out in agony and threw his head back, striking Pental flush in the face.

As the vampire stumbled backward, the Claw spun about and dove at his opponent. A blade that Indie hadn't seen before was suddenly in the Berrat's hand. He thrust it repeatedly into Pental's chest. Indie was now barely a step away when he heard the vampire's guttural voice. Blood sprayed from his mouth with each word he spoke.

"Finish him." Pental thrust his hands forward, clutching onto the Claws' wrist. "You can't let him live. Kill him." The vampire had willingly given his life to kill the Crow leader. He seemed willing to die, just to end this man's life.

Indie's blade was already in his hand. He didn't recall drawing the weapon, but it was there just the same. With the Claws' back to him, he took a wide arcing swing, throwing every ounce of strength he had into it. His obsidian long sword sliced cleanly into the Berrat. It bit deeply, slicing through flesh and bone alike. The Berrat spun towards Indie. He had nearly been chopped in half and yet he was raising his blade, preparing to strike. Pental appeared behind the Crow and wrapped his arms around his chest, pinning the Claw's arms to his sides.

"Remove his head." Pental's face was deathly pale. Without thinking, Indie raised his blade and swung it at the Berrat's neck. A quick spray of blood splashed across his eyes obscuring his vision. He couldn't tell if he had been successful or not.

"Well done," Pental called out. "You have only King Karter to deal with now."

Indie ran his fingers across his eyes, wiping away the thick, warm liquid. He blinked rapidly, trying to rid himself of the remaining blood. When his vision cleared, the Berrat leader lay dead on the ground, his head several feet from his body. Pental was nowhere to be seen.

Chapter Thirty-Three

And the Evil Shall Burn

The assembled soldiers from both sides stood transfixed, confused by the events that had just unfolded. Kit looked for her cohorts. Many were perhaps two dozen paces to her left. She could see Danny, Indie, and Runt. To her right were Treedale, Mukale, Breayn, and the unknown Berrat man. At her side, Lump stood proud and tall. His shaggy hair hung over his eyes, giving him a devil may care look, but she knew there was so much more brewing just under the young man's skin. Lin stepped up on Kit's right with the three horses still in tow. Calian moved in silently beside her. Between Indie and Kit was Coldforge, standing shoulder to shoulder with his dwarven clan.

"What are you all doing standing there?" King Karter screamed out. When none of his soldiers moved, he threw his helm to the ground, his teeth bared, his jaw clenched. "Kill them!"

A griffin rider stepped forward. He held his white scarf in his hand, keeping it from dragging on the ground. The man was immense. "If you want us to continue following you, deal with these people yourself."

Ulip and Yuka had landed amongst the hawk riders. The giant's bulk appeared out of the darkness, shrouded in a cloud of smoke the fire drake had streaming from her nostrils. He walked up to the commander and stood shoulder to shoulder with him. Kit expected the pair had found some sort of accord. When Ulip's fist snapped out like a cobra, catching the hulking commander cleanly in the temple, Kit realized she was wrong. The commander's body went stiff on contact and remained that way until he bounced off the ground.

"You have none who will stand against the Fire Drake Clan," the giant said. "You don't have the witch with the poisonous words to assist you, to warp our minds, to force us to do your bidding."

"You've lost." Kit said, stepping forward. "I don't know who you are, but we are going to rip you from that body, and we will..."

"You will, what?" King Karter's chest swelled as he stepped forward. He might have been shorter than Ulip, but he was well over a head taller than Kit, and he was not above putting it to his advantage. "Do you think I need these mortals to deal with the likes of you? Do you think..."

The man's words were cut short when Kit slammed her battle hammer into his ornately carved breastplate. He staggered back a few steps and quickly hurled a fireball at Kit. She did nothing to evade the attack. The spell exploded on her chest, its flames quickly engulfing her. She took a deep breath and smiled as the blaze receded. It was only at that moment she noticed her armor was barely hanging off her. When the griffin had raked her back, it had ripped it completely through. Anger welled up inside the girl's chest. The armor had been a gift from Fenrir herself, and now it was ruined.

"You are a curiosity, little priest. I have yet to discover your secret, but I will." Kit smiled and stepped closer to King Karter. She let her armor drop to the ground, revealing the thin white shirt she was wearing beneath.

"I will share my secret with you, deceiver. I am your better. In fact, almost every living soul around you is your better. You are a spineless worm. You can try to fight all you like, but you will lose. We are fighting for justice and freedom, and you will never keep us down."

"I have your mother." King Karter's statement was pure truth, and it cut Kit as deeply as any blade could. "I was planning to just leverage her power, but instead, I will make sure her last days are spent wailing in torment."

Kit burst into flames. The heat from her body was so intense that all but Lump, who had shifted back into his dragon form, retreated. Indie moved in from her left, his body wrapped in golden scales. King Karter threw his arms up in front of his face to shield himself from the heat.

"Impressive," he chortled. "No wonder my fire attacks did you no harm. So, the little abomination has finally discovered her true nature."

Kit was about to step forward when Indie grasped her by the shoulder. She wheeled on him, her flames intensifying. Despite the look of pain on the man's face, he refused to release his grip. "If you kill him, you'll never find your mother." The flames that had engulfed the pair subsided. When they were fully extinguished, Kit nodded.

"Ulip," Kit said, her voice sweet but tinged with venom. "Can you detain this man? I would like to bring him inside for questioning." Ulip grunted and slowly stalked toward King Karter. He rested his hand on the man's shoulder and squeezed. The would-be prisoner spun about and struck Ulip cleanly on the chin, staggering the giant. Ulip grinned slightly before pouncing on the man. The two rolled around on the ground, with the smaller man delivering several vicious blows. The look of self confidence had long since disappeared from Ulip as the man continued to best him.

Coldforge chuckled and tossed his ax to the ground. "Let me have a go at him." Throwing caution to the wind, the dwarf waded into the melee and threw himself onto King Karter, swinging his rock-fists at the enemy. With such a thick beard, it was difficult to see any facial expressions, but the dwarf's eyes were wide, showing signs of panic. "He's much stronger than he looks," Coldforge grunted out as he tried to get a clean hold on the enemy.

From Kit's left, Breayn appeared. It looked like she, too, was going to jump into the fray. She was tall for a Berrat, but she was no physical match for these men. Even so, she moved in close. "Hold his arm," she called out. "I need his hand."

Kit didn't understand what was going on. What hope could the Berrat woman have, joining into this brawl? When she caught sight of gold glinting in Breayn's hand, her curiosity doubled. The Berrat man Kit didn't know moved in beside her.

Despite their best efforts, Coldforge and Ulip couldn't get a clean grip on King Karter's arm. He twisted and turned like a constrictor while he continued to rain down blows on his enemy. The Berrat man standing beside Breayn suddenly shifted into a great brown bear. He curled his lips back and bellowed out a challenge. There was a slight pause in the fighting as all three combatants turned towards the tremendous roar. With surprising speed, the bear lurched forward and seized King Karter's forearm in his jaws. The man screamed out, but he could not extricate himself from the bear's grip. Coldforge and Ulip immediately grappled the King to the ground, completely subduing him. The dwarf nodded to Breayn, who jumped forward and grabbed King Karter's fingers, wrenching them backward like she was trying to snap them. As soon as she had a single finger isolated, she jammed a ring upon it. It was a small, unadorned circle of gold. Instantly, King Karter's body went slack.

"What did ye do to him?" Coldforge asked. He stood up from the ground and inspected the man. "Did ye suck the life from him?"

"I did nothing like that," Breayn said with a victorious smile. "I merely slipped Rusty's ring on him; the one the Hobgoblins had created to subdue her father's spirit. That little piece of gold is a prison, trapping whoever is inside this man until we take it off him."

Ulip picked himself up off the ground. His face was badly bloodied, and his mood appeared even more battered. Having been bested by a human had crushed him. "What are you going to do with him?" He motioned to King Karter. "My drake would like to eat him. The others have offered to help, even though no help is needed."

The great bear changed back into his Berrat form. Breayn gave him a quick smile. "Thank you, Ryn. What would I ever do without you?"

"And what will we do with his soldiers?" Indie asked, moving in beside Kit. "They still heavily out number us and it's not like we can take them prisoners."

"I don't know." Kit said. A golden aura pulsated around her hands. She moved towards Ulip to heal him, but he held his hands out to keep her away. She understood. It was a lesson that Sister Gale had taught everyone in her combat classes. Wounds are a steady reminder of what you did wrong. The aura dissipated, and Kit sighed. It felt like the weight of the world rested upon her shoulders. "Let them go. If any want to stay, tell Rusty to find them a place. I cannot tell friend from foe, and I'm too tired to interrogate them all."

"I can tell," Danny said. "Or at least, the phoenix can."

⤛⤛⤛⟡⤜⤜⤜

Kit climbed onto Lump's back. She could swear that he was larger than the last time she rode him, barely an hour ago. The horns on his neck were definitely more pronounced than they had been. They were now easily large enough to be used as handles. She slipped her necklace over her head and called out to the gathered soldiers.

"The Split Crow leaders are all dead. Lay down your arms and you will be spared." From her back, Kit could hear the cheers of her army. In front of her were hundreds upon hundreds of stern faces. The little priest didn't know what to do. In every other battle she'd fought in, once the leadership was removed, the soldiers changed allegiances. These soldiers were standing strong. The only thing that wasn't clear was why they weren't attacking.

Danny strode up beside Kit. "I can change into my phoenix to see who is still against us."

"They are all against you," Calian said. Kit's eyebrows went up a notch when the woman sidled up next to Danny. "I can smell the fear pouring off them in waves. They want to attack, but without someone to urge them forward, they won't."

"How many of the soldiers who witnessed the defeat of their leaders are still truly against us?" Indie looked out at the gathered soldiers. Many were confused, many more looked terrified. The news of the leaders falling had spread through the attackers like wildfire.

Danny shrugged at the question. "I'll need to be in phoenix form to say for sure." Breayn stepped in close and put her hand on his forearm.

"Can you call upon the phoenix without completely giving in to her? She may give you her sight without fully transforming." Danny's eyes turned to flame, tiny wisps of smoke curling up from their corners.

"All of them are our enemies," Danny said. "But two of them stand out from the rest." Danny continued to survey the front-line soldiers, who were slowly forming a half circle around the group. The Berrat strode forward, heading for a slender Nomad female. "What is your name?" The woman jutted out her chin, refusing to answer the question.

Kit, still sitting astride Lump, came strolling up to her. "Was the question too difficult for you to answer?" The woman shuddered at the sight of the gold dragon but remained steadfast in her silence. Indie moved forward, putting himself between the woman and the others. He quickly noted that she was dressed in fine armor, much too elaborate for her to be a regular soldier.

"My lady, my name is Indigo Willowbrook." The woman's bearing didn't change, other than perhaps to add a sneer to her already haughty demeanor. Lin slid in beside Indie. She brushed him lightly as she stepped past.

"You are clearly a woman of distinction," Lin began. She did not bow but still showed the woman significant respect. "My name is Lady Aithlin of House Arthure. Now that the Crow's leadership has been – removed, we will seek to install new leaders. Based on your bearing and demeanor, you are clearly a woman accustomed to wielding power, ready to keep people in line."

The woman's chest swelled, and her nose rose in haughty derision. "And what place do you see for me in this new hierarchy?" Lin pursed her lips at the question.

"That would entirely depend on your leadership experience and your standing." Lin practically yawned out the words.

Kit couldn't help but marvel at Lin as she conducted herself. The woman's actions were smooth as silk, but she knew her friend was as dangerous as any viper.

"I am Baroness Eldrite, ruler of Moresby. King Karter promised me a seat on his small council should I bring my army to him. This act of generosity on my part came at substantial risk and at an even greater cost. I command seven thousand soldiers and I rule a barony of over twenty thousand people. I supply King Faol with over two thousand slaves each season, even in the harshest of winters." The woman gave a dismissive wave. "Even if over half of those *animals* die in transit, he still gets more from me than any other ruler."

"You lying sack of entrails." A man of perhaps forty summers, with long blonde hair, stepped out from the assembled crowd of soldiers. He was dressed in even more elaborate armor than the woman was, but the way he moved across the ground told Kit he was a skilled fighter. The way his fingers were moving reminded him of Lin when she was casting a spell.

"You don't command half that many soldiers and it doesn't matter if it's winter or summer. Your slaves die because you don't know the first thing about moving people across the lands of the north." The baroness' mouth flopped open, and she sputtered. "That was the most intelligent and honest bit of uselessness that has ever spilled from your mouth. Do everyone a favor and keep your trap shut."

"Now, now, Lord...?" Lin smiled sweetly at the man as he neared. She looked down at his hand as he continued to weave a spell of some sort. "You are among friends." Lin's eyebrows shot up and a wicked smile crossed her face. "I don't know what spell you intend on casting, but I'm guessing that this dragon or this phoenix can immolate you before you can finish speaking the words."

The man's finger gestures stopped immediately. His face grew flush, making his blonde hair stand out all the more.

"I am Baron Weysel, ruler of Cassiar. The vast majority of this army is my own. I am to be King Karter's Master General in his new hierarchy, while the baroness will probably be nothing more than a bedwarmer for the king. Her mouth reeks of fish and garlic, but she is a comely thing."

"You're just jealous because he doesn't find you attractive." Baroness Eldrite stuck her nose in the air while her face soured.

Lin smiled and inclined her head just enough to be respectful. "Oh, I'm sure you both excel at whatever you do, and I am more than confident that you can both hold a seat of power in the new regime. Please accompany me to the manor so that we can discuss this in more detail. I'm sure our underlings can get the rabble back in lockstep once again. You must be tired and hungry after your journey. We have wonderful facilities set up that I'm sure you'd enjoy."

"Allow us to assist, Mistress Aithlin." Jayne gave Sellina a nearly imperceptible signal. She nodded lightly and motioned for several dozen of the Auctioneers to follow.

Lin remained quiet until the prisoners were well out of earshot. "Danny, were Baroness Eldrite and Baron Weysel the two you identified as enemies?" The Berrat nodded briskly, his impish grin on full display.

"Nothing has changed amongst the others, though," he offered. "They're still our enemies. They don't trust us."

Kit touched the pearl necklace that hung from her neck. "Soldiers of House Eldrite and House Weysel, I welcome you to Cormorant. We know that some of you no longer wish to be slavers. We know that most of you were put in the untenable position of following orders or dying. Tonight, you are no longer slavers. Tonight, you are free. You can choose to return home or to stay with me and continue to fight until all slaves are freed, and the land is returned to the Berrat people."

The bulk of the soldiers who stood before Kit brandished their weapons and surged forward. Lump immediately flamed, melting everyone within a dozen paces. Despite the carnage, the soldiers continued to press into combat. Danny shifted into his phoenix form and joined into the fray. Moments later, the sky was filled with fire drakes, drenching the ground in their own fiery attacks.

In minutes, the area looked like the remains of a forest fire.

"Hold," Kit called out, the power of her magnified voice echoing across the grassland. "Hold," she called out again. Danny and the fire drakes returned, landing next to Kit.

Kit pulled off her necklace. "How many of the remaining people are still against us?" she asked.

"Many," Danny replied. "But they are running. The forest is filled with them."

"And those who are not running?"

"Most of those who remain have changed their allegiances." Kit nodded while she considered Danny's words.

"Wait until we have those who are not hostile to us out of the way," Indie said to Danny. "Then set the forest ablaze. We cannot let them escape."

Kit's face blanched. She looked to the east, where the sky was brightening. A new day was dawning. A new day without slavery in the north. "Burn them all," she said. "They are beyond redemption."

Runt and Coldforge walked up to the group, the dwarf dragging the lifeless body of King Karter behind him. "He just went limp. Yer wolf was guarding him. He was fightin' and strugglin', and then he just went limp. He still breathes, but there is no fight left in him."

A blinding light erupted in the middle of the field's charred remains. It continued on for several seconds, making it impossible to look into it. From within the brilliance came a slow, thunderous clap. While the rhythm of the clapping remained unchanged, the sound became louder and louder. When the light finally dimmed, a blue giant appeared. He was easily a head taller than Ulip and just as muscled. His body was covered in a thick layer of ice, or perhaps he was entirely made of ice. It was difficult to discern skin from armor. Everything appeared to be seamless.

An enormous dire wolf stood at his side with several dozen more dire wolves at his back. The lead wolf's lips were pulled back, exposing his vicious canines. Streams of drool poured between his terrible teeth. From behind Kit, Runt stepped out. His hackles were raised from the tip of his head to the base of his tail. A low snarl rumbled in his chest while, like the massive wolf before him, he put his own teeth on display.

Kit's heart was thumping in her chest. As big as Runt was, this wolf was bigger, and he looked more than capable of taking on the young pup, even if he had been blessed by Fenrir. Indie's concern turned to terror as more and more dire wolves continued to appear at the larger wolf's back. They spread out in a semicircle.

Lump looked over the wolves and bellowed out a roar with enough force that several of the dire wolves turned tail and bolted. Runt barked and snarled at the dragon. He looked to be chastising his friend. Kit's thoughts were confirmed when Lump slunk back, leaving Runt on his own. She slid down from the dragon's back and moved in beside Runt. She gently placed her hand on his back. The wolf's body stiffened in response.

Ymir, the ice god, stepped closer to his own wolf. He pulled his trident from its sheath and waved it at Kit. "Don't you think it would be fun to let these two determine who is the Alpha of the north? Shade here has garnered the support of the dire wolf population, but the grays are not yet willing to declare their allegiance to him. It would have been so much easier had Fenrir named a new alpha, but since she didn't, Shade has taken the position himself. It seems your wolf is the only challenger worthy of the post."

CHAPTER THIRTY-FOUR

THE ALPHA AND THE OMEGA

Amilta, in her small female gray wolf form, appeared from behind Runt and took up a position on his right flank. She snarled at Shade, her tongue licking out from between her fangs, saliva dripping from the corners of her mouth. A dozen more wolves of varying sizes gathered behind the pair. Another gray, much larger than Amilta, took up a position beside the smaller female. As large as this wolf was, he was dwarfed by Runt. The trio held their ground, waiting for the dire wolf, Amaruq's Omega, to do something.

"Isn't that sweet," Ymir cooed. "Your pup has friends who want to help him fight the big bad wolf."

Runt snarled and snapped at the two grays by his side. The larger male backed away, but Amilta, the much smaller female, held her ground. This seemed to amuse Ymir all the more.

"It's cute how this little bitch thinks she can make a difference." Ymir was practically giddy. "It looks like the son of Amaruq has a mate, or is she just an admirer, I wonder?"

A small Berrat girl with tight white braids and skin covered in blue whorls moved up beside Kit. She was shaking her head, looking up at the ice god with a mixture of pity and disdain.

"Your life has run its course," Fenrir said as a group of small dire wolves moved in around her. One wolf stood next to Kit and rubbed her shoulder against her. The little priest absentmindedly stroked the wolf's head, letting her fingers run through its thick, silky fur. These wolves looked so familiar. Kit had only met a few dire wolves in her lifetime, so it seemed unlikely that she'd ever laid eyes on these particular animals. Nevertheless, she recognized them. It wasn't until the jet-black female she was stroking nuzzled up under her arm that she understood.

"Hello there," Kit whispered, still scratching the wolf's head. "It's been a long time since I've seen you. Oh, how you've grown." This was Runt's sister, the one who'd helped him track down the rest of his littermates. The wolf gave Kit's hand a quick lick.

"If only Runt's mother was here to witness this." Amaruq's words resonated in Kit's mind. His voice was filled with pride, but there was also a hint of concern. She was certain of it. *"It is true that I am worried about my son. Not because he cannot defeat this Omega, but because he's afraid. He doesn't trust himself. Without faith in his abilities, my son will fail."*

Kit's golden aura immediately burst forth. She was about to step up beside the wolf pup, but a quick hand and a look of disapproval from Fenrir stayed her actions. The wolf god slowly shook her head, and the little priest closed her eyes and nodded. Kit understood what the god was telling her, even if she didn't want to hear it. Runt needed to do this for himself. He could not receive assistance from anyone.

Kit's teachings in the Temple flooded back to her; how each priest must stand alone, even if they are a part of a larger community. It's not the destination, it's the journey that's important and, right now, Runt's journey required him to either face his opponent, or back down and let him claim the leadership of the wolves. Shade would become the Prime Alpha. Runt was too young for such a decision. She didn't think he was ready. Is that what her mother thought as well when Kit left her village to travel to Aarall? She was only eleven cycles when Riva let her set out on her own. The woman was likely watching her along the way, but she still let Kit decide her own fate. With a worried sigh, the little priest put aside her fears and threw her full support behind her pup. "We're with you, Runt," she said, pulling her golden aura back into herself. "Have faith in yourself like we have faith in you."

Shade snarled at Kit's words and snapped the air in front of Runt's face. The wolf-pup cringed away, a small whimper escaping as he tucked his tail tight under his belly. The small female at his side renewed her snarls, taking a step back to keep close. A look of victory spread across the larger wolf's smug face.

"You are nothing," Kit said to Shade. "You are, Omega." Whether this was her talking or the wolf spirit within, Kit didn't know, but Shade's reaction was completely expected. The dire wolf leapt at Kit, ready to separate her head from her shoulders. He was mid-flight when Runt latched onto his throat. The pair landed roughly on the ground, but Runt maintained his grip. Shade twisted and turned, eventually landing on his back with Runt straddled over him. The enormous wolf raked Runt's belly with his claws. While the wolf's thick black fur offered some protection, Shade's razor-sharp nails got through to the soft flesh beneath. Runt released his grip with a startled yelp. He backed away with his tail again clenched firmly between his legs. The small female backed away, giving the larger males room to move.

Shade leapt to his feet and lunged. To avoid the attack, Runt dodged to the side, slamming into the wall of dire wolves that had gathered around the fighting pair. They snapped at him, driving the young wolf back towards Shade. They yipped and barked frantically and closed the circle even tighter, giving Amaruq's heir even less room to maneuver.

Runt's siblings barked frantically, either in warning or perhaps to cheer their brother on. As a group, they all moved in, almost closing the circle that had been forming. Lump, now back in his natural wolfdog form, joined the circle, moving in beside Amilta. There was an unsteady truce between Shade's pack and Runt's siblings. The addition of Lump and the small gray upset the balance. Several of the dire wolves made a move towards the wolfdog. Their movement quickly halted as several dozen grays moved in, taking up a position at their backs.

Runt and Shade circled one another, each wolf continuing to put on a display of strength. With their heads low and their hackles high, they snarled. With their lips pulled back to show off their array of formidable teeth, the two wolves almost looked unnatural. Kit had seen Runt bare his teeth before, but he had never looked like this. She winced when she noticed Shade's tail was held high and Runt's was still tucked tight between his legs. Her pup was putting on a good show, but he was terrified. Despite his fear, he was not backing down.

A dire wolf, a member of Shade's pack, snapped at Runt, clipping his haunch. The pup snarled and snapped at the attacker, trying to force him back. In that moment of distraction, Shade was on him. He had the pup in his jaws, his teeth clamped tightly around his waist. Shade picked the smaller wolf off the ground and tossed him at the wall of his supporters. They quickly mauled Runt before pushing him back in Shade's general direction. Another fight broke out between the dire wolves and the grays. Kit could feel the daemon within her losing control, wanting to be free to unleash its terror upon the pack that would dare to hurt her friend.

"Be at peace," Amaruq said to Kit. *"They are gauging each other. Omega needs to prove he is superior to my son in every way. He is not trying to kill him, not yet anyway. He seeks to embarrass him. It's the only way he will earn his leadership over the other wolves."*

The wolf spirit's words did not comfort Kit. She did not want to see Runt humiliated or killed. She wanted him safe and warm with her. She wanted to protect the pup and deliver justice upon any who would do him harm.

More gray wolves appeared beside Kit and Fenrir. There were now well over ten times as many grays backing Runt as there were dire wolves supporting Shade. Some joined in the battle between the grays and dire wolves while others yipped and barked. They seemed to be cheering Runt on.

"After my wolf kills yours," Ymir said with a mocking tone, "it will be my turn to kill you, little priest."

"Why wait?" Kit drew her hammer and gave it a spin. "Runt will have no difficulty in defeating this lowly Omega. He's only playing with him right now, showing the other wolves that he is the true Alpha. My guess is, he will humiliate your worthless wolf before giving him a chance to run. I'm also guessing that, like you, your wolf is too dull-witted to know when the fight is over."

"We will fight in good time, little priest. We will have our battle soon. I don't want to miss a moment of the entertainment." He tapped the shaft of his trident with an icy finger. "First Shade will defeat this pup, and then he will kill Fenrir. I wish to bear witness to both battles. I will watch as Shade relishes his kill, just as

I will relish killing you. I will savor it. I will drink in every one of your screams. I will inhale your dying breath as I subsume your essence."

"I'm sorry to tell you, traitor. You won't get the opportunity to fight her." Indie had his sword drawn and was moving towards Ymir. His actions seemed to amuse the ice god. He held his trident out before him, freezing Indie in his tracks.

"I can accommodate your wishes. I will gladly fight you first." The ice god's eyes widened. They had a horrible gleam to them. His cold, cracked lips curled up into a sinister grin. "I think it will be most delicious to watch the little priest's heart get crushed when I kill her love." Runt snarled at the ice god and shook the foam dripping from his lips. Again, Shade took advantage of the distraction and seized the opportunity. His body coiled before his hind legs thrust him forward. With his maw opened wide, and his claws outstretched before himself, he sought to end Runt's life. He would become the Alpha Prime.

There was a flash of white and a howl of agony. As Shade closed his jaws to get a killing grip on Runt's neck, the young wolf dropped low and rolled to his back. With his own bite, he lashed forward, catching his attacker by the throat. The pair tumbled and rolled. Shade twisted this way and that, but Runt held on. The larger wolf raked Runt with his powerful hind legs. Multiple times his claws ripped through soft flesh, and still, Runt held on. Like the Omega he was, the older, larger wolf cried out for help. He whined, begging for the others to step in. Through it all, Runt held on.

With the bulk of his body straddling Shade's, and with his teeth worrying their way into the larger wolf's neck, the fight was over. Shade's body went limp beneath the young wolf. Runt held his death grip for several more seconds before releasing. Shade's breathing was rapid and erratic, his once gray neck-ruff now soaked with crimson. He eyed the wolf who had defeated him, still standing over him. Slowly, he rolled to his side, and even more slowly rose to his feet. The defeated wolf stumbled momentarily while he tried to regain his composure.

"Attack," Ymir screamed! His voice was panicked, almost frightened. He repeatedly slammed the butt of his trident on the ground. He looked like an infant throwing a tantrum. "Attack. Kill him. Are you the Alpha or are you nothing more than an Omega, the lowest of the low?"

Fenrir, now in her Berrat warrior form, lightly placed her hand upon Kit's shoulder. "Listen," she breathed. Soft, soothing magic washed over Kit. "Listen and learn." The voices of every wolf suddenly filled Kit's mind. They were in chaos. There were too many words coming all at once. It was like listening in on a crowd of people, all trying to yell over one another.

"I am no Omega," Shade snarled.

The voices in Kit's mind immediately went silent, all except for Shade's.

"I am Shade, a wolf of the north. I stand before Runt, son of Amaruq, the true Alpha." Runt barked back a series of shrill, short yips. Lump and the small gray female also barked out. There were no words behind the vocalizations, but every wolf present understood their meaning.

"You have embarrassed our kind," Runt said as he closed in on Shade. "The moment you took up with this coward, your fate was sealed. Your shame will be your punishment. You are free to live on these lands. You are free to join any pack you choose. So long as you follow the teachings of Fenrir and the laws of the north, no harm will come to you."

"I will do as you say. I will follow the words of our god and I will do no harm. I will seek to protect the laws of the north, the laws of our kind." Shade bowed before Runt. All the dire wolves that had accompanied him followed his lead. With his head still low, Shade closed his eyes. "I would ask you for a second chance, my Alpha. Allow me to join your pack as your Omega. Allow me to earn my place once again."

Runt bowed back in response. "You must first prove yourself worthy. When you do, you will be welcomed back into the great pack once more. Opportunities abound if you keep your eyes and your heart open to them."

"He is his father's son, and he's going to be an outstanding leader," Fenrir said to Kit. The wolf god smiled warmly at the young priest, whose eyes were already brimming with tears. "When he's old enough, that is." Kit nodded briskly, wiping her cheek with the back of her hand.

A deep, rumbling laugh filled the night air. Ymir swung his trident out in front of himself, releasing a thick spray of ice as he did. The dire wolves, caught in the frost blast, yelped in pain. Their natural resistance to cold could not protect them fully. They bolted from their place, taking refuge behind Runt and Fenrir.

Kit ignited her hands in flame and brandished her battle hammer. "We will end this now, Ymir. I will give you a traitor's death and I will do everything in my power to make sure you suffer when I deliver justice unto you. You will feel the pain and anguish of those you've tortured, or whose lives you've ruined. I will ensure that tonight is the last night of your existence."

CHAPTER THIRTY-FIVE

A DUEL OF FIRE AND ICE

Ymir scoffed at Kit and pointed his trident at her face. "Those little magic tricks you pull are just that, tricks. You bested me once because you surprised me, and I was stuck within the confines of that limited body. Now I am in my true form, and you will not fool me a second time."

"You were King Karter? It was you in his body when I defeated him?" Kit smirked and rolled her shoulders. "I beat you once. I can beat you again."

"Your confidence will be your undoing, child." Ymir took two steps toward Kit before Indie cut him off.

"You killed my father. Today, I will have my vengeance." Indie brandished his sword and took a fighting stance. Ymir gave the young man a bored look.

"Out of my way, orphan. I have killed many fathers. I'm sure yours fell as easily as all the others. I could destroy you with a thought. The little girl, though, she may provide me with some entertainment before I eviscerate her."

"You're a coward. You didn't even have the courage to face my father yourself. You had to send diseased wolves to do your dirty work for you. If you believe I am no challenge, then do your worst, traitor." Ymir drove the tines of his trident towards Indie's chest. With practiced grace, he parried the attack and moved into a different fighting stance. "You'd think for a god you could to better than attempt a lame thrust. Perhaps you have relied on your godly powers for so long that you've forgotten how to fight like a man."

Indie's taunt enraged the ice giant. He thrust his trident forward again, this time with enough force to drive it entirely through Indie's chest. Indie stepped back and used his sword to deflect the blow toward the ground. He spun to his left and sliced at the giant's thigh. His obsidian weapon scored a clean blow but barely even chipped the giant's ice skin.

"You fight better than I expected," Ymir said, his voice dripping with sarcasm. "Perhaps I should just let you swing at me until your arms grow tired and then crush you under my foot."

Kit took a stance next to her man, her war hammer ready to strike. Indie's face turned purple with rage. "He's mine. I don't need your help."

"Oh, isn't that precious?" The sarcastic tone in Ymir's voice thickened. "Your little friend here is going to protect you."

"And who is going to protect you?" Indie asked, sweeping Kit behind him with his arm. "You no longer have your little wolf friends to call to your aid."

"Why would I need wolves when I have Ice Giants?" From well behind Ymir, a group of Ice Giants strode forward, each of them several feet shorter than Ymir. Like the ice god, they were a mixture of white and blue. Their skin looked like frost stretched over muscle. If they were wearing armor, it was impossible to discern. Ymir's face brightened as many of those gathered stepped away.

"I wonder," Ymir said, cocking an eyebrow. With a voice that feigned caring and dripped with sarcasm, he continued. "Shade told me he had killed a family of humans. Were they yours? Tsk, tsk. He told me how he'd killed a blubbering woman and a wee girl who bleated like a lamb when he sunk his teeth into her. He said she was particularly delicious. Too bad your father was too weak and too cowardly to protect them. He couldn't even protect himself." Indie flew into a rage at the man's words.

"My father was a great man, but you wouldn't recognize greatness if it bit you in your frosty ass. You are the coward, hiding behind the strength of others. Stop procrastinating and fight me." Ymir rolled his eyes and flung a fireball at Indie. It was big enough to engulf his entire body and took several seconds to dissipate. When it did, Indie was still standing right where he had been, still holding his obsidian blade. Only now his body was covered in golden scales from head to toe. At the sides of his neck were rows of tiny horns, just like the ones Lump had.

"Oh my," Ymir said, stabbing his trident's pole into the ground and leaning upon it. "Do we have ourselves another dragon wannabe? Did you know gold dragons are extremely vulnerable to the cold? I'll bet you didn't."

Indie pushed the point of his long sword into the ground and leaned on the pommel. "How powerful you must look to your pets, unable to beat a simple human in combat without resorting to magic. I expect the Ice Giants of Jotunheim would be disappointed by your weakness. These giants who stand behind you are not like the ones my father spoke of. My father spoke of their magnificence and their bravery. He spoke of their intelligence and their loyalty. You show none of these qualities. I'm not really sure how you can get anyone to follow you. You're a simpering coward. You're not a good fighter, and you're too stupid to know when you've been bested."

No sooner had Indie said the words than a brilliant flash of multicolored light appeared. It was immediately followed by a deafening crack of thunder. From the residual rainbow-haze, eleven more Ice Giants emerged. They were much larger than all the others, even Ymir.

"We are most disappointed." An Ice Giant, who easily stood a head taller than Ymir, stepped to the forefront. His voice dripped with icy contempt. "Tell us, Ymir, why can you not best this human without the aid of magic? Tell us why you have brought *our children* into your war."

A deep grimace contorted Ymir's face. His look suggested that, even though he was a god, he feared these people. Perhaps Indie had it right. Perhaps Ymir truly was a coward. The ice god's stone-cold gaze shifted from the giants, back to Indie. He adjusted his grip on his trident, practically strangling it as he crushed its bone shaft between his frosty fingers. Indie smiled and took yet another fighting stance, his footing wide and strong, his sword raised above his head, the tip pointed at Ymir.

With a single grunt, Ymir brought his trident around in a wide arcing swing. Indie stepped back, easily avoiding the attack. He watched as the tines slid past. He was not looking for the broad blue foot that followed, striking him cleanly on the side of his head. The impact sent Indie careening across the ground. Kit instinctively moved forward to divert the Ice Giant's attention. Ymir reacted, wheeled around, and swung his trident at Kit. In a move similar to Indie's, she stepped back, allowing the weapon to swish harmlessly before her. Unlike Indie, she was prepared for the subsequent foot attack. She stepped under the kick and delivered her own to the inside of the giant's knee, causing him to buckle and drop to the ground.

"Leave him to me," Indie screamed. The golden scales that covered his face reddened. His voice was filled with rage. "He is mine to defeat. Don't you dare take this from me." Kit paused and watched Indie pick himself up off the ground. His eyes were glassy, unfocused. His footing was unsteady. "I need to do this."

"I don't want to see you die." Kit put herself between Indie and Ymir. "Let me help you."

"No. I need this. I have to do this on my own." Focus had returned to Indie's eyes; his footing became more stable. "I let my parents and my sister down once. I need to finish this if I'm ever going to be able to live with myself. I won't let him kill me."

The Ice Giant rubbed his knee and gingerly got back to his feet. "You won't *let* me kill you?" His laughter sounded like an avalanche. "I will kill you both, together or separately. It's your choice." Kit looked to Indie. He stared back, his eyes pleading, his expression one of total resolve. Kit rolled her shoulders and smiled at Ymir.

"Indie doesn't need my help. I expect you'll either cheat or run away before he kills you."

Still encased in golden scales, Indie moved up beside Kit. "Thank you." She didn't look at him as she stepped to the side. Indie took a few more steps forward and took another battle stance. He dispersed his weight between front and back foot. He held his sword low at his waist, wide from his body.

Ymir grinned. If he was even the slightest bit afraid, he didn't show it. A knot grew in Kit's stomach. Something about Ymir suddenly felt off.

Fury's words to Kit were barely more than a whisper. "Give me to Indie. Let him use me to defeat Ymir." Kit sensed a deception in Fury's words. He wasn't lying, but he wasn't telling her everything either.

Before Kit could say anything, Indie lunged with his sword. In a series of intricate maneuvers, he thrust and slashed, and bobbed and weaved. Ymir countered each move, almost like he could predict what Indie was about to do. As Indie moved in for the killing blow, Ymir struck out with the butt of his trident, catching Indie fully in the side of his head, staggering him once again.

With a flick of his wrist, Ymir brought his trident around and thrust its tines at Indie's throat. By the grace of Titan, the young man got his sword up, deflecting the blow to the side. Again, Ymir's foot followed the attack, kicking Indie flush in his ribs, toppling him over, sending him sprawling onto his face.

"Get up, boy. Face me and I'll make this quick." The Ice Giant's taunts clearly stung. Indie grimaced and gritted his teeth together. He popped back to his feet, but with effort. Kit wanted to go to him, to heal him, to help him defeat the ice god and restore whatever was missing inside the young man.

Indie grinned and struck the same pose as he had a moment ago. His stance was balanced, his blade held wide from his body. The knot in Kit's stomach tightened.

What are you doing, Indie? If you don't change your tactics, he'll... Kit nodded briefly and turned her attention to Ymir. Like her, he saw Indie repeating his previous stance. In a similar fashion, he renewed his own stance. In a heartbeat, Indie lunged with his sword. Ymir parried it easily. Each move Indie took in his series of intricate maneuvers, the ice god countered. Even as the speed of Indie's movements increased, Ymir continued to easily parry them. As Indie went to take his final killing blow, Ymir struck out, anticipating the attack. His eyes bulged, and a smile broke across his chapped, frozen lips. The ice giant thrust the trident at Indie, intent on burying the tines deep into the young man's chest.

Indie ducked and threw his weight to his left, allowing the trident to come dangerously close to his head. One tine caught his scaled cheek, slicing it wide open. As the thrust continued past him, Indie spun inside Ymir's guard and thrust the tip of his obsidian blade under the chin of the giant and into his brain.

What should have been a killing move only resulted in Indie's sword shattering. His blade fell from his hand, its pieces clattering across the ground like broken glass. Ymir threw his head back in triumph. He was invincible to this boy's attacks. The outcome of the battle was now inevitable.

Kit's heart raced but her man's resolve didn't waver. Despite being weaponless, Indie's attacks continued. He pounded on the Ice Giant with kicks and punches, each attack faster and harder than the previous. Indie was in too tight for Ymir to use his trident. He freed up one hand to throw a punch, which Indie easily avoided. The young man stayed close to his opponent, continuing to unleash a barrage of strikes.

Ymir continued to throw punches. He swung wildly, seeking to end the confrontation with a single blow. Indie avoided each looping swing. With each miss, Ymir's anger grew. Tossing his trident to the side, the Ice Giant moved to grapple the human annoyance before him. Each time the giant tried to grasp Indie, the young man evaded him. Ymir was strong and powerful, but Indie was quicker. He slid clear of each attempt, infuriating his attacker more with each passing moment.

Sweat poured from Ymir. He was overheating from the exertion. His breathing was becoming erratic and labored. His movements slowed.

Take him, Indie. Take him now. Kit found her grip on her hammer so tight that she threatened to break it. Her own breathing was rapid, out of control. She seemed to mimic Indie's actions without her feet ever moving.

Indie stepped aside, evading another of Ymir's awkward attempts to grapple him. He jumped behind the giant and practically scampered up his back until he wrapped his arm around Ymir's neck. The sweat pouring off Ymir made him slick, allowing Indie's arm to slide fully under his chin. The young man's muscles bulged as he tightened his grip.

Ymir clutched at Indie's forearm, his actions desperate, his fingers clawing at the dragon-man's scale-covered skin. The giant staggered forward.

"Yield and I will give you a merciful death," Indie growled. The comment made Ymir chuckle in a strangled sort of way. While Indie continued to squeeze the giant's neck, frost appeared on his arm. The glistening ice crystals continued to form across his golden-scales and over his obsidian armor.

Despite the biting cold, Indie seemed unphased. He inhaled deeply, set his jaw, and slowly blew out his breath. With each breath, he stoked the fire in his chest. With each exhale, the layer of ice that had encased him lessened and his scales became brighter and brighter. The perspiration that had covered Ymir returned. His body was now dripping with sweat, tiny rivulets pouring down his neck and chest.

Indie took another deep breath, stoking his flames until his body was practically glowing. He opened his mouth and blew a torrent of golden fire onto Ymir's head. The giant howled as the flames seared his frozen flesh. Ymir staggered forward, his arms now flailing about as he tried desperately to latch onto Indie. The man's grip tightened further while he continued to bathe Ymir in golden flames. The giant dropped to one knee while he continued to sweat rivers of pale blue water. He threw himself to the ground in a last-ditch effort to rid Indie from his back, but the young man's grip never faltered while he continued to bathe the ice god in flames. A moment later, Ymir's body lost its integrity and exploded in a wave of blue-gray water.

⚜

The largest of the Ice Giants glided towards Indie, his hands outstretched by his side. The dragon-man moved into a ready stance, preparing for the worst. Likewise, Kit moved near, her hammer poised to strike.

"I am Aurgelmir, Master of Jotunheim, ruler of the Jötnar, or the Ice Giants, as you prefer to name us. I mean you no harm, Indigo, son of Kihew Willowbrook. You are your father's son. Of those who served in the Temple of Jotunheim, he was among my favorites. It saddened me to hear of his passing. It infuriated me that Ymir was connected to his death." Indie lowered his fists and his breathing eased. The scales that had covered his body melted away.

"You knew my father?"

"I did. I believe I knew his heart and that it was true. You have his spirit and his courage." The Ice Giant bowed deeply to the young man. "You may not know it, but you did us a great service today. Long have we hated Ymir. If it wasn't for the protection afforded him by the spider god, we'd have dispatched him many cycles ago."

"Arachnielle was backing Ymir?" Indie looked at Kit, her eyes widened in response. The little priest couldn't fathom why the spider god would help Ymir at all. Her ruminations must have been obvious, for it drew a deep, hearty laugh from the Ice Giant.

"You know the spider god's name, but I expect you know nothing of her. She is cunning and ruthless, but her heart yearns for her true love, Bael. She will stop at nothing and sacrifice anything to see him return from beyond the Veil. This land we stand upon is above the thinnest, most vulnerable part of the barrier that prevents her love from returning from the Underworld, assuming the spider god did not lie about this. She put the wheels in motion to strike this location, to destroy the Veil and allow Bael and the inhabitants of Helja to flood onto the land. Imagine her surprise when the lot of you were actually helping that event come to pass."

"We did no such thing." Kit railed against the giant's words, the flames in her eyes appearing before she realized.

"Oh, but you did. Unwittingly, no doubt, but you have been aiding her just the same."

"How?" Indie moved closer to Kit. She didn't need him to fight on her behalf, but it warmed her heart to know that he stood with her, no matter what.

"This remarkable young woman is going to free Titan. That act, in of itself, will most assuredly result in the Veil's collapse. Together, you two freed the dark elves and the earth elementals they were with. Arachnielle had not anticipated King Faol would waylay the entire lot of them by enslaving them. By your own hand, you freed them from the vampires and allowed them to go back to their intended work."

Kit swallowed hard. What the giant was saying was making a lot more sense now.

"Last, but not the least of all, you are at the cusp of freeing the dragons. They cannot tear down the Veil on their own, but in their rage, they will destroy everything on these lands. In doing so, they will kill those who are actively protecting the Veil. Without their constant support, the Veil will fade and all of Helja will be freed. Ragnarök will come to be, and all will perish. There is simply no chance of survival when the dragons and the demons lay waste to the lands."

"You don't know that." Kit's voice wavered. She knew the giant believed every word he was saying. Whether he was correct was irrelevant. The fact there was a chance of it happening made the contents of Kit's stomach churn. Is this why Arachnielle's followers were in Ashcroft? Did she send them there to drag Kit into this conspiracy? Could the spider god actually see that far into the future, or did she simply put many plans into motion, hoping that at least one of them would succeed?

The color drained from Kit's face. Tyr had willingly given her a cane that held a piece of Fury. Was he in on these plans with Arachnielle? Had he given her the first piece of the puzzle designed to free the dragons? Of course, Fury would play along. He would get his freedom, something he wanted more than anything. He likely didn't care what the outcome of the world would be, so long as he was free. Free to be with his love, Siku.

Eris' words also flooded back. She said she wasn't sure which side she was on. Did that mean that she was aiding Arachnielle in some way? Was she helping Tyr to free the dragons? Was she actually helping Kit to free Titan? So many of the Fate's actions led directly to Kit's successes. It was by her hand that Danny became the phoenix.

The Ice Giant laughed. "You are a pleasure to watch, young celestial. I can see you considering the events of the recent past. Your eyes reflect your confusion. Your heart breaks at the thought of your trust being abused. Know this, little angel. You don't know the half of it." The giant took a knee in front of Indie, allowing him to speak with him as an equal. "Tell me, young Dragonheart, what boon would you seek from us? We wish to reward you for the service you have rendered unto us."

"A boon?" Indie glanced at Kit. She pressed her lips together and shrugged. Closing his eyes for a moment, the young man considered his options. "I wish you to free Kit's mother from the Temple and return her here." Kit's eyes bulged, and the giant smiled.

"What do you mean, *free my mother*? Where is she? Who took her?" Kit's mind was racing out of control. Who would do such a thing? Whoever it was, when she found them, she would eviscerate them.

Indie ran his hand over his head as he struggled to find the right words. "Ymir took your mother from her hut. He took her to Jotunheim. She has been gone for a couple of days, I think. I only just found out a short while ago, too."

Ymir had taken her mother. The words rolled around inside Kit's head for several moments while she tried to process them. How could she deliver justice upon a man who was already dead? The daemon within flared, furious that it could not exact its revenge.

The Ice Giant ignored Kit's questions and her outrage. "You would ask for nothing for yourself, young Indigo? We have many things we could offer you." Indie shook his head, slowly at first, and then became more assured.

"No, I want nothing for myself. I just want Kit to be happy. Please return her mother to her." Again, the giant smiled. For someone who looked carved from a block of ice, he had a surprisingly warm face.

"Okay, I will grant you your boon, but not exactly as you asked." Indie's brow furrowed. Kit couldn't fully read his expression, but she feared he was about to say something he shouldn't. Again, the giant smiled, this time even more broadly, stretching his frozen face into weird, obtuse angles. "Rest easy, son of Kihew Willowbrook. I will honor your request in spirit, but I wish to give you something... more."

Indie's expression turned stoic. The way his hand was twitching, it was obvious that the offer intrigued him, excited him. The giant reached to his waist and drew a dark-gray dagger. The morning sun had fully risen now. It was bright and warm, but the blade reflected none of its golden rays. It was as though its steel absorbed the light that struck it. "This dagger has been in my family for many generations. The creator of the blade has long since been forgotten. The metal from which it was formed is foreign, unlike any I have ever seen or heard of in tales of wonder. By day, it is dull and lifeless. It absorbs the light of Pele when presented to the sun god. When Pele leaves and Medeina tracks across the night sky, the blade shines a pale red. We believe it allows Pele to speak of his love to the moon god. It is rare that the pair are ever in the sky together, but, with the help of this blade, Medeina can see Pele and feel his love for her.

Kit sniffled, drawing the attention of Indie and the giant. "That's beautiful." The words came out with a choked voice.

"Thank you," Indie said, not sounding totally sincere. His eyebrows were cocked, and a small frown pulled at one corner of his mouth. "How does giving me this blade free Kit's mother?"

"Because, my young friend, this blade can summon the Bifrost, the rainbow bridge." Kit and Indie's mouth flopped open in unison. The Bifrost was a thing of legend, a story told to children in all cultures. It spoke of a method to travel anywhere the heart desired. "You need but think of where you want to go, and the bridge will transport you there." The giant chuckled lightly. "Be wary of your first few travels, though. The experience can be... upsetting."

CHAPTER THIRTY-SIX

JOTUNHEIM

Kit struggled to wrap her head around the news of her mother having been kidnapped. Had she been injured? Had the ice god tormented her the same way that Brother Powder had tortured Miyuki? She couldn't think that way. She couldn't allow her fears to warp her emotions. She needed to remain calm. She needed to get to her mother and free her. Only then would she know, with certainty, what had happened to the woman.

While Indie talked with Aurgelmir, Kit wandered over to where Ymir had fallen. Amid his melted remains lay the ice god's trident. The weapon was at least one and a half times Kit's height. She couldn't help but think Amara would appreciate such a weapon, even if it was neither hammer nor ax. It was a magnificent work of art, carved from the bones of a great yeti. It was that act of skill and bravery that convinced Titan that Ymir was a suitable candidate to free him. That the ice god had squandered his gift infuriated Kit. All for what? Power? Why wasn't the power that Titan had offered him enough? What drives someone to seek more than they need? His lust for more had led him to his ruin. The thought of Kit's daemon self crept into her mind. That part of her was raw, undiluted power. When it surged through her, she felt indestructible. There was no opponent she couldn't stand against and prevail. It was intoxicating, and she wanted more of it. Even now, with the heat of battle still pounding through her veins, the daemon called to her, desperate to be released. They had singled out two of the leaders, but she knew, deep within herself, that there were more monsters among the gathered soldiers. Too many of them enjoyed what they did, asserting themselves over others, lording their power over the weak.

Kit took a deep breath and exhaled slowly. Was that the problem? Was it the thirst for power that warped the minds of people? Was it an insatiable beast that consumed every lick of decency in a person? Was Ymir the example she needed to see that fault in herself? Was that a warning of the daemon within and how she should treat it?

The little priest absentmindedly snatched the trident from the ground. As soon as she wrapped her fingers around its bone shaft, a bolt of cold shot up her arm, numbing her muscles. The weapon was cursed, and it had corrupted Ymir. That had to be it. How could Titan have chosen his rescuer so badly? Was she now doomed to the same fate?

The feel of the trident in her hand washed away the doubts that had crept into her mind. She remembered this numbing cold. She had felt it before, and it was like none other. This was the cold of the North Sea, deep beneath the waves where her god was locked away.

This is the key!

Kit yelped when Indie tapped her on the shoulder.

"Aurgelmir has explained how to use the blade to open the Bifrost." The excitement in Indie's voice was palpable. "Kit, we can go free your mother and bring her back."

"I need to go to Lilloet." Kit hadn't really listened to what Indie had said. She had heard the words, but she had just found the key to freeing Titan, and it was utterly consuming her.

"Did you hear me? We can go rescue your mother in Jotunheim. I know how to get her." Kit gave Indie a stunned look.

"What?" Kit stared down at the trident. "Did you say, my mother?" Indie's words had finally sunk into her consciousness. "We can free my mother?"

"Yes," Indie said. "Aurgelmir told me how this sword works. He told me how to summon the Bifrost and how to command it to take me where I want to go." The air whooshed out of Kit's lungs. She wouldn't be able to go if it only transported the holder of the sword.

"How will you return with my mother if the rainbow bridge only transports one person?" Indie shook his head at Kit's question.

"I can transport many people." Indie stared down at his feet for a moment. "I don't know how many, but the way Aurgelmir described it, everyone within the Bifrost circle will be transported to wherever it is I want to go."

"How big is the circle?" Excitement was once again welling up in Kit's chest. They could use the rainbow bridge to go get her mother, and then they could use it to travel to Lilloet. She didn't know how she knew, but it was where she needed to be to free Titan.

"I didn't ask Aurgelmir. I didn't think to."

"Can you ask him now?" Indie shook his head at Kit's question, again giving his boots a good inspection.

"They're gone. They left while you were examining Ymir's remains." Indie nodded towards the trident. "It's an impressive weapon. Is it heavy?" Kit looked at the weapon in her hands. A pain ripped through her belly. She didn't want to hand it to Indie, even if it was just to feel its weight. This was the key to freeing Titan, and she didn't want to let it go.

"No," Kit replied, clutching the weapon close to her body. "Its surprisingly light for its size." Her heart thumped hard against her ribs when Indie held out his hand, asking to hold it himself. "You can't touch it." The words blurted out of her mouth before she had a chance to even consider what she was saying. It had been a while since her mouth had gotten away from her, but there it was again. As usual, the timing of her impulse was extremely bad.

"I'm sorry." Kit quickly tried to cover up her impulsive response. "I... I feel this is the key to freeing Titan. I'm afraid to let it go." Indie smiled warmly at his love and looked down at the blade in his hand.

"I know how you feel." Indie motioned to the group that had formed at Kit's back. "If we're going to get your mother, we should go. Who do you want to bring with you?" Kit turned to see Danny, Calian, Bango, Ulip, Coldforge, Amilta, and Fenrir. Behind the lot of them, Runt and Lump waited patiently to be called.

"I don't know," Kit replied. She wanted to bring everyone, but something told her that was wrong. All she could think of was one word – family.

"I need you all to remain here and get everyone settled. Much has happened and the people of Cormorant will be frightened." The entire group nodded their understanding, except for Runt and Lump. They both appeared heartbroken. Kit's heart melted. The word in her head was family. They were as much her family as Riva or Aurora were. She looked up at Indie and smiled. So did Indie. The trident thrummed in her hands. She was on the right path. This is what she needed to do.

"Runt, Lump, let's go." The look of dismay vanished as the boys' eyes brightened and they both gave Kit a full doggie smile. The pair immediately bounded through the crowd that was separating them from their person.

Indie motioned for Kit and the boys to move away from the large gathering. "I don't know how big the circle is. We need some space." Kit nodded and followed along as Indie moved away.

The little priest turned back to the others. "I'll return as quickly as I can. Hopefully, I'll have Titan at my back when I do." She spun around and sprinted to catch up to Indie and the boys.

"Are you ready?" Indie held the blade in his hands. "Aurgelmir said the experience can be unsettling." Kit nodded and gathered the boys close to her. She wanted to hold them, but she also didn't want to let go of the trident. Panic suddenly ripped through her, fearful that somehow she and the boys might become separated. Was this a trap? Was this all an Ice Giant ruse, perfectly planned and executed to destroy Kit and her family?

"Take us to the Great Hall of Jotunheim." Indie spoke the words before Kit could finish her thought. Almost instantly, a brilliant kaleidoscope of lights appeared, completely blinding her. Winds whipped around her. There was a brief feeling of being airborne, but it was swept away by the sensation of her spine being ripped through her belly. Her mind couldn't comprehend. The rainbow of colors continued to intensify until they blurred into a blindingly pure white.

With a pop, the brilliant light vanished, only to be replaced by a darkened room filled with a deep, penetrating cold. Her head swam as she tried to maintain balance. The walls continued to spin for several seconds and when they finally stopped, she had a nearly uncontrollable urge to vomit. A soft, warm body leaned against her side.

"Runt?" The dire wolf licked her face. "Are you okay?" The oversized pup nuzzled her. A wave of reassurance filled her heart. "Lump? Indie?"

"Over here," Indie said. He was on his hands and knees. It appeared he could not withstand the urge to vomit. Lump was standing beside him, licking his face and neck. "Stay where you are. I'll come to you."

"Don't be ashamed," Kit said, ignoring his request and moving by the young man's side. "I had the exact same urge." Indie groaned. Perhaps telling him she had been able to withstand the impulse didn't help the situation. "Where are we?" She had hoped changing the subject would help.

"You are in the Great Hall of Jotunheim," replied a silvery, smooth voice from across the room. It seemed to echo off the walls, like a scream in a deep canyon. Was it some sort of trick? Perhaps it was an after effect of traveling across the rainbow bridge. "I knew you'd come for me. I see by the trident that you have defeated Ymir."

"Mother?"

"Hello, sweetness." Riva was sitting comfortably upon a red silk cushion in the middle of the expansive room. She looked to be perfectly at peace. Kit threw herself at the woman, practically bowling her off her large cushion. She hugged her and squeezed her with all her might. She didn't let go until Riva made a muffled cry, letting Kit know she needed to breathe.

"Mother, are you hurt? Did they..."

"I am fine, Kitten. I didn't appreciate the way Ymir stole me from my hut, but he never physically harmed me." The woman regarded Indie. "I hadn't expected to see you. Not right now, at any rate." The woman shook her head and chuckled to herself. "It seems my visions are much less precise where you two are concerned. Perhaps my heart gets in the way, coloring my interpretations.

Perhaps I only see the best and fear the worst. Perhaps the gift Gaia bestowed upon me is faulty."

"Oh, I doubt that anything Gaia ever does is faulty." A voice echoed down the hall from beyond the room. It was followed by the sound of delicate feet treading upon a tiled floor.

Kit peered into the darkness. All she could make out was the silhouette of a slender creature with six arms striding towards them. Kit swallowed hard and tightened her grip on the trident. Runt and Lump growled and padded forward.

"Hello, Sister." A voice, smooth as silk, emerged from the darkened recess of a massive set of doors leading into the great hall. From out of the shadows, a tall, thin woman with blue-gray skin and four spider legs protruding from her back stepped into the room. A thick mist clung to her feet as she glided forward. It seemed to swirl playfully about her ankles, barely dissipating at all until her knee-high boots clacked against the stone floor.

Lump and Runt immediately moved further forward, putting themselves directly in harm's way, guarding Kit and Indie from the approaching woman. While Runt's growls turned to slobbering snarls, Lump's changed into a throaty roar. His dragon self had appeared, ready to meet any challenger head on. Again, Kit couldn't help but think he was getting bigger. Perhaps it was only after he changed, since he was now so much larger than his wolfdog self.

"Kit, this is Arachnielle, the spider god." Riva's words were calm and carefully measured. There was no hint of fear in her voice, nor was there any hint of malice towards the misshapen woman. "You're going to want to listen to what she has to say." A hint of a smile pulled at the corner of the spider god's ruby red lips.

"How very kind of you." Arachnielle inclined her head slightly to the Berrat woman seated on the thick, plush cushion in the middle of an otherwise nearly empty room. "You have wonderful companions," the spider god cooed. "So strong. So handsome." The woman took a knee and called Runt to her. The dire wolf's snarls faltered. He circled back and pressed his body against Kit, his bright jade green eyes waiting for the little priest to give him instructions. The wolf's behavior made Arachnielle laugh. It was much sweeter than Kit had expected. The woman was beautiful beyond reckoning, but with the four spider legs protruding from her back and the six extra eyes sitting upon her brow, she was also a thing of nightmares.

CHAPTER THIRTY-SEVEN

ARACHNIELLE'S REVELATION

"You have something to say to us?" Kit stepped up beside Lump, motioning for him to stand down.

"No, not you, sweet child. At least, not yet." The woman pointed a long slender finger at Indie. "It's you I wish to speak to. It's you I want to thank."

Indie was still holding onto Aurgelmir's blade. He kept it low at his hip as he moved forward, taking a stance beside Kit. "I neither deserve nor want any thanks from you."

"Oh, sweet boy. No need to be modest. No need to put on a false bravado in front of your lady love." Kit noticed Indie taking a much tighter grip on his blade. So did Arachnielle. "Do you plan on using that on me? I have shown you no hostility, none whatsoever, and yet you are ready to attack. Why is that?"

"You kidnapped this woman." Indie didn't sound as sure as usual. The spider-woman had immediately gotten under his skin and Kit wasn't sure why. Arachnielle shook her head at Indie's accusation.

"It's bad form to make such declarations when you know nothing of what you speak. I had nothing to do with Riva's kidnapping. In fact, I petitioned Ymir to release her. He might still be alive had he listened." A wicked grin forced the woman's mouth into a thin line that nearly split her face. Her ebony black eyes seemed to get larger, more intense. "Then again, I knew he wouldn't listen to me. I knew his choice would lead to his ruin and it would open the door I so desperately desire to step through."

"And what door is that?" Kit slipped her hand onto Indie's wrist, gently applying pressure against it. She needed him to calm down, to allow the woman to speak. Her mother had said they should listen to Arachnielle, and for that to happen, there needed to be a conversation.

Kit's action wasn't lost on the spider god. "The door into Helja, of course. Like you, I wish to be with my love. Right now, he is trapped beyond the Veil and cannot return to me. I have done everything I can to see the Veil fall. I have spun an intricate web across the kingdom. I invited you all into it, and you so graciously accepted my offerings."

"What offerings?" Indie's voice had a sharp edge to it. Kit considered calling upon her inner angel to calm him, but she knew that wouldn't go well. She also didn't know how much the spider god knew about her, and she didn't want to tip her hand too early. "We accepted nothing."

Arachnielle slowly closed her eyes and held them shut for several moments before slowly reopening them. "Not you, young man. I offered you nothing. But you did me a great service in killing Ymir. You handed his trident to the little priest here, and that trident is the key to bringing down the Veil. She will use it to free Titan and with it, she will also free the dragons. When their magic is unleashed, the Veil will collapse, and my love can return to me."

"And how will the trident help free the dragons?" Kit looked at the weapon, not knowing what she was doing. "I sense it will free Titan, but I don't see it being of any use in freeing the dragons."

"Perhaps you don't." Arachnielle practically purred the words. "But your friend Fury understands." Kit freed up a hand and drew her battle hammer.

"Fury, do you know what she's talking about?" The visage of the draken appeared beside Kit. He leveled a look of pure hatred toward the spider god.

The strange woman covered her mouth, feigning shock. "Oh, Fury. Did I ruin your surprise?" Kit looked from Arachnielle, back to Fury.

"Fury? What is she talking about?" The draken sighed at the question. His lip curled into a sneer.

"The trident holds the last piece of my soul. With it, I can be whole again."

"Why didn't you tell me?"

"I don't know. I should have. You have treated me well since the first day I met you. You aren't like the others who seek power at all costs. I should have trusted you." Kit snarled at the draken.

"You're only telling me a half truth. What are you not saying?" Fury pulled back his scaly lips, exposing his own formidable teeth.

"I really hate that side of you. It makes it extremely difficult for me to be my dragon self."

"What are you not saying, Fury?" Kit had raised the hammer over her head like she was ready to strike him with it. She didn't really know what she would do, it just felt right. She immediately wondered what would happen to Fury if she struck him with the hammer he inhabited.

"Put that down," Fury said, his own anger abating. "What I haven't told you is that I cannot make myself whole without a host strong enough to hold me. My body is the best vessel, but another would suffice until I can reunite myself with it. There is also the problem with my current incarceration. Even if I was whole, I would be trapped in my mountain domain. I need the key to the collar of command. I need to free Ouroboros and only then will I, too, be free." Kit's face went slack halfway through Fury's explanation.

"That's why you wanted Indie and Lin to be one of those Dragonheart things, or people, or whatever they are. You wanted one of them to host you when you were whole. Your entire plan to turn Indie into a Dragonheart, or whatever they're called, was all about giving you what you wanted." Kit wheeled on Indie, while rage blossomed in her heart. "Did you know this? Was this your bargain with him all along?"

"He would only inhabit me long enough to free his body from the mountains. In return, he would make me a true dragon. I would be like Lump and Danny. I could switch between forms. I could be human when I wanted to be, and a dragon when I needed to be."

"You will never need to be a dragon!" Kit struggled to find her next words. Her daemon desperately wanted to come out, to take over, to wreak havoc on the foolish man standing in front of her. "You and me, by ourselves, just as we were. That was enough for us to face any challenge. We never needed to be more than that. I love you, Indigo Willowbrook. I love you, the man. I don't need or want anything more from you. I just want you as you were."

"He doesn't need to be anything more than what he is to be a useful vessel," Fury said, interrupting Kit. "Even Lump would do just fine for my purposes."

Kit swung her battle hammer at Fury, intending on striking him in the knee. She wanted to knock him down so she could bash him over the head. She hadn't expected the hammer to pass through him as though he was completely insubstantial.

"I'm not actually here," Fury said with his draconic smile. "I can't manifest like I used to. I am using too much magic just trying to keep myself from leaking out of the hammer. I don't know why you're so angry with me. I've told you all along that I want to be whole, and I want to be free. Why does it bother you so much that I need help to do it?"

"I don't know," Kit yelled. "It just does." She really didn't understand why it upset her so much. Was she protecting Indie? Was she jealous of Fury, worried that he'd take her love away and never return?

"Perhaps it's because you'd rather have the dragon to yourself?" Arachnielle's voice was sweet as honey, and it made Kit's skin crawl. "Perhaps you don't want him to be free?" Kit didn't like the way this was going. The woman's words had a ring of truth to them. Was Kit actually being selfish? Was she trying to keep Fury with her, to horde Indie and the boys all to herself?

"What offerings?" Kit asked Arachnielle, changing the subject, not wanting to confront her feelings. She didn't understand how she felt, and she certainly didn't want to think about it right now. "What offerings did I accept?" Arachnielle's black eyes lit up and her lips pursed.

"Do you truly need me to lay it out for you, child? Can you not suss it out for yourself?"

"You're wasting my time." Kit turned to her mother, offering her a hand up from the cushion she was sitting on. "I have a job to do."

"Yes, you do," Arachnielle purred. "You've had many jobs to do, and you did them all admirably. Did you never wonder why my followers were in that dusty little town? Did you never wonder why you specifically were sent to investigate?"

Kit's brow furrowed. She hadn't really considered it, she'd only reacted. Why had Grams let her grandson be taken? She was a powerful priest of Titan. She felt her strength. She knew it from the first time she met the woman.

"Setting you on that path took a lot of planning, and the cooperation of many others." Arachnielle was now standing beside Kit, her spider legs tucked in behind her back. Sweet Titan, the woman was tall. Kit hadn't noticed until she was standing next to her. Everything about this woman was alluring, sensual. Kit's head snapped to Indie to gauge his reaction. The man's face was stern. He was holding his weapon low and wide from his body. He was ready to strike at a moment's notice. It made Kit's heart beat faster.

"My actions were my choice," Kit said with conviction. "I was influenced by nothing." Her statement made the spider god laugh.

"You dangled from my thread the entire time. You might as well have been a marionette. But I have to say, it was not all my doing. I had a great deal of help. Some were unwitting, but others were only too happy to provide you the extra push you needed." Kit swallowed hard. Everything this woman was saying was the absolute truth. There wasn't a hint of deception in her words.

"Who?" Kit demanded. "Who has been helping you?"

"I have," Fury said. There was a hint of shame in his voice. Kit hadn't ever heard him be anything other than arrogant or condescending. "I helped her to guide you in the right direction. As did Eris."

"Eris? The Fate? She's been manipulating me? How? Why?"

"We all want the same thing." The shame in Fury's voice vanished, replaced with a slow-burning hatred. "We want to be free, unshackled from the chains that hold us. Is that too much to ask for?"

The draken's words reverberated through Kit. This whole time, ever since she'd left for Ashcroft with Lin, she had been on a path to free people from slavery, from oppression. She had heard the tales of the Fates and how they'd been forced to care for the Travelers like some sort of nanny. She knew of the dragons and their mountain prisons, trapped there for fear they would destroy the Travelers.

"Who else?" Kit demanded. "Who else has been in on this? Who else has been pulling my strings?"

"That is not their story to tell." The familiar voice of Tyr drew Kit's ire. "Not all have been playing you, little sister. Some were trapped in the same web as you, but these two will not tell their stories. You're a clever girl. You can figure it out for yourself. Just know this: the path you are on will save many, not just us selfish gods."

"I'm not surprised you're behind this." A sneer twisted Kit's upper lip, and she glared at Tyr. "It seems you're living up to your reputation as a master of trickery."

"I never tried to trick you or deceive you. I was tasked with looking over you, but I saw you didn't need me. I found that quite stimulating. Even though it wasn't necessary, I chose to keep my eyes on you." Kit didn't know how to react to that. Why did she need to be watched over? Her eyes widened.

"Who tasked you to watch over me?" Tyr smiled at the question. He paused and tilted his head back slightly. He gave a slight nod and returned his attention to Kit.

"That is not my story to tell. But I will tell you it's time for you to leave. Someone is waiting for you on the shores of the North Sea, just north of Lilloet. It's best you go there before it's too late."

"Too late for what?" Kit practically yelled the words. Anger flared up within her when Tyr simply smiled and vanished with a pop. In the distance, a coyote howled. "I hate it when he does that."

Kit spun around to face Arachnielle. "Too late for..." The spider god was also gone.

"We need to leave." Riva's voice was gentle but commanding.

"Mother, what do you know of this? Did Arachnielle tell you anything?"

"I know much, little piece of my soul, but now is not the time. The Veil will soon fall, and you best free Titan before it does."

"I don't know how?" Kit's lower lip was trembling. Was her mother in on this deception as well? Why was she at the center of this conspiracy? How many people were hurt just to push her into this situation? The memory of the deaths at Templeton came flooding back; the terror on their faces as they fell into the chasm she had created. The sound of their cries as they tumbled to their deaths still haunted her dreams.

"You will know what to do when the time is at hand. Trust me, Kitten. I am your mother and I love you beyond reckoning. Trust in me as I am trusting in you."

"I don't know where Lilloet is," Indie interrupted. "I can't take us there."

"Show him the way," Riva said to her daughter. "You have it within you to share everything of yourself with this man. You have already sealed the bond between yourselves. All you need to do is access it." Indie and Kit stared, dumbfounded by the Berrat woman's words.

With barely a hint of hesitation, Kit took Indie's hand in her own and slowly closed her eyes. She searched her feelings. They guided her, showed her the way. Kit's golden aura burst outwards as she reached into her soul, finding two hearts beating as one. An echo sounded in her mind, and then another. The feeling of love was overwhelming. It was all-consuming. There, bright as the morning sun breaking over Mount Toka, was Indie. Every feeling, every emotion, every aspect of Kit's heart was being poured into the man. She felt his hand tense as he accepted her gift. When she opened her eyes, Indie was weeping.

He gave his sword a quick glance before gazing back at Kit. "Take us to Lilloet, to the North Sea."

CHAPTER THIRTY-EIGHT

TRITON AND AKUA HONU

Kit's stomach lurched as she stared out at the North Sea. The second time traveling over the rainbow bridge wasn't any easier than the first. Indie, who was standing right beside her, didn't look any better than she felt. His mouth was clenched tightly while he tried to regain control of his stomach.

Lump, Runt, and Riva all looked just fine, unaffected by the vortex that had just whisked them from Jotunheim to Lilloet. A pang of envy ripped through Kit, but it faded as quickly as it had arrived, thankful that the people she loved had not suffered the way she and Indie had.

"Hello," said a voice from behind Kit. She turned to find Triton, the water god, standing behind her. "I was expecting you." Kit blinked at the water god's words. She wasn't sure how she felt about Triton. He was condescending and arrogant the first time they'd met, but he seemed different after she had helped rescue the magicked water used to create Titan's statue at Mount Toka. He had said that it was within his nature to reflect those who stood before him. Had she been arrogant and condescending? Why was she thinking about this, rather than wondering how he knew she'd be coming here at this exact time? As though the god of the seas had read her mind, he chuckled.

"I knew you'd be here because everything that has happened since the first time I met you was designed to lead to this very moment." Kit's grip tightened on the trident.

"Why are you lying to me? Who are you?" Indie immediately moved closer to Kit and took an aggressive stance, followed by Runt and Lump. Kit couldn't see what Riva was doing. She hoped her mother was safe behind the shield they were creating for her.

Triton laughed, but it was a weak and somewhat guarded sound. "Your powers are improving. It's difficult to know if a god is speaking true, and yet you do it with ease."

"You didn't answer my questions," Kit said, her anger flaring in her chest. Lump immediately changed into his dragon form, the heat from his body warming the area.

The sea roiled and churned. Immense waves crashed upon the shore. "I am Triton, and you would be wise to calm yourselves lest I call upon the sea and its creatures to swallow you all."

Triton was who he said he was. Kit recalled that he reflected whatever was around him. Right now, he was being met with hostility and he reflected that back at Kit and her cohorts. She lowered her weapon. "Be at peace. This is Triton and he means us no harm."

Lump was the first to respond, his dragon form melting away, revealing his golden retriever self. Runt followed shortly thereafter. Indie was the slowest to respond, his chest still heaving when he finally lowered his blade.

"Why did you lie to me, Triton?"

"I didn't mean to, not exactly anyway. You have been destined to free Titan since the day you were born. I was destined to be here, to provide you with a means to reach his prison. The events that led us to this moment were not as they had been prophesied." The god surveyed the group standing before him and chuckled. "No, not at all like they were prophesied."

"What was to happen?" Kit asked, curious to know what he believed the prophesies to be. Triton pursed his lips to hold back a grin. He slowly shook his head.

"They are no longer relevant and not worth worrying about." Triton raised his arm, motioning to the sea behind Kit. "I have summoned your carriage, *Akua Honu*. She does not belong in this sea, but she is the only creature who can take you where you need to go."

The roiling seas had abated, leaving the surface as smooth as glass, its near black water looking like a giant sheet of obsidian. Kit scanned the horizon, searching left and right for the creature who would carry her to Titan's prison. Her pulse raced when a great green dome broke the water's glassy surface. Whatever it was, it was heading to the shore at a tremendous speed. As it neared, a smooth head featuring an enormous beak slowly reared out of the water. This was the creature from Kit's dreams, the giant sea turtle who had carried her to Titan's prison. A sudden shiver ripped through Kit's body. She remembered the dream like she had just awakened from it.

"Akua Honu is here to bear you to Titan's prison. She can only carry one. Your friends must stay behind."

"Where Kit goes, we go." Indie stepped forward, ready to challenge the god's words. Triton's demeanor soured.

"You cannot, nor can her mother, nor can her canine companions. This is her fate, not yours." The god's words were firm, yet not without compassion. Triton tilted his head back and closed his eyes. "Your fate lies here on the shore, young Indigo."

"What does that mean?" Kit said, leveling the trident on him. "What are you planning on doing to him?" Fury appeared beside Kit before Triton could respond.

"Indie's fate is to stay here with me. I cannot come with you on your journey." Fury paused as he considered his next words. "I will share with you something that no dragon has ever shared with any other being." Kit simply stared, not wanting to give the draken the satisfaction of knowing that she was touched by his words. Fury drew a deep breath and slowly exhaled.

"We dragons cannot enter deep water. It would extinguish our flame and we would perish. It is our only real weakness, and I am trusting this knowledge with all of you. You are my family, as much as it pains me to admit it."

Triton practically fell over. "I am not your family, and yet you entrust me with such knowledge?" Fury bowed his head slightly.

"I do trust you. If I did not, I would not allow Kitten to accept your generous offer. Akua Honu is far from home, and she would not consider leaving her domain lightly. She trusts you, and she is willing to bear a celestial into a sea guarded by one of the fiercest creatures to inhabit this world. If I could enter the water, even in my full glory, I would not want to face the leviathan in his own domain."

Kit didn't know what to make of this exchange. This was not Fury's normal behavior, not by a long shot, but every word he spoke was the truth. Admittedly, however, his description of the leviathan weakened her knees more than she'd like to have admitted.

"Time is of the essence," Triton said to Kit. "The Veil will soon be breached and all Helja is literally about to break loose upon the lands. Freeing Titan can change the outcome."

"Breached? Breached how? How will Titan change the outcome?"

"The dwarves will break through the Veil before the sun sets. They seek to free their god, Gimlie. They seek to free their kin. Many were trapped in the underworld when the Veil came to be. They have worked tirelessly to break through. With the help of Arachnielle, they will succeed."

"And how will Titan change the outcome?"

"I don't know, but when he is freed, he is going to want retribution for what was done to him. His wrath knows no bounds. He may simply wipe the life from the entire world. He may keep his promise to you and help the peoples of the north. Not even Anu can fully predict how he will respond."

Kit had to think back. Anu was the little man she met on the strange island floating amongst the stars. He was an odd fellow, but he was very likeable.

"I will give you to Indie," Kit said to Fury. "You best return yourself to the hammer before I do."

"Good luck," Fury said before unceremoniously vanishing.

⁂

"You must leave, little angel. Time is of the essence." Kit quickly nodded to Triton and raced back to where Lump and Runt stood. She drew them close and wrapped her arms around their necks.

"I love you both, with all my heart. I will be back soon." The boys responded with whines and licks and a few more whines. Kit pulled herself away before her tears started to flow. She dashed to her mother and took her hands in hers.

"I remember the day of my Rite of Ways. On that day, you offered me your advice, your love, and your courage. Every day of my life, you have been with me, just like you were on that night. Even when I couldn't see you, you stayed with me to make sure I'd be safe." Riva nodded weakly and swallowed hard. "I don't know if this is the future you feared, but every day of my life seems to have led me to this moment. I'm glad that you're beside me now, still giving me your love and support. I love you, Ananak, more than words could ever express."

Riva cupped Kit's cheeks in her hands. "May Gaia be with you and protect you. Until we meet again, I am with you, now and forever." Kit smiled and turned to Indie. The man's eyes were wet with tears, but he did nothing to hide it.

"Come back to me," he said, the words mostly sticking in his throat. "I cannot live without you." Kit smiled and raised an eyebrow. She handed him her battle hammer.

"Be wary of Fury. He wants nothing more than to be free and he will do anything to get it." Indie's expression darkened. At that moment, a million thoughts raced through her mind. Why did that upset him? Was it that her last words were a warning to him, rather than an expression of her undying love for him? Why did she have to say that? Did she not trust him? Did she not trust Fury? She thrust the shaft of the trident into the soft, sandy ground and threw her arms around the man, embracing him enthusiastically.

"I love you with all my heart. I would be nothing but an empty shell without you. I pledge my life and my heart to you. I will be with you until I die, or until you tell me to leave. I am yours, Indigo Willowbrook." She pressed her lips against his. The passion that flowed from the man stole her breath. The world spun, making her lightheaded. She had experienced this feeling before. It's what had happened when Anu called her to him. She didn't want to leave Indie. Not now. Not ever. She waited for the inevitable trip to the island in the stars.

It didn't happen. She just continued her embrace while her world continued to spin about her. When the kiss finally came to its end, Kit was flushed and breathing hard.

"I am yours, too, Sister Kit Standing Bear." Indie's voice was quiet, reverent. "For now, and for all eternity. No matter the challenges. No matter the obstacles, I will be with you forever." This was the strongest magic Kit had ever felt. Nothing could be more powerful. Fearing she'd break the spell, she spoke not a word, grabbed the trident, and darted towards Akua Honu.

Kit struggled to climb up onto the great turtle's back. Her shell was wet and slick, making it exceedingly difficult to get solid footing. When the little priest finally clambered to the top, where it was reasonably flat, she patted the turtle's back.

"Take me to Titan," she said, offering a quick wave to those she was leaving behind.

The turtle pushed off the beach and spun to the north-east. Kit nearly slid off as soon as she did.

"Titan's snowballs. This is going to be impossible."

⚬⚬⚬⚬⚬⟨⚬⟩⚬⚬⚬⚬⚬

Akua Honu flapped her great flippers, carrying Kit out to sea at a tremendous pace. It seemed like only a few minutes before there was no land in sight. The sea had been calm, with only a light spray of the frosty water coming off the great turtle's shell as it cut through the still surface. As they got further and further from shore, the water became rougher. Waves were breaking over the turtle, threatening to wash Kit off her back and into the turbulent sea.

The endless swells continued to pound Kit, soaking every inch of her. Without the armor that Fenrir had made for her, she was completely exposed to the elements. The winds, whipping over the near frozen water, bit at her, chilling her all the way to the bone. Her joints were seizing up, with each new wave becoming harder and harder to resist. Soon, one would wash her away and she'd quickly perish from the deep cold.

Her teeth were chattering badly, and her fingers struggled to find purchase on the turtle's now frost-covered shell. Kit swallowed hard as she watched an approaching wave. She had to crane her neck to see its top. Knowing this would be too much, she dropped to her hands and knees, trying desperately to find a grip somewhere on the turtle's shell. Something that would save her from being swept away.

In the dying seconds before the wave crashed upon her, Kit's life flashed before her eyes. The images came faster than she could process them. The memory of her time in the catacombs where Brother Rimes had tortured her father and murdered Sister Miyuki invaded her thoughts. Her daemon self came bubbling up. Whether she was in control of herself didn't matter. Fire burned within her heart, warming her body, melting the ice that turned the shell into a slick platform. Obsidian claws replaced her fingertips; long, sharp and hooked. She looked up at the wave as it was about to break over her, and she dug her claws into the turtle's back. The creature did not cry out in agony. It did not flinch. Kit could only hope that she was not causing injury to the one bearing her in these ungodly, freezing-cold waters.

The wave crashed over Kit with a force like nothing she'd ever experienced. The water roiled and churned. With all her might, she grasped onto the shell. They may have been rolling beneath the turbulent sea, but Kit couldn't tell for sure. Everything was a torrent of eddies and currents and bubbles. Time had no meaning, but the way Kit's lungs burned told her she needed the turtle to surface or she would drown. She considered pushing herself off the shell and swimming for her life, but she had to trust that the creature understood what she needed. After all, turtles needed to breathe, too, didn't they?

Panic took hold. They were still beneath the surface. With only pitch blackness around Kit, crushing in on her, she had no way of telling how deep they were. Oh, how her lungs burned. One deep breath and the pain would be gone. Everything would be gone. But what of her family? They would be devastated. She promised she'd return to them. She promised herself to Indie. She promised she would be with him forever. He had made the same promise to her. She couldn't give in to the pain.

The turtle belched.

It was a deep, horrid sound that reverberated in the water. It sounded like a great door being opened, dragging across a rough stone floor. It was... Kit was suddenly enveloped in an air bubble. It clung to the head and back of the turtle. Was this how she survived deep beneath the ocean surface? Kit knew nothing of this creature. She knew nothing of its ways, how it survived. Did it create this pocket of air for its own benefit or for Kit's? Was the air in the bubble breathable?

Kit's lungs were now a raging ball of pain. Holding her breath any longer was not an option. Her lungs craved air, and she was going to take a big gulp from the bubble, whether she wanted to. Spots danced in front of Kit's eyes.

The little priest gasped, relief spreading through her as the sweet, reasonably fresh air filled her lungs. As quickly as she sucked in a breath, she blew it out and sucked in a second one. The panic that had taken her earlier was still there. It screamed at her to continue sucking air as fast as she could. It took everything within herself to not listen to that voice. She closed her eyes and calmed herself. She slowly exhaled and, even more slowly, took her next breath.

Safely ensconced in the giant bubble, Kit finally took a moment to look beyond her current dilemma. It was impossible to tell how deep she was, but with her daemon self in the forefront, she could peer deeply into the darkness. As she strained to cast her eyes into the icy depths, a shadow passed overhead, blotting out what little light there was penetrating the gloom.

Ever so slowly, the darkness passed over. It created a current so strong the turtle was forced to dive deeper in an effort to remove itself from the shadow's turbulent wake. With a single beat of the creature's broad flat tail, it disappeared, its body swallowed up by the darkness.

"We'll be okay." Kit didn't know if the turtle understood the words, but felt confident that she could understand the feeling in them.

The turtle continued swimming, the strokes of its long, spade-shaped fins thrusting them forward at a steady pace. Kit had wondered how long they'd be beneath the surface on the way to Titan. She also wondered how long the bubble would last.

From out of the depths, the gargantuan creature appeared once again. It moved closer to Kit and Akua Honu until it was alongside, barely a dozen paces away. Kit's hand fell to where her battle hammer usually hung. Disappointment ripped through her when she found it wasn't there. She desperately wanted to call upon the hammer's light, to get a better look at the creature that was shadowing them. With her improved dark vision, she could see it was there, but not well enough to make out any of the creature's details. A smile pulled at Kit's lips.

She stuck her arm up over her head and called upon her flames. A fire ignited in her palm, illuminating the surrounding area. A gargantuan eye, easily twice as tall as Ulip, peered at her in the darkness. Reacting to the sudden burst of light, the creature's pupil rapidly contracted. It was then Kit noticed the animal's blue-black skin. It looked like a Makara, only many times larger than the biggest one she had ever seen in the Gaelinora Sea.

The creature turned towards Kit, exposing its gargantuan spiraled horn. It was definitely a Makara.

The animal continued to turn, bringing its primary weapon to bear. When it contacted the bubble cocoon, the icy water came gushing inward, threatening to sweep Kit off the turtle's back. Much worse, that was Kit's only air supply. At this depth, she was going to drown and there was nothing she could do about it.

Kit's concern for breathing was instantly replaced with a crushing pain. Her ears felt like there were ice picks being rammed into them. Her chest felt like it was going to explode. She exhaled, releasing the building pressure. The agony in her chest lessened, but her ears still ached with the sharp, stabbing pain.

Kit was going to die down here, but she would not be the only one. She yanked her trident around and thrust it at the leviathan. The Makara avoided the attack and thrust forward, attempting to skewer the little human. Fighting underwater was nothing like fighting on land. All of Kit's movements were slow and sluggish. The Makara was in its element. It lived in this wondrous, watery world. It moved quickly, able to deal death with its horrible horn.

Maybe that's its weak spot.

What was she thinking? The horn was easily three times as long as Kit was tall. Its point appeared to be needle sharp.

Okay, it will not be weak.

Kit's lungs were burning again. She hadn't taken a breath for a while. She was going to die soon.

Pushing down the urge to take a breath, Kit pushed off the turtle's shell and launched herself away from it. There was no need for it to die as well. Perhaps it could escape while she dueled with the leviathan. With her hands now tightly wrapped around the trident, Kit called upon her daemon powers. She was going to light herself up like a bonfire. Maybe she could burn the Makara, kill him that way.

The daemon wouldn't come. She called upon it again, but it was nowhere to be found. Had she lost her connection with it? Was it the cold of the depths? She had lit her hand just a few moments ago, but now she couldn't feel it at all. Was it the turtle? Was it because she had been standing on it the whole time?

The pain in Kit's lungs was getting worse. She needed to breathe, but if she did, her life was over. Why wasn't the Makara attacking her? Was it drawn to the turtle? Is that where it had gone, to devour the poor creature who had come to Kit's aid?

Kit's golden aura burst forth, turning the dark frigid waters a deep green. The wonder of it all disappeared when Kit gulped a substantial amount of water. The pain in her chest lessened and her golden aura diminished.

This was how she was to meet her end.

I'm sorry that I failed you, Titan. I'm sorry that I will not be returning to my family.

A great shadow passed before Kit's eyes and her body went limp.

CHAPTER THIRTY-NINE

A BEACON OF HOPE

Someplace off in the infinite distance, a pinpoint of light peered through the darkness.

Was Titan calling Kit for her to return her essence to him? Is this what it felt like to be dead? It didn't feel any different from being alive, except for the impenetrable darkness that was crushing in on her. She could feel the light calling to her. It promised peace and tranquility. It promised love and comfort. It was a beacon of safety.

The darkness became turbulent; her body caught in a vortex that tossed her about like a rag doll.

Sweet Titan, I'm alive. I'm floating in the sea.

Kit took a deep breath. The cold water filled her lungs. It felt refreshing, invigorating. She exhaled and drew another breath. It took a bit more effort than she was accustomed to, but she was breathing water.

What magic is this?

Kit called on her aura. It burst outward, illuminating everything within a hundred paces. It illuminated the blue-gray skin of the great Makara. It illuminated its spiraled horn that it was threatening to impale her with. Thankful that she still had the trident in her hand, she held it out before herself, pointing its tines directly at the oncoming Makara. The sea creature's horn looked to be ten times the length of her trident. It was going to impale her long before she could stick it into the animal's head. At the last possible moment, Kit realized her attack would be useless. She turned her body to the side and kicked her feet.

Her last-minute movements helped her avoid the horn, but it did nothing for the tooth filled maw that was immediately behind it. The leviathan's mouth was big enough to swallow a ship. A little girl wouldn't likely even register as a morsel.

She held the trident out before herself and kicked her legs frantically. It was a useless gesture. She would not out-swim the Makara.

Again, Kit was tossed about in violent currents. She assumed she was being sucked into the animal's mouth. She thrust her trident blindly, hoping to score a hit, perhaps dissuading it from making a small meal out of her.

With each attack, all she hit was water. The Makara was gone. The tiny pinprick of light seemed brighter than it had been before. She wasn't sure why, but Kit felt a desire to swim for the light, so swim she did.

Holding the trident made it more difficult, but she continued heading for the tiny illumination. She continued kicking her feet with as much power as she could muster. At an onerously slow pace, the light grew. It grew brighter. It grew warmer. A feeling of confidence blossomed in her chest. She was doing exactly what she needed to be doing.

This was Titan's prison. She was sure of it. With renewed vigor, she swam forward. She pushed herself harder and harder, but her progress had seemed to stop. The light wasn't coming any closer.

Kit stopped kicking to consider the situation. As soon as she slowed, the light grew smaller.

I'm fighting a current, an immensely powerful current.

If only she could swim faster, kick harder. She was about to call on the strength of Amaruq when she had a thought. She hadn't called upon Titan's strength in a while. Had enough time passed? Was this why Titan granted his gift of strength? Was it to give his rescuer the ability to fight the relentless current?

Kit started kicking again, swimming with all her might to make it to the prison.

Titan, hear me. In your lonely prison cell, cut off from those who worship you, I call upon you. In this the hour of my need, I call upon your strength.

A moment passed, followed by another. Kit feared not enough time had transpired and her prayers would not be answered. She was about to call on Amaruq when her body was wracked with a cold so intense that she feared it would kill her. She gasped and gritted her teeth. Never had she ever felt such intensity. Her golden aura again burst forth, tempering the cold, helping her to catch her breath.

With the strength of Titan coursing through her muscles, she renewed her kicking. The light grew brighter as she closed in on her destination. The currents were intensifying, desperately trying to keep her from her goal. The light grew so intense that it became difficult to see, and nearly impossible to concentrate. Its brilliance was mesmerizing. She tried shielding her eyes with her arm, but to no effect. No amount of protection could stop the light from burning into her senses, into her soul.

Kit took a deep breath, pulled her arm away, and fully opened her eyes. For the briefest of moments, the searing pain was both excruciating and elating. She continued to hold them open, defying the agony, refusing to let the torturous ache stop her from seeing her goal.

Suddenly, everything stopped. The current dissipated and the blinding light diminished. Kit stood before a simple gray square box that was no taller than she was. Was this the prison that held her god? Had she reached Titan?

Thin, nearly imperceptible runes covered the container. As Kit neared, the lines became more visible. Pulsating blood-red light seeped out from the runes, making the vault look like a giant, beating heart. A deep cold emanated from within the tomb. With each pulse of the red runes, waves of ice-water washed over Kit. The young priest's body was nearly frozen solid, but there was no fear of death.

Her god was before her, yet unseen.

She placed her hand upon the vault's surface. It was pleasantly warm. Despite the runes etched into the metal, it was surprisingly smooth. The warmth of the box seemed to draw her closer. It provided a welcome respite from the bone-jarring cold of the deep-sea water. The warmth slowly faded. Was it Titan providing the warmth? Was he dying? Is that why the heat was being washed away with the currents? Waves of cold pushed away what little warmth re-mained. Ice quickly formed around Kit's hand, locking it against the box's metal surface. The cold quickly became unbearable. Frozen blue crystals crawled up her arm, threatening to encase her entire body.

Kit called upon her daemon self. Her hand lit in red flames. Her fires merged with the pulsating lights. They seemed to add to them, to magnify them. The runes changed. The lines moved across the surface, like thin rivulets of molten iron. They flowed towards Kit, gathering around her hand. They seemed to sway to the rhythm of an unheard melody. Unsure what to do, Kit pulled her hand back and the dancing runes halted.

Beneath her hand, a small white circle appeared. Like the runes, its light pulsated. The circle seemed to expand and recede several times before it split into three separate rings. The trio spun about each other until they settled into a perfect row.

What am I to do?

Kit didn't know who she was speaking to in her mind's eye, but she hoped for an answer. The circles meant something. They were important. She knew it in her bones, but the solution eluded her.

The rune-covered box suddenly pulsated with an intensely bright light. Kit twisted her head to avert her eyes. From the depths behind her, the leviathan was swimming aggressively towards her. With her daemon self at the forefront, she could see him clearly. He would be upon her before her racing heart could thump out its next beat. As the creature's lance-like horn was about to puncture her chest, Kit turned sideways, allowing it to pass harmlessly by. There was a resounding clang, like a clapper striking an enormous bell.

The sound of the impact was dwarfed by the screams of the Makara. It thrashed wildly, as though being held by some unseen force. Its great eyes were wild.

Over Kit's shoulder, she saw the reason for the animal's reaction. Its horn was lodged in one of the three holes. Kit remembered the insane cold that had emanated from the box when she'd touched it. Perhaps the Makara was experiencing the same thing. Perhaps this was the opportunity she needed to defeat the creature. Perhaps it was Titan himself, who was holding the Makara, refusing to release it until Kit could destroy it.

The little priest held the trident at the animal's head, poised to strike. The Makara's thrashing immediately stopped. It made a sad, almost pleading noise before it closed its eyes. Was it accepting its fate? Was this all a part of what needed to be done to free Titan? Was the horn the key to the prison?

Kit looked back to where the creature was caught. The very tip of its horn was embedded in the center of the three holes. She looked at her trident and blinked. Was this the answer? Was the trident the key to the vault? Was the Makara trying to prevent her from using the trident to free Titan?

You're a guardian. You are here to prevent Titan from being freed. Kit looked back at the prison, her brows now drawn tightly over her eyes. *You weren't trying to kill me. You were only trying to stop me from reaching my goal. That was what you were doing all along.*

Kit swam over to where the horn had penetrated the cube and compared the size and distance of the circular holes to the distance between the tines of her trident. They were a perfect fit.

"I don't want to kill you. Please, if you can hear me, remove yourself so that I can complete my mission."

The leviathan didn't move. Its eyes opened, gazing at the small girl carrying a large trident. The magnificent beast's tail continued to undulate, perhaps pushing its horn deeper.

"I'm sorry. I must complete my quest."

Kit drew back her trident and sucked in a deep breath, filling her lungs with the icy cold water. Her daemon self vanished, and her golden aura burst outward. With a single swing of the trident, she sliced through the horn. Kit's body wracked with pain as she grabbed the Makara by the horn, just beyond where she had cut it off. She poured everything she had into healing the wound she had just inflicted. The great Makara thrashed for a moment before it relaxed, allowing Kit to continue. As quickly as the pain had struck Kit, it diminished, only to be replaced by the most wonderfully euphoric sensation she had ever felt. The Makara backed away, drawing its horn from Kit's hand. The euphoric feeling immediately faded, leaving Kit wondering if it was a gift from the Makara for having healed it.

The young girl stared at the piece of horn that was still embedded in the prison wall. A sinking feeling in her stomach made her pause. What if the horn was stuck and she couldn't remove it?

Only one way to find out.

Kit wrapped her fingers around the protruding piece of horn and, with a twist, pulled it from the hole. She smiled weakly and stared at the spiraled dagger she held in her hand. The trident in her other hand vibrated. A feeling was pouring off it. It felt—excited. Kit nodded to it and rammed its tines into the holes of the box. A blinding flash of light overloaded Kit's senses just before everything went dark.

"Welcome, Sister Kit Standing Bear, bringer of freedom."

⨾⨾⧬⨾⨾

Kit opened her eyes to find herself lying on a great sheet of ice. In her right hand, she held the trident. In her left, she held the small tip of the Makara's horn. In the distance was a peak that dwarfed Mount Toka. Carved into its cliff-face was a statue of Titan. Like the mountain that supported it, the statue was at least twice the height of the sculpture at Toka, the one that had supplied the water to create Lake Titan.

A look of unbridled wrath was etched into the statue's face. Great manacles adorned its wrists. A heavy linked chain attached the shackles to the icy ground. The god's muscles strained against his bonds, intent on yanking them free from the glacier holding them.

Across the ice expanse, between the towering legs of her god, a sliver of yellow light poured through a doorway. A back-lit figure stood just outside the entrance, casting it in dark shadows.

"Come to me, Sister Kit Standing Bear. Come to me so that I may reward you for your efforts."

Kit stood motionless. She didn't fear the figure in the distance, but her feet felt frozen in place just the same.

"My brother's patience may not be what it used to be. You best hurry." Kit turned to the voice, only to find Triton standing behind her.

"Your brother?" Triton smiled warmly at the little girl standing before him. "When we met, you said that Gaia was your mother." Triton's smile broadened and his eyebrows raised slightly. It was then that Kit noticed the scar on his forehead. It had not been there before. Her eyes widened when the realization struck her.

"It was you all along? You were the great Makara?"

"I needed to be sure that Titan's teacher was pure of heart. It was my final test." Kit blinked. These revelations were coming too fast, and she was struggling to keep up with them.

"If Gaia is your mother and Titan is your brother..." Kit's nose scrunched up as she puzzled the pieces together. "Gaia is the mother of Titan?" Triton nodded. His blue eyes swirled as she continued to stare at him. The look of confusion on Kit's face redoubled.

"You called me Titan's teacher. That makes no sense."

"It makes perfect sense, if you would but open your heart to the possibility." The water god's words crept under Kit's skin. Even though he appeared pleased, to Kit's ears, that sounded like an insult, like she was too dim to understand.

"Sweet angel, no. I meant no disrespect." Triton huffed and ran his hand over his face. "Since the day you attuned yourself to my brother, he has witnessed your feelings, your actions, everything you have thought."

"Attuned? What does that mean?"

"What you called the Rite of Acknowledgement. You reached out across the plain of existence. You reached out for my brother, and he accepted you. It's not something that is easily achieved. In fact, you are the first.

"That's not true," Kit said, even though she felt no deception in his words. "Father Hoarfrost was also acknowledged. He told me so himself."

"Did he now? Are you sure?" Suddenly Kit wasn't sure. If it wasn't him, who told her? She quickly pushed the thoughts aside.

"What boon will you ask of my brother? It is within his power to grant you anything you desire."

"He promised to free the people of my village from slavery, from the relentless attacks of those who would do them harm." Triton smiled again.

"Why do you want to help them? They were nothing but cruel to you." The little priest lowered her head while she considered the question. It was true. The villagers had hated her. They'd mocked her, ridiculed her, kept her at a distance. They...

"They acted the way they did out of fear. They had been subjected to countless cycles of cruelty and torture at the hands of humans. I am human. It was difficult for them to not project their fears and their hatred onto me." Kit raised her chin. "The Berrat were not always as they are now. They once welcomed the Nomads with open arms. They taught them how to live in the north, to live *with* the north. It was fear that drove them to behave badly."

"Admirable." Triton said. "You are willing to see past the actions of others and look at their motivation. Even when their actions are reprehensible. But you will have to find something different to ask of Titan."

"Why?" Kit's jaw stiffened. "He promised me he'd free my people."

"They are already free. There is nothing more for my brother to do." Kit's jaw slackened.

"They are?" Triton nodded. "All of them?" Triton nodded again and then shrugged.

"No, not all, I suppose. But those who are still oppressed will probably be free of their captors before the new moon. Even so, it may take them generations before they are free of the scars they will carry after the harm the peoples inflicted upon them." Kit considered the god's words.

"Can Titan heal their scars?" Triton shook his head. "Why not?"

"That's not how our magic works. We can create and we can destroy, but we cannot change the way people feel. It is through patience and by example that you can heal them."

"Because I'm an angel?"

"No. Because you are a beacon of hope." The look of blissful peace on Triton's face suddenly turned grim. "I'm afraid I've kept you too long. My brother appears to be quite angry."

CHAPTER FORTY

TITAN'S BOON

The chains holding Titan's statue shattered, sending enormous shards in all directions. Pieces large enough to make the ground tremble landed paces away, sending up showers of ice and snow. Kit turned to Triton, only to find he was gone. The earth shook with such intensity it knocked Kit from her feet, sending her skittering along the ice field she was standing on. Before she had time to react, a great hand scooped her from the ground, carrying her thousands of feet into the air. The tormented look on Titan's statue was gone. It was now filled with undiluted wrath.

"The Veil has been opened and yet you ignore me so you can spend time with my brother?" Ice and snow fell from Titan's face with each word he spoke. The sound of his voice thundered in Kit's ears.

"The Veil has been opened because I freed you. Everyone warned me it would happen, but I made a promise to you, and I keep my promises." Titan's icy forehead furrowed. His thick shaggy eyebrows knitted together, sending more ice and snow to careen down his body. Kit held her trident in both hands, almost daring the god to smite her. The unbridled fury in the god's face lessened. He threw his head back and laughed. His entire body shook, sending multiple avalanches crashing down to the ground below. The very mountain itself shook at the power of his laughter.

"I knew I had chosen well with you. Like Fenrir, you were true to your word. Unlike Ymir, who sought only power, you sought justice." Kit stared at the god, unsure if she should speak or simply listen. "What boon do you ask of me?"

Kit took a knee and lowered her head. "I ask for nothing, my god. You have already given me that which I needed. My people are free." Titan's laughter stopped.

"You attribute your successes to me?"

"Who else should I attribute them to?" Kit's question was her honest reaction. "Through the gifts you gave me, I was able to attain so much in such a short length of time." Titan stared down at the small girl in his palm. "Everything I have," Kit continued. "Everything I have, I owe to you. Had you not visited me as a child, I don't know how my life would have turned out. I would not have learned of your greatness. I would not have ever met Father Hoarfrost, my friend and mentor. I would have never met Indie, the love of my life."

"I will bestow a gift upon you, and you will accept it. I promised you a boon and a boon you shall have."

"But I've already received what I asked for." Titan's expression shifted to anger once again. Perhaps he was taking her refusal as an insult. Many cultures thought that way, and yet Kit didn't understand why that would make someone angry. She looked at the now reddening eyes of her god and nodded.

"If you wish to grant me a boon, grant me the power to defeat King Faol." The anger in Titan's face intensified.

"Why do you continue to ask for what you already have?" The god's nostrils flared. He looked to be on the verge of exploding.

"I don't understand," Kit said. She felt the truth in Titan's words, but she couldn't comprehend what he was saying. The meaning was lost on her. "He threatens my city with an army of vampires. How can my friends and family stand against that? Surely, the feat is impossible."

"Freeing me was an impossible task, and yet you did it. I say again, you already have everything you need to defeat Faol." Titan's eyes suddenly brightened. "I know what to give you."

A surge of excitement welled up in Kit's belly. She wanted nothing from her god, but he had chosen a gift for her. Whatever it was, it would be amazing. Kit's memory flashed back to her sixteenth birthday and the gifts that her friends, and her father, had given her. Never had she ever received a feeling of such love, of such... belonging. Wasn't that what she had always wanted? Was that the underlying feeling she felt that day? Was that what made her so happy?

Every happy emotion that Kit was feeling instantly vanished. Titan turned his hand to the side and dropped Kit, sending the little priest to her death thousands of feet below.

"Why? I haven't finished my task. I still need to help my people."

The icy ground below was racing up at Kit. What of Indie, her mother, and the boys? They were waiting for her in Lilloet? What of Father Hoarfrost and her father, trying to stem a tidal wave of enemies ready to knock down the walls of Aarall? What of Danny and every Berrathian? They need me. I need them.

I will not fail them.

Great white wings sprung from Kit's back. They thrust outwards, slowing her descent, but not by enough. She was still falling at a terrible rate. The image of Lump and his early attempts to fly flooded into her mind. All he needed to do was to be a dragon, to be himself.

Kit flapped her wings with all her might. With each stroke, her descent slowed. With each wingbeat, her confidence soared.

"I'm an angel," she screamed out in delight. "I can fly!"

It was as though Kit's acceptance of her true nature set her free. Her wing-beats were now sure and powerful. She dipped and banked. She beat her wings again and immediately gained altitude. She circled the legs of Titan, climbing up to his waist and then to his chest.

The memory of the first time she rode Angel flooded back. When they'd jumped over the chasm, the feeling of undeniable exhilaration had filled her soul. This was the same feeling, only so much more.

She saw that Titan was still holding his hand aloft, his palm now turned upward. With instinctual grace, she lighted upon his hand like a songbird might land upon a branch.

"I am pleased that you like my gift to you." Titan's wrath was replaced with joy, and it was pouring off him in thick, warm waves.

"I am. Thank you." Kit took a knee and bowed her head.

"You understand, I still haven't given you anything you didn't already have." Kit smiled warmly.

"You don't understand." Her eyes were bright as she stared up at her god. "Sometimes the greatest gift of all is helping someone realize who they are. This is the gift that you have given me. From the first time we met, you have been helping me realize this."

Titan's lips parted slightly. His face seemingly frozen.

"Thank you." Titan took a knee and bowed his head to the little girl. "Thank you for being my teacher. When I dropped you, you faced certain death. You didn't know what you were capable of. But, in your last seconds, you thought of others. You always think of others. You put their wellbeing ahead of your own. I... I didn't know how to do that. I never knew the value of such emotion."

The ground shook violently, staggering Titan.

"Go now. Return to Lilloet with haste. Gather your family and return to Cormorant. The Veil has been breached and my brother's minions seek to wreak havoc upon the lands." Titan tossed Kit into the air. "Fly. Follow your heart to your loved ones. Trust in your friends and your family. They will be your salvation."

Kit had no idea how far she needed to travel to reach Lilloet. She wasn't sure where it was or what direction she needed to fly to get there.

Follow your heart. That's what Titan had said.

Kit banked left and beat her wings. The wind whipped over her face as she sped forward, trusting her instincts, trusting her heart.

⸘⸙⸘

The little angel had no idea how long it took her to fly from Titan's temple to the north shores of Lilloet. She reveled in the sensation of flight, the way the air raked over her body, the way her wings caught the wind. The sun's rays caressed her skin, warming her, rejuvenating her.

When the north shore of Lilloet came into view, she could see her mother, Indie, and the boys standing almost exactly where she had left them. As much as her heart soared while she was flying, it was nothing compared to what she felt seeing her family.

With simple grace, she landed lightly on the ground, only a few paces from her receiving party. Kit's eyes were bright as excitement rushed through her. Every one of her senses was heightened.

"Titan is free." They were the only words that came to mind. Everyone was staring at her with their mouths open. No one said a word. No one moved. They just gaped at her. Her mother was the first to react. She closed her mouth and raised her eyebrows.

"I wondered how long it would take for you to get your wings." Riva's blank expression was wiped away by her smile. "When the vampires took me in Cormorant, I thought that you would achieve your full potential. In my death, I was to ignite your soul." Riva chuckled awkwardly. "In a sense, I suppose I did. That was the day your daemon half came out."

Runt and Lump leapt forward, slamming their bodies into Kit. They whined uncontrollably as they continued their greetings. Kit gave them both a thorough rub-down while the boys sniffed at her silky white feathers. The little angel looked up at Indie, who was still staring at her with the same dumbstruck expression he had when she'd landed.

"Aren't you going to say something?" Kit spun around to show him the full beauty of her wings. When he still said nothing, she spun around again. Her look of joy turned to ash, filling her mouth with the taste of dread. "Indie? Is there something wrong?"

"I knew you'd be fun to be around." Kit's head snapped back at the words. What in Helja did that mean? Indie's face suddenly flushed. Riva moved in beside her, taking Kit's hand in hers.

"It's not Indie, my sweet. It's..." Before Riva could finish the sentence, Kit brushed her aside. The little priest's angelic demeanor vanished, along with her bright white feathers. Her skin turned into molten rock while her wings became obsidian, just like her eyes. Small, hooked horns appeared on her forehead. Her hair turned into a mane of pure flame.

"I will destroy you for this." Kit's voice was low and guttural. The trident ignited in her hand, bathed in bright blue flame. The shard of the Makara's horn she held did not melt. It did not burn. It turned into a glowing, blue-gray dagger covered in strange markings.

"Kitten, wait." Her mother's voice barely registered in Kit's ears. All she wanted to do was rake her now four-inch claws across this man's face, his neck, and his ribs. She wanted to open him from chin to groin and bleed him like a lamb.

"Kitten, please stop." Her mother's voice echoed through the recesses of Kit's consciousness. It was like an anchor, holding her back from attacking Indie. She loved this man with all her heart and soul. Why would she want to eviscerate him?

"Kit, he had to save Fury. It was the only way." The rage that had gripped her washed away like dust from a statue. Her breathing slowed and her vision cleared. "It was the only way," Riva repeated.

Kit's head swiveled towards Indie, her daemon appearance still on full display. "Explain."

Indie swallowed and took a deep breath. "It was the only way to save me."

"What do you mean, save you?" The inky blackness of Kit's eyes flashed like they were the gateway to the abyss. "To whom am I speaking?"

Indie bowed deeply and held the pose for several seconds. "It is I, Fury. I will be forever grateful to Indie for what he did for me. When you left me with him, I could not contain myself in the hammer. I no longer had your magic to assist me. My soul was leaking out. Had he not offered to help me, I would have perished." Kit couldn't tell if he was lying or not. While the daemon gave her amazing powers, her ability to distinguish truth from lie was gone.

"I want to speak with Indie." Fury shook his head.

"I cannot let him have control." Fury eyed the trident and the piece of horn in Kit's hand. "May I see those?" Kit held them back and shook her head.

"I want to speak with Indie." She let go of her anger and allowed her angelic self to return. It was like breathing in a field of lilacs and lavender, a stark contrast to the scents of brimstone and magma that the daemon gave her. Again, Fury shook his head. This time, a bit more slowly. "Now." Kit's eyes flashed golden as she issued the command. Fury flinched.

"I'm afraid." Fury said. Kit's heart stuttered. He wasn't just afraid. He was terrified.

"Why? What do you have to fear if you give Indie control of himself?"

"I'm afraid I'll be lost forever. The young man is incredibly strong willed and with you here to help him, he could easily suppress me." Fury continued to eye the trident and horn. "Please, may I have a closer look at those?" Kit shook her head.

"Let me speak with Indie first."

"And then I can have them?" Kit's eyes narrowed and her grip on the trident tightened.

"You said you wanted to see them more closely. What are these items to you?"

"I'm not sure," Fury said. "I won't know for certain until I hold them." Kit took a step back.

"Tell me what you think they might be." She paused for a moment, reading the man's expression. "Tell me what you *hope* they are." Indie blew out a deep breath and shook his head. "The Veil has been broken and the denizens of Helja are spilling out. People are likely dying while we are playing word games. Tell me what they are, or I'll simply leave you here."

"The trident holds the final piece of me. I can feel it calling to me, but the magic that contains it is incredibly powerful. What you are calling a horn, I believe to be the key to the Collar of Command. It is what we dragons have been seeking for so many cycles. It will free us from our mountain prisons."

"Let me speak with Indie. If he acknowledges that he willingly accepted you into him, I will consider giving you both items. We can travel to Cormorant, deal with the Veil, and the Hobgoblins can work their magic and return you to your body."

Indie slumped slightly. Kit dashed to his side to offer her support, but with a weary look, he pushed her away. "I'm okay. It was just... how do Rusty and Breayn do it? It felt like I was suffocating the entire time."

"Did you *let* him do that to you?" Kit's voice was soft, but her tone was razor-sharp. Indie sucked in a quick breath and slowly exhaled.

"Fury said he couldn't maintain his hold on the hammer. He said if his soul leaked out, he would be gone forever."

"And he forced himself into you? Did he leverage his position because you're his apprentice?" Kit's voice was not so soft, and the sharpness of her tone increased significantly. Indie just shook his head.

"No. It was nothing like that. He demanded nothing. He just asked." Indie got a sad look on his face. "He was scared, and I helped him."

"Do you still want to help him get his body back, to free him from the mountains?" Kit plunged the trident into the ground and hitched the piece of horn into her belt. She took both of Indie's hands in hers while her golden aura poured out over them. Kit could tell lie from truth, but she wanted to be sure who it was she was still talking with. Indie nodded lightly to the question. "I need you to speak the words aloud. I need you to tell me if that's what you want."

"It is." Indie squeezed Kit's hands tightly. "For good or for ill, I made a promise to help him. What kind of man would I be if I wasn't true to my word?" Kit tensed at the question. It seemed she had made a remarkably similar declaration to Titan not so very long ago. A hint of a smile crossed her lips. She slowly slipped the horn from her belt and handed it to her man. In a similar fashion, she pulled the trident from the ground and extended it to him.

"You willingly give these to me?" The way Indie was shaking, Kit knew instantly who was in control of his body. "You would choose to make me whole, to set the dragons free?"

Kit gave Fury a weak smile and the slightest hint of a bow. "I do. I trust you will not make me regret it?" Indie nodded his head.

"I will." He motioned for Riva and the boys to draw near. "Let's get you to Cormorant. I hear there may be a demon uprising there."

CHAPTER FORTY-ONE

FROM BEYOND THE VEIL

Great clouds of smoke belched up from a tremendous crack in the ground. Bodies of dwarves and hobgoblins were strewn about, interspersed between the blackened husks of creatures unknown to Kit.

"Demons," Indie muttered. "They've made it to the surface."

Kit's eyes were locked on the fissure that stretched from the beach all the way into the city. Her stomach knotted. It looked suspiciously like the cracks she had created when she called upon Titan to cast her earthquake spells.

A thunderous boom from somewhere beyond the dock warehouses drew the attention of the dwarves who seemed to run aimlessly in front of the Port Authority buildings. They were dressed in heavy armor like nothing Kit had ever seen before. In moments, they were clomping their way into the city, marching precariously close to the gaping rent that had opened up in the land.

"What do we do?" Kit looked to Indie for his martial advice.

"I need to get to the manor," Indie said. "I need to get the Hobgoblins to make me whole." Kit groaned. In the bedlam, she had forgotten that Indie wasn't Indie. He seemed lost in his own thoughts, perhaps trying to plan how to deal with this situation, perhaps thinking only of himself. Whatever was going on inside his head would need to wait. Runt and Lump snarled and took off at a dead run to Kit's right.

"Sweet Titan." There were six or seven creatures clawing their way up from the fissure. Their skin was black as night, their eyes fire-red. Wicked claws hung from oversized hands while rows of pointed teeth filled their awful maws. "Boys, no!" Whether they didn't hear, or whether they didn't want to hear, Kit didn't know. The pair of canines were running at top speed when they crashed into the group of demons. Lump knocked a demon backwards, sending him careening into the hole from which he'd just come. Runt took a demon's head full into his mouth and began shaking him. It raked at him with its claws for a moment before going limp.

Lump switched into his dragon form and immediately flamed as many of the demons as he could. They didn't seem to be affected by his dragon-fire, at least not significantly.

"Feel for the magic within you," Indie screamed as he ran forward, his trident held wide from his body, the leviathan's horn held close to his chest. "Call upon the magic. Unleash it with your breath." Lump dropped his body low to the ground and extended his wings. With his muscles tensed, he appeared ready to pounce. A moment later, his mouth opened in a great yawn, unleashing a light so bright, Kit was forced to shield her eyes. A great torrent of golden flame poured forth, engulfing the three demons standing in front of him. Their eyes bulged momentarily, just before their brains liquified and poured from their skulls as a gray sludge. The rest of their bodies fared slightly better, lasting another two or three heartbeats before turning to ash.

Runt had two demons on him. One he plucked off, crushing it in his mouth, while the other raked at him with its wicked claws. With each swipe, a bright spray of blood flew from Runt's neck. Despite how powerful the dire wolf was, he could not withstand that much damage for long.

"You'll need this," said a voice from beside Kit. She turned her head to find Riva, holding her war hammer out to her. "It's time." Kit didn't understand the emotion that rippled through her, but she accepted the hammer and turned to find Runt. Indie was already beside him, his trident embedded deep into the demon who was ravaging the dire wolf's neck. Holding the creature several feet above his head, Indie opened his mouth and unleashed a heavy stream of brilliant blue flame, crisping the demon in mere seconds.

Runt was staring over the edge of the rent, snarling and barking as he did. His coat was matted with blood that continued to ooze from the wounds on his neck and back. Without thinking, Kit beat her wings and flew over to the wolf's side. His head snapped towards Kit for a moment before immediately returning to his obsession down below. Kit gently placed her hand on Runt's head. Her golden aura burst out, engulfing both the angel and the wolf. The wounds had been severe, and yet, there was no pain. Kit didn't need to accept the damage into her body. She simply healed him.

The dire wolf released a series of quick barks. He was still focused directly on the chasm and whatever it was he was seeing down below. Kit moved next to the rent and peered over the edge. A blood-red light glowed deep within the chasm, casting hundreds of bodies below in a bizarre macabre. Runt continued barking frantically.

A rush of wind nearly knocked Kit over the side. She watched in horror as Lump soared into the abyss with Indie straddling his back. Runt's barks got louder and higher pitched. His feet were scrambling about like he was looking for a way to go down into the hole. He turned to Kit; his eyes filled with panic. Without thinking, Kit wrapped her arms around the dire wolf and threw herself over the edge.

⚮

Runt's body was fully rigid in Kit's grasp. She remembered how he'd struggled to jump a small river, and how his fear had made it impossible for the wolf to trust himself enough to jump a deep chasm. In her arms, as they sailed headlong into trouble, he trembled uncontrollably.

"You're safe with me," Kit said as she maneuvered her way through the rift. The walls were uneven, with great boulders sticking out from its sides at irregular intervals. Some places appeared too narrow to navigate, but her angel-wings guided her safely along. Runt whined in response.

"Oh, sweet Runt. You trusted me when you were but a small pup. You put your faith in me, and I put mine in you. I promise you will not fall. I will see you safely to our destination. I am with you."

The tension in Runt's body melted away. The pair was fast approaching the bottom. The crevasse had opened up into an enormous cave. Along its ceiling, green slime shone, lighting the cavern with its sickly glow. At the far end of the room, a jagged crack had opened in the stone wall. An ominous red glow poured out of it. From a distance, it looked like a demented smile. From out of the opening, demons were crawling out by the hundreds. As soon as they emerged, hordes of Dwarves and Hobgoblins fell upon them.

Blue lightning crackled and arced across the cavern. It struck the bodies of the demons. It seemed to make their bodies transparent, illuminating their skeletal forms from within.

A thunderous boom rocked the cavern, knocking many of the combatants off their feet. The demons stopped coming through the hideous red smile. In their stead, dwarves poured out in an endless stream of gleaming silver armor. Hundreds upon hundreds of them had passed through before their numbers ceased. The red crack wavered before it suddenly darkened. A dwarf of enormous proportions crawled through the hideous smile. He stood several feet taller than a Gigas, but his proportions were perfectly dwarf-like. His body was wide and heavily muscled. Blindingly white armor encased him from head to toe, exposing only a face that was completely covered by wild orange hair. In his right hand was a double-bladed ax, of what appeared to be pure mithril.

"Father!" a voice boomed out. "Ye are free!" Kit watched with dumb fascination as Coldforge sprinted across the cave, knocking anything and everything out of his way with his glowing white ax. The dwarven prince must have already been in the cavern before Kit had flown down. It was only at that moment the little angel realized she still had Runt in her arms, hovering a dozen feet above the ground.

Lump swooped low, clearing a path through a throng of demons who were working to block Coldforge's progress. He blew golden flames on any demon in his way.

"Let's go help them," Kit said to Runt as she lowered him to the ground. The little angel drew her war hammer and sang out a war cry. Her golden aura exploded outwards, much to the dismay of a gang of demons who were headed their way. They clutched the sides of their heads and howled in agony. In seconds, Kit and Runt were racing across the cavern's uneven stone floor, making their way to Lump and Indie.

With a grunt, the oversized dwarf threw out his war ax. It spun through the air, barely above the ground. Every demon in its path exploded on contact. The ax suddenly went airborne and returned to its owner's hand.

"By Gimlie's beard," the dwarves all called out in unison. "All will be saved!"

Runt surged ahead of Kit, his strides carrying him twenty paces at a time. A group of demons had taken up position at Lump's rear. They were hurling swirling spheres of blackness at the dragon while he was dealing with another gang of demons hacking at him from the front. They had been joined by another, much larger demon. Each time Lump blew out his flames, the larger demon's voice screeched out, deflecting the dragon's golden fire around his comrades.

The dire wolf threw himself into the enemy, his teeth a blur of white and red. He fought like he was possessed. He seemed to instinctually know exactly what to do, how to move. He avoided counter attacks with ease, using his bulk to knock his opponents off balance.

"He has found his courage. He is no longer consumed with fear." The voice of Amaruq filled Kit with pride. *"You gave that to him. It is yet another reason I will be eternally grateful to you."* She wasn't sure that was true, but it warmed her heart, anyway.

The next few minutes were pure chaos. Kit could barely keep track of everything that was happening around her. With hammer in hand, she smote any demon who came within her reach. She sang her angelic song, sending the demons scattering. While they made disorganized retreats, the Dwarves and Hobgoblins fell upon them, striking them down with ax and magic. Great billows of ash clouds filled the air, obscuring Kit's view.

When the smoke finally dissipated, there wasn't a single demon left standing.

"By Gimlie's beard," the dwarves intoned and took a knee. They all genuflected before their god as he strode through the throng.

"What have we here?" Gimlie called out, his deep voice echoing off the chamber walls. His facial hair twitched as he eyed Lump, Indie, and Runt.

"Have the dragons been freed?" He slid his battle ax into its sheath at his hip and stepped closer to Lump. "Me eyes tell me yes, but me heart tells me no." His eyes twinkled as he cast his gaze upon Indie. "And yet, a dragon in a boy's body sits upon that which appears to be a dragon of gold."

"These are my friends, father." Coldforge called out. "The fine young man's name is Indie. The dragon he sits upon is a wolfdog named Lump. The magnificent wolf standing beside them is Runt. I have enjoyed many glorious moments with this young wolf." The dwarf's face slackened. Even behind his mass of orange hair, Gimlie's shock was obvious. "And this wondrous creature standing behind them is me friend and rescuer, Sister Kit Standing Bear. While I was not looking, she has gone and become a full angel."

Gimlie laughed. It was a joyous belly laugh that echoed off the walls. He continued until it seemed the entire cavern was going to come crashing down around them.

"She is no mere angel, me son. She is so much more." The dwarf god took a knee before Kit. "The grace of Titan adorns you like snow on a mountaintop. You would be a sight to behold without it, but it still enhances your beauty. While me children freed me from me Underworld prison, I suspect it was ye that made it all possible."

Kit stared up at the enormous face before her. Coldforge was the spitting image of this man. The likeness was incredible. "Thank you," she finally said after several excruciatingly long moments. "I am pleased to meet you... your godliness."

Again, Gimlie laughed. He gave his beard a tug and shook his head. "If yer a friend of me son, then yer a friend of mine. I would be honored if you would call me by me given name."

"His name's Gimlie," Coldforge whisper-shouted at Kit. Everybody within earshot, which was pretty much every living person in the cavern, laughed at the dwarf's words.

Kit spread her wings wide and bowed deeply. She took on the drake's pose when they humbled themselves before their queen. "Thank you, Gimlie, God of the Dwarves." She raised her head to the god and smiled. "You may call me Kit."

Indie cleared his throat. "As much as I would like to spend time getting to know all of you better, I have a long journey ahead of me and I still need to get my soul reunited."

"Gimlie," Kit said. "The body of the young man astride the gold dragon is Indigo Willowbrook. However, the person speaking from within the man is the dragon lord, Fury."

"Fury?" Gimlie's voice changed, instantly shifting from joyous to suspicious. "How did a dragon lord escape his prison? Why does his spirit linger in the body of a human?" The dwarf god considered the trident in Indie's hand. He sniffed at it. "Ye hold the staff of Ymir, and within it, is a piece of yer soul. Do I have the gist of the situation?"

"You do, Gimlie, god of the dwarven realm. My soul was taken from my body, split into pieces, and its parts were placed within four artifacts. Three pieces of my essence now dwell within this young man who has willingly accepted to be my host until I can be returned to my true body. The final piece of me lives within this trident. I plan to seek the help of the Hobgoblins to transfer the last of my essence into this host. When I am whole, we will travel to the Mithril Mountains and unlock the Collar of Command."

"And in doing so, ye will free Ouroboros." Gimlie cocked a bushy eyebrow.

"The only way I can be free," Indie said, lowering his head, "is to free my master. The magic that holds the great black dragon holds all dragons."

"Let me speak to the boy," Gimlie said. Indie's eyes widened and his face paled. He stole a glance at Kit, who nodded in response to the non-verbal question. Indie nodded to Kit and then to Gimlie.

"I am myself," Indie said with a shudder before quickly bowing his head.

"Young man," the god said. He spoke slowly to make sure Indie understood his words. "This dragon lord cannot be trusted. Like his master, Ouroboros, he seeks only to fulfill his own needs and desires. I don't know what he offered ye in return for hosting his essence, but if he were to become whole, he may never leave ye. He may choose to use ye until your body can no longer sustain him. When that happens, he will move on in search of another host."

Indie's face contorted at the dwarf-god's words. Kit couldn't tell if it was Indie who was upset, or if it was Fury, or if it was the two of them fighting an internal struggle of their own.

"Enough!" Indie yelled out, his face red from his exertion. "I understand, Fury. Let me speak, would you?" The conflict in the young man's eyes drained away and his body relaxed.

"Yes, Gimlie, I understand and accept the risk of hosting this dragon lord. Kit and I both believe he will do the right thing when the time comes. I will stake my life on it."

Kit's golden aura poured forth and clung to her body. She stepped close to Lump and patted him gently on his front leg. "Fury?" She stared up at the man sitting on the dragon's back. The change from Indie to Fury was almost imperceptible, but Kit immediately knew to whom she was speaking. "Do you swear to release Indie and return to your body in the most expedient way possible?"

Indie crossed his arms over his chest and cocked his head to the side. "It hurts me you would so carefully phrase your question. I have already given my word. Asking me to speak it again is insulting."

Kit smiled brightly and batted her eyes. "Do me the service of telling me one more time. I wish to bask in the wisdom and grace of your words." Indie chuckled, placed his hand to his heart and bowed his head.

"Since you asked so nicely, little Kitten, I will leave this young man's body at the first possible moment. When my soul is united and whole once again, I will make haste to Ouroboros' domain and unlock the Collar of Command. Assuming he allows it, I will immediately return to my mountain to reunite with my body. When I do, Indie and I will both be free and his debt to me will be paid in full."

Kit looked at Gimlie, giving him a questioning look. He blew out a breath, making his mustache flutter. "I trust ye know what yer doing, little angel." The dwarf-god held out his hand, motioning to Indie to give him the trident. With reluctance, Indie gently placed the shaft in the oversized hand. Gimlie closed his eyes and breathed upon the weapon. A dim blue aura appeared. It swirled about, coalescing at the weapon's tines. The aura brightened. Shimmering shades of blue swirled while the aura shaped itself into a perfectly formed miniature dragon. It flapped its wings and gazed about, confused by its surroundings. When its eyes fell onto Indie, the tiny dragon blew out a thin ribbon of flame. It spun several times before taking flight. With a couple of wingbeats, it sailed directly into Indie's chest.

Indie's head flew back. Veins stood out on his neck. Every visible muscle wracked. His golden scales burst out and covered his body. He let out a blood-curdling scream. His golden scales suddenly morphed. The brilliant gold washed away, slowly replaced by a sky blue so strikingly clear that one might expect a midday sun to appear. Great leathery wings sprouted from Indie's back, and he launched himself into the air. With a couple of powerful strokes, he circled the cavern, raising clouds of dust as he did. After several passes, he landed next to Gimlie and took a knee.

"Thank you," Indie said, his head bowed low. "You will not regret this. I swear it on my life."

The ground rocked. Large chunks of the ceiling came crashing down, obliterating several dwarves in the process.

"Cave-in," somebody shouted. "Make for the surface!"

The dwarves immediately scrambled away and began scaling the cavern's stone face, making their way up through the fissure to the surface. To Kit, they resembled spiders scurrying up a wall. An enormous molten arm came reaching through the crack that resembled a demented red smile. From beyond the Veil, a clawed hand stretched through the crack and into the room. Lava dripped from its fingers as it clamped onto the floor.

"Gorgaraeth comes," Gimlie bellowed. "Make for the surface. I will hold him back as long as I can."

"By Gimlie's beard," many of the dwarves responded, as they continued working their way up the impossibly steep cliff.

"Leave, all of ye," Gimlie bellowed. "Ye cannot stand against this foe. He is the destructor, the bringer of Ragnarök. I will try to drive him back and seal the crack. Leave!"

CHAPTER FORTY-TWO

UNTIL THE LAST DEMON DIES

The heady stench of sulfur and brimstone filled the cavern. With every breath, the taste of ash coated Kit's tongue. The air was so thick, it made it difficult to breathe. Gorgaraeth was pushing himself through the slash in the wall. From within the crimson glow, dead, lifeless eyes peered out.

"I'm not leaving," Kit screamed at Gimlie. "If he breaches the barrier, he'll not be able to move well. He's too big for this room. We're best to fight him here and now."

"Girl, get out!" the dwarf god yelled back. "Ye don't know what yer doin'. Ye cannot fight him. Ye cannot defeat him. The demon god is pure evil, and he cannot be stopped."

Coldforge, sitting astride Runt's back, raced towards the molten hand. He leapt from Runt's back as they neared and, in a two-handed overhead swing, brought his ax down upon the demon-god's hand, severing a finger.

"Ah son, now why'd ye go and do that?" Gimlie gave the dwarf a look of exasperation. "Ye only served to make the situation worse."

Coldforge stared at his ax while its metal head melted from the handle. A look of dismay crossed his face before he tossed the useless piece of wood to the side. His dismay turned to horror when the severed finger laying next to him coalesced into a horned demon of pure molten lava.

"Don't let it touch ye," Gimlie called out. "The two of ye get away from that thing."

Runt wasn't so quick to back away. The demon thing was moving on his friend, and he would not allow it. The dire wolf barked and snarled, desperately trying to draw the creature's attention. The fiery demon, for a moment, seemed confused, unable to decide which of its two adversaries it would attack. Before it acted, Lump raced forward and engulfed the demon in a bath of golden flames.

From within the inferno, the demon squealed. Lump continued his attacks for several more seconds, only stopping when the creature's wails ceased. When the dragon fire abated, a puddle of magma lay on the floor.

"Ye shouldn't have done that either," Gimlie said. "Ye all should heed me words and get yer arses out of here. Ye don't understand what yer dealing with." The dwarf god had barely finished speaking when the puddle of magma bubbled and spit, and reformed back into the demon. This time, it was a few feet taller than it had been a moment ago.

Runt immediately began barking at it again. He moved his fur-covered body between Coldforge and the demon, baring his teeth and snarling menacingly. The demon laughed at the wolf's antics as it took a step forward.

"Runt, get out of there," Kit screamed out, near hysterics. She flapped her feathered wings and launched herself forward, intent on intervening, intent on protecting her wolf. She unleashed her angelic song, hoping it would hurt the magma demon the same way it had the others. Her music rolled over the demon, and it screeched out, either in pain or in anger, but it didn't stop it. Black wings sprouted from its back, and it lurched forward for Runt.

The wolf dodged the attack, barely avoiding the rake of the creature's claws. Runt barked again, darted forward and then instantly retreated before making contact. Kit's heart rose into her throat, fearing the worst. With her hammer raised, she was about to throw herself at the demon when Indie slammed into her, knocking her from the air. The two tumbled hard to the ground, locked in a tight embrace. When they came to a stop, Indie was straddling Kit, a look of wild fear in his eyes. Rage bubbled up within Kit's soul, her body instantly shifting into her daemon form.

"That's my girl," Indie said. "It wasn't time for the angel." Kit threw Indie off and launched herself into the air. Runt and the demon were about to engage. She wouldn't get there in time.

With wings unfurled and claws extended, the demon launched itself at Runt. The wolf held his ground and opened his mouth wide, inviting the demon into his maw. A heartbeat later, a stream of frost blew from Runt's mouth. The ice struck the demon and instantly turned into steam. The demon screeched out and Gorgaraeth bellowed. His gargantuan voice rocked the entire cavern.

When the steam cleared, there was a small iron statue of the demon, frozen in the exact pose it held before launching itself at Runt.

⁂

"Is that it?" Kit called out. "Is that the secret to defeating Gorgaraeth? Is cold his weakness?"

"I don't think the cold killed it, but is sure slowed it down," Gimlie said.

"Perhaps deciding to show himself in the north was not a good plan for him," Indie said. Kit gave him a sidelong glance. Her rage had not fully subsided yet, but she could think clearly enough to understand why Indie had attacked her, knocking her from the air.

"What's next?" Coldforge asked.

Gorgaraeth pulled his arm back from the bizarre smile in the wall. He bellowed out in frustration, seemingly unsure how to deal with the situation. Excitement grew in Kit's chest, thinking they had beaten back the demon god. Knowing his weakness would be the key to defeating him. Discovering a way to leverage the knowledge would be the hard part. Even with her and Runt working in concert, there was no way they could produce enough cold to freeze the god.

Cracks formed on the demon statue's dull gray surface. From within those cracks, deep lines of red appeared.

"It's as I feared," Gimlie said. "The wolf's breath didn't kill it. It only slowed it down."

Runt immediately released another stream of frost at the statue, once again returning it to its solid state.

"Maybe," Kit said as she strode up to the rock-solid demon, "it just needs to be made much smaller." She pulled back her leathery black wings and hoisted her battle hammer over her head. With all her might, she brought the weapon's mithril head down on the demon. There was a brilliant flash of light on contact, shattering it into tiny shards that scattered across the room.

"What did ya do, girl?" Gimlie reached out as if to punish the small daemon. "Ye can't kill him like that. Ye only made things worse."

Kit ignored the dwarf-god's rant and picked up one of the larger pieces of the demolished statue. It barely fit in her palm. She gazed at it for several moments before a bright red flame appeared. It licked over the demon shard, almost caressing it. In seconds, the hunk of debris in her hand melted into a small pool. A moment later, it evaporated into a dense black smoke.

"I don't think these pieces will reform," Kit said, smiling brightly up at Gimlie. "Perhaps it's my hammer that is the key to destroying Gorgaraeth. Maybe because it's made of mithril?"

"Nay," Coldforge said. "I don't think so. I think it's the enchantments held within the weapon. Let me give it a look." The dwarf held out his hand, his fingers convulsing while he waited to hold the hammer.

"I did say I would give it to you," Kit said brightly. "You kept your word and I'll keep mine. It's yours."

Coldforge was practically salivating when she held the hammer out to him. He cradled it carefully, holding it like a father might hold his child. "'Tis a wondrous weapon, girl." He spun it over in his hands while he inspected the runes on the face of its mithril head. "Father, this weapon has been imbued with *brilliance*. The enchantments were not particularly strong, but they were surprisingly effective. Do ye think it is the key to defeating Gorgaraeth? Maybe if we gave yer ax a proper enchantment, ye could use it to smite his sulfurous arse?"

Before Gimlie could answer, Runt barked furiously. Waves of demons were pouring through the gap in the wall. Many of them were huge and barely fit through the demented red smile.

"There are too many for us to fight," Indie said. "We need to get to the surface."

Kit didn't want to run. She wanted to fight. Her daemon self was at the forefront, and it wanted to be unleashed.

"Fury's right," Gimlie called out. "Me kin are above. We will face the enemy there." Kit chortled at the dwarf-god's words.

"That doesn't sound like the dwarven way to me." Kit turned to Indie and motioned to Runt. "Get him out of here. I'll buy you time."

Without hesitation, Indie snatched up Runt and flew up for the surface. Lump didn't follow. He belched out massive fireballs, incinerating demon after demon.

"Lump, go. I'm right behind you," Kit yelled, just before turning herself into a human fireball. Lump continued his assault on the demons, breathing great gobs of golden flames across the ground. It took Kit several moments before she realized he was laying down a wall of dragon fire.

Two winged demons slipped through the horrible smile and took flight. Kit beat her wings and made for the newcomers. The flames that engulfed the daemon seemed to make her lighter, faster than her angelic self. She tried to unleash her angelic song, but it came out sounding more like a great belch.

Okay, then. I'll need to try a different tactic.

Kit had no weapon as she flew at the winged demons. She threw her obsidian claws out in front of herself just as she reached the first enemy. The demon responded in kind. It wheezed out as Kit continued forward, throwing the full weight of her tiny body into the creature's chest. The demon wrapped its leathery wings around Kit, its own claws biting into her back. Within the cocooning wings, the air became thick and heavy with smoke. Thinking that it was the demon that was burning, Kit dug deep into herself and drew upon her daemon fires. The pair exploded in a fireball. The demon never even had a chance to scream.

Kit chortled and made her way towards the second winged creature that was flying directly for Lump. The dragon dog launched himself into the air, meeting his attacker head-on. There was a thunderous collision, and the pair plummeted to the ground, landing with a tremendous thud on the earthen floor beneath. They tumbled and rolled about with the demon grappling for the dragon's wings. Perhaps the demon understood it was Lump's weakest point, or perhaps they were the easiest thing to grab onto. Whatever its reasoning, Lump simply grabbed the demon in his toothy maw. The creature thrashed for a moment before the dragon's jaws clamped tight, cutting the winged monster into multiple pieces.

Looking like the demon left an unpleasant taste in Lump's mouth, he shook his head to rid himself of the flesh that clung to his teeth and immediately got back to laying down a wall of flame.

Kit took a quick look at the opening up above. Gimlie and Coldforge had just crested the lip of the crevasse. Indie and Runt were already gone.

"That's good enough, Lump. Let's go."

The dragon ceased laying down the wall of flame and took flight. He circled the cavern once before turning his nose skyward. With just a few flaps of his wings, he was gone.

Kit hovered in place, watching as the demons tried to breach the wall of flame. Several tried to run through, only to be burned up before they could make it across. They screeched with rage, shaking their fists at the daemon who watched their failure. Kit could feel another joyous chortle growing in her chest. Before it could be released, she swallowed it down. From beyond the hideous red smile in the wall, a man crawled out. His body was covered in flame as he emerged, but they receded as soon as he had passed through the crack in the Veil. He rubbed his bald head and flexed the muscles in his arms, shoulders, and chest. He stretched his neck from side to side as though trying to work out a deep kink in his bones. He looked up at Kit and smiled. There was nothing friendly about the grin that split the man's face.

"Hello," he called up to Kit. "I hope you're having a good day, for it will be your last."

Something in the man's voice was unnerving, like she had heard it before. It sounded so familiar, but she couldn't call upon the memory.

The man walked toward the wall of flame. The demons all laid themselves prostrate at his feet as he passed them by.

"Arise, my children. Your purpose is at hand. With your fire, you will cleanse the earth of all who dwell here. You will unleash your malevolence upon the lands. The world will shudder as you burn the life from it."

"You will never leave this cavern," Kit called out. She gathered a ball of flame in her hands and hurled it at the self-important man as he glided across the ground, heading directly for the dragon fire. The ball struck him on his shoulder. On contact, it exploded into flaming bits, starting tiny fires on the surrounding ground. The man brushed off his bare skin where the fire had struck him and gave Kit a look of annoyance. Without breaking stride, the man continued into the wall of fire, stepping through the inferno unharmed.

He gave Kit a cocky smile and passed his hand over the dragon flames. They instantly receded, allowing the demons who had gathered behind him to come racing through the gateway he'd created.

There was a blinding flash of light from behind Kit, and a thunderous voice filled the cavern.

"Foul! Foul, I say."

The advancing demons immediately halted as though frozen in place.

"Mephitis, Arbiter, I call for a ruling," a deep, rage-filled voice from behind Kit called out.

A bubble full of brilliant green gas appeared before the man who had just walked through dragon fire. There was a pop, and the bubble vanished. The green mist clung to the odd creature within. Mephitis, in her bizarre yet strikingly beautiful form, stood before the man. Her thick green hair, consisting of hundreds of small water snakes, writhed on her head as if measuring the person standing before her. A hint of a smile crossed the woman's face, stretching her alligator-skin ever so slightly. She reached out with her swamp rat hand and invited the man to stand closer to her. Her long rat tail swished slowly behind her as she waited. When the man didn't move, she unfurled an enormous pair of forest green, leathery wings.

"Come to me, Bael, and be judged."

Sweet Titan, it's Bael?

"Not my proudest moment as a father," a voice whispered in her ear. "It's not the way I would have liked you to meet him."

"Titan?" Kit spun around. From within the bright light that had appeared behind her was her god. She could not see him, but she could feel his presence.

"I declare you to be in breach of the rules set out for this game," Mephitis called out. "I declare these playing pieces forfeit."

"No," Bael cried out. It almost sounded to Kit like he was whining. "No, I did nothing wrong. I never cheated."

"You took direct action on the situation here to the benefit of your position. That clearly violates the rules, and my judgment is final." With a swipe of her rat-like hand, the entire group of demons that were crossing through the opening vanished. The wall of flames that Bael had extinguished burned once again. This time, they were even taller than they had been. "A penalty for your actions."

Bael's face contorted with rage. He reached out and grabbed Mephitis by the throat and throttled her.

"Enough," Titan called out. "Let her go or I will mete out your punishment." Bael continued to throttle the strange-looking woman. She clawed at the god's hands, struggling against his grip.

"Bael, release her now or I will... undo you. I brought you into this universe and I can take you out of it." The bright white light behind Kit disappeared, reappearing a moment later in front of Bael. It immediately vanished, leaving Titan standing there. "Bael, I will not give you another warning."

The god's mouth twisted into a bow and his lower lip quivered. He pushed Mephitis away, sending her sprawling onto the ground. The god's body was shaking as he stared up at his father.

"Consider your next action before you take it," Titan said. "It is a game we are playing, nothing more. We have lost many times, and we have never broken the rule of non-interference." Bael's hands clenched into fists.

"You cheated," he said, thrusting his chin out at his father. "You cheated all the time. You gave this one power. You filled her with your magic, made her stronger than she was. Mephitis, I call for a ruling. Did my father cheat or not?"

Mephitis picked herself up off the ground, refusing to dust herself off. She gave Bael a look of pure loathing.

"Despite the way you have manhandled me, I will render a fair and impartial verdict." She glared at Bael and raised her eyebrows. "Will you agree to my arbitration on this matter?"

The look of anger on Bael's face melted away, replaced by worry. If you are found to be making false accusations, you will forfeit your place in this game. You and your pieces will be removed from the game board, and you will participate no longer.

The god swallowed hard as he considered the Arbiter's words. From behind the Veil, things could have been skewed. He might not have seen what he thought he had seen. He turned to face his father, who was shaking his head slowly.

"Don't do it, son," Titan said. "This has been our best game ever. Don't spoil it with your petty ways."

Titan's comment made something inside Kit snap. She flew down from her place and landed next to the god. With all her might, she shoved him, knocking the god off balance.

"You're going to continue playing this *game*? You're going to let this maniac's demons come spilling out on the lands and wreak havoc upon its peoples. You called me your teacher. Have you learned nothing of love, kindness, or decency?"

"Be at peace, Sister Kit," Mephitis said. "They are bound by forces beyond their control. They cannot simply stop the game. It must play out."

"I don't understand," Kit screamed. "You can declare them forfeit, or whatever it is you said. You can stop the game. You can prevent everyone from being killed."

"No, little angel, I cannot. If I were to declare the game ended, everything the Travelers have wrought would be destroyed, annihilated, like it never existed. Their essence would be returned to its source, and everything you hold dear would be no more. You, sweet child, would be no more."

"I would disappear?" Kit looked to Titan, hoping he would refute the claim.

"You are the indirect result of my creations." The god's eyes were glassy as he spoke. "You, too, would be returned to me."

"What am I to do?" Kit asked. "How can I stop Ragnarök?"

Titan's lips parted as if to speak. "You cannot tell her," Bael screamed out. "Mephitis, tell him to be silent." The strange lizard-rat-woman glared at Titan.

"Win the game," Mephitis said to Kit with a matter-of-fact voice. "Only by winning the game can you save the ones you love."

"How do I win?" Kit asked. She thought back to her time at Silverhawk when she was forced into playing a game of cards for the lives of three prisoners. Now she was playing for the lives of millions. "What are the rules? How is victory decided?"

"The rules are quite simple," Mephitis said. "The game is over when the players concede defeat."

"And when do they concede?" Kit asked. She was glaring at Bael, who had a dangerously sly look on his face.

"I will never concede," he said. "I will not stop until I have achieved victory."

Kit looked to Mephitis, hoping she would say he couldn't do that, or it was an illegal action, or something. Anything that would give her hope that she might win. The Fate shrugged in response.

"There is no rule that says he must concede," she said. "You must defeat the demons, fight them back until they lose the will to fight on."

Bael roared with laughter.

"They will never back down. They will fight until their very last breath."

CHAPTER FORTY-THREE

INTO THE ABYSS

"Bael has been freed," Kit said to Gimlie. The dwarf-god looked about, ready to climb back down into the chasm to find out where he was.

"Did ya have ta fight him?" Coldforge asked. He spun his shiny new battle hammer in his hand and gave it a sour look. "Ya should have had yer weapon with ya. I should have never accepted it."

"No, I didn't have to fight him and no, you were right to take the hammer. I promised it to you, and I don't break my word." Kit stared up at Gimlie. "Titan and Mephitis were there, too. Bael tried to break the rules, but Mephitis put a stop to it. Titan threatened to dissolve him, or whatever happens to gods, if he cheated again."

"How did he cheat?" Coldforge asked. He was still eyeballing his new hammer.

"Lump, put down a wall of dragon fire to hold the demons in the cave. Bael waved his hand, and it disappeared. As soon as the demons stepped through the wall, Titan called foul and Mephitis showed up. She made the demons just... evaporate. They vanished like they had never even existed." Kit's eyes went wide, and she made an exploding-like gesture with her hands. "They just went poof!"

Simultaneously, Gimlie and Coldforge blew out a long breath. Both of their overly hairy mustaches fluttered out over their lips.

"What are we going to do about Gorgaraeth?" Lump asked. He had switched from his dragon form into the shaggy-haired human now standing before them. "I don't think my fires will hurt him." Runt rubbed against Lump's side and whined. "No, my friend, I don't think your icy breath is going to hurt him, either. We're going to need a lot more cold than any of us can produce."

"Where's Indie?" Kit asked, her head swiveling about as she looked for her man.

"The boy left," Gimlie said. "He said he's keeping his promise and that he'll be back to you as quickly as he can."

Kit's brow furrowed. She scrubbed her hand down her face and groaned. "He didn't need to leave right now. We could have used him here." Kit sighed and looked out over the Gaelinora Sea. There was a stiff wind blowing in from the north, turning the water into a froth. Gigantic waves pounded in against the shore.

"Me kin approach," Gimlie said, motioning towards the city. Kit turned towards the warehouses and office buildings that lined the shore. Down the main road, a stream of Dwarves, Hobgoblins, Berrat, and Nomads were marching towards the beach. At their lead were Bango and Calian, their mouths somewhat agape as they stared at the oversized dwarf standing next to Kit.

⊙

"Bango, Calian, this is Gimlie, God of the Dwarves." Kit's gaze jumped between the two women, waiting for one of them to say something. They both continued to gape at the giant-sized dwarf.

"Ah, girls, ye know it's rude to stand there catchin' flies in yer mouths." Gimlie seemed to enjoy the women's state of dumbfoundedness.

"Hello, Gimlie," said the small voice of a Berrat child. Her skin was a golden bronze and covered in blue whorls. "The wolves sing songs of you and your heroism." Runt and Lump immediately bounded over to the girl, greeting her enthusiastically. Runt caught sight of another small Berrat girl and quickly gave her a similar greeting. Amilta squealed with joy when Runt bowled her over.

Gimlie's beard twitched several times as he considered the small girl with blue whorls standing before him. "Ye are more than ye seem," he said, taking a knee.

"Gimlie, this is Fenrir, God of the Wolves, Titan's chosen one." Kit bowed to the small Berrat girl as she made the introduction.

"She's a fine woman," Coldforge said, "but today she is dressed in the cloak of a small child."

"I can imagine," Gimlie said, inclining his head. "Now that we have dispensed with the pleasantries, perhaps we should get to the business of Gorgaraeth, and the growing crack in the Veil. That wall of flame won't keep them out for long. Even now, I can feel the earth move beneath me feet. The demon god is working his way through."

"Sister Kit," Bango said as the army continued to approach. "We have eliminated the demons who had escaped from the hole. Danny, Breayn, and Ryn are searching the area to make sure none were overlooked. Breayn and Ryn are using their great hawk forms to conduct the search. Anything they spot, Danny will take care of."

No sooner had she finished speaking than the cry of the phoenix sang out overhead.

"Ye have the phoenix fighting fer yer cause?" It was Gimlie's turn to appear speechless. His head swiveled about as he watched the trail of the firebird as he swooped across the skies.

While the rest of the army stayed back, the dwarves gathered near the leaders. They had reported they'd taken heavy losses, but they also told how they had single-handedly eradicated the last of the escaped demons. Kit could tell they were stretching the truth, but from the sounds of it, her army had taken no significant part in killing the demons. She glanced at Bango, who replied with an eye roll and a thin-lipped shrug. Apparently, she thought they were taking credit for everything as well.

Breayn was the first to land, followed shortly by Ryn and then Danny. The introductions continued for several minutes. Breayn and Ryn gave a detailed report of their search while Kit gave the others a full account of what had happened beneath the surface.

"The yetis might be able to help against Gorgaraeth," Calian said. "They've got a cold attack, too. They are eager for another fight. After all, they were responsible for dozens of kills others are claiming as their own." She glared at Garragh, who was taking way too much credit for their successes against the foul creatures. "They were a thing to behold, as they ravaged their way through a pack of at least twenty demons."

"It won't be enough," Kit said. "It took Runt everything he had to freeze a single finger. Anyway, we don't know if it was the cold that hurt Gorgaraeth or if it was the *brilliance* enchantments on my hammer." Kit's eyes suddenly brightened. "Breayn, what about Boreas? Can you use the North Wind to freeze him?"

"Boreas is free," Breayn said. "But I don't think he could do it, anyway. He can make the air freezing cold, but I don't know if he can do what you are asking." The woman turned to face the north and inhaled deeply. "I can ask him, I suppose."

"Didn't you just say he was free?" Kit was more than a bit confused. "How can you ask him if you no longer hold his spirit?" Breayn gave Kit a playful smile.

"The North Wind is everywhere up here, and we have an arrangement."

Breayn looked toward the north and closed her eyes. "Boreas, if you can hear me, and if you are able, I need your help." A stiff breeze almost immediately kicked up, causing the sea to turn to a froth. The waves increased in size, crashing in rapid succession upon the shore. Froth blew across the faces of those gathered, freezing upon their skin. The wind continued to strengthen, and the temperature continued to drop.

"Boreas says he won't face Gorgaraeth, but he will help if he is able." Breayn had to shout to be heard over the storm that had picked up out of nowhere. The way her jaw was set, she was not too pleased with the North Wind.

Kit shivered. Without her armor to help keep her warm, her skin was exposed to the ever-increasing burn of the ice as it clung to her body. Her daemon wanted to help warm her, but the little priest found the intense cold to be invigorating. Goosebumps covered her flesh. Her lips were turning blue.

"I have an idea," Kit said. "We don't need Boreas to fight for us. We have everything we need right here." She motioned her hand towards the sea. "If the dwarves can open up the rift a bit more, the sea will pour into the cavern. It's not cold enough to freeze Gorgaraeth solid, but I'll bet it will slow him down."

"Maybe it will drown the demons, too," Danny added. "I doubt they're used to living under water."

"It's not advisable," Gimlie said. "The water will pass through the crack in the rift and travel directly into Helja. If Orth's core is cooled, it could be catastrophic. It would likely rip the world apart." Kit gasped at the dwarf-god's words.

"Maybe that's been Arachnielle's plan all along? I'm guessing it was likely Bael's plan, too. This was all set up for us to bring about Ragnarök. They expected us to destroy the world ourselves." Kit stopped talking. Her stomach was churning uncontrollably. She had to forcibly swallow down vomit before she spewed it across the ground. "I almost did it. I almost caused the end of the world."

"Nah," Coldforge clapped her on the back, nearly knocking the girl off her feet. "I doubt the spider god could have planned this. Ya had a bad idea. We have all had at least one of 'em in our life." The dwarf stared up at his father and smiled. "Me, myself, I've had more than me fair share. It's why we have friends. They help us to not do stupid things."

Kit blinked at the orange-faced dwarf. She wasn't sure if she had just been called stupid. She always recognized that she was a blunt instrument, but she never considered herself stupid.

Why do I keep saying stupid?

"Look," Gimlie said. "We have no plan, so we're going to have to wing it."

"Thank you, Boreas," Breayn called out. "We'll take it from here." The wind immediately died down and the temperature started returning to normal.

"Wait," Kit yelled at the sky. "You can help."

The wind swirled around Kit, causing her flame-red hair to spin about her head.

"Can you make enough waves for the water to flow into the chasm? I just want it deep enough to make it hard for anyone down there to move around, but not so much as to flow into the crack in the Veil."

Once again, the wind whipped across the sea, driving frozen pellets against everyone's skin. A huge swell appeared offshore. Driven by the growing gale, it surged towards the beach.

"Everyone, get back," Bango yelled. "Head for higher ground." Nobody moved. They all stood transfixed, staring out at the massive wave that threatened to wipe everyone off the beach. Bango clutched her necklace and bellowed out. "Get away from the water!" The force of her voice only made the pelting ice that much worse.

"Go," Kit yelled at the woman. "Join the others. You can't stay here." Bango gave Kit a look of confusion. When she looked back at the sea, her eyebrows shot up. With a quick nod, she raced for the city and its higher ground. "Wait," Kit yelled out again. "Can I borrow your necklace? I don't have mine with me." Bango pulled her necklace over her head and tossed it to Kit.

"Grab onto it," Bango yelled to her. She mimicked, clutching the tiny pearl in her hand. "It's how the magic is activated."

Kit nodded and called her wolf to her. "Runt! Come!" The dire wolf bounded to her side, gazing up expectantly at the young woman. "Do you want to stay with the people up here or come down with me? I'll carry you down again if you want to come." The wolf yipped back at her and sat. He didn't need to speak to her for Kit to understand, *"I'm coming."*

"Coldforge," Kit called to her friend. "Get to higher ground. You can't help us down there." The man gave her a look that suggested she was insane.

"I'll not miss out on the best scrap in the history of this world," he clapped back. "Ya must be daft if ye think I'm goin' ta..." He caught the mischievous look on Kit's face and burst out laughing. "Oh. I like ya, girl."

"Lump, can you carry Coldforge?" Kit asked.

The wolfdog immediately morphed into his dragon form. He laid himself flat on the ground, making it easier for Coldforge to climb aboard.

From the sky above, a series of high-pitched screeches peeled through the air. Kit immediately recognized Ulip sitting on Yuka. With him were nearly a dozen fire drakes and a half dozen blue-white ice drakes.

"No time to waste," Gimlie called out. "That wave will be here before we know it." He held his hand out to Fenrir. The little girl changed into her warrior persona. An exquisitely crafted blue-white hunting bow appeared in her hand as though she had drawn it from the aether. That weapon was familiar to Kit. She was certain she had seen it before, but she couldn't remember the time or place.

"To higher ground, Amilta," the warrior said. "Today is not your day to fight." The small girl pouted, stamped her foot, and crossed her arms. When Fenrir's face hardened, Amilta melted into her wolf form and raced across the sand toward the rest of the soldiers leaving the beach. When she was safely out of harm's way, Fenrir accepted the giant dwarf's hand and climbed up onto his shoulder. Before Kit's angelic wings could fully unfurl, Gimlie was over the edge of the cliff.

Everyone else morphed into their flier forms and lifted off into the sky.

"Wait for the water to recede," Kit screamed out.

In moments, a great swell rolled across the beach. Icy water poured down into the crevasse. Within the torrent, many flashes of blue-black color caught Kit's eye. In seconds, the wave receded, and the wind calmed.

Screams peeled up from the rent in the ground. Kit clutched onto Runt, gave each of her cohorts a quick nod, and with a flap of her wings, dove headlong into the rift.

⌖⌖⌖

Chest-deep water filled the bottom of the cavern. Demons thrashed about, screaming as though they were in agony. They clambered over each other, trying to find any crack or crease in the wall to find purchase. It seemed the cold water was more effective against them than Kit could have imagined. She watched with morbid fascination as a demon tried to scramble up a large rock that protruded from the water. It seemed slick, making it difficult for him to keep hold. He had nearly gotten himself clear of the water when a Makara leapt up, snatched him from his perch, and disappeared back under the surface.

A wave of fear washed over Kit. The water was too deep and too dangerous for Runt. He couldn't be here. She was about to fly back to the surface when Runt whined. He pointed his snout towards the water and blew out a blast of frosty air. Ice crystals formed and spread out, forming an island in the ongoing chaos. He wiggled frantically, making it nearly impossible for Kit to maintain her grip on him.

"Okay," she said finally, lowering him to the island. "I trust you." Kit released the dire wolf onto the ice patch. He immediately got to work expanding it outward. Demons saw the island and swam for their refuge.

"Titan, hear me," Kit whispered. She thrust her hands out towards the oncoming demons. A rush of cold coursed through her body. She held onto it, letting the power build up within her. Her muscles burned in protest as her body seized. When she felt she could hold it no longer, she unleashed an arctic blast so intense that it created a frozen path that stretched across the entire cavern. Any demons who had been in the blast's way were turned into a block of ice.

A frozen bolt flew past Kit's head, striking a flying demon who was approaching her from the rear.

That's polar fire!

The image of Old Sky Eyes flashed through her mind. When she was but a child of five, when the slavers had raided her village, Sky Eyes called upon his favorite weapon. It was a blue-white bow that shot arrows of flaming frost.

Fenrir, who was standing on a ledge well above the water's surface, flashed Kit a quick smile and returned to her task of killing demons. Each time she drew her bowstring, a frost covered arrow materialized. Each time she released it, the arrow streaked across the room, finding its mark, burying itself in a demon's chest.

Kit paused for a moment, taking in the scene unfolding around her. Great hawks plucked demons from their places against the walls, dropping them to the waiting Makara below. The phoenix was engaging the demons who were continuously pouring out of the great red smile on the wall. He flew through their bodies like they were nothing more than a sheet of vellum. Each time he struck one, they exploded into a ball of ash.

Lump was leading the drakes. They were circling the room, engaging any demon who looked like it might escape. The frost drakes used their frozen breath attack to halt their ascent while the fire drakes picked them off the walls and crushed them in their clawed feet. Coldforge had hooked up with Runt once again. The dire wolf raced across the ice-covered surface, carrying the dwarven prince close enough to smite any demons within range. Each time he struck one, his hammer unleashed a flash of brilliance.

All the while, Gimlie stood by the rip in the Veil, perhaps waiting for Gorgaraeth to emerge.

A blinding flash of light filled the room, immediately followed by a heart-stopping, thunderous roar that echoed through the cavern. It shook the walls. It cracked the ice. It ripped open the grotesque red smile, turning it into a gaping yawn. The floor of the cavern gave way, and much of the water disappeared. Kit watched helplessly as Runt and Coldforge tumbled into the darkness.

Sweet Titan, no!

The little angel inverted herself into a dive, flapping her feathered wings with all her might. Unbidden, her body morphed into her daemon self, her leathery wings propelling her even faster into the darkness below. A golden blur blew past her.

Get 'em, Lump. Good boy.

A moment later, another golden flash sped past. Had she imagined it? Did her fear of losing Runt and Coldforge finally cause her to lose her mind?

Kit's blood was pounding in her ears when an erratic movement caught her eye. It was Lump, carrying Coldforge in his mouth. The dwarf lay limp, unmoving. The dragon-dog was flying him to the far end of the cavern, where its floor was still intact.

Runt? Where's Runt? Why didn't he save Runt?

Kit's heart shattered. Her wings simply ceased to function and, like the lifeless body of Coldforge, she fell limp into the inky abyss.

The little daemon tumbled through the air. She caught brief glimpses of what was happening above, but she didn't care. Grief clutched her heart and refused to let go. There was another flash of gold that passed by. Was Lump coming to save her? Her descent suddenly slowed. A pair of jade-green eyes appeared, followed by a slobbery tongue that scraped across her face.

"I've got you."

At that moment, Kit was sure she had passed into the Great Cycle. The green eyes looked like Runt's and the deep, soothing voice sounded like Indie's. Maybe it was a dream? Runt was dead and Indie was on the other side of the world for all she knew.

"This is no time to sleep, my love."

An unexpected warmth pressed against her lips. It made no sense, but she leaned into it, letting its tenderness fill her soul. She opened her eyes to see Indie staring intently back at her, his eyes filled with worry.

"Gorgaraeth is free of Helja," he said. "I thought you might like to help me kill him."

It had to be a dream or something like it. Indie was covered with golden scales, with great leathery wings flapping slowly behind him while they hovered. He had Runt under his left arm. The dire wolf was unharmed, smiling back at Kit with his tongue lolling out the side of his mouth.

"Okay," she said. "How?"

"I used the Bifrost." He said the words like they explained everything, and yet they explained nothing. "Can you fly on your own?" Kit nodded. The truth of the unreal situation slowly brought her back from the brink. She nodded again and pushed away from the man-dragon, who was hovering effortlessly over a terrifyingly deep abyss.

"Get Runt to safety," Kit said. "We've got a demon god to kill."

Chapter Forty-Four

The Fallen Angel

Gorgaraeth stepped out of the gaping yawn in the wall. The demon lord's body was living, liquid magma. From his skull protruded two heavily ridged horns that hooked around his pointed ears and along the side of his head, following his jawline. His eyes were two pools of swirling red and black. His lipless mouth was a misshapen mass of iron and granite protrusions that might have been teeth. At his back were obsidian wings that rivaled that of Siku. The god threw back his head and bellowed. His voice rocked the cavern, opening the rip in the Veil even further.

The weird red smile in the wall was gone, replaced with a hole that could have easily been mistaken for a mouth that could swallow your soul and carry it straight to Helja. Kit held her breath, hoping the demon god would take a misstep and send himself over the edge of the great crater that had nearly swallowed Runt and Coldforge. Unfortunately, life was never that accommodating.

With a thirty-foot horned creature of molten magma at their lead, demons continued to pour out of the hole in the wall. There seemed to be an endless supply of the foul beasts. With guttural voices, they yapped and snarled at each other as they scrambled to make their way past their god of fire and ash. They would occasionally curse at the flying heroes who were staying out of their reach. Their deep, guttural voices raised the hair on Kit's neck. She wondered if she sounded anything like that when she was in the throes of her daemonic rage. She quickly shook off the feeling and gasped as Gorgaraeth swiped at Gimlie with his disfigured hand. The giant dwarf leapt backwards, avoiding the attack with surprising deftness. He countered, swinging his double-bladed ax, missing his target spectacularly.

The demons were running hard towards where Runt and Coldforge were engaged in battle. Despite how effectively the pair fought together, the demons would overrun them in seconds. They could not survive against such impossible odds. Indie must have seen the danger. He flew over the line of demons, belching fireballs at them. His flame was nothing compared to Lump's, but it was enough to drop several of the demons and send dozens more scurrying to get away from him.

Lump, with Ulip and Yuka at his side, led the rest of the fire drakes in an aerial attack on the demon horde. Even if the drakes' fire was not hot enough to burn the demons, the group laid down enough flame that the ground itself liquified. The demons became bogged down in the molten floor. They slogged along, the liquified ground nearly up to their waists. It didn't kill them, but it slowed their progress dramatically. Not far behind, the ice drakes circled and blew out blasts of frost, instantly cooling the melted rock, hardening it once again, trapping every demon in the solidified ground.

Winged demons squared off against the phoenix and the great hawks. Ryn and Breayn were ill-equipped to fight these creatures. As deadly as their talons and beaks were, the flying demons were too agile in flight. Fenrir's frost arrows did a good job of felling the enemy, but there were too many and their flight patterns too erratic. The phoenix was barely more than a blur as he picked demons out of the sky. With each pass, he could explode one or two, but there were just too many.

Kit stole a glance at the confrontation between Gorgaraeth and Gimlie. The dwarf was giving ground, but he did not yet seem to be in any trouble. Indie had peeled off from his attack on the ground demons and was flying to help his Berrat friends. The golden scaled man flew dangerously close to one of the great hawks. It was impossible to be sure, but it looked like he was trying to talk to whomever it was. Kit couldn't tell Ryn from Breayn in their hawk form. Whoever it was, the hawk banked away from Indie, nearly slamming into its cohort. A moment later, the two raptors beat their wings and quickly gained altitude.

Indie broke away from the pair and flamed the first of the winged demons who was giving chase. The other demons, like a flock of birds, took off after the hawks. Frost arrows flew into the flying mass of demons, sending them tumbling to the ground below. Lump followed the flock, flaming them from behind.

The pair of Berrat shapeshifters dove past Kit, their wings held close to their bodies. A half dozen demons were hot on their trail, but they could not match the hawk's speed. Kit flapped her angel wings and launched herself toward the group. Like the hawks, she put herself into a dive to gain enough speed to catch up with the fiends tailing her allies. The hawks disappeared into the crater. The demons followed the hawks, and Kit followed the demons.

"Titan, hear me!" she called out, thrusting her fists forward. A spray of ice pellets flew from her hands into the darkness. The cries of demons said she'd hit her mark, but she had no idea how many she had taken out. Kit's angelic aura burst forth, lighting the enormous sinkhole. Ryn and Breayn were heading her way, flapping hard to stay ahead of the pair of fiends still tailing them. The two hawks split apart, flying past Kit on either side of her. Hovering in place, Kit wrapped her hand around Bango's necklace and unleashed her angelic song. Her voice echoed off the walls, drowning out the cries of agony from the two remaining demons. They clutched their heads for a moment before they disintegrated into a cloud of smoke and ash.

I'll take it. She had no idea her voice had such power.

With no enemies in sight, Kit beat her wings and followed her cohorts out of the hole. When she emerged, the battlefield had completely changed. Lump, Ulip, and the drakes were hovering near the gaping hole, attacking demons before they could fully make it through. Dwarves and Hobgoblins were coming out, along with the demons. While the heavily armored Dwarves engaged them in the melee, the Hobgoblins unleashed lightning storms upon the enemy. Breayn and Ryn flew to where Runt and Coldforge were, killing off the demons who were trapped in the floor.

Indie and Danny were engaging Gorgaraeth, providing distractions for Gimlie to get in devastating strikes, sinking his enormous ax into the demon god's thigh. With each hit, torrents of molten iron poured from his body. The dwarf-god's arms and legs were covered in severe burns from where Gorgaraeth's blood had splattered on him.

Kit clutched her necklace again and flew into the fray. She inhaled deeply and threw every bit of herself into her angelic war cry. The power of her voice slammed into Gorgaraeth, sending him stumbling into the cavern wall. His face contorted with pain and rage. With his eyes closed, he thrashed at the air, hoping to rid himself of the creatures buzzing around him. Frost bolt after frost bolt slammed into his neck, turning his forge-red skin a dull gray.

Using his body like a battering ram, Indie flew at the demon-god, slamming his shoulder into the side of the creature's head. Gorgaraeth stumbled again, crashing hard against the cave's wall. The demon-god bellowed, throwing his arms out aimlessly, flinging bits of magma with each swing.

Again, clutching onto her necklace, Kit unleashed another battle-cry. The entire chamber reverberated with her song. Like a harsh counterpoint, Gorgaraeth wailed in response, dropping onto his hands and knees. Gimlie seized the opportunity and buried his ax into the side of the great demon. A torrent of blood sprayed out, covering the dwarf-god's face and neck in liquid iron. He screamed out in agony, clutching his burning skin.

With lifeblood pouring out of the gaping hole in his side, Gorgaraeth tried to right himself. With each movement, the demon renewed his bellows. He balled his hand into a tight fist and raised his arm, preparing to smash Gimlie into the ground. The phoenix flew forward, nearly slicing the demon's arm in two. Indie, in a fashion similar to his last attack, used himself like a battering ram and crashed into the back of Gorgaraeth's head, driving his face into the ground.

Without a second thought, Kit flew to Gimlie, her golden aura already reaching out to engulf the dwarf-god's wounded body. Her aura faltered at the sight of Coldforge riding Runt, racing toward the fallen demon. Runt was spraying out a thick cone of ice pellets, targeting Gorgaraeth's head. Frost bolts struck the same location. The god's flaming head turned a dull gray.

With a war cry of his own, Coldforge leapt from Runt's back and brought his war hammer down on Gorgaraeth's skull. A brilliant flash of light and an ear-splitting crack echoed through the hall.

When Kit's vision returned, she witnessed the last of the demon-god's death throes. His headless body shuddered one last time before going still. Screams and cries of anguish followed as the demons watched the death of their god. Those who were not engaged in combat immediately retreated for the yawning hole in the wall. The Dwarves and Hobgoblins gave chase, mowing down the creatures as they routed from the battlefield.

Kit's aura burst forth again, reaching out to heal the severely burned face of Gimlie. The pain was excruciating, beyond anything she had ever felt before. Kit's wings failed her, and everything went dark.

⸺⊰◊⊱⸺

A light touch caressed Kit's cheek. It was pleasant and warm. It called for her to return from wherever it was her mind had taken her. She opened her golden eyes to see the faces of Indie, Lump, and Runt staring down at her. The boys both gave her a quick lick, leaving a trail of slobber dripping down the side of her face.

"Ye can't be doin' things like that, girl." It was difficult to tell where the powerful voice came from. It almost sounded like it was echoing inside her head. "Ye nearly sent yerself back to Gaia behavin' like ye did."

The face of Gimlie came into focus. He was standing well back, giving Kit's family plenty of room to be close to her. She blinked away the last of the haze that had been obscuring her vision. Riva was standing over her as well, a look of cautious optimism painted on her bronze skin.

"Hello, mother," Kit said with a weak smile. She turned to gaze into Indie's adoring eyes. "Did we win?"

"Ay, we did," Coldforge said, pushing his face between the boys. "It was a glorious battle. I hope you were still awake to see Runt and me finish the foul demon off."

"I did," Kit said, the memory of the battle now flooding back into her consciousness. The last thing she remembered was trying to heal Gimlie's horrid facial burns. Her eyes reached out beyond the sea of faces hovering over her to the Dwarf-god standing in the back. Much of his facial hair was gone and his face was badly scarred, but he seemed otherwise healed. Kit tried to push past her onlookers and sit up. A searing pain ripped through the right side of her back. She could barely maintain consciousness.

"You broke a wing when you fell," Indie said, trying to restrain Kit before she injured herself further. "You hit the ground awkwardly."

She had no recollection of falling. The only thing she could recall was trying to heal Gimlie.

"Back away, all of you," Lin said as she pushed her way between Coldforge and Runt. "My special healing potions weren't enough to fully restore Gimlie," she said with a shrug, "but they might help a little angel and her broken wing. Open up." Lin held her mouth open, mimicking what she expected Kit to do.

Kit obliged, opening her mouth wide enough for Lin to pour a potion past her lips. The liquid was honey sweet. It warmed her mouth and as she swallowed, the warmth spread down to her throat and belly. Her pulse quickened as the elixir's power coursed through her. Kit lightly shrugged her shoulder, testing for pain. There was none. She flexed her muscles, wincing as she did. The expectation of pain was unfounded.

"I think it worked," she said to Lin. "I need to stand up to know for sure."

Indie immediately thrusted his hand in her face, offering to help her from the bed. How did she get into a bed? They were in a cave just a moment ago.

"How long have I been unconscious?" she asked. She was in her room at the manor. Every one of her friends was there, hovering over her like she was on her deathbed.

"About an hour," Lin said. "Nobody could revive you in the cave, so Indie carried you here."

Indie's eyes were red and swollen from tears. Kit gave him a warm smile and took his outstretched hand. He slowly guided her to the side of the bed and helped Kit to her feet.

"Any pain?" he asked. Kit stretched out her injured wing, wincing slightly when it reached its full extension.

"No," she said. "It's okay."

"Liar," Lin said, holding out another vial for her to drink. "It took the oversized dwarf seven before he stopped whining like a big baby." She looked over her shoulder to look for Gimlie's reaction. A hint of a smirk appeared on his face.

The Dwarves really do enjoy their verbal sparring matches.

Lin shook the vial, directing Kit's attention back to the healing potion. "I've got a lot more of these. Drink as many as you need. The war isn't over."

Kit popped the stopper and downed the contents. When the liquid's warmth faded, she stretched her wing again. She retracted it and tried it once more.

"Much better," she said, handing the vial back to Lin. Kit's brow furrowed. "The war continues? Are the demons still coming from the hole?"

"Nah, girl, we beat them back," Gimlie said enthusiastically. "Me kin are working with the Hobgoblins to free the rest of our kind. When Gorgaraeth fell, the demons returned to Helja. I don't think they'll be returning."

"Then what war do we need to fight?" Kit looked about the room, questioning everyone's concern.

"I fear the battle for Aarall is going badly, my sweetness," Riva said.

"She had another vision," Fenrir added. She and Amilta had been waiting further back from the rest of the group. "Tens of thousands of soldiers have amassed outside your city. Catapults are pounding the fortifications. The walls cannot withstand such an attack for long."

"What are we waiting for, then?" Kit asked. She caught a deep sadness in her mother's eyes. Unspoken words passed between mother and daughter. Death awaited Kit if she returned home. She gave her mother a thin-lipped smile and acknowledged her understanding.

"We were waiting for you," Indie replied. "We were waiting for our leader to wake up."

Tears were stinging Kit's eyes. She quickly blinked them away and set her jaw. "Let's get going then. There is no time to waste." She looked over at Runt and raised her eyebrows. "Are you coming?" The dire wolf replied with a broad doggie smile. "Will you let me carry you?" Runt's smile faltered slightly.

"No need," Indie said. "Not when we've got the Bifrost to carry us there."

CHAPTER FORTY-FIVE

UPON THE BATTLEMENTS

In the dying light of the day, the wind whipped Aurora's white-blonde hair about her face. She hooked a group of unruly strands with a finger and tucked them behind her ear. The scowl that marred her face had been getting deeper ever since King Jordain's full army had arrived at Aarall a few hours earlier.

The king had started his assault by sending nearly five hundred soldiers to break down the main gate, a small percentage of his total army. Three mountain trolls had pushed an enormous battering ram against the iron-clad doors while soldiers armed with longbows tried to keep the City Watch off the parapets. As the archers kept the City Watch busy, the trolls repeatedly slammed the end of the enormous ram against the great oak doors. Had they not been dealt with quickly, they'd have breached the gates in no time at all.

Aurora had flown out over the trolls, distracting them and their archer-protectors while the City Watch and the Temple Priests slipped out through one of the smaller exits beside the main gates. Sister Gale and Aurora made quick work of the trolls while Captain Harding led the remainder of the team against the archers. With sword and shield and a great deal of magical support from the priests, Captain Harding and his people routed the enemy, sending them scattering back towards the main army. As they retreated, archers from atop the battlements felled them before they could escape.

After the battering ram attempt had failed, the king's army changed tactics, switching to catapults. They began by hurling giant boulders over the walls, but they gave up on that tactic shortly after it began. The catapults had done significant damage, but the king could not conquer the city using that strategy. He needed to get his soldiers past the main gate and inside the city before they could seize control. A siege was possible, but it was unlikely they'd be patient enough to wait it out.

The enemy quickly changed its tactics yet again and used the catapults to pound the walls near the city's main gate. The fortifications were extremely thick there, but if they could break through, the enemy soldiers could swarm into the main square and the city would quickly fall.

The constant barrage had gotten under Aurora's skin, and she was about ready to do something foolish to make it stop.

"Do you suppose they'll just keep doing this until they finally breech the wall?" Aurora blew out a tired breath. From the look on her face, she didn't really care if she got an answer or not.

"As long as those trolls keep digging up stones, they'll keep tossing them at us." Captain Harding rubbed the back of his neck. "As much as they're dragging down our soldiers' morale with these attacks, they likely could have swarmed us had they just done a full frontal assault."

"They're waiting for King Faol's army," General Ormand Gabryl said. "When they get here, their vampires will simply fly into the city, kill who they have to, and then open the front gates to let the rest of the soldiers inside."

"How can you be sure, Ormand?" Sister Gale asked. She had changed out of her priestly robes and was dressed in light leather armor.

"Because King Faol leads them," Grams said. "He wants to be here to see Father Hoarfrost and me die."

"What? Why?" Captain Harding looked to Aurora. Perhaps she had some idea of what the old woman was talking about.

"Because Galahdes and her elves have been a thorn in King Faol's side for hundreds of years," Aurora said, giving the old woman a warm smile. "I just want to know why you're back in this disguise of yours. As the elf queen, your beauty is timeless, and yet you insist on pretending to be an old woman."

Grams smiled brightly in response. "My time in this world is drawing to an end. I do not expect to survive King Faol's attack. This aged body reminds me that our time here is fleeting and that we should enjoy every minute until our last breath."

"Besides," Father Hoarfrost said, "I think she looks adorable, like a wrinkled, sun-dried peanut."

"Is that how you see me, old man?" Grams said, poking the aged priest in his soft belly. "You were so handsome and smooth skinned in your youth. Now..." She waved her hands up and down before the high priest. "You're just as handsome, and my love has never been deeper."

"Alright, already," Tyr said with his rheumy, cracked voice. He had popped in behind the group, surprising nobody. He was in his Brother Snowbank persona, perhaps to fit in with the elderly impersonators. "Have you discovered a way to defeat this army? I'm rather counting on your success against King Jordain and King Faol. All of us Fates are, I'm guessing."

"What do you want, Trickster?" Grams had to crane her neck to look up at the false priest. "Unless you're going to help, off with you."

"You know I cannot take part, Galahdes. But maybe you'd like to see me face the power of four? Perhaps you wish me to be sent to oblivion?"

"What do you want, Tyr?" Captain Harding said, putting his enormous frame between Tyr and the others. "In case you haven't noticed, we're busy."

"Me, want something?" Tyr waved his hands in front of his face, dismissing the captain's question. "I'm here to give you news of your daughter."

"What of Kit?" Aurora said, pushing past the captain. "Tell us what you have to say and begone."

"Oh, it's not much." Tyr toed the ground with his rough leather boot. He stuffed his hands into the pockets of his robes and hummed a random tune. "I thought you proud parents might like to know that she got her wings today."

Aurora's hand flashed to her mouth as she tried to hide her glee at the news. Captain Harding cocked an eyebrow at her reaction. "What do you mean, she got her wings?" He gave Aurora a questioning look. "You mean she's an angel, like you?"

"No, not like her mother," Tyr said, his shaggy white eyebrows popping up high on his forehead. His beady black eyes shifted between the two parents, while a grin crept across his face.

"She's a daemon?" Aurora's golden skin paled. "My little girl's a daemon?"

"Not entirely," Tyr laughed. His eyes got a wild look in them. His smile became creepy, almost sinister, the way it was twisting up his face. That smile disappeared quickly when Captain Harding's fist smashed into it, knocking Tyr over the parapet to the city grounds below. A moment later, he reappeared in front of the captain. Blood was dripping heavily from his nose and mouth.

"I guess I deserved that, human," he said, wiping the bit of blood away before more dripped onto his cassock. "That is the only reason I'm not turning you into a lump of clay or a pile of dung."

"Well, that and the power of four," Father Hoarfrost said. "He's too important to remove from the game board, and you know it." The Fate disappeared with a pop. A moment later, a coyote howled in the distance.

Captain Harding's eyebrows raised as he gawked at the high priest. "I'm too important?"

"Oh, go ahead and thump your chest," Aurora said, her voice dripping with playful sarcasm. The captain chuckled and returned his attention to the gathering army. The bit of levity seemed to have lightened the mood and provided a welcome respite from the impending battle.

"Grams!" a high-pitched voice called out, drawing everyone's attention from the battlefield. Captain Harding took a double take as five forest animals with feathered wings came scampering down the battlement. "Grams, we need to speak."

"What do we have here?" Captain Harding called out, blocking the sprites' progress.

"Let them be, Captain," Grams said, tapping the man on the back. "They're friends of mine."

"Friends?" Sister Gale said. "What are they?" Misty's eye twitched at the priest's comment. She pulled back her lips to expose a set of tiny needle-sharp teeth.

"What are we?" Midnight repeated. "What are we?"

"We are sprites," Triss said, smacking the rabbit on the side of the head. "Forest creatures from the Elven realm."

Feigh folded his arms across his tiny mouse chest and huffed. "And it's because of insensitive reactions like yours, priest, that we tend to not make ourselves known to the regular human population." Hobbs was about to race past and show the humans exactly what they were, but his progress was halted when Misty snagged him by the back of his leather armor.

"Be still, Hobbs," she said, stepping past everyone. Her cat-snarl never left her face until she stood before Grams. "I've spoken with our friends in the south." Misty whispered through clenched teeth and motioned with her head.

"I know," Grams said with a smile. "You can speak freely here. You are among friends." The sprites stared up at the gathered leaders. Triss' face went slack when her gaze fell upon Aurora.

"You're a... celestial, aren't you?" Aurora took a knee and smiled warmly at the mouse-sprite.

"And you are an elf, transformed by magic, aren't you? I've heard many tales, but I didn't expect to meet any of you in my lifetime."

"We aren't difficult to find if you know where to look," Misty said. "I take it you are Aurora Windsong. It is my pleasure to meet you."

An enormous boulder struck the wall barely a dozen paces from where the group was standing. The top of the parapet exploded, sending large chunks of stone spraying down upon the city square below.

"Is everyone okay?" the captain called out, choking on the thick cloud of dust.

"I think so," Father Hoarfrost said. "They're aim is improving."

"What is it you needed to tell me, Misty," Grams said, still coughing up bits of dust.

Misty cringed away from the old woman. "The Wood Nymphs won't come here. There isn't enough greenery for them to hide in. They took heavy losses trying to slow down King Faol's army. They said they won't fight in the open and there are too many soldiers by the lake to transport there safely."

"You tried to get the Wood Nymphs to fight?" Father Hoarfrost asked. "You said you couldn't afford to let them leave the... tree."

"The Tree of Life is safe right now," Grams said. "With Faol's army split between here and Berrathia, there is little chance he will attack the Elves."

"Except they're not coming," Feigh said. "The Wood Nymphs aren't nearly as potent outside of the forest realm."

"Midnight," Grams said, her expression serene. "Can you tap into Lake Titan from here?"

Midnight reached into the aether and drew out his staff. He held it aloft and faced the great lake to the east. His breathing slowed as he concentrated on the large body of water. He extended his other hand and waved it in a small circle. With a flourish, he spun to his right and pointed at Hobbs. A large bubble of water appeared over the squirrel-sprite's head. It hovered for barely a moment before it burst, drenching the little creature.

For several seconds, not a sound could be heard among the gathered cohorts. The silence was finally broken when Hobbs spoke.

"Thank you, Midnight. I was hotter than I realized, and that water was refreshingly clean."

The entire lot burst out with laughter. When Misty smacked Midnight across the face, the group laughed harder still.

"I'd say he can tap into the lake," Father Hoarfrost said. "What did you have in mind, my love?"

The laughter died out immediately as everyone gaped at the old man.

"Oh, grow up, the lot of you." Father waved a dismissive hand at them.

"I will bring the forest to Aarall," Grams said. She had a deep blush creeping up her neck that was a perfect match for the rosy circles growing on her cheeks. "Hopefully, the enemy doesn't think to set it on fire."

"You can't," Father Hoarfrost said. "You don't have the strength. Not this far away from the tree."

Grams shook her head and patted the old man's hands. "The trees of Orth are all connected. I just need to be next to any tree, preferably an old one. I should be able to draw enough magic from it to grow a new forest for our warrior friends."

"Let me help you, Galahdes. Don't do this on your own." A look of profound sorrow clouded Father Hoarfrost's features.

"You are not allowed, and you know it. Besides, you have too little strength left in you for such a feat, my love. You knew we would not survive this cycle, but if all goes according to plan, our people will live on."

"Let us help, my Queen." Misty took a knee before the old woman. The other sprites immediately followed suit, bowing their heads in deep respect for the Elf god. "Let us make amends for the harm we have caused. Let this be the day we can return to our home in the Elven Realm."

"You are too sweet, my friend. I would gladly accept your help, but in your current state, I fear you could not offer much additional magic."

"It's not just us who came, Grams," Feigh said, hopping close to his queen. "All the *shamed* are here. They all came to heed your call. Together, we will have magic to spare." Grams' eyes glistened when she heard the news.

"The great oak behind the Temple is the oldest tree in all of Aarall," Father Hoarfrost said. "Gather your brethren and meet us there. Lady Galahdes and I will be along shortly."

"As you wish, Ollin, my god." Misty motioned to the others and the group of sprites disappeared over the side of the wall in seconds.

"Do you really think they have enough magic in them to summon a forest?" Father Hoarfrost asked. Grams smiled and shook her head.

"They were the most powerful mages in the entire realm. Had their spell not failed, the Veil would have been permanently impenetrable. The resulting burst of wild magic transformed them, but I don't know how much of their powers they lost in the catastrophe. You saw what Midnight did. That was not a trivial feat."

"Okay then," the old priest said. "Let's go make a forest."

"Grams." Feigh darted up beside the old priest and tugged at her sleeve. He whispered something to her, and the woman nodded in response. Feigh pulled out his favorite amulet, closed his eyes, and vanished.

"Does anybody else have any idea what just happened?" Captain Harding looked like a lost boy as he watched the two elderly priests walk over the damaged parapet and down into the city below.

"No, not really," Aurora said. "I've seen the Elves pull off some amazing magic in my time with them, but never have I ever heard of them growing a forest."

Sister Gale shrugged. "I saw Silverleaf conjure an orchid once, and he's only a half elf. I'm guessing the Elven queen and her most powerful cadre of mages might be able to do something... bigger."

"So, just to be clear," Captain Harding said. He was shaking his head in disbelief. "They're planning on growing an entire forest in front of the city walls? Using magic? I sincerely doubt the kings are going to wait for that to happen before they attack."

"You need to have faith, Captain." Ormand patted him on the shoulder. "I think you should take advantage of this break and get a bit of rest. I will stand watch through the night. Get some sleep."

Aurora ran her fingers through her hair and twisted it around her wrist. "The sun will set soon. Even if they travel through the night, it will be at least another eight hours before King Faol's army arrives. You all get some sleep and I'll keep watch. You too, Ormand. Even vampires need to sleep."

"So do angels," the captain said. "I'll post sentries. They'll come get us if anything changes."

CHAPTER FORTY-SIX

GALAHDES AND OLLIN

The leadership made their way to the City Watch barracks. The captain led them to a common room that was lined with cots. "They're not much to look at, but they're surprisingly comfortable."

Sister Gale laughed. "Compared to the stone-slab beds in our cells, this will be a slice of paradise."

The group quickly selected their cots and were asleep in no time. The tension of the situation had drained them, and the respite was a welcome break. The nonstop pounding of boulders hitting the city walls did nothing to dissuade them from drifting off.

"Captain," a tiny voice whispered in the big man's ear. "Captain, I need to speak with you."

The man opened his eyes to find a small Tahr staring down at him. She gave him a shy smile when his vision came into focus.

"Yes, Iba? I had wondered where you'd gone off to."

"Where I have been doesn't matter," she said, her voice still a soft whisper. "I need you to promise me something." The captain groaned and propped himself up on an elbow.

"If I agree, can I go back to sleep?" He rubbed his eyes and yawned. The little Tahr nodded her head. "Good. I agree with whatever it is. Let me sleep." He closed his eyes and pulled his thin woolen blanket under his chin.

"But I haven't told you what I need." Iba gently shook his shoulder. When he didn't respond, she shoved him.

"What is it you need, Iba? I need a bit more sleep."

"I need you to promise that you'll help find a home for the displaced Lupien."
The captain propped himself up on his elbow again.

"What? What's a *lu-peen*?"

"Lupien. Lu-pee-en." The captain's eyes glazed over as she carefully pronounced the wolf-gizmo's proper name. "You know them as Hill Gizmos. The
wolf people?" The captain's eyes cleared, and he sat up on his cot. He scrubbed
his face with his meaty hands.

"What do you want for them?"

"A proper home and a promise that they'll be left to live in peace with... with
the other Gizmos."

"Why are you bringing this up to me now?"

"Because I convinced them to fight with us. They're going to fight against
King Jordain and King Faol. Not just them, all the Gizmos in Aarall, and Two
Peaks, as well. I told them that if they fought with us, you'd make sure they'd get
their homes back."

The captain scratched the top of his head. "Are you telling me you convinced
the entire Gizmo nation to fight with us? After everything we did to them,
they're going to help us against our enemy?"

"Yes." Iba nodded. "You know, the two kings are not just *your* enemy. They
are the enemy of every free person in the north. You're fighting for the freedom
of everyone."

"Is the sun even up yet?" The captain stretched, forcing himself to stifle a
yawn.

"Soon. The eastern sky lightens, but Pele has yet to show his face."

"You have returned to the old gods?" Sister Gale was lying flat on her back,
staring up at the dark ceiling.

"I had never left them," Iba said. "That doesn't mean I don't have faith in
Titan. Can it not be possible that many gods can have our best interests at
heart?" Aurora stretched and moaned loudly.

"People in power often put their own interests first. If it also assists those
beneath them, then that's more of a lucky happenstance than it is anything else.

I likely fall under that category as well." There was a long moment of awkward silence following Aurora's statement. "I want to help the people of Arnnor, but freeing my sister and killing Faol are my true priorities. I will not harm others to meet that goal, but it is my true purpose for doing what I do."

"I see where our daughter gets her humility from," Captain Harding said with a laugh. "You two inspire thousands to follow you. You both lead by example and, regardless of your motivation, you always put others ahead of yourselves." Sister Gale growled and popped out of bed.

"Okay, since it seems we will not be getting any more sleep, why don't we see if there is any food in the kitchen? I hate fighting when I'm hungry."

⚬⚬⚬◆⚬⚬⚬

"Red sky," Ormand said, pointing to the east. "It's an ill omen."

The captain stepped out from the dining hall, stared up at the eastern sky, and nodded. "It is. An exceptionally ill omen indeed. Our enemy is about to have an exceedingly bad day."

The vampire chuckled and pulled the hood of his black cloak over his head.

"How long until Faol's army arrives?" He stretched out his shoulders as he walked beside the general.

"They're already here," Ormand said. He picked up his pace as he headed for the barracks' gatehouse.

"What? Wait. Why weren't we woken?" Aurora and Sister Gale came sprinting up beside the pair.

"There was no need," Ormand replied, still not bothering to turn around. The group of followers had to run to keep up with the vampire's ever-increasing pace. Almost as an afterthought, he turned back to the captain and gave him a wry smile. "You'll see why when we get to the battlements."

The captain shielded his eyes as he came out of the guard-tower's dark interior and stepped onto the parapet. The sun was just breaking over the horizon, igniting the landscape with its morning glory. The trees below were cast in colors of amber and gold, reflecting the early rays. Beyond the forest, tens of thousands of soldiers appeared to be standing motionless.

"She did it," Aurora said as she followed the captain onto the walkway. She rested her hand on the gap between the wall's protective crenels. "Had Galahdes said she'd have it finished before the sun rose, I'd have not believed it."

"Who?" Captain Harding asked. He was busy looking at the vast mass of soldiers in the distance. They had no hope against such an army.

"Galahdes," Aurora repeated. "Grams? The old priest who is also the queen of the Elves? Does any of this ring a bell for you?" The celestial's words finally got through to the captain.

"What are you talking about?"

"Oh, sweet Titan. Are you truly that blind? Your eyes are open and yet they see nothing."

"My eyes see just fine," he said, rounding on the woman. "What are you going on about?" Aurora dropped her chin to her chest and growled.

"What do you see between here and the enemy's army?"

"A forest. What of it?" Aurora looked up to see the blank expression on the man's face as he cast his gaze across the landscape. "Sweet Titan, they did it."

"They more than did it," Sister Gale said. "If I am not mistaken, they didn't just create a forest. They recreated the *Amberwood Forest.*"

"What's an *Amberwood forest?*" the captain asked. He was still marveling at the scene below.

"It's the forest we decimated when we failed our spell," Misty replied. Her cat-eyes were red and swollen, her fur frazzled. "We spent everything we had to bring it here, to heal it. The enemy cannot burn it. It will be fed by the waters of Lake Titan, and it will live forever." The cat-sprite wobbled. "We leave the rest up to you and the Wood Nymphs. I expect the woods are teaming with them by now. It's why Faol's army has stopped outside the forest's edge."

"Thank you," Aurora said. "By your actions, you may have just saved the world." The cat smiled weakly back at the angel.

"If we win the day, Galahdes promised to welcome us back into the Elven Realm. We will probably live as servants, but we will be home."

"Why as servants?" the captain asked. "I'd think you'd be welcomed back as heroes."

"We will be *scuds*. Elves without magic. We sacrificed it all to bring the forest. We did so without reservation or regret. We had a great debt to repay." The cat's eyes were glassy as she spoke. "Please make our sacrifice worthwhile. Please help us return home."

"We will," Aurora said. "I promise." The cat nodded and leaned against the wall. "Go now. Find peace and sleep." The cat slid down the wall until she was curled up in a ball on the dust-covered stone floor.

"That's not what I meant," Aurora said to the captain. "I had hoped she would find a place that wasn't in the middle of the battlefield."

"I'll take her to the Temple," Sister Gale said. "I expect Father will have found a place for all of them there."

"Allow me," Aurora said, scooping up the cat-sprite into her arms. Misty purred and snuggled her nose into the angel's armpit. "I'll be back shortly." And with that, a pair of magnificent white wings sprouted from the celestial's back. With a couple of wingbeats, she was airborne and heading for the Temple.

"She is something, isn't she?" Captain Harding said, his eyes locked on the angel receding in the distance.

"She is," Sister Gale replied, giving the man an elbow in the ribs. "So is your wife." The captain's face reddened at the comment.

"We may win this war yet," Ormand said, jarring the pair with his presence.

"Captain!" a wide-eyed city watch guard poked his head out from the guardhouse stairway. "We have company. There is an army of green women standing outside the main gate. They wish to be allowed entry into the city."

⌘

Captain Harding and Sister Gale stepped out from the iron door that led from the City Watch gatehouse to the city wall's exterior. As soon as they exited, the door was slammed shut and barred from the inside. These had been the captain's orders. If the women at the main gate were the enemy, only two people would suffer for their folly.

"Who goes there?" The captain called out to the band of one hundred women waiting impatiently for the portcullis to be raised. The sound of bow-strings being drawn caused the captain and the priest to stop their forward progress.

From the group of women walked a tall, beautiful warrior with pale green skin and forest-green hair. "I am General Gaelira Magdan, of the Queen's Royal Army. In the absence of the Queen or the High Councilor, I am in command."

"It's a good thing that your queen is here then," Captain Harding said. The general showed no reaction to the captain's statement. "I doubt she would be pleased that you would threaten the safety of the Captain of the City Watch with your overzealous warriors."

"Queen Galahdes is here?"

"You know she is," Sister Gale said. "Who else do you think could have created this magnificent forest overnight?"

The general closed her eyes and nodded. "I would seek her council. We are here to protect your city. My archers will stand upon your accursed stone walls and prevent the spawn of Faol from breaching its perimeter."

"The queen is unavailable." Captain Harding inclined his head slightly. "But we welcome you into our home. Your help is much needed, and your arrival couldn't be timelier."

The general waved her hand at the portcullis. "Then move this abomination so that we may pass."

"So, it's true then." Sister Gale held the green woman's gaze. "You are vulnerable to iron." The general sneered.

"The retched metal burns our skin. It stinks of dung. It leaves a nasty taste in our mouth just being close to it." The captain raised an eyebrow at the woman. "I have nearly three thousand more warriors in the forest that surrounds us. No enemy will pass through this gate while we draw breath. Within the depths of the Amberwood trees, we are unmatched."

The captain blew out a breath and rolled his shoulders. "Open the gates," he called out. "Reinforcements have arrived."

Within seconds, there was a loud groan, followed by the sound of chains clanking. With each turn of a crank, the iron gate lifted. As it raised up, the two iron-clad doors swung open.

"Follow me," the captain said as he moved in beside the general. "Welcome to Aarall, the high seat of Titan."

***

The captain, Sister Gale, and the Wood Nymph army were greeted by the entire City Watch and what looked to be every member of the Temple's faithful. Amara and Silverleaf stood at the forefront, with Brother Rimes and Brother Snowpack at their side. They perhaps numbered two thousand.

"Please tell me this is not the entirety of your army," the Wood Nymph general said. Her voice was filled with derision. Her expression was a perfect match to the tone of her words.

"It is," the captain said. "We had no reason to expect a war against our own king. We could not have anticipated his treasonous acts. We lost many good people fighting the traitor. I am honored to fight beside those who remain."

"Very well." General Gaelira Magdan turned to her people and raised her chin. "The situation is even more dire than the *shamed* led us to believe. But we are the queen's best, and we will not let her down. Take your place upon the stone structures. Space yourselves fifteen paces apart. No enemy shall pass these walls while you stand guard."

As though on queue, three of the Wood Nymphs drew their longbows. Golden arrows appeared out of nowhere as they pulled back on their bowstrings. In perfect unison, they launched the arrows over the battlements at what looked like a cloud of insects. There was a blood-curdling screech when the arrows passed through. The dark cloud coalesced into a man just before he fell from the sky, landing amid the gathered soldiers with a sickening thud.

"Our weapons are attuned to vampires, as are my warriors." She sniffed the air. "There is one among your group. An ally?"

"General Ormand Gabryl of the King's Army." Ormand stepped forward, drawing the attention of a half dozen drawn bows.

"Lower your weapons," Captain Harding barked. "Raise a hand against my people again, and I will skin you alive." The Wood Nymph general laughed at the captain's words.

"You couldn't lay a hand on any of us before we ended your already short life." The captain's fist met the woman's face with a resounding crunch, sending her to the ground in a heap. A ribbon of dark green blood dripped from her nose and into her teeth as her smile broadened. "I stand corrected, Captain." The woman popped back to her feet. "I might suggest that you caught me unaware, but I am never off guard. I will gladly fight by your side. Maybe, after we've defeated Faol, you and I can spar properly." Her gaze fell upon Sister Gale, who had her hand resting comfortably on her narrow hips. "I am guessing that you'd like to join in. I will gladly fight you both at once. Or, if you'd prefer, one at a time. I will let you choose." The Wood Nymph shrugged. "It's good to practice with worthy opponents. It's how we learn."

Any sense of joviality on the Wood Nymph's face disappeared and was instantly replaced by a granite-like veneer. "Take your places upon the wall," she barked out. The woman's warriors immediately broke for the stairways leading to the parapets. With unsurpassed precision, they climbed up to the walls and spread themselves out at fifteen pace intervals. With stiff backs and chins high, they stood watch over the forest below.

"What are we to do, Sister Gale," Amara asked. "We are ready to do our part."

"You will be bait," General Gaelira Magdan stated, her voice completely devoid of emotion. "We will follow the road to where the enemy stands. We will harry their soldiers and invite them to chase us. The trap is set. We have but to spring it upon them."

Amara looked to the captain and Sister Gale, her eyes wide. "You wish to use us as bait?"

"Her plan has merit," Sister Gale answered quickly. "We cannot fight the enemy in the field. They have the numbers. If we do, we will lose."

"Don't forget our allies," Iba said, appearing out of nowhere. "I cannot speak to their numbers, but I can tell you they will fight with honor."

"A Tahr," General Gaelira Magdan said, nodding her head in approval. "This land is full of many surprises." Iba rolled her eyes at the comment.

"When the warning bells peel, it will signal for them to come."

"How long until they arrive after we sound the alarm?" The captain was still mulling over the plan to use his people and the Temple's faithful as *bait*.

"I don't know," Iba said. "When the bell is struck, they will light the signal fires. All will be made aware in minutes. How long they take to muster is unknown."

"They won't take long to arrive," Aurora said, right after touching down. She folded her angelic wings away and gave the Wood Nymph general a terse nod. "I saw their movements in the mountains while I was on patrol. They are wary of King Jordain after his act of treachery upon them. When his army mobilized, they were immediately on high alert."

"Ring the bells," Captain Harding said. "We'll take the fight to the enemy and draw them in." He turned to Amara. "Spread the word. We will sally forth as soon as the warning bell rings."

"It will be glorious," the Wood Nymph general stated. Her eyes were filled with zealous fire. "In the names of Galahdes and Ollin, we will prevail."

CHAPTER FORTY-SEVEN

THE END GAME DRAWS NEAR

The Temple's warning bell's peel rang out. With each clang, a wave of fear ripped through the city.

Only those who lived under rocks and floorboards didn't know there were armies amassing outside the city walls. Only those who were too dim to realize Aarall's forces were heavily outmatched hadn't made plans to survive the city's fall. Perhaps many believed Father Hoarfrost would perform a tremendous miracle and keep the enemy at bay. Perhaps they hoped the world for Aarall's people would go on like nothing had ever happened.

The rhythmic, ear-piercing ring of the warning bell removed all doubt about what was to come. The city was in trouble and war was at hand.

A tall, slender man of advanced age strode towards the front gates. He wore gray plate armor, carried a pole-hammer, and a kite shield that was half his height. A straggly beard hung from his chin, the only real bits of hair the man had on his head. At his side walked a lithe, Elven woman with olive green skin and penetrating yellow eyes. She wore leaves for armor and carried an exquisitely carved longbow slung over her shoulder. Galahdes, the god of the Elves, could have easily passed for one of only twenty cycles, but the worry on her face and the wisdom in her eyes suggested she was much older. Beside the pair walked another person, dressed in a green-gray cloak that covered everything except her alligator-skinned face and a rat-tail that dragged along the ground behind her.

"You cannot take part in the battle, Ollin," Mephitis whispered. "The rules will be adhered to, or you will be found in violation and your playing pieces will be removed." The old man glowered at her, his eyes threatening to end her life where she stood. "Nor can you act against me. The protections your parents put upon us are also binding. So long as we are acting in your service, we are free from repercussions."

"I will not fight," the old man growled. "But I can influence. Those are the rules, and I will not break them. If my people draw inspiration from me, there is no foul." Ollin looked over at the woman and brushed his arm against hers. "However, Galahdes is free to fight, as are all of our chosen ones."

"You cannot give her any more of yourself than you already have," Mephitis said. She was careful with her phrasing. She would not allow the old man to twist her words to get her to agree to something that was out of bounds.

"I am not trying to trick you, Arbiter. I am tired and I am weak. I will bear witness to this, the ultimate battle of the final game. I will see my creation through to the very end, be it in victory or in defeat." Ollin hoisted his hammer higher, adjusting his grip to make the weight more bearable. "This game was cruel and we should have never started playing it."

"And yet, you did," Tyr said, popping in on Ollin's other side. He was in his youthful Nomad persona. Like Ollin and Galahdes, he was dressed in a full suit of armor. It was simple, soft brown leather that featured the head of a howling coyote embossed over his left chest. "I think we made a wise choice, creating this game for you to play. It wasn't our fault you took so long to learn the lessons it carried."

Ollin glared at Tyr, his lips pulled into a sneer. "We were young and inexperienced. You didn't have to let so many innocent people die horrible deaths just to teach us a lesson."

"No, Ollin, we didn't." Mephitis' voice was calm and measured. She spoke to him like how a mother might talk to a petulant child, giving him a chance to calm himself. "Other teaching methods could have been successful, but they would not have prepared you fully for when your true powers come to the forefront."

"Our true powers?" Ollin's eyes lit up at the comment. "We will get new powers?" Tyr's eyes widened and a mischievous grin spread across his face.

"Oh, Mephitis, you have said too much." The sing-song way he spoke suggested she had said exactly what he was hoping she might say. "You know they will have to wait until they've fully matured before their new powers will manifest."

"What do you mean, fully matured?" Ollin asked, demanding an immediate answer. A contented purr rolled in the back of Mephitis' throat. Tyr waggled his eyebrows at her.

"Quit teasing him," said a voice from behind the group. Tyr turned to see the round face of a robust woman; her patchwork flesh hidden in the dark shadows under the hood she had pulled tightly over her head. Wisps of black smoke clung to her feet as she walked.

"We're only having a bit of fun, Eris. Lighten up or leave." Tyr turned away from the Fate, grinning wildly.

"Angering our charges is not in our job description," Eris said, pushing herself between Ollin and Tyr. "Today promises to be interesting, though. With Gorgaraeth's body destroyed, his shade will have nowhere to go should Faol be defeated. Bael will lose his best piece and there will be nothing powerful enough to stand against Ouroboros when he arrives."

"The dragons are free?" Ollin's face went deathly pale. Tyr's eyes brightened significantly at the news.

"Never have we ever seen such a confined endgame," said another voice from behind the group.

"The outcome usually takes years, but this one will end in less than a moon," said another voice.

"We didn't expect to see you two," Tyr said brightly. He was still excited about having heard the dragons were freed from their prison. Tyche and Tiamat nodded to the others when they'd finally acknowledged their presence.

"When will you play your best card, Tiamat?" Eris pulled back her hood far enough to reveal her weird, yet remarkably beautiful, patchwork face. "I can't wait to see the little brat's face when you yank her off the game board."

Tiamat shrugged and smiled. "I don't know," she said with a sly grin. "Maybe I'll just let her play her role. After all the effort you and Tyr put into getting her to do your dirty work, it seems a shame to not let her see the game to its end. Just because she gave me her life to save another's, doesn't mean I can't give it back to her."

"You can't remove Kit," Ollin said, his voice low and threatening. The old man's head swiveled about like he was making sure nobody was listening in on their conversation. "She has been groomed for this. She is this world's only hope for survival."

"Nonsense," Tiamat said, rolling her eyes. "The outcome of this battle is irrelevant. You and your parents have learned what you needed to learn from us. We have already met the terms of our arrangement." She shrugged and smiled warmly at the old man. "We just want to see how the game finally ends. Even without us putting our fingers on the scales, the humans may yet prevail once again, but right now, I'm pinning my hopes on Bael. He simply refuses to give up even though his most powerful piece has been removed. He thinks Faol's new vampires will defeat the humans, the Elves, and those accursed were-creatures in Lycos. If he does, he will roll across the landscape with his ever-growing army of bloodsuckers and the world will fall to him."

"Let's not forget Arachnielle's spider folk," Tyche said with something of a laugh. "The Arachne and the Anansi are already laying waste to the southern continent. There are none who can stand against them so long as the Forest Trolls fight with them."

"They are of no consequence," Tyr said. "When Faol is destroyed, Gorgaraeth's shade will be destroyed with it. Without the vampire lord at their helm, his children will wither and perish. I suspect that if he dies, so will they. Bael will see that he has no hope of winning and he'll concede."

"The dragons will prevail, and Titan will win," Eris said. "Ouroboros is without equal. These pitiful armies that have gathered here will be incinerated in a single breath. Faol will die. Kit, the Savior of Aarall, will die. Hope will be lost, and Titan will have won. The dragons will sweep across the lands and set the world ablaze. Those who survive will be enslaved and, that vile black creature, Ouroboros, will do whatever he wishes."

"None of that will happen," Ollin said. His voice rumbled like the thunder of a distant summer storm. "Faol will fall. Ouroboros will fall. The people will prevail, and the game will end in a stalemate. Nobody will win and life will live on."

"A stalemate?" Mephitis' eyes widened and her mouth dropped open. "You're playing for a draw?"

Ollin and Galahdes smiled wryly at the Arbiter. "We don't need to win," Galahdes said, "we just need to not lose. Neither Titan nor Orth have an appetite for this game anymore. All we need to do is see that Bael cannot win."

"His demons will never stop," Tyr said. "They will need to be defeated before Bael will quit."

"Nonsense," Ollin said, waving a dismissive hand. "They have already been pushed back into Helja and Gimlie is working on closing the rip in the Veil. The dwarves and Hobgoblins have been freed, and those who have survived will be content to live their lives rooting around in the Underworld, seeking precious stones and shiny metals."

"My people will continue to strengthen and maintain the Veil, and life will live on," Galahdes added. "Bael's pieces will be removed or nullified. He will soon get bored and quit."

"He is immortal," Tyr said, shaking his head. "The star that this world revolves around will die before Bael concedes."

"Either way, the people will be free, and life will live on." Ollin's words had a ring of finality to them. He was finished talking to the Fates. He wanted the end game to begin. One by one, the Fates disappeared until only Tyr stood with the couple.

"I wish you luck, Ollin and Galahdes. I hadn't expected you to be my teacher, not today, at any rate. I would have never expected you to play for a deadlock. Genius. It's the only word that properly expresses how I feel about your gameplay. Pure genius." Tyr bowed his head and disappeared with a pop. In the distance, a coyote howled.

"Open the gates," Ollin called out. "The enemy is at hand. Let us make them regret their decision to darken our door with their shadows. We will cast our light upon them, and they will tremble in fear."

The assembled soldiers stood dumbfounded as Ollin and Galahdes approached. None moved. None cheered. The city gates remained closed.

Ollin hung his head and groaned. His body shimmered for a moment, and his persona was replaced with the more familiar form of Father Hoarfrost. Galahdes did the same, returning to her form as Grams.

"Open the gates," Captain Harding bellowed. "Today we fight for freedom." The gathered soldiers cheered wildly, and the gates swung open. Their collective cheers drowned out the sound of the portcullis as the City Watch guards worked the great cranks.

"You look wonderful, just the way you are," Grams said to Father Hoarfrost, giving him a wink. "When it is my time to fight, I will return to my Elven form." She took the old man's hand in hers and gave it a tight squeeze. "Regardless of the outcome today, never forget how much I love you."

"Do not leave me," Father Hoarfrost said. "I cannot bear the thought of living for eternity with a piece of me missing."

"If I die, I will return to you. We will never be apart."

"You know what I mean, my love. Do not die. Return to me in this form or as your true self. It doesn't matter. Just come back to me."

The pair paused. They waited while Captain Harding, Sister Gale, and General Gaelira Magdan led the soldiers and the Temple's faithful out the gate and into the Amberwood Forest beyond. It was the beginning of the end. With every prophecy shattered, the outcome was unknown, but it would be determined before the sun set on the day.

CHAPTER FORTY-EIGHT

THE BRIGHT LIGHT OF SALVATION

Within minutes of the first ring of the Temple's alarm-bell, fires ignited in a chain reaction across the kingdom of Arnnor. The first of the bonfires ignited outside the Spiderwood Forest to the southwest of Aarall. Another fire started to the southeast shortly thereafter, and another due east from there.

The fires lit up across the Mellandile mountain range, the impassible series of impossibly steep mountains which separated Arnnor from the Elven kingdom. From the mountaintop of Two Peaks, the seat of the kingdom's monarchy, another fire ignited. Several more fires lit up the sides of Mount Toka shortly thereafter.

"My people know to come," Iba said to Captain Harding. "The signals now spread to the north."

"They are too far away to do us any good today," the captain replied, "but if we prevail, your people will all know that we fought together as one." Iba grinned up at the captain, nodded, and scampered off into the trees.

The roadway that led into Aarall was surrounded on both sides by the Amberwood Forest. The trees were so densely packed and their canopy so thick, it was as dark as a moonless night beyond its edges. The captain didn't like the feel it gave him. He trusted the Wood Nymphs were fighting with them, but would they be able to find the enemy, using the forest for cover to hide their attacks? He wanted to believe the Elven queen knew what she was doing, but his doubts gnawed at his stomach.

He gave Sister Gale a quick glance. Her face was solemn, but she showed no signs of fear. The rage that had filled her heart when the Wood Nymph general disappeared into the forest seemed to have passed. He couldn't help but wonder, though, what she might say or do when the general returned, if she returned at all.

"Captain?" Amara said, her deep baritone voice carrying a noticeable edge to it. "What will we do when we get to the end of the woods?"

"We will engage the enemy and then quickly retreat into the forest. If we can draw them in, get them to follow us, the Wood Nymphs will deal with them." The Gigas priest nodded, her reaction stoic.

"I don't like it," Silverleaf said, drawing a look of ire from Sister Gale.

"Let him speak," the captain said, shaking his head at the combat instructor. "We are asking a lot of our people. We need to hear their thoughts."

"We are not all trained to fight vampires. Even though we've all been equipped with blessed weapons, most of the priests are not trained to use them. Even if we cast *Archer's Blessing* upon them before the battle, I don't think it will help. Once the vampires come, fear will take over. Kit told us how fast the creatures are, how they can be somewhere one moment and, in your face, the next. If they can do that, how are we to escape back into the forest?"

"We won't," Sister Gale said. The captain saw the look of pain on her face. None of their people had been told they were going on a suicide mission. Sister Gale had insisted that the soldiers and the Temple's faithful be given the full details of what they were doing. The captain argued against telling anybody. The safety of the world outweighed the lives of the few. The mission was too important, and he feared the soldiers would balk. Everyone needed to be fully committed or the plan would fail. In that moment, seeing the look on Silverleaf and Amara's faces, he questioned the wisdom of his plan.

"I understand," Amara said. Her heavy forehead creased as her brow lowered down over her eyes. "When the general said we would be bait, she meant it literally. We are to be food for the vampires, and while they feed, the Wood Nymphs will kill them." Silverleaf made a strangling noise as his giant friend spoke.

"I wish I had known this," he said, staring up at the much taller woman. "There are too many things left unsaid, left undone. I would have liked to have remedied that before we came out here today." The giant looked down at the half elf and nudged him with her hip.

"Not everything needs to be said or done. Knowing is enough." Silverleaf smiled at the priest's comment, but it was the saddest thing Captain Harding had ever witnessed. Life was precious. Much too precious to throw away, hoping a plan might succeed.

"I'll not do it," the captain said. He gritted his teeth and set his jaw. "I will not lead us to our demise. Not like this. I will fight to the death if I have to, but I'm not leading our people like lambs to the slaughter."

"What do you have in mind, Captain?" Sister Gale motioned ahead to where the road exited the forest. Only three hundred paces away was an army larger than any of them had ever seen.

"When we get near the forest's edge," he said with a shrug. "We'll wait for Aurora to return. Hopefully she'll have news of the Gizmos' movements."

"And if she doesn't?" Silverleaf asked.

"Then we'll cross that bridge when we get to it," Sister Gale said.

⋘⋙

The captain's stomach knotted. Aurora should have been back by now. "We can't just wait here."

Sister Gale nodded and looked back at their people. "Let's move up closer to the edge and then spread out in the forest. We step out, fire our bows, and step back inside. If the vampires attack, hopefully the Wood Nymphs are going to stop them before they get too close."

"You're going to need to split up your priests and acolytes to keep them with my soldiers. I have many good archers, but your people are less adept." Captain Harding caught Amara's look, reaffirming what she had said earlier. She was carrying the biggest hunting bow the captain had ever seen.

Sister Gale turned to the Temple's faithful. "We are going to take the fight to the enemy. I want each of you who can cast either Archer's Blessing or Ranger's Mark to take a group of ten soldiers with you. We will spread out along the forest's edge, and we will harass the enemy until they give chase. When they do, everybody retreats into the forest. Once you're inside, take cover and let the Wood Nymphs get to work."

"Does anybody have questions?" the captain called out. He waited for a few moments to see if anybody was going to speak up. When nobody did, he turned and sprinted up the road towards the enemy.

There had been some confusion about splitting up the priests and acolytes, but between the captain and Sister Gale, they'd gotten everyone organized. When they were about one hundred paces from exiting the forest, half the group split off to the right and the other half to the left. Sister Gale and Captain Harding stayed on the road and stepped out past the forest's edge. The captain checked the skies for Aurora, but she was nowhere to be seen. Fifty paces behind them on the road, two people approached. Father Hoarfrost was dressed in robes of brilliant white, while Grams had shed her old-woman skin and was back to her tall, Elven self as Galahdes.

"Sweet Titan," the captain hissed. "What are they doing here?"

"We will not let our people fight without us," Father Hoarfrost called out. The couple's pace quickened.

The captain hissed, trying to cover up a string of curse words. "Sister, speak to him. Maybe he'll listen to you."

"I don't know who he is anymore." Sister Gale shook her head. "I have no idea what to say to a god who once posed as our spiritual leader."

"You need not say anything," Father Hoarfrost said. There was a profound sadness wrapped around his words. "I am the same person you've known for most of your life. Nothing has changed except your perception of reality. You have trusted me in the past. I only ask that you trust me now."

"Father, you're not allowed to fight." Captain Harding's face was reddening badly. "They'll kill us all if you do."

"I have no plans on fighting," the old man said as he walked up to the captain. He patted him on the shoulder plates of his armor and kept right on walking.

"What is he doing?" Sister Gale asked Galahdes. "He can't be here."

"Do as Father asks. Trust him."

"King Faol," Father Hoarfrost's voice carried across the mass of enemies who covered the ground as far as the eye could see. The man's voice was incredibly powerful. "King Jordain. I know you are both cowering behind your wall of people, and I know you can both hear me. You will not survive this day. Tell your people to lay down their arms and return to their homes. They need not die with you."

Three swirling masses of black dust raced across the hundred paces that separated Father from the front line of the enemy. They swirled and twirled, changing directions this way and that, but with each passing heartbeat, they neared. When they were less than ten paces away, arrows flew out of the forest. The masses of smoke screamed, coalesced into humans, and fell in a tangled mass on the ground at Father Hoarfrost's feet.

Captain Harding ran out to stand beside Father. "Defenders of Aarall," he bellowed. "Kill them all."

The soldiers who were hiding within the forest stepped out, filled the sky with arrows, and slunk back into the woods. More black clouds of ash came flying forward. Many flew towards Father Hoarfrost and the captain, but at least half flew to where the soldiers had retreated into the foliage. Again, arrows flew into the swirling clouds of ash, and again, dead vampires fell to the ground.

"How long do you think you can keep this up?" Galahdes gave the captain a playful smile. "Eventually, they're going to figure out that we are hopelessly outnumbered."

"It's not as bad as it was," Aurora said. Her face was flushed. "I've circled the city several times now. I couldn't tell you how many Gizmos are coming, but there are a lot. They're ridiculously difficult to track from above. I also killed several vampires who thought they could take me from the sky. There is another army coming from the south-west. It's not large, perhaps five hundred strong. It looks to be composed of Berrat and Cormorant soldiers."

Captain Harding looked up and down the edge of the forest. "Archers, at the ready," he yelled out. The front ranks of the enemy banged their shields in response. "Archers, send them to Helja!"

Like the first time, City Watch, priests, and acolytes stepped out of the forest and filled the air with arrows. The enemy responded with screams and cries of anguish. The captain surmised the Temple's faithful had done a better job with their spells this time.

"We may win the day yet," Sister Gale said with a nervous laugh.

"Archers at the ready," the captain called out again. Before he could issue the order to fire, the enemy surged forward. There was no need to tell the soldiers to unleash their attack. The sky was immediately filled with arrows. There was a brief pause before another volley was issued.

"People of Aarall, retreat!" The captain watched as volley after volley of arrows flew out across the sky. Enemies were dropping at a horrendous rate.

Galahdes drew on her bowstring and a golden arrow magically appeared. "Children of the forest," she called out. "Attack!"

From out of the forest, thousands of Wood Nymphs emerged. Their golden arrows streaked through the air, striking the front ranks of the attacking soldiers. The enemy's vanguard collapsed as hundreds upon hundreds of bodies fell face first. Those who were behind them either tripped or fell to the constant onslaught of arrows that continued to rain down on them. They had barely moved fifty yards when the mass of soldiers came to a halt. They constructed a wall of shields in front of themselves. While the golden arrows occasionally found their mark through small chinks in the enemy's defenses, most of the attack bounced harmlessly away.

"Cease fire," the captain bellowed out. There was no use in continuing their attack while the enemy was turtling.

"Oh, sweet Titan," Sister Gale said. The sky went dark as a massive cloud of arrows came flying from behind the wall of shields.

"Take cover," the captain screamed. "Everybody, get into the forest."

The captain's people tried to retreat, but not before hundreds were killed or injured in the blizzard of arrows. Sister Gale had erected a protective bubble around their group, deflecting the projectiles away before they could do any damage. There was no break in the enemy's volleys. The arrows continued to rain down by the thousands. In less than a minute, the area looked like it was covered with porcupine quills.

When the arrows finally stopped falling, Sister Gale released her spell, and the protective bubble disappeared. She was sweating badly. "We need to retreat. I can't do that again."

"Nonsense," Father Hoarfrost said. His voice was grave, but full of hope. "Our salvation is at hand."

From the sky above, a tremendous burst of blindingly bright light crashed upon the ground to the north of the enemy. It created a kaleidoscope of brilliant colors. The wall of shields suddenly collapsed, and the army surged towards the tower of light.

The captain couldn't make out what was happening where the brilliant pillar had appeared, but whatever it was, the enemy was being drawn to it like moths to a candle. From the forest, the surviving archers stepped out and unleashed their arrows.

"What was that light?" Sister Gale said. "What's happening?"

"Like I said." Father Hoarfrost grinned at Aurora and Captain Harding. "Our salvation is at hand. The Savior of Aarall has arrived."

"Kit's here?" Aurora said. The high priest nodded. Aurora gave the captain a single look that spoke volumes.

"Go," he said. "Be with our daughter. Defeat the enemy."

Without a word, Aurora's wings unfurled, and she launched herself skyward.

"What do we do?" Sister Gale said as she watched the army that was barely fifty paces away, charging north.

"We harry their flanks," the captain said. "We cause as much grief as we can for as long as we can. An army cannot effectively fight on multiple fronts."

CHAPTER FORTY-NINE

SAFELY IN THE ARMS OF A DRAGON

The roar of the Bifrost while transporting soldiers from Cormorant all the way to Aarall was near deafening. Kit, Indie, Feigh, and the boys were the first through the portal. Kit and Feigh were riding Angel while Indie and Lin sat upon their own horses, Char and Whistler. Fenrir, Riva, Amilta, and an extremely large number of wolves arrived moments later. Lin, Coldforge, Calian, and Danny followed shortly behind them. Bango, Mukale, and Treedale were the last to arrive, along with the rest of the military commanders and the bulk of the army.

"That's no way for a dwarf to travel," Coldforge said. His orange beard twitched wildly on his face. It looked like he was going to say something else, but no words came out, only vomit. "Thank Gaia, me father wasn't here to witness that."

"That's a lot of soldiers," Indie said, pointing to the enormous army that was charging towards them. He looked back over his shoulder while more and more of the Cormorant army continued to arrive through the portal. Kit had decided they should land north of Lake Titan. It was the largest plot of flat land that wasn't being farmed in the area. It was mostly rock and sand there, making it impossible to grow anything of value.

Nobody remembered there being a vast forest in front of the city.

"Danny, go see what we're facing here," Kit said. "I need to know if we have the numbers."

"I'll go," Indie said. "I..." Kit placed her hand on his arm and shook her head. "I need you here with me." Danny summoned the phoenix and in moments was a burning blur speeding headfirst towards the enemy.

"I want you and Lump to lead the drakes." Kit gave her boyfriend a tired smile. She was weary of the obvious jealousy Indie was showing, despite Danny having found a mate for himself. Yuka's screech announced Ulip's arrival. Neither the Gigas, nor his mount, looked very well. As Kit surveyed the other drakes, they all appeared ready to hurl.

"Take deep breaths," Coldforge said. "If ye want it to pass quickly, take yerselves a lot of slow, deep breaths." Yuka screeched out something, perhaps passing along the dwarf's words to the other drakes.

"Ulip," Kit called up to the big man. "Can you visit Siku? If she's free to leave, perhaps she will come and fight on our behalf."

"The dragons will not fight with you," Yuka said. "But we will."

"Why won't the dragons fight with us?" Indie asked. That the dragons would betray the people responsible for freeing them seemed absurd, and the fire drake's comment obviously got under Indie's skin.

"The dragons will seek domination over the lands," Yuka replied. "Since you freed them, they may let you live in their world, but they will not be your ally. They will be your master."

"Let it be, Kit," Fenrir said. "The dragons are dragons, and they will do what they will do. I will take your mother, Amilta, and the wolves east. We'll flank the army. The wolves will be of little use in a head-on clash." In a moment, Fenrir was in her wolf form and taking the wolf pack east.

"Bango, ready the soldiers," Indie yelled out. "Get the archers prepared for when the enemy comes within range. Spread out as much as you can."

"We know what to do, Indie," Bango yelled back. "Look after yourselves. We've got this."

"You two, be careful," Lin yelled at Treedale and Mukale. "I will not face Grams' wrath for not bringing you home safely." The pair gave the woman a nod before disappearing into the crowd of advancing soldiers. The overaged acolyte, who was normally as sure as steel, appeared frazzled. Lin's eyes went wide, and she pointed to the sky to the west. "Kit, up there!"

Aurora touched down in front of the young priest only seconds later. She gave her daughter a quick hug and a warm smile. She stole a glance over her shoulder at the incoming army. "We have much to discuss, but it will need to wait."

"When did that forest happen?" Kit asked, motioning toward the Amberwood Forest that had not been there when she had left Aarall.

"Galahdes and the Elves, but we don't have time to speak of it. The forest is filled with Wood Nymphs. They are fighting for us." Feigh was practically dancing in the saddle upon hearing the news.

"Grams did it," the mouse-sprite said, clapping his hands gleefully. "She grew the forest overnight."

"She had a lot of help, my winged friend," Aurora said with a chuckle. "The *shamed* did a wondrous thing. Thank you for coming."

Yuka screeched and blew a fireball into the air.

"Kit," Indie screamed. "We're in trouble."

From over the heads of the enemy, a dark cloud of ash and dust flew towards Kit's army. They looked like a swarm of locusts flying towards a field of grain, intent on stripping the crops bare.

"Vampires!" Aurora called out. She brandished her longsword and took flight. Ulip and Yuka, along with the rest of the drakes, were in the air in moments. The phoenix unleashed its song just before it cut through the dust cloud. The vampires burst into flames as the firebird flew through them. Several singed bodies fell from the sky. It was likely that many of the vampires Danny had collided with had burned up on contact. The cloud suddenly swirled and shifted around the flaming missile, avoiding the phoenix's attacks all together.

Kit slid down from Angel and patted her on the neck. "Get Feigh to safety. Take Char with you." Angel nickered in response.

"You fight better when we're together. Don't make me leave."

"I need to fly." Kit was quickly becoming frustrated. She needed her horse to run, to get clear of this battle. She needed to know Angel was safely out of harm's way.

"You need to stay on the ground, trust me." Angel shook her main.

"Angel, I need you to..."

"You need me to carry you into battle. Use your voice. Rally the soldiers. Lead them into the mouth of the enemy. You will be their inspiration and you need to be on the ground for that to happen."

"Char doesn't want to leave, either," Indie said. "We're running out of time."

Lin wheeled Whistler around. She held one of her flaming swords aloft, swinging it in slow, wide circles. She gave Kit a quick smile before digging her heels into her horse's ribs. Whistler reared up and sped off toward the oncoming army. Coldforge was already on Runt's back. He tossed Kit her hammer.

"Ye can give it back when we're done here." The dwarf's eyes were wild. He thrust his stone fists into the air. "I've got what I need for this scrap, girl. You get yours and I'll get mine." Coldforge whooped several times and Runt leapt forward, racing to catch up to Lin and Whistler. Lump had already changed into this dragon form. He roared and belched out a series of fireballs, most of them directed at the incoming cloud of vampires. With a push of his hind legs, he was airborne and unleashing a firestorm as he winged towards the enemy.

Bright golden scales instantly covered Indie's body. "Be safe!" he called out with a playful grin. He drew the Bifrost blade and Char bolted forward.

Kit hopped back onto Angel's back. She raised her hammer over her head and galloped back and forth in front of her army. They cheered and brandished their own weapons as she did. The little priest wrapped her hand around her necklace and called out. "For freedom!" The army echoed her call. "For freedom!" She bellowed it out once more, and again, the army echoed her words.

Bright white wings sprung from Kit's back. She turned to face the oncoming army and unleashed her angelic song. The power of the pearl amulet magnified it a hundredfold. The cloud of vampires coruscated wildly before they dropped from the sky, landing hard on the ground in their human form.

"For freedom!" Angel lurched forward, forcing Feigh to take a tight grip on her mane. The mouse-sprite's ears were flapping wildly as the little roan gained speed. Sparks flew from the horse's hooves as they beat upon the ground. In moments, the land was being set ablaze as they streaked into battle. The wind rushed by so quickly that Kit's eyes were tearing up. She could barely see. She sensed an incoming attack and swung her hammer. There was a blinding flash of light and a vampire exploded.

Indie, who was several horse-lengths behind Kit, was unleashing his own dragon fire upon the vampire horde. Even if it wasn't as impressive as Lump's, he still toasted a good number of the blood suckers. Meanwhile, his Bifrost blade flashed, slashing and beheading several more vampires who'd gotten too near the dragon-man.

Kit's heart sunk when she saw a riderless Runt blowing a steady stream of frost at the vampires who were surrounding him. She strained her eyes, looking for Coldforge. The dwarven prince couldn't have fallen. A loud whooping noise drew Kit's attention to her right.

The dwarf's hands were glowing blocks of stone. They were flailing about, seemingly at random, with each swing making solid, bone-crushing contact. Angel turned abruptly, making her way towards Runt. Feigh was nearly lost in the sudden change in direction. Something of a mousy shriek escaped his lips. A winged shadow passed over Kit. She had expected to see Lump or the drakes, but nothing was there.

"My ride is here," Feigh said. "Be safe."

Before Kit could react, the shadow passed over her again. Feigh was suddenly airborne and heading to the east. She had no idea what had happened, nor did she have time to consider it. She brought her hammer to bear just as Angel burst into the crowd of vampires who were attacking Runt. The horse had to dodge Coldforge as he, too, came to Runt's aid. Vampires grabbed him and threw him to the ground, but he quickly turned the tide. The dwarf resembled a tiny tornado, raising dust and dropping enemies at a frightful pace.

Lump flew low, flaming the area with his golden fire before launching himself skyward again. Over and over, he turned and dove, and flamed and climbed.

Two great hawks appeared high above the fray. They were circling the battle, searching for the enemy's leaders. They were among the last to arrive. At Kit's request, they were to stay away from the fighting and to use their superior vision to scout the area.

The main bodies of both armies slammed into each other in a deafening clash of steel and skin. Screams of pain filled the air as hundreds of warriors fell to ax and sword. Kit's stomach roiled at the catastrophic loss of life. With each passing second, dozens more fell in the heat of combat. Their lives were being cut short so that a few people could rise in power. Bones were shattered. Blood was spilled. Fathers and mothers, brothers and sisters, sons and daughters on both sides were dying violent, horrible deaths. And why? So that one man might declare himself ruler of all. It was utterly senseless.

"Follow Ryn and Breayn," Kit said to Angel through their bond. *"They will lead us to King Jordain or King Faol."* Angel turned to the south and crashed into the enemy army. Kit bellowed out her angelic cry. Through the sheer force of her will, the soldiers parted like a river rushing around an indomitable boulder. Kit couldn't see it, but her people were hot on her heels.

⚭⚭⚭◈⚭⚭⚭

Where are you going? Indie's mind raced as Kit and Angel flew headlong into the enemy's ranks. *"Don't let them get ahead of you."* Indie could not speak to Char as Kit could speak with her roan, but the two instinctively understood each other. The black stallion's hooves beat upon the ground like war-drums as he thundered forward, desperately trying to keep pace with the angelic blur up ahead. Coldforge's whoops told him than he and Runt were right behind him. He had to assume that Lin and Whistler were keeping pace. There was no time to look back to find out. Guilt ripped through his belly. He couldn't just assume she was still there. He had to know if she was okay. The woman drove him crazy, but he couldn't leave her behind.

Indie glanced over his shoulder. Whistler was behind him, but Lin was not on her back.

"Stay with Kit," he said, his leathery dragon wings bursting out behind him. They yanked Indie off Char's back and with a couple of quick beats, he was in the air and flying back toward where Whistler was coming from. He flew over the horse, blowing golden flames over any enemy who dared to near her. Whistler passed beneath him, steadily galloping after Char. Perhaps fifty paces further back, Lin was fighting off a half dozen soldiers. She had both blades drawn, their flaming steel blazing as she thrust and parried the heavily armored enemy. The woman was dressed in nothing more than leathers and a black cloak. When it seemed all hope was lost, a black mist whipped about her feet, carrying her above the soldiers. Lin was unsteady as she hovered above the enemy. The young man had forgotten about the enchanted items Coldforge had crafted for her.

Indie's heart raced as a vampire dressed in similar apparel materialized at the woman's back. He was about to launch a fireball at him when Indie recognized him to be Ormand.

"Lay down your weapons and surrender," the vampire called out to the soldiers below him. "The fight is over."

Indie shouldn't have been surprised. He understood the power of compulsion. It still amazed him when over fifty soldiers dropped their weapons to the ground and stood motionless. The general nodded to Lin, turned into a cloud of ash, and blew south as though carried by the wind. The look of astonishment on Lin's face reflected the feeling that was gripping Indie.

"Need a hand?" he called out as he flew to the still hovering woman. "Our horses are heading to war without us. I can take you to them." Lin held out her hand, offering it to the dragon man. Indie flew behind the woman, wrapped his arms around her, and took off.

"Careful where you put your hands," Lin said, her familiar annoying banter instantly grating on Indie. "I don't want to get between you and your lady-love."

"My hands are only holding you to prevent you from falling. If you'd prefer, I can let go of you."

"No, please don't." There was a laugh in her voice. "You're very warm and I feel safe for the first time today."

Indie didn't know how to process that comment. He flapped harder, speeding himself to his destination.

CHAPTER FIFTY

THE KINGS' GAMBIT

Angel carried Kit through the enemy forces. She was barely more than a blur as she galloped through their thinning ranks. Where they had been heading east towards the Cormorant army, the enemy soldiers were now heading south, away from Aarall and the new Amberwood Forest. They appeared to be in a panic, nearing the brink, ready to rout from the field. The little priest only needed to look more closely to see why. Gizmos, by the hundreds, had engaged in the melee. There were Tahr, and Lupien, and a few other races that Kit couldn't identify. She didn't know why they were attacking the enemy, but she was glad for their help. The kings' soldiers may have had the numbers, but the Gizmos made up for it with sheer ferocity. Memories of Iba and her tiny vorpal blades came to mind. Even powerful spell casters stood little chance against the girl's speed and agility. She never tried to overpower her enemy. Iba simply used the gifts she had to exploit a target's weaknesses.

What weaknesses do you have, King Faol?

Ryn and Breayn had flown to the south of the enemy ranks. Angel changed direction, following the great hawks. They must have located one or both of the kings, or at least whoever it was commanding the kings' armies.

"If I have to leave your back, get yourself to safety." Angel huffed at Kit's words.

"I'm not leaving. I go where you go."

"Angel, please. I need to know that you're safe." There was no reply from the little roan, only silence. *"Think of Char and your unborn child."*

"You're cheating," Angel said. Kit breathed a sigh of relief. She could hear the resignation in her horse's voice. *"But I understand. I will steer clear of trouble, as best I can."*

"Thank you."

The private moment between horse and rider had distracted Kit from the battle raging on in front of her. Her soldiers had penetrated more deeply into the enemy lines than she'd realized. Berrat warriors, armed with bow and blade, were being led by Treedale and Mukale, and a female dire wolf she didn't recognize. The wolf wasn't attacking, at least not directly. She was providing something of a shield for the Berrat warriors, using her size and speed to keep the enemy off balance. They were doing well, but if the enemy's army continued to move in their direction, the small band of warriors would soon be overrun.

Beyond Treedale and Mukale was the true source of the disturbance. A sea of gray, black, and brown poured over the enemy forces, drowning them in a frenzy of tooth and claw. In the middle of the fray was a great white wolf with blue whorls. Fenrir had used the wolf population to tear down the enemy's southern flank. What looked to be a lopsided battle, with the wolves on top, was about to take a turn for the worse.

A wave of death poured across the battlefield. The smell of rot and decay was so thick that it coated Kit's tongue. A large group of red-haired humans was speeding towards Fenrir. Kit instinctively knew who they were. She had to slow their progress as they moved toward the wolf god.

"Put us between Fenrir and the vampires." Angel immediately changed course, turning to intercept a band of red-haired bloodsuckers.

Kit wanted to leave Angel's back so her horse could escape, but she knew Angel could run much faster than her white feathered wings could carry her. The pair raced through the regular soldiers, choosing not to engage until they met their intended enemy. With her battle hammer held high, Kit called upon her angelic song. Her voice slammed into the vampires, drawing hisses from the entire group. There looked to be nearly fifty of them and something about them shook Kit to her core.

Three of the vampires broke off from the group, looking to intercept the little priest. Angel veered slightly towards them, intending to clash with them head on. The bronze-skinned, redheaded human vanished. Remembering what Indie had told her of vampire tactics and how their desire for blood forced them into certain behaviors, Kit pushed her hammer out and called on its light. A brilliant flash burst outward, illuminating the three redheaded vampires. They had surrounded Kit mid-flight. Their features changed at the moment of their attack. Black eyes, impossibly long fangs, and obsidian claws were only a part of their transformation. Their brows and jaws had enlarged to exaggerated levels, making them look more monstrous than human.

Despite how fast Angel was running and how quickly these creatures were closing on Kit, everything was moving in painfully slow motion. It was as though the world had simply stopped. This wasn't the first time the little priest had experienced this. A vague memory spilled from the back of her consciousness. A fight in tunnels beneath the ground. Enemies and friends alike all fell to her uncontrollable rage. The sight of Indie's mangled body and her blood-soaked claws slammed into her mind.

Her daemon self had emerged, but she refused to let it take control of her. She would allow her unbridled rage to be unleashed, but she would not lose herself to it.

The moments ticked on, each one lasting an eternity. She watched in painful detail as the vampires' claws reached out, their teeth practically extending from their faces as they closed on their prey. Kit's heart lurched. They weren't attacking her. They were attacking Angel. She had been too slow to see their plan. There would be no time to react. Her horse, her friend, her confidant was about to die a horribly violent death.

The world turned to a crimson so deep it was almost black. The daemon was now in full control, and Kit didn't care. She would let it do what it must in order to save the horse that so willingly carried her into battle.

The next moment made no sense. Her eyes saw, but her mind couldn't process it. The vampires were barely a pace away, ready to tear her little roan to pieces when their bodies changed shape, contorting into a bizarre pose, like they had just slammed into an invisible wall.

The image was surreal. An impossibility was unfolding before Kit that her brain simply couldn't fathom.

A winged mouse floated above the vampires. He held a bow that was launching a golden arrow. He was moving too quickly. His arrow passed through the neck of a vampire. The monstrous thing's black eyes instantly went dead. An inky cloud flew from its mouth and promptly disintegrated.

Was that Feigh?

If it was the mouse-sprite, he had just saved Angel's life. With her right hand, Kit smashed the head of her hammer into one of the two remaining vampires, while her left hand snatched the other by the throat. Her clawed hand easily dug into the creature's bronze flesh, practically severing its head from its shoulders. The burst of brilliance of her hammer obscured the damage it inflicted on the third, blinding Kit momentarily.

Angel steered towards the remaining group of vampires, intent on cutting them off. She would not let them get to the wolves. Kit called upon her angelic song, but all that came out was a throaty roar. The surrounding air became stifling. Angel's mane was on fire. Flames licked from her ears.

Oh, sweet Titan, what have I done?

Horse and rider were a churning ball of flame. They slammed into the band of red-headed vampires, immolating them on contact. The vampires split up, trying to stay clear of the inferno that was cutting through them. Some avoided the flaming duo, only to be engulfed in a golden firestorm. Others fell to more golden arrows launched from somewhere above the fray. The phoenix appeared from nowhere, using its flaming body to explode a set of vampires who had conveniently lined themselves up. Runt and Coldforge worked in tandem, tearing apart another that had escaped Lump's dragon fire.

In mere minutes, there wasn't a single vampire remaining.

Kit's flames died out, as did Angel's. The small roan appeared uninjured, but the little horse was drenched in sweat. Char and Whistler, both riderless, trotted up alongside. A knot gripped Kit's stomach. Where were their riders?

Lump landed heavily beside Kit, distracting her from her worries.

"Our quarry lies ahead," Fenrir said, pointing to the south. Kit's gaze followed to where the wolf-god was indicating. The knot in her stomach tightened harder.

Guards had surrounded Indie, Lin, and a tall man standing next to her. He wore a black cloak and hood, making it impossible to tell who he was. She couldn't hear them at this distance, but they were exchanging harsh words with a pompous-looking man dressed in ridiculously colorful armor. His long blonde hair was tied into a top knot. A ring of gold sat upon his head.

It had to be King Jordain.

Well away from King Jordain stood another man with pale skin and slicked black hair. Three women clung to his arms. Two were human. The third was Berrat. Of the two humans, one had black hair, and the other had hair so blonde it was almost white. The Berrat woman had flaming red hair, just like Danny's. The group was staring directly at Kit. They all appeared to be amused.

"King Faol, Annabella, Hope, and a woman I don't recognize," whispered a voice. Kit's head snapped around to find her mother. She was a gory mess. Her wings looked badly battered. "Jordain is nothing. Ignore him. Faol carries Gorgaraeth and Annabella carries an unknown demon. Hope is not possessed, but she is extremely dangerous. Do not underestimate her."

"Gorgaraeth is dead," Kit said. "Coldforge killed him. I saw it happen."

"That was only the demon-god's body. Faol carries his shade, the true power of Gorgaraeth."

"What do we do?" Kit's eyes flashed back to Indie and her mother. Despite the number of guards around them, they didn't seem to be in any danger. She looked back at Faol. The man was laughing. The situation amused him.

"We burn them," Danny said. "We burn them all." The Berrat gave Kit a roguish grin. "Fire seems to be our go-to method."

"I doubt that even Lump's flames can hurt Faol," Fenrir said. Calian slid in beside Danny. Blood coated her face and bald head. The gore obscured most of the tattoos that covered her exposed skin.

"He's not unbeatable," the dog soldier said. "If he was, he wouldn't have bothered to bring an army with him. He'd have taken the city on his own." Treedale and Mukale showed up just moments after Calian. Like the woman, they, too, bore the marks of excessive violence. No one involved in this battle would leave untouched by its carnage.

"This was only a testing ground," Aurora said. "He wanted to see how his creations would perform in a true battle. I don't think he expected this much resistance."

"I don't plan on waiting for him to act first," Kit said. She slid down from Angel and patted her on the neck. *"Stay clear of the battle. Take Char and Whistler with you. Run if you must."* The little roan didn't respond.

While the battle continued to rage on, Kit led the small group of heroes forward. She didn't know how she was going to do it, but the war was going to end, here and now.

⁓⊷⊙⟨⊙⊶⁓

Lin had been screaming at her father, the king, for several minutes. Indie was wondering if she was ever going to take a breath. Based on the look of detached amusement on King Jordain's face, he may well have been wondering the same thing. He stole a glance at General Ormand, who was standing at Indie's side. He had been silent the entire time, allowing Lin to do all the talking. The king had flushed when the vampire general had appeared shortly after Lin and Indie. The guards were about to move on them, but a quick flash of Ormand's teeth and a single phrase telling them to be still kept the entire lot at bay.

"You are a horrible, disgusting, worthless excuse for a human being and you are definitely not fit to lead a kingdom." This was perhaps the fourth time Lin had berated the king. If the situation wasn't so dire, Indie would have found it amusing. He had wanted to fight at Kit's side, but when Lin saw the king, she insisted he fly her to him. Had he not, he would likely have been the recipient of the woman's wrath.

"Still your mouth, woman," a tall guard dressed in golden armor said. "The penalty for such insolence is to have your tongue removed and your body burned at the stake."

"Shut it, Goldie," Lin screamed. "I shall speak to my father in whatever manner I deem fit. If you'd prefer that I first carve out your eyes, I'd be happy to do so." Lin had her sword drawn and at the frivolous guard's throat before his own blade cleared its scabbard.

"Put your weapons away, Aithlin," the king said. Had he yawned as he spoke, he wouldn't have sounded any more bored. "My safety is assured. Neither you nor your *friends* will do me any harm, lest you wish to see your mother killed."

Lin's blade was still pressed against the golden guard's neck when she turned to her father. Indie instinctively knew that threating the life of her mother was an extremely bad play. It might buy the man some time, but it would definitely make his demise even more unpleasant for him.

"I would suggest that your threat is empty," Lin said as she drew her sword away from the golden guard. She flicked her wrist slightly as she did, giving the man a non-lethal scar to remember her by. "But I don't think your heart is filled with anything but pure blackness. She bore you a daughter and a son, but you would never consider marrying her. You left her and your children to the devices of Lord Arthure, another cruel and heartless man, just like yourself."

"Lady Jaquine was a lot of things, but she was no lady," the king said. His tone was filled with a mixture of lust and loathing. "She was good enough to warm my bedchamber, but she was not fit to sit beside me on the throne."

The golden guard's eyebrows shot up and he gave the king a sideways glance. Had this been Lin's plan all along? Was this whole confrontation a ruse to get the king to admit that she was his daughter? The woman grated on Indie, but his appreciation for her wiles jumped dramatically. She was undeniably crafty.

Lin smiled at the king and bowed. "Thank you, father, for showing me your true colors. I believe you when you say mother is in danger. I will allow you to leave here unharmed. Run back to your palace and hide beneath your bed. When I finish with Faol and his underlings, I will come for you, and I will kill you. Slowly."

Lin held her hands out by her side, palms raised to the sky. A swirl of dark smoke gathered around her feet as she lifted from the ground. The thick stench of decomposing flesh rolled off her as she rose into the air. Ormand followed the woman's lead, mimicking her ascent.

Lin clutched her breast and laughed. It was a deep throaty laugh that spoke of a promise. The sound of her laughter burst outward, knocking the king and his entourage off their feet.

"Come, Indigo, my pet," she called out. "We have a vampire king to kill. I will deal with this one at a time of my own choosing."

Even though Indie knew of the magic Lin carried that allowed her to perform these illusions, he wondered if the woman might actually be a vampire. Perhaps Ormand had turned her. He gave his head a shake, chasing away the thought before thrusting himself into the air. The dragon-man blew out a series of fireballs, striking the ground harmlessly around the king's people. He hadn't intended on hurting anybody, but he wanted to remind them that drawing their bows came with life-shortening consequences. When it appeared their retreat was safe, Indie took Lin by the hand and sped her towards Kit and the vampire king.

CHAPTER FIFTY-ONE

COURTING DEATH

Indie, Lin, and Ormand landed next to Kit and Aurora. With Coldforge riding Runt, and Lump still in his dragon form, they made a formidable-looking group. Danny walked a few paces to their left, along with Calian, Treedale, and Mukale. Fenrir, Amilta, and a band of wolves walked at their back. High above, Ryn, Breayn, Ulip, and the drakes circled. They seemed to be in a holding pattern of sorts, waiting for the inevitable outcome of the meeting.

"Hello, General," Annabella called out. "I had thought you were dead. After you fled Two Peaks five cycles ago, you were not heard from again."

"I'm here now," Ormand clapped back. "I'm not quite the same as when you turned me." The woman sniffed the air like a bloodhound.

"No. You're not. You're weaker. And what of this trollop at your side? The one who pretends she is one of us, one of the chosen few." Ormand laughed and placed his hand on Lin's shoulder.

"The rightful heir to the throne is no trollop. Perhaps you are projecting how you feel about yourself onto her? As the daughter of the most vile man to have ever walked the lands, it would not surprise me you have self-esteem problems."

Kit had no idea where this conversation was going, nor why it had even gotten started, but it was grating on her. She wanted to kill Faol, not have a verbal sparring match with him. The group was only ten paces from the man now. The little priest was fast, but she doubted she could sprint at the king before the others intervened.

"It must frustrate you, daughter of Aurora, to see me so close, and yet too far to strike me."

How had Faol known what she was thinking? Could he read her mind, or was he simply reading her expression? She desperately wanted to end this man's life. It was more than likely every bit of her body language screamed that very thought.

The man licked his lips. His purple tongue spoke of just how vile he was. Like Annabella, he sniffed at the air, pretending he was in the throes of ecstasy. "I cannot imagine just how delicious you would all taste. I've never had the pleasure of draining a celestial, but I have dreamed about it. I wonder, little wolf god, would you taste as sweet as you look? Perhaps I could take all three of you to my bedchamber for a little fun and a late-night snack."

Runt snarled at the man's choice of words. Saliva poured from his mouth. Like the vampire king, he slowly licked his lips. The dire wolf's reaction made Kit smile.

"I think my friend here wonders what *you* would taste like, King of Depravity. You stand there, all high and mighty, when really you are nothing more than a vessel for something truly powerful, something much more than yourself. Without Gorgaraeth, you are just a weak little man."

"I can only guess, girl, with that infuriating grin on your face, that you don't understand the danger you and your petty little group are facing."

"She's heard prattlin' like yers more often than ye might think, ye pointy toothed gutter scum. I killed yer precious Gorgaraeth once. I can kill 'em again. If yer head happens ta git in the way of me fist while I'm doin' it, all the better." Emboldened by Coldforge's words, Runt took a step forward. Lump followed in kind. Kit could feel the heat building in the gold dragon's body.

"Hope," Aurora called out. "Leave this man's side. Come home to your family. Don't do this."

"King Faol raised me. He loved me, cared for me. In his home, I wanted for nothing. What do you offer me, sister, other than a life of hardship and strife?"

"The man you say loved you and cared for you also killed our parents. He brutally murdered them right before your very eyes. You may have only been a child, but surely you remember. Surely you know I speak true."

Aurora's words struck a nerve. Kit saw it in the woman's eyes, her aunt's eyes. It only lasted for the briefest of moments, but it was there.

"How many more has this man killed while you watched?" Kit asked. "How many have suffered so that he might rise?" Hope sneered in response. Kit had no connection to this woman. Trying to make one now was futile. A rush of wind blew Kit's hair about. To her left, several feet past Danny, Ryn, and Breayn landed, now back in their Berrat form. King Faol's back straightened. He took several steps toward the couple.

Breayn locked her gaze on the redheaded Berrat woman. Tears welled up in her eyes as she spoke a single word. "Mother."

"Oh, what a gift I have been given," Faol said. His eyes were wide. He was practically vibrating with excitement. "I have searched for you, Breayn, for so many years. Your pure blood will feed my army for eternity."

Kit gasped. She hadn't noticed until just this moment. The red-haired Berrat woman standing with King Faol was the spitting image of Breayn. They were absolutely identical.

Danny took a protective step in front of his cousin. "You won't lay a hand on my family ever again, lord of darkness."

"Ooh, lord of darkness." Faol practically cackled. "I like that name. I may have to adopt it as my own." The vampire rubbed his hands together and gave a mock shiver. "Your parents were inferior, but effective. Perhaps the carrier of the phoenix will be the key to the perfect vampire. Perhaps it will be your cousin. Either way, I hadn't expected either of you to just drop into my lap like this. I hoped you might be here, which is why I brought this Berrat woman's shell." He motioned to Breayn's mother and gave the pair an overly exaggerated bow. "Thank you, to both of you."

From Kit's right, a wisp of black smoke flew past. It seemed to dodge and weave its way through the assembled body, working its way up to where King Faol and his entourage stood. When it slipped behind Hope, it materialized into

Pental. He wrapped his arms around the woman, placing his left hand over her heart and his right hand around her throat. His fangs were fully extended, ready to sink them into the woman's creamy, tanned skin.

"Wait," Kit screamed. "Don't!"

The vampire king glanced back at Pental and Hope. He shook his head and groaned. "Is this how you repay the one who granted you immortality? I made you the most powerful Berrat in all the lands, and what did you do with my gift? You squandered it. You used it to launch your personal crusade against those who would bring food for my people."

"Surrender, Faol," Pental said. Kit could feel the power in his words. He was trying to use compulsion on the man who'd sired him. "Surrender, and I'll let this one live. I'll let her have a chance at a normal life."

Faol's body quaked. His fingers extended into impossibly long claws. His mouth became filled with rows of razor-sharp, needle-like teeth. Great hooked horns grew from his head, curling around until they were level with his jaw. "You would dare to use the gift I bestowed upon you? You dare to use it on me? I am evil incarnate. I carry the demons of Helja. I am legion. I am Gorgaraeth, the destroyer. I will set this world ablaze and I will feast on the remains of the slain. Kill the girl. She is nothing but a plaything, a pretty bobble to keep around for my amusement."

Hope's eyes widened. She glanced at Aurora for a moment, then at Kit. Pental's face twisted into a sneer before she spun around to face him. Before he could react, she slammed her fist into his chest, knocking him back several feet. The vampire lunged forward, intent on ending the woman's life, but she was too quick. She clutched his wrist, spun herself to be behind the man, and wrenched his arm up his back. When his shoulder finally dislocated, she kicked him just above the knee, shattering his leg. She brought her fist down on his skull, knocking the mangled vampire to the ground, unconscious.

In the mayhem, Kit seized the moment and threw her war hammer at Faol. The weapon hit him flush in the chest, exploding in a burst of brilliant white light. Expecting everyone to be blinded in the next moment, she darted forward, ready to engage the vampire king before he recovered.

The next thirty seconds were complete bedlam. Breayn, Ryn, and Danny dashed to secure Breayn's mother. Aurora leapt for Annabella, followed closely by Runt and Coldforge. Lin and Ormand went to help Kit against Faol.

"Kill Faol," Indie said to Lump. "Try not to burn Kit."

A screech from above drew Indie's and Lump's attention. Ulip, Yuka, and the other drakes were being engaged by an extremely large white dragon. Indie stole a glance at Kit in combat with Faol and shook his head. "We need to keep the dragon off them," he said. "If it lands, it will kill us all."

Lump kicked off, and with a few wingbeats he was gaining altitude at a tremendous rate. Indie was staying close behind.

⁓⁓⁓◈⁓⁓⁓

"*She is Siku,*" Lump said. The dragon-dog's words echoed inside Indie's head. It made his brain hurt. He'd felt nothing like it before. He tried, ineffectually, to cover his ears with his hands. "*Sorry, I spoke too loudly. The dragon is Siku. She is Fury's mate and our friend. She is warning Ulip that Ouroboros is coming.*" There was a pause in the words. "*Siku is hurt. Ouroboros has blinded her. Fury is dead.*"

Indie's heart skipped a beat. Ouroboros killed Fury? Why would he do such a thing?

"*Sorry, he's not dead. Fury is fighting Ouroboros. The black dragon was hurting Siku, and he attacked him. He helped Siku escape, and the dragon lord said he'd kill him for his interference. I can't make out everything she's saying. Siku is speaking too fast for me to get all the words. They are atop Mount Toka. We should help Fury. Maybe we can defeat Ouroboros if we fight together.*"

Indie reacted without forethought. He beat his leathery golden wings and made for the top of Mount Toka. Lump flew under him.

"*Get on my back, I'm much faster than you are.*" Indie lowered himself until he could drop the last few feet onto the dragon's back. He latched onto the enormous horns that protruded from Runt's neck.

"*Go! I'm ready.*"

It took no time at all for the duo to fly to Toka, and it wasn't difficult to find the pair of dragons. They were standing nose to nose, circling one another, sizing each other up. Whatever it was, Fury looked like he was in trouble. The sky dragon was big, almost as big as Siku. But the black dragon, Ouroboros, was monstrous. He was easily twice the blue dragon's weight. Indie didn't understand why he wasn't attacking. Why was he prolonging the battle?

"Look," Lump said. *"The black dragon has already struck a blow. Fury's side is bleeding badly. It may be fatal."*

Indie's thoughts jumped to Kit and her healing powers. His heart raced. He'd left Kit to fight the vampire king. Why was he here helping a dragon lord when he should be fighting by his love's side?

Ouroboros lashed out, catching Fury's neck in his jaws. The blue dragon cried out as the much larger black tossed him against a cliff face. Fury tried to fly, to put some distance between himself and Ouroboros, but he couldn't get away fast enough. The black dragon was on him again, sinking his teeth into the joint where the wing met the dragon's body. Again, Fury cried out in pain.

Lump beat his wings, turning himself into a golden missile. With every beat, his speed increased. Indie's eyes were watering up as the wind buffeted against his face. Neither Fury nor Ouroboros knew they were coming. They'd get one chance at this. If they failed, it likely meant death for the both of them. Indie had an idea. It was a stupidly dangerous idea, but it was the only one he had.

"When we're close, hit him with as much fire as you can. Shape your attack into as large a fireball as possible."

"If I make it tight, it will be hotter."

"It doesn't need to be hot. It needs to be big. I don't want Ouroboros to see us. I don't want him to know I'm here."

Lump took a deep breath, fueling the fire in his chest. Despite being covered in his dragon scales, Indie could feel the intense heat. It was becoming unbearably hot. His idea was becoming less and less plausible by the second.

"When I say now, I want you to break away. You need to steer clear of the black dragon. Do you understand?" Indie was pleading with Lump to obey him. His idea was dangerous, and he didn't want the pup to lose his life over it.

"If I steer clear, I can't help you fight."

"Tell me you'll do it." There was no response. They were drawing dangerously close to the fighting dragons. *"Lump, tell me you will."*

"Okay." A rolling ball of flame came out with the word. The wolfdog's annoyance with the request to break away fueled the inferno building in his chest. All Indie could see was an enormous rolling ball of golden flames. He drew his Bifrost sword.

"I love you, Kit. Lump, now! Break away."

Indie leapt from the dragon's back. He launched himself to where the black dragon had been just before Lump unleashed his fire attack. In a moment, he'd be entering the firestorm. He could only hope his scales would protect him long enough to sink his blade into the dragon's skull. He could only hope his weapon would be long enough to penetrate his brain.

With his sword raised above his head, ready for a double handed strike, the fire cleared. The black dragon's gaping, tooth-filled maw was there, and he was about to drop directly into it.

Titan's snowballs.

Indie's gold leathery wings snapped out, slowing his descent enough that he could fly wide of the dragon's mouth. He had lost most of his forward momentum. He doubted he would have the strength to drive the blade into his skull without it. The black dragon's eye suddenly dilated.

I surprised him.

The wide-eyed response to his arrival gave Indie an alternative. He shaped his wings to bring himself dangerously close to Ouroboros' mouth, but it was the only way he'd be able to bring his blade to bear. He careened off the dragon's snout, rolled across his thick, incredibly smooth inky black scales until he was next to the big green eye. The eye that still seemed to be surprised. With both his hands wrapped around the blade's handle, he thrust it into the dragon, instantly blinding him.

Ouroboros bellowed out in agony. He spewed tremendous torrents of flame everywhere, desperate to incinerate whoever would dare to attack him. He would obliterate the one responsible for marring his otherwise perfect form.

The heat from the flames was unbearable, and he was blowing them away from Indie. Ouroboros hadn't seen him drop directly in front of himself, landing between his scaly front legs that were the size of... Indie had no idea what they were the size of. Outside of the Temple, he'd seen nothing this big in his life.

"Leave," Fury bellowed at him. "Save yourself." The blue dragon leapt onto Ouroboros' neck, sinking his teeth deep into the flesh beneath his nearly impenetrable hide. Again, the black dragon screeched out. The two dragons threatened to drop onto Indie and crush him under their gargantuan weight. He darted between the black dragon's legs and launched himself skyward. Lump, who was supposed to have left, flew underneath him, ready to accept his rider once again.

Indie pulled his wings to his body and dropped to Lump's back. The gold dragon immediately pumped his wings. Indie stole a look over his shoulder to see a flaming ball closing on them.

"Drop. Drop now!"

Lump didn't ask questions. He dipped his tail and dove, keeping his body close to the mountain's ice-covered surface. The fiery ball of instant death flew harmlessly overhead. With his wings fully extended, Lump glided along, barely skimming the snow that covered the treeless mountaintop.

Again, Indie looked over his shoulder. The black dragon was careening down the side of the mountain. An avalanche was forming beneath him as his hulking mass stumbled down the sheer cliff's face. Ouroboros' pitch-black wings sprung from his back, practically blocking out the sun.

"Lump," he screamed out. *"Fly, Lump, Fly. As fast as your wings will carry you."*

CHAPTER FIFTY-TWO

DARKNESS FALLS

Kit cursed under her breath. She wished Lin had not joined in to fight Faol. Even though she was equipped with a blessed bow, and even though she could fly, she was no match for the vampire king and his demon-god shade. Bloody Helja. Even Kit was no match for him, but she was desperate. The man had to be stopped, and this was the best chance they had.

Faol swiped at Kit's face. She dodged at the last moment, barely avoiding the attack. She needed to stop worrying about Lin and concentrate on the enemy standing in front of her. An arrow whizzed past her ear and sank into Faol's shoulder. It didn't even seem to hurt. Outside of the annoyed look on his face when he snapped the shaft off in his hand, he appeared unharmed. A second arrow whizzed past, and the vampire lord simply avoided it.

Kit swung her battle hammer, hoping the distraction provided by the arrows would be enough for her to land a blow. The mithril head struck with a satisfying thud against Faol's ribs. From within the burst of light that followed, the man screamed. It was more likely from rage than from pain, but Kit didn't care. She'd scored a strike. She quickly followed it up with her angelic song, hoping it might provide an additional effect. The man's hand launched out, snagging Kit by the throat. His grip was unbelievably strong. He effortlessly hoisted the little priest into the air.

Ormand appeared behind Faol. He wrapped his right arm around the man's throat, locking it tightly beneath his chin. He used his left arm to push Faol's head forward, applying even more pressure. The technique was referred to as a blood-choke. It was one of the many hand-to-hand techniques that Sister Gale had taught in her combat classes. The attack forced Faol to release his grip on Kit. She dropped hard to the ground, struggling to catch her breath.

From her prone position, Kit watched in horror as a black shadow emerged from Faol. It gave a ghastly laugh as it pulled itself from the vampire king's body. With its long, spindly hands, it took Ormand by the face and forced itself into his mouth. It was shoulder-deep when a golden arrow passed through its insubstantial form. The shade shuddered momentarily before continuing to force itself upon its would-be host. Another arrow flashed through it, and another. When the fourth arrow struck it, the shade exploded into a puff of ash. Kit stole a look, finding Feigh sitting astride a great white-winged stallion. Lin was sitting behind him. Her blessed bow had been replaced with one of the Wood Nymph's magical bows.

Ormand released his grip on Faol and stumbled backwards. The demon shade's assault on him had left him disoriented. The vampire king spun around, ready to rip him to shreds, but Ormand dissolved into a dust cloud and blew away. Gorgaraeth's shade screamed out in frustration. The voice may have come from Faol, but it sounded just like the demon-god she'd fought in Cormorant. Kit wondered how many demons Faol carried within his body. He had declared himself *legion*. Surely, he didn't hold a thousand such creatures.

⚬⚬⚬◇⚬⚬⚬

Aurora leapt back, using her wings to help speed her escape. Annabella lunged forward, thrusting her pair of three-pronged daggers at the celestial's face. The angel swept her sword in front of herself, trying to parry the weapons away.

Coldforge snatched at the woman's waist while Runt blocked her from moving any closer to Aurora. The dire wolf tried using his frost-breath on her, but he could not hit her with it. Annabella was incredibly fast. She was practically disregarding the wolf and the dwarf who were harrying her. She seemed utterly focused on ending Aurora's life.

Annabella swiped at Runt with one of her strange daggers. The tip of the center tine clipped his ear, but the wolf used the opportunity to bite at the woman's wrist, catching it in his powerful jaws. He closed his mouth tightly, eliciting an unearthly scream from the woman. She brought her second dagger to bare, sinking it deep into Runt's shoulder. The wolf shuddered, but he refused to release his grip.

For a moment in time, Annabella was tethered to the wolf. With steadfast determination, Runt held her wrist. He was twisting his body, trying to force the woman to the ground. Coldforge, with surprising quickness, seized the moment and slammed his stone fist into the side of the woman's head. Her legs buckled and Runt successfully brought her to the ground.

With their opponent down and out, Aurora leapt forward with her blade, ready to end the life of Faol's daughter. Her sword was mid-arc when an unseen force slammed into the angel, sending her sprawling. The pair tumbled for a moment, with Aurora ending up on her back. Hope was sitting on her chest, holding down her sister's arms with her knees. In a blind rage, she brought her fists down, repeatedly striking the angel in the face. Hope's hands were barely more than a blur as she rained down devastating blows. Spots were dancing in front of Aurora's eyes. She would lose consciousness any moment.

"I forgive you," Aurora said, just as a fist smashed into her temple and the spots gave way to complete blackness.

⬥

"Mother," Breayn screamed. The red-haired doppelgänger flashed a smile as her child raced towards her. The woman held her arms out wide, welcoming the girl she had given birth to. Breayn's arms were extended, ready to embrace the woman she had been desperately searching for.

"Beware." The soul of Breayn's mother cried out in her mind. *"That is my body, but she is not me."*

Breayn was deaf to the words, blinded by the sight of the woman who'd raised her. The Berrat woman slammed into her mother, the pair falling to the ground in a tight embrace. Pain blossomed in Breayn's shoulder. It was a searing, tearing ache. Her brain told her she must have landed awkwardly. The pain was getting worse. She pulled herself away from her mother to get a look. The woman's face was blood-soaked. Had she injured her mother, as well, when they'd fallen? Breayn's mother's mouth opened wide, exposing a set of terrible fangs.

"That fiend has turned me into a vampire." Breayn's mother's voice was filled with outrage as it echoed in her mind. *"Kill me. Don't let my body live on as this abomination."*

"No," Breayn screeched out at the vampire she was clutching onto. "I won't kill you. I need you."

Ryn grasped Breayn by the back of her armor and yanked her away. Danny threw himself between mother and daughter to create some space between them. As soon as his cousin was clear, the phoenix burst into flames. Breayn and her mother both screamed out, one in pain and the other in horror.

"Don't kill her," Breayn cried out, her arms flailing wildly against her mate's grasp. "Danny, for the love of Gaia, don't kill her."

"She's gone," Ryn said, clutching the desperate woman, preventing her from throwing herself at the phoenix. "She's gone."

Danny was about to incinerate the woman when a black shadow passed out of her. He held back his flames for a moment. The woman continued to writhe beneath him. A second shade emerged, and a third. The body of Breayn's mother stilled and her eyes went vacant.

Ryn released Breayn and waved his arms at the shade that was floating towards them. Breayn pushed Ryn aside and screamed at the shadow, drawing it towards her. Danny pushed away from the husk of a woman he was on, instantly transforming into the phoenix. The three shades closed in on Ryn and Breayn. The phoenix called out, unleashing its song. The high-pitched cry stunned the shades long enough for Danny to launch himself at them. The phoenix lurched forward, igniting the shades one by one as the firebird flew through them. Their demonic forms became unstable and a moment later, they turned insubstantial and blew away with the wind, nothing more than piles of burned ash.

Breayn, seeing her mother laying motionless on the ground, sprung forward, wrapped her arms around the woman, and wailed inconsolably.

<div style="text-align:center">~~~◈~~~</div>

"Lump," Indie yelled, forgetting he could communicate with the dragon in his head. "We need to split up. I'll distract him and you get away."

"Don't get off my back," the gold dragon said. *"I think I can outmaneuver him. I think I'm faster than he is. Even now, the distance between us is increasing."*

Indie looked back. Lump was right, they were slowly pulling away.

"Stay low," Lump called out. They were approaching a large copse of trees and the gold dragon appeared intent on flying into them. Indie grasped Lump's horned back tighter as the pair crashed between the trunks of the huge Berrathian pines. The long needle-covered branches threatened to sweep Indie off his mount's back, but he held on just the same.

"What if Ouroboros sets the forest on fire?"

Hardly a dozen seconds had passed when the forest erupted in flames all around them. Had he just given the black dragon a way to flush them out? Had he just betrayed Lump's location with a thought?

Lump didn't respond. He continued to flap his wings as he sped between the trees. The gold dragon flew so low his feet touched the ground. He used his legs to help avoid the massive trunks. Indie swayed heavily to the right when Lump deked hard to his left. The dragon pushed off a flaming tree to make the turn as sharp as possible. The crafty wolfdog was using the fire for cover. As hot as the blaze was, it was not enough to cause either of them any harm.

The sound of the black dragon crashing through the burning forest told Indie that he hadn't seen the duo make the turn. He wanted to tell Lump to circle around so they'd be at the dragon's back, but he didn't want to speak for fear of Ouroboros hearing his thoughts. Lump continued on his path for several more seconds before he launched himself skyward and out of the forest fire.

Thick black smoke filled the air as the green-needled trees continued to burn. The air was acrid, making breathing difficult. Indie suppressed a cough, fearing the black dragon might somehow hear it. Lump banked hard to the left, circling around until he was behind their rampaging opponent.

The gold dragon flew close to the top of the trees, staying within their flames. The air here was insanely hot, but the feel of the fire in Indie's lungs was almost pleasant. His scales were absorbing the heat. The feeling was exhilarating. Beneath the duo, the black dragon continued to speed forward, leaving a path of destruction in his wake. The ribbon of dead, burning trees made him desperately easy to follow. Lump was now only a few dozen feet above him, maintaining the black dragon's speed. Indie drew his sword and patted Lump's neck. Their exchange was wordless, but they both knew what was going to happen next.

With a soundless cry, Indie leapt from Lump's back. He raised his Bifrost sword over his head, ready to drop the point down in a devastating, two-handed strike. The thrill of the hunt surged through the young man's body, filling his muscles with adrenaline, fueling his desire to end this confrontation here and now.

The gold dragon-man landed at the base of Ouroboros' skull as he brought his blade-tip down with every ounce of strength he had. This would be the moment he would slay the most feared dragon in all of Orth. This would be the moment his value would be known to all. He would finally be worthy of Kit.

The Bifrost blade slid easily through the dragon's scales, but it was too short to have any significant effect. The dragon lord's skull was simply too thick for the weapon to penetrate his brain. Ouroboros roared, releasing a torrent of white-hot flames. Indie yanked his blade free and kicked off, using the heat of the raging inferno to help propel himself away from the great dragon. Lump somehow put himself under the young man and whisked him away to relative safety.

A great black shadow emerged from the burning forest. It turned towards them and blew out another stream of flame in their direction. From above, the body of Fury fell upon the dragon lord. The pair smashed against the mountainside, disappearing beneath the smoke and flames.

⌒⌒⌒⌒◇⌒⌒⌒⌒

Kit's heart was thrumming in her ears. She had seen Aurora fall to the vicious beating her aunt was giving her mother. She desperately wanted to come to her aid, but she had her own battle to fight, and it wasn't going well for her. The billowing black smoke pouring off the side of Mount Toka distracted her for a moment. She hadn't seen the hand that had reached out and grasped her throat. She wasn't prepared for the strength behind it. Her back exploded in pain as she was slammed to the ground.

Faol rammed his knee into Kit's chest as he continued to press down on her throat, preventing her from taking a breath. A golden arrow flew past the man's face, narrowly missing him. He chortled as he continued to squeeze the life out of Kit. She wanted to scream out, to release her angelic song, but it was impossible.

The daemon in Kit burst forth, transforming the girl into a human torch. The smell of the vampire king's searing flesh filled her nostrils. Acidic ash filled her mouth. The man was burning up, but he refused to release his grip. Kit's black claws dug into the vampire's wrist. Her white skin, covered with black runes, seemed to glow, basking, as her flames caressed her body. Despite what had to have been excruciating pain, the vampire lord continued his deep, obscene laughter.

Kit clasped her hands together, raised them over her head, and brought them down onto Faol's wrist. The grip on her throat lessened enough for the girl to draw a shallow breath. She quickly pulled her hands up and slammed them down yet again. She sucked in another breath and repeated her attack. She didn't stop until she heard bones shatter.

Faol howled as he pulled his hand back. He brought his other hand down, smashing Kit in the face. The impact stunned the little angel. Suddenly, there were three vampires hovering over her.

Where did the other vampires come from?

In perfect unison, the vampires pulled back their fists and brought them down square onto her face. Just before hitting her, the three fists merged into a single pale-skinned set of knuckles. Kit's vision failed her. Everything went dark. She slashed out with her clawed hands, but they found nothing. She swiped out again, hoping to slash the man before he brought his fist down on her a third time. Again, her efforts were wasted. She held her breath, expecting another strike, but none came.

⤛⟩⟨⤜

Indie watched with morbid fascination as the two dragons tumbled down the mountainside. He allowed himself a few moments to take in the view of the battle that raged on the ground below. The armies were so tightly entwined that it was unclear who was winning. His gaze moved south to where Kit was, but she was too far away to tell what was happening.

"Can you see Kit and the others?" Indie strained to get a look, but he couldn't make anything out.

"We need to go," Lump said. There was fear in his voice. Even while battling Ouroboros, Indie sensed no anxiety from the pup. In this moment, the gold dragon wasn't just scared. He was terrified. Indie's stomach knotted up. He shouldn't have left to help Fury. He should have stayed with Kit. He was not worthy of her love.

"Go!" Indie hunkered low on Lump's back, trying to keep himself as close as possible. He could feel the panic rising in the dragon-dog as his wings continued to beat frantically, propelling them towards their friends. Their speed increased as they descended. Indie had to shield his eyes to prevent them from watering up as the wind whipped over his face. The scene came into view, everything snapping into crystal clear clarity.

They were still five or six hundred paces away. They would not arrive in time to save Kit.

CHAPTER FIFTY-THREE

FAMILY HAS MANY SHAPES

The phoenix threw himself at Faol. It was the only way he was going to stop the vampire king from eviscerating the unconscious body of Kit. Unlike other victims who had fallen to the phoenix's flaming feathers, Faol's body was impenetrable. Danny slammed into him. It felt like he had run into a stone wall. The phoenix's flames dissipated, returning the Berrat to his natural form. His ineffectual attack had bought Kit a few precious seconds, but now his own life was in mortal peril.

Golden arrows thumped into Faol's chest, one after another after another. He bellowed out, enraged by the audacity of someone, thinking they could fell the lord with mere weapons. With a swipe of his clawed hand, he snapped the shafts off himself, only to have them replaced by three more arrows.

Feigh and Lin were hovering some twenty feet above the vampire on the back of the pegasus. Faol's eyes burned with hatred. A hatred he planned on satisfying when he fed upon the insolent beings who would dare try to hurt him. His loathing showed on his face. His disgust was apparent in his snarl. The vampire crouched slightly before pushing himself into the air. His convulsing clawed hands stretched out before him, intent on ripping the pair from the back of the flying horse.

The pegasus shimmered and disappeared, along with his riders. The vampire clutched at the air, his claws raking wildly. He was committed to ripping open the insignificant beings who had dared to attack him. In rapid succession, dark shades poured out of his body. Several lasted only moments before they turned to ash and blew away. Others dipped and dived, perhaps searching for the pegasus who had been present barely a moment ago.

A deafening roar filled the air, followed by a cry of agony. The high-pitched voice drew the vampire lord's attention. His precious daughter was trying to fight off the relentless attack of a great brown bear. The animal pressed forward, using his weight to his advantage. While his thick coat absorbed Hope's attacks, he shredded her pale white skin with his devastating claws.

Ryn's intervention bought Aurora enough time to recover from her sister's vicious assault on her. The blonde woman clambered to her feet, unable to effectively maintain her balance. In a stupor, she watched the bear attacking her sister. Aurora's eyes were opened, but they were unfocused.

The angel's face suddenly changed. The dimness that had filled her eyes was gone. Her eyes flashed golden as she threw herself at the great bear. She clutched onto his thick fur, desperately hoping to hurt it enough that it would break off its attack. When she decided there was no way she could outmatch its strength, she drew a dagger from her hip and buried it up to the hilt into the animal's back. Ryn roared out in anger and pain. There was no way he could see his attacker. He threw himself onto his back, hoping to crush whoever it was beneath his tremendous bulk.

Aurora jumped clear of the falling bear and sped over to her sister. A golden aura burst out from the angel, enveloping Hope. Aurora screamed in pain as she accepted the girl's wounds as her own. Despite her sister trying to help her, Hope lashed out, punching Aurora repeatedly with hammer-fists. The angel clasped her arms around her sister, clutching her to her chest. A moment later, Aurora dropped to the ground, leaving Hope breathless and confused. Her bear attacker lay motionless on the blood-soaked soil. Only his rapidly rising and falling chest gave any sign he was still alive.

⸎

Kit blinked the world back into focus, somewhat. Her head was pounding. Every inch of her body hurt. With a groan, she rolled over onto her belly and raised her head. Aurora was engaged in combat with Faol, while Hope watched like a spectator. Danny lay on the ground, unmoving. Breayn was hovering over the body of Ryn while her mother stood like a statue a few feet from the mated couple.

Runt and Coldforge were standing over the lifeless body of Annabella, fighting off a pair of shades. Coldforge's attacks appeared to be having little effect, as were Runt's teeth. The shades whirled about, trying to gain advantage over the dwarf and the wolf. The pegasus appeared out of thin air a dozen paces away. Lin and Feigh were both wielding bows, shooting arrows through the shades' insubstantial bodies. After many successful strikes, the demon spirits turned to dust and blew away.

From above, Lump and Indie were flying towards Kit. The gold dragon, with his gold rider, was coming in much too fast. They were going to crash. Her body tensed, fearing the pair would hit the ground with a life-ending thud. Lump's wings suddenly sprung outward, and their forward momentum came to an immediate halt. They landed feather-soft upon the ground. In a moment, Indie was off Lump's back and by Kit's side.

"Help Aurora," Kit said, directing the pair to where her mother was engaged with Faol. The vampire king was in a full rage. He was screaming at Aurora. The only word that was discernible was *Annabella*. Had her mother killed her?

Shades poured out of Faol. As they left his body, they took corporeal form and fell upon Kit's mother. Her sword cut through them like a scythe through winter wheat. Kit didn't fully understand what was happening until a shade with curled horns emerged from the vampire king. Gorgaraeth himself had left his host. His spirit did not become substantial. It stayed in its ethereal form. It flew at the angel and grappled with her. Aurora's attacks did nothing. They passed harmlessly through the disembodied spirit while it gripped at the back of her head. The shade was trying to enter the woman's body through her mouth.

Arrow after arrow passed through the shade. None of them appeared to have any effect.

Kit and Indie leapt for Faol. They grabbed his arms, trying to overpower him with sheer strength. Lump joined into the fray. He pressed an enormous, clawed foot against the king's chest and pushed him to the ground. The spirit of Gorgaraeth broke away from its quarry and returned to the vampire king. Faol's body swelled with energy as the demon-god's life force took hold of its host. With a mighty scream, he forced his attackers off him, sending them tumbling backwards.

Faol ignored Kit and lunged for Aurora. He grabbed the woman and threw her to the ground. His attempt to separate the angel's head from her body was halted by a hand that clasped onto his wrist.

"You'll not harm my sister," Hope called out. "Your reign of terror ends now."

The vampire king slashed out at the woman he had once called daughter. His claw ripped through the woman's chest, her lifeblood gushing out of her. Aurora threw herself at Faol. She wrapped her arms around him, binding him with every ounce of strength she had. With a few flaps of her wings, she carried the man into the air. Higher and higher they rose.

Kit flew to her aunt's aid, immediately reaching out with her healing aura. It took all her concentration to maintain control. Hope was trying to push her aside, her eyes filled with terror as they searched the skies above.

"Aurora, no!" The words came out of the woman in a choked whisper. Kit had turned in time to see her mother and the vampire king locked in a deadly embrace while Aurora plummeted headfirst towards the ground below. Kit barely gasped before the pair slammed to the ground. A blinding flash of gold burst outwards. When the light subsided, all that remained was a small cloud of dust where the pair had fallen.

From out of the cloud, Gorgaraeth's shade floated out. Red eyes flashed just as the entity became substantial. Its head swiveled about, perhaps seeking another host. It caught sight of Hope. A large tooth-filled gash appeared on the demon-shade's face. His jaws stretched open in a grotesque display. The burning magma that filled its mouth made it look to be a gateway straight to Helja. A horrific sound poured out. It took several menacing steps forward before breaking into a run. Kit was about to intercept when a flaming bird tore through the rampaging fiend. The gaping hole in the demon's chest sizzled and burned.

Gorgaraeth wailed and took a wild swing at the phoenix. A series of golden arrows slammed into the demon's chest, its semi-corporeal body offering enough resistance that they didn't pass cleanly through. Runt leapt forward, a blast of frost pouring from his mouth as the dire wolf crashed into the shade. Parts of Gorgaraeth's body exploded into tiny shards.

Kit's body failed her. She wanted to step forward, to finish Gorgaraeth off, but the sight of her mother's mangled body stole her breath. Faol's remains were twisted in with hers in a bizarre embrace. The sound of Hope's screams drew her attention back to the battle. Her aunt's eyes blazed as she ran at the badly injured body of the demon-god. She leapt through the air; her fist drawn back and ready to strike. The woman threw herself at Gorgaraeth, smashing her fist against his face in a devastating blow. A golden flash burst outward.

When Kit's vision cleared, the demon-god was gone. Her aunt was on her hands and knees, her chest heaving uncontrollably. Kit raced to her side, her healing aura once again pouring out of her.

"Get away from me," Hope screamed out. "I can't look at you. I..." The woman's grief at the death of her sister overwhelmed her. She craned her neck up at the sky and wailed. Kit wrapped her arms around her, pouring every ounce of herself into the hug. In part, she was trying to console the woman, but perhaps more so, she was sharing in her grief. The little priest's heart was shattered. Her aunt was the only piece of her mother that she had left. No matter what the woman said, she would not let her go. She would not get away from her. She was going to hold on to her for eternity if she had to.

"Kit," Indie said, his voice urgent. The little priest could hear his words, but she didn't care. Nothing was more important than this moment. She was going to share her grief with her aunt, and nothing else mattered.

"Kit!" Indie screamed. He wrapped his arms around both women, beating his dragon wings with all his might.

"What are you doing?" Kit screamed at him, trying to push the man away. Her rage quickly subsided at the sight of two dragons, locked in their own deadly embrace, plummeting to the very ground they had just been standing on.

There were cries of terror as everyone tried to clear the area.

The ground shook from the impact, sending a shock wave across the land. The earth rolled like ripples on a pond. A thick wave of dust and debris exploded outwards.

Ouroboros lifted his great black head and roared out a challenge, daring anyone to defy him. He placed his enormous, scaled foot onto the head of Fury and ground it into the earth. He roared again and blew out a towering blast of dragon-fire into the sky above.

"We need to help him," Indie said. Kit understood. She could feel the hurt in him, the worry that Fury was dead. She knew what hurt was like. The first time she'd ever truly experienced it was with the death of Sister Miyuki. Today, the feeling was magnified. The death of her mother drove the feeling even deeper. Kit didn't know if she would ever recover from it. If she could save Indie from that pain, she would. If not, she would at least try.

"Go," Kit said, "I'll carry Hope to safety, and I'll come."

Kit wrapped her arms around her aunt and nodded to Indie. He gave her a quick kiss on the top of her head and released his grip on the two women. The pair plummeted for several seconds before Kit's silky white wings extended outward. She took Hope a safe distance away from the dragons and dropped her off. Not wasting a moment longer, the angel leapt into the air and sped back to Indie. Up ahead, Lump was speeding to Fury's aid, with Indie straddling his back.

The horror of Kit's mother's death was sinking in. That loss gripped her, paralyzed her. It shredded her resolve. Fear seized her as she watched Indie and Lump flying towards certain death. What hope could they have against such a creature as Ouroboros? Her angelic self transformed into her daemonic persona. She looked down at her rune-covered body as her flames licked over her skin. The warmth of her fires burned away the worry, replacing it with the desire to destroy.

From high above, the familiar screech of drakes cut through the sky. Were they coming to the black dragon's aid? It would be bad enough to face the monstrous creature on his own, but if the dragon lord had assistance, there could be zero chance of victory.

"The drakes are not attacking. They are surrounding Siku, screeching out their location to her. Ouroboros has blinded the great white dragon. The drakes are leading her to the black dragon and to her fallen love."

Even though she wasn't riding him, Lump could still communicate with Kit. Tears stung her eyes. The heat of her flames instantly turned them into mist. Her daemon wings surged, speeding the girl forward. In moments, she had caught up to Indie and Lump.

"Don't get in Siku's way," she said to the duo. *"She won't know we're there."*

"Yes, she does," Lump responded. *"I just told her."*

⚜

Indie's heart raced as Kit flew past him and Lump. She was taking a direct path to Ouroboros. He remembered the daemon and the heartless attack it had made on him. He could not reason with it. It was pure wrath, vengeance personified. The little daemon was flying headlong to her doom.

"She'll be okay," Lump said. *"She is no longer that person. Her powers no longer control her. She is the master of them. She will wield them like she does her war hammer, with deadly effect."*

Indie breathed easier after hearing the dragon-dog's words. He really was a smart puppy.

Kit's body became totally ensconced in flame. In this form, she looked too much like the phoenix. Not so very long ago, that similarity would have bothered Indie deeply. At this moment, he was okay with it. The phoenix was powerful, perhaps even more than Kit's daemon. The dragon-man groaned. Another flaming missile was flying towards Ouroboros. Had he somehow summoned the phoenix just by thinking about him? Indie nodded and patted Lump's neck.

"We're going to need him," Indie said. *"It pains me to say it, but I'm glad he's here."*

"It does my heart good to hear you say that," Lump said. *"He is an important person in Kit's life, and in my life, as well. We are... family."* Indie smiled.

"Come on then, Lump. Our family needs us."

Dragon and rider sped forward, flying directly into the jaws of certain death. Ouroboros caught sight of the incoming streaks of flame and blew out his own firestorm to greet them. Kit and Danny didn't slow down. They both flew directly into the blazing inferno.

"Please, Titan, let them survive." Indie rarely prayed, but it seemed like a good time to ask for a favor of the god whom Kit had devoted her life to. The man's heart sank when the black dragon's flames subsided and neither the daemon nor the phoenix were within sight.

Indie set his jaw and tightened his grip on Lump's horn-covered neck. *"Into Helja we fly, my friend. If we don't make it through the day, I'll meet you in the Beyond."*

"Our day is far from over. Our family still lives. Kit and Danny both live."

The pair had flown past the great dragon and were flying next to Siku. The drakes started their descent, their cries continuing to fill the late afternoon air.

"Traitors!"

The voice of Ouroboros boomed in Indie's head. Lump's wings failed him for a moment, and he lost some altitude. The black dragon's voice must have echoed in the mind of every dragon on Orth.

The dragon lord reared up from the ground and unfurled his wings, casting dark shadows across the land. He belched out a series of fireballs directed at the drakes escorting Siku. All but one avoided the attack. The frost drake that had failed to evade the fireballs became charred. Her bright white scales turned a dull gray, and it plummeted from the sky. Ulip and Yuka maintained their position, but the other drakes scattered. A moment later, Kit flew over the great white dragon and dropped onto her back.

"Kit will be her eyes," Lump said. *"She will guide her in. Yuka will be her vanguard. Ulip will be her herald, announcing Siku, the Dragon Queen."*

Ouroboros unleashed another firestorm at the approaching queen and her herald. Siku responded in kind with her frost breath weapon. The meeting of fire and ice exploded into billowing clouds of steam. Vision would be impossible within the mist.

The steam cloud suddenly swirled away. Ouroboros beat his wings, clearing the mist with but a few beats. He continued to hold them outspread, almost inviting Siku to come into their embrace.

Lump surged forward. The black dragon was too busy watching what was in front of him to see the speeding gold dragon and rider coming from his rear. Indie kept his mind clear, fearful that he may somehow announce their arrival to the dragon lord.

Lump blew out a narrow stream of his golden fire. It struck the black dragon's wing, just below the knuckles, where the bones all merge at the wing's apex. The pair flew through the expanding hole in the membrane.

Ouroboros screeched out, flaming wildly at the gold dragon. With a deft turn, Lump avoided the fires before heading skyward.

Danny must have seen what Lump had done. Indie watched as the phoenix mimicked their maneuver, blasting his way through the dragon's other wing. Again, Ouroboros cried out and tried to flame his attacker. The black dragon's preoccupation with the smaller assailants blinded him to Siku's approach. She slammed into him, gripping onto his back with four clawed feet. She beat her wings, raising enormous clouds of dust as she climbed, carrying the great black dragon with her.

The phoenix circled around, ripping through the dragon lord's wings again and again.

Indie's heart was beating out of control. Kit was no longer on Siku's back and Yuka was nowhere in sight. Ulip was seated on the great white dragon's neck. He must have replaced Kit as the dragon's eyes. Where was Kit? Where was Indie's little angel?

CHAPTER FIFTY-FOUR

A DRAGON'S BLACK HEART

Kit had dropped from Siku, landing between the two rows of pointy ridges that ran the length of Ouroboros' back. The black dragon was struggling to break free of the white dragon's grip on him, but she would not give up easily. With all the thrashing, it was difficult for the little daemon to clamber her way up the dragon's back to his head. She had tried to use her claws to dig into his scales, but they were impossibly tough.

The two rows of ridges gave way to a single line of horns at the dragon's neck. The closer to his head they were, the larger they became. The ones near the base of his skull were several times taller than Kit.

Doubt crept into her mind. What chance did she have to harm this massive creature? His armor plating was likely a foot thick, if not more.

"His eyes," Siku's voice whispered in Kit's mind. *"They are his weakness. One eye has already been blinded."*

She could attack his one remaining eye and blind him the way he had blinded Siku. The poetic justice of this thought made the daemon in her chortle. Getting there would be the problem. The dragon's scales were tough and slick. Once she got up to his head, she would have nothing to hold on to. How would she lower herself into a position where she could strike his eye?

You can fly.

Kit blushed. She really was just a blunt instrument. The chortled died away with her embarrassment. Resolute in her plan, Kit pulled out her battle hammer and spun it in her hand.

It's too bad Fury isn't here for this. He'd have enjoyed destroying this vile creature's remaining eye.

Her daemon wings unfurled, and Kit lifted off Ouroboros' body. She had no difficulty keeping up with Siku's speed. With the burden of the black dragon, the great white dragon was barely maintaining altitude, let alone forward momentum.

Kit pulled her arm back, ready to bring her hammer down. She flew up along the right side of Ouroboros. The daemon was nearly in position when the black dragon's head thrashed, slamming into her, knocking Kit out of the air. She tumbled and fell, hurtling towards the ground below. The daemon regained control of her body, thrust out her wings, and halted her descent. She stared back up at the two dragons and beat her wings. She quickly gained altitude, doing her best to avoid getting rammed a second time. The black dragon's thrashing motions were becoming somewhat rhythmic. If he would only maintain the pattern, she could time her arrival and take her swing.

Not yet. Not yet. Not yet... Now!

Her daemon flames exploded and in moments, Kit was at the dragon's head. She pulled back her hammer to strike. Her stomach twisted. She was attacking the already blinded eye. She needed to strike from the other side. The moment of inaction cost her as the dragon thrashed. Making solid contact, he sent her toppling through the air once again.

"Stand down, Kitten." The voice of Fury grated in her head. The sky dragon was flying her way. He was struggling to stay true. His body kept listing to the side. *"I will finish this."*

Kit shook her head. She would not let him do this; not on his own, at any rate. *"You're in no condition to fight. Let me help you. Let us help you."* Fury was silent. She took it as his approval. With hammer in hand, Kit flew up to Ouroboros' head. Blinding him was still a good plan. The trouble was, in order to use her hammer effectively, she needed to approach him head on. He would see her coming. He would flame her to a crisp before she could get close enough.

Lump and Danny burst through the dragon's wings yet again. They were now badly torn. Great flaps of loose skin fluttered in the wind as Siku continued to drag the dragon lord away from the battlefield.

Kit stole a glance at Fury. He was closing the distance, but his flying was still erratic. His left wing wasn't working properly. His right wing was trying to compensate. Had he broken bones in the fall? Kit knew very little of dragon anatomy. Well, nothing really, but she understood what an injury was. Maybe that was the right course of action. Maybe she should try to heal the sky dragon, help him be at his best when he faced the dragon lord.

The girl broke off from Ouroboros and started making her way to Fury. Her daemon wings transformed into their white feathered counterpart. The runes that covered her body faded away and her golden skin returned.

"What do you think you're doing?" Fury said. He didn't need to ask. He knew exactly what Kit was doing. He had seen her healing powers in action too many times. *"You can't heal me."*

"You don't know that. I don't even know if I can, but I don't see why I couldn't. You're a person, just like anybody else I've ever healed. You're just... bigger. I'm going to need you to steady yourself if you can, so I can land on your back."

Fury's wings stopped beating. He stretched them out and held them steady. The strain on his scaled face said just how excruciating it was for him to hold this position. Just as Kit leveled out over him, she tucked in her wings and her golden aura erupted. She dropped onto Fury's neck directly behind his head. The angel pressed her body against the dragon's scales, letting her aura seek the injuries. There were too many. How he could fly was beyond her. Most of Fury's bones were broken. Many of his organs had been smashed.

Fear gripped the girl. He was so big and there was so much to heal. She didn't know if she could take all the damage into herself without it killing her. She had to try.

"I forbid it."

Kit's head snapped around, searching for whomever it was speaking to her. It was a woman's voice. It was familiar, but she hadn't heard it in a long time. Tyche. It had to be her.

"I will not let you risk your life to save this one," she said. "Your life is mine to do with as I please, and I will not allow you to throw it away like this."

Kit ignored the Fate. She reached out with her aura, letting it seek the injuries and envelop them. She took them on and absorbed them into herself. Pain wracked her body. Her vision went blurry.

"No! You cannot. I forbid it."

The golden aura receded. She didn't do it on purpose, nor did the Fate have anything to do with it. Kit's vision cleared, and she reached out again. She was about to take in the pain when a voice of reason spoke to her. It wasn't someone external. She didn't really know where it was coming from. It was almost like it was her own heart speaking to her. *You cannot heal everything at once. You got to this moment fixing one problem at a time. You didn't do it by yourself. You had help. You are not alone.*

"Titan, hear me," she whispered. Her golden aura brightened as her priestly healing powers melded with them. "One problem at a time." The entirety of Fury's injuries appeared in her mind. His internal damage was severe, but it was the broken bones in his wings that were preventing him from flying properly. Her aura reached out like golden tendrils. It slithered over the dragon's iridescent blue scales, gently caressing his body as they spread. The main wing bone, the one that connected to his dragon body, looked just like a human arm. She let her aura wrap around it, felt for the damage, and accepted the pain.

Oh, sweet Titan, how the pain came. It flooded through her. It threatened to rip her apart. The yellow aura of her priestly power accepted the pain and wrapped itself around the white-hot agony, shielding Kit from the devastation it would have unleashed upon her. In a moment, the pain was gone. Then the angelic aura reached out, seeking its next injury. Kit breathed a sigh of relief. Fury's flying was improving with each passing second.

⁂

"Lump," Indie cried out. "Watch out!"

Ouroboros and Siku rolled in the sky. The wing the gold dragon had been looking to shred was now tucked into the black dragon's body. If they flew into it, they'd ram into the dragon's side. Lump blew out a torrent of flames, striking Ouroboros' flank. It may or may not have hurt the great dragon, but the intent was to have the intense heat give Lump extra lift. It worked, mostly. The duo avoided slamming into the immovable object. Lump's feet landed on the dragon. He scampered across the enormous body before kicking off, launching himself back into the air.

"Titan's snowballs," Indie cried out. The pair had nearly flown directly into Fury. The sky dragon had extended his clawed feet, intent on grabbing hold of Ouroboros. He would share the burden with Siku.

Lump rolled onto his back and dove out of the way. The phoenix zipped past, barely avoiding a midair collision.

Ouroboros bellowed out, flaming the blue dragon that had just latched onto him. Fury seemed impervious to his attack, enraging the black dragon all the more.

"I'll destroy you all," Ouroboros screamed. "I will rend you to pieces. I will feast upon your bones. I will..."

The phoenix slammed into the mouth of the black dragon. Indie couldn't tell if it was intentional or not, but the dragon finally stopped espousing how he was going to end everyone's life. Danny's body dropped past Lump's left. The gold dragon broke off and made his way to the unconscious Berrat, who was plummeting to his death. Lump snatched the young man from the sky and quickly leveled off. They were flying just a few paces above Lake Titan.

"Get him to shore," Indie said. *"We need to get back into the fight."* Lump flew up and turned north towards Aarall. While he made his way, Indie watched the titanic battle raging above. Siku maintained her grip while Fury was working his way up to Ouroboros' neck. The great black dragon continued to flame at him. Indie didn't understand how he could withstand the direct attacks. Even dragons were not immune to that much concentrated heat. Nobody was.

"Oh, sweet Titan." Indie's pulse quickened. Amid the writhing dragons, a tiny spark of gold illuminated Fury's head. Kit was riding the sky dragon. Like him, she was taking the full brunt of Ouroboros' attacks. By some unknown miracle, like the blue dragon she rode, she was not being incinerated by the firestorm.

Indie hadn't even noticed Lump dropping Danny off. He hoped he hadn't just dropped him, not really anyway. A wry smile crossed his face as the picture of the Berrat's body flopping on the shore popped into his mind's eye. He shook his head, banishing the thought. Lump would never do it. Kit would be devastated if he did.

"What do you want to do?" Lump asked, snapping Indie out of his silly revelry.

"Take us close and wait for an opportunity to present itself."

"Do you think Siku and Fury can kill him? It looks like they're dragging him over the lake."

Water. Deep water. It was a dragon's only true weakness.

"I know what they're doing. They're flying him over Lake Titan to drown him."

"They'll all die," Lump said. *"That's not a good plan."*

"I don't think they care. I think they want to destroy Ouroboros at any cost." Indie's voice was filled with resignation. He appreciated Siku and Fury's willingness to sacrifice themselves for the greater good. Despite his pompous attitude, Indie liked Fury. He had committed himself to helping the dragon, and he was true to his word. Indie's commitment had not ended. He was still going to help him. He didn't know how, but he would.

"Hang on," Lump said. Indie barely had time to tighten his grip before the gold dragon sped forward. Again, Indie could feel the dragon-dog's fires billowing up in his chest. With each breath, he stoked his flames. The heat was becoming unbearable, but he had no intention of trying to hold Lump back.

The gold dragon slammed into Ouroboros' head. With his clawed feet, he grasped onto the fine scales on the black dragon's snout. Between the rows of impenetrable armor, he found purchase. Ouroboros continued to flame. The air was awash with the bright red blaze. Sulfur. The smell of sulfur was so thick it made Indie gag.

"Strike his eye," Lump said. *"Strike his other eye and blind him."*

"The Bifrost blade is too small. I need a better weapon."

"Use your hands if you have to. We cannot let him see. He must be blinded."

"Kit," Indie called out. "Kit, I need your hammer." He had no idea if she could hear him. They were fighting in utter chaos. The rush of air and the constant flames had likely burned away his voice long before the words had reached her ears.

"She's coming." There was a smile in Lump's voice. Indie didn't really understand it, but he was happy that the puppy could so easily communicate with Kit. *"You can, too. All you need to do is call to her."* Indie forgot that Lump could read his thoughts. He wondered if Kit could, too. He also wondered why he couldn't read hers.

Kit jumped from Fury's neck and used her wings to guide her down to Lump. "I've got this," she screamed out. With her angel wings unfurled and her bright red hair whipping about her head, she looked like a goddess.

What thing did I do in my life to deserve such a gift?

With Lump holding onto Ouroboros' snout, Kit clambered up the black dragon's face. He shook his head wildly, trying to dislodge the winged girl. Fury clamped onto the dragon lord's neck, desperately trying to hold him still. Even though Indie had never conveyed his plan to the blue dragon, Fury obviously understood what they were doing.

Indie's heart was beating out of control. He wanted to be the one to blind the dragon, but nobody knew how to use that mithril hammer better than Kit. The girl used her wings to maintain balance as she ran.

"No, don't! I'll leave peacefully." Ouroboros' scream was almost pitiful. Indie couldn't imagine what it would be like to live sightless, unable to gaze upon the beauty of his loved one. He had no idea whether Kit felt any remorse for what she was about to do. She burst into flames; her feathered wings replaced by leathery black ones.

Probably not.

"I will relent. I will leave. I will not exact vengeance upon you. I will live a solitary life. Don't do this, I beg you."

Kit didn't buy it. She was still in her angelic form when the black dragon promised to leave. She had turned into her daemon self just moments later. The dragon was lying, and she knew it.

The flaming daemon wasted no time. When she got into position, she drew back her hammer and brought it down with righteous vengeance. There was a familiar flash of white light, followed immediately by bellows of anguish and utter despair. Ouroboros' thrashing redoubled as he screeched out in pain. The dragon lord transformed into a whirling tornado of scales, and claws, and teeth. Kit beat her wings, trying to put some distance between herself and the winged-god who would obliterate her.

"Let him go," Lump screamed. *"Let Ouroboros go!"*

"Why?" Fury asked. The blue dragon was struggling desperately to maintain his grip. The trio of massive dragons were losing altitude, unable to maintain proper flight while the black dragon continued his thrashing.

"Siku, release the dragon lord. I will kill the bawling dragonet myself," Lump called out. There was a moment of silence in Indie's head. Either they were considering the dragon-dog's demands, or they were simply ignoring him. Whatever it was he was thinking, it was insane. A moment later, Siku and Fury released their grip on the black dragon and pushed away.

Ouroboros immediately righted himself. With his front legs now free, he reached for his snout and the little gold dragon who was perched upon it. Lump flamed the blinded dragon's ruined eyes and leapt out of danger's way.

"You're nothing," Lump said, taunting the dragon. *"I am right in front of you. Catch me. Kill me if you can."* Lump had dived before he had finished the thought. The black dragon released a spray of fire. He let his head sway to the left and right, doing his best to create as large a swath of death as he could manage.

"You missed," Kit called out. Her voice boomed with such power that Ouroboros' flight became unstable. Indie watched as a great flap of a torn wing fluttered in the wind. The dragon's wings were a tattered mess. He and Danny had ripped them to shreds.

Kit dove and Lump followed. *"Catch us if you can,"* Lump taunted. *"Surely the great and powerful dragon lord can destroy a tiny dragon such as myself."*

Ouroboros belched out a series of fireballs in random directions. Kit sang out, her angelic voice loud and clear. She had left her daemon self behind. The black dragon screeched out and dove, desperately seeking his prey. Lump dove and circled off to his left. Ouroboros' head snapped in the same direction. He banked hard and followed. He was gaining on them.

"He has picked up my scent." Lump said. *"He doesn't need his eyes to follow if he can smell us."* The gold dragon went into a steep dive. He pointed his nose straight down and beat his wings with all his might. *"Split apart,"* he said to Indie. *"I'll lead him away."*

"No," Indie said. There was no way he was separating himself from Lump. If nothing else, he could be his eyes. He would look behind them and tell Lump how close the black dragon was to them. Indie's eyes bulged when he looked back. Ouroboros was extremely close and getting closer by the second.

"Lump, pull up!" Kit's voice echoed in Indie's ears. *"Lump, pull up. You're going too fast."*

Indie spun around. They were barely thirty paces above the lake's surface, and the black dragon was even closer. He understood what Lump was doing. With all his strength, he gripped the horns on the gold dragon's back and spread his dragon wings wide. They were traveling so fast. Too fast. Lump dropped his tail and spread his wings, desperate to slow their fall. Indie could feel his body being driven into Lump's back when he pulled up. The black dragon didn't know he was out of time.

Lump's toes were barely skimming the lake's surface as he pulled out of his dive. Ouroboros crashed into the water, unable to save himself with his tattered wings. A tidal wave of gargantuan proportions exploded out in all directions. The gold dragon pumped his wings, trying desperately to clear the duo from the wall of water. The dragon-dog was fast, but not fast enough.

⌘

The lake frothed as Ouroboros thrashed in his death throes. Deep water was a dragon's only weakness. Great sprays of steam had filled the air as soon as he'd contacted the lake's surface. Kit's heart exploded in her chest as she watched the tidal wave swallow Lump and Indie before the entire scene was obscured by a thick cloud of mist.

The angel dove to where the deluge had swamped the golden duo. She tucked her wings into her body and sliced through the surface. The water was clear but terribly dark. The shroud of fog covering the lake stopped any of the day's dying light from penetrating the surface. Kit thrust out her hammer and called upon its powers. She pushed her own angelic aura into it. Her light flooded out, illuminating the crystal-clear water for hundreds of paces in every direction. There was no sight of them.

Fear gripped Kit. Being in their dragon forms, had the water killed them the same way it had destroyed the dragon lord? They couldn't be dead. She refused to believe it. She would not lose them, too. Grief took her. It wrapped its fingers around her heart and crushed it.

No! I refuse to give up. I refuse to lose hope.

She kicked her feet as hard as she could and dove deeper. She pushed more of herself into her aura, desperate to increase its range. Hope sprung up in her chest. Perhaps thirty paces below were two figures. One was Indie's size. The other was much too small to be the gold dragon. The tightness in her chest worsened.

She kicked harder still. The muscles in her legs were burning from the exertion, but nothing was going to keep her from pressing forward. The two forms came into view. It was Indie and Lump. The wolfdog was his normal golden retriever self.

Titan, no.

With renewed vigor, she swam to the pair. She scooped up Indie in her left arm while gripping her hammer in her right. She couldn't hold on to it and Lump at the same time. Without a thought, she tossed it aside and grabbed the dog. She held his lifeless body close to hers, rubbing her face into his soft golden coat.

Kit used her wings to help her rise to the surface. She mimicked the movements of the great turtle that had borne her in the North Sea. She erupted from the lake like a phoenix rising from the ashes. Seconds ticked by as she sped for the shore. Each heartbeat sounded like thunder in her ears. The muscles in her back were screaming in agony as she pushed herself beyond her limits. Her wings could fall from her back for all she cared. She only needed them to last long enough to make it to shore. After that, the gods could have them.

The trio crashed onto the grass just beyond the lake's edge. They skittered and skid across the ground until they came to a stop. Kit's healing aura extended around all three of them. She poured everything into her healing powers. She poured her entire celestial life-force into them. Her breathing was becoming labored and ragged. Her vision blurred. She didn't care. All she cared about was the people she loved, and she would not let them down. Not now. Not after they had come so close to finishing everything they'd started.

Kit's vision faltered. The feel of wet grass hit her in the face. Everything in her body hurt, but none more so than her heart. It was beyond repair. There was nothing left in it.

⟨⟩

"Kit?"

Was she dead? Had she passed to the Beyond, or wherever it was she was to go when she died? The voice sounded like Indie's, but it couldn't be. He was dead and so was Lump.

"Kit? Open your eyes."

She didn't want to open her eyes. She didn't want to see what the Beyond was like if it didn't include her family and the people she loved. The voice did sound like Indie's, though. Perhaps Titan had granted her this boon, that she and Indie would spend eternity together in the Beyond.

A warm cloth scraped across her cheek. It was familiar. It was Lump. She was sure of it. Titan had let him come, too. She would be with Indie and Lump for all eternity. The shred of joy that had welled up within her was suddenly squashed. What of Runt? What would he do without her? What would she do without him? Surely Fenrir would care for him. He was just a puppy, after all. He had only seen one winter. She didn't want him to be with her, here in the Beyond, but she would miss him. She'd miss him for eternity. Her heart ached.

"Kit, my love. Open your eyes. Come back from wherever it is you are." A warm hand ran over her brow. It felt nice, welcoming. She breathed deeply, letting the smell of wet dog wash over her.

Wet dog?

Kit willed her eyes to open. Dark shadows hung over her. Dark, dripping wet shadows.

"There you are." That same warm hand stroked Kit's brow once again. It was so warm, so inviting. Another shadow neared, obscuring her view of the world. A wet tongue scraped across her face from chin to brow. Kit's heart thumped hard against her ribs. It kept beating faster and faster. The shadows came into view. A golden retriever and a young man were looking down at her. They were dripping wet. The feel of the water falling on her skin was refreshing.

"Hi," Kit said. A look of recognition crossed her face. The corners of her mouth pulled up into a small grin. "You're okay?"

"I feel very odd," Indie said. "But I am good." Lump barked.

"You were dead." Kit sat up. "You were both dead. I found you at the bottom of the lake."

"I guess you saved us then," Indie held out his hand, offering to help Kit to her feet.

"No, thank you." She pushed the man's hand away. "I'm good right here."

Lump laid down next to her, placing his head on her chest. She gave him a scratch behind his ear. "Where's Runt?"

"I'm not sure," Indie said. His voice was calm, almost reassuring. Wherever Runt was, he was okay. He had to be okay. Kit knew it in her heart that he was fine. She just wanted to rest. She had no energy. It was like she was completely empty. An empty, hollow shell. She closed her eyes and let sleep take her.

CHAPTER FIFTY-FIVE

THE GUEST PARADE

Indie hovered over Kit, holding her hand. He hated the Temple's infirmary. It was so white and empty and sterile. Brother Snowpack had just left. Even though he had insisted Kit was fine and that she just needed rest, Indie felt something was wrong. The girl's red hair had turned bone-white. Her golden skin was a deep tan color, like it had been when he'd first met her. The gold in her eyes had been replaced with a deep mahogany color. She was no less beautiful, but it was a stark contrast to the girl who was slaying demons and dragons only a day earlier.

Father Hoarfrost walked in with Grams at his side. They had left their Ollin and Galahdes personas behind, returning to their more familiar forms. Most everyone knew who they were, but they seemed happier and more at ease when they appeared as the aged couple.

"How long, Father," Indie asked. "When will she wake up?" Father Hoarfrost only shrugged and smiled. "What happened to her hair, her skin, her eyes?" Again, the old man simply shrugged. Grams elbowed him in the ribs.

"I can't say for certain, but she will awaken when she's ready. I cannot imagine what she endured that would cause these changes, but she is who she is. It's all she's ever been and all she'll ever be."

Grams gave Indie a sad look. "Have no fear, young man. Your love is safe and warm, and she will return to you. You just need to have a little patience."

Coldforge came bursting into the room. He was dressed in bright green leathers and was wearing a pointed hat with a red feather in it. His clothing stood in stark contrast to his vibrant orange mustache and beard. "Ye don't mean to tell me the girl is still snoozin'."

Runt jumped up from the floor and raced over to greet the dwarf. Neither he nor Lump had left Kit's side since she was brought into the ward. The bed was too small for them both to be on it, and Lump had hopped up first. The dire wolf barked out a greeting and raced back to be by Kit. He gave the golden retriever a stern look. Indie was certain he was telling him to get off. It was his turn on the bed. When Lump didn't move, he barked again, and again.

Kit's eyes fluttered open. She stared blankly at the gathered crowd. "Hi," she said.

Runt, no longer willing to wait his turn, hopped onto the bed, straddled the girl, and gave her an exuberant face washing.

A chill ran down Indie's back. She wasn't reacting. Not at all. She just laid there while the dire wolf covered her in slobber. It seemed Runt didn't like Kit's lack of reaction as well. With his face barely inches from hers, he barked. Lump pushed his way in beside the wolf, stepping on Kit, and joined in. The pair continued barking for several seconds before the girl beneath them stirred.

Kit blinked again. A smile spread across her face. She quickly wiped the disgusting amount of slobber away with her sleeve. Her smiled brightened even more.

"What are you all doing in my bedroom?" Kit blinked several times, like she was trying to figure out what was happening.

Indie was the first to laugh. The others joined in shortly thereafter. Kit's gaze wandered around the stark room. She knew where she was. She had spent many a day recovering here, especially after Sister Gale's combat training. The girl suddenly sat bolt upright on her cot. "Is the battle over?"

"It is," Father Hoarfrost said. "The two kings' soldiers were nearly ready to rout after the vampires were…"

"Neutered," a deep voice said from behind the old priest. "When Aurora killed Faol…" Captain Harding's words paused. He couldn't seem to get the words out.

"The vampires ceased being vampires," Father Hoarfrost finished. He placed his hand on the big captain's shoulder, guiding him forward. "It might have been when Hope killed Gorgaraeth. Either way, the vampires lost their powers, and they were washed away in the turning tide."

Kit's lower lip quivered, and her shoulders shook. Indie's heart broke as he watched the heartache of Kit's mother's death come crashing into her mind. He understood the pain she was feeling, the incredible, unrelenting grief that came with losing a parent. He slid in beside her on the cot and wrapped his arms around her, desperately wishing he could take Kit's pain away, the same way she had taken the pain from so many others. His world had become a sea of sorrow. Her grief threatened to swallow him as well, but he didn't care. Kit hugged him. Even in the grips of despair, she tried to ease his pain.

"Who else?" Kit asked, giving Indie another squeeze.

"Who else, what?" Indie wiped the tears from his eyes and sniffled.

"Who else did we lose?"

"We lost over half our army," her father replied. He, too, wiped tears from his cheeks. He cleared his throat and rolled his massive shoulders. "Most of the City Watch was decimated when we attacked the front lines. Many of the acolytes fell as well. Brother Rimes was the only priest who perished."

Indie watched Kit's reaction to Brother Rimes' death. She had grown up hating the man. The girl's eyes welled up at the news.

"He was heroic," her father said, continuing to describe the outcome of the battle. "There had been a barrage of arrows. They came by the thousands. Those who had not retreated into the woods immediately fell. The brother threw up a barrier and went to retrieve those who had not yet passed. He dragged dozens to safety. He continued his actions until his barrier could no longer protect him. He saved dozens of people. He saved Silverleaf."

"Silverleaf's okay though?" Kit asked. She looked around the ward. All the beds, except for the one she was sitting on, were empty. "Where is he?"

"The wounded are all in the barracks' infirmary. He is there now, but he's not bedridden. He's mostly helping Brother Snowpack and Sister Amara tend to the survivors. Lin's been trying to make healing potions for them, but she can only make them so fast."

"Lin's okay?" Kit sniffed and wiped her nose with the back of her hand. Indie nodded and rubbed her back.

"Your friends are all safe and whole. They've all been here to check on you, at least twice."

"I had to keep pushin' their arses out the door," Coldforge said. "If they didn't get back to work, nothin' was goin' to get done and ye'd not be getting the rest ye needed."

"You're a good friend," Kit said with a smile. "I don't know what I'd do without you."

"Well, yer goin' ta need to figure it out, girl. I need to get back to me people. Me father isn't goin' ta do all the work himself. We've got a kingdom to rebuild. Without that damned black dragon interferin' with our diggin', we'll have Mitril up and running in no time." The dwarf's fuzzy orange beard twitched a bit. "Ya don't suppose ya could let the big fella come with me, could ya?" He glanced over at Runt, who was snoozing soundly at the foot of Kit's bed.

Kit's face crumpled.

"I don't think our pup is going anywhere," Indie said. "His home is here with us." Kit was already crying again. She rested her head against Indie and took a deep breath.

"Runt can go where he wants. If he would rather leave with Coldforge, it's his decision. He came with me by choice. He can leave the same way."

"What da ye say, boy?" Coldforge was packing as much excitement into his voice as he could muster. "Do ya want to come with me to the mountains? Do ya want to see me home?" Runt lifted his head and smiled. His tongue lolled out of the side of his mouth, his jade-green eyes bright and cheery. He gave Kit a quick look, perhaps asking for her permission to go with him. Indie wasn't sure.

"It's up to you," Kit said, the words barely coming out of her mouth. Runt wined. He leapt from the bed, knocked Coldforge to the stone floor and gave him a thorough licking. Indie could feel Kit's shoulders shaking. He tightened his arm a bit more, offering her additional support. A moment later, Runt stepped away from the now slobber-covered dwarf and jumped back onto Kit's bed. He placed his massive black head on her lap and closed his eyes.

"Are you sure?" She asked him, giving his ears a scratch. The wolf responded with a snore. Indie didn't have the same connection with him as Kit, but he understood the wolf's meaning completely. He wasn't going anywhere without her.

"Ah, it's a shame," Coldforge said. His face was a mass of slobbery orange hair flying off in a thousand different directions. "But I understand. Family comes first." The sadness in his voice was apparent, but Indie knew the strange little man only wanted what was best. "Oh, and just so ye know, me kin will stay here for another day or three. They'll have that Temple fixed up as good as the day it was built. It really wasn't so bad. Who knows, maybe they're finished already." The twinkle in the dwarf's eyes was back and on full display. He strode across the room, using his broad shoulders to push through those who were blocking him from getting to the bedside. He took Kit's hand in his. Indie marveled at how small her hand looked in the man's massive fingers. "It was a pleasure meeting ya, girl. Ya gave me the best adventure of me life."

"Do you have to leave?" Kit asked. "Can't you stay here? We've got mountains that have never been mined." She gave him a shy smile. "Maybe you can stay and help us rebuild our cities." Coldforge chuckled.

"Ye don't need the likes of me hangin' around ye, all whoopin' and smashin' like I do."

"I don't want you to go. Runt might not have chosen to go with you, but he loves you. I love you, too."

Coldforge wiped his nose with the back of his hand. Indie had never seen this side of him.

"Maybe I can stay for a while longer," the dwarf said with a laugh. He gave Runt a scratch behind his ear. "I don't want the big feller to miss me, ye know. He's awfully sensitive."

Kit ripped herself out of Indie's arms and threw herself at Coldforge. She knocked his silly green hat off his head and kissed him soundly about his cheeks and ears.

Now that Kit was awake, she had a steady stream of people coming to check on her recovery and to thank her for what she had done. She was growing weary of the attention she was getting, but she recognized the visits were as much for them as they were for her. The girl's mouth dropped open when Captain Tym Windspeak came through the door. She hadn't seen him since they'd gone to Templeton and had liberated it from the would-be slavers. He gave Kit an amiable smile and a shrug.

"I came to help," he said, sounding somewhat sheepish. "I brought nearly five hundred soldiers, but by the time we got here, most of the battle was finished. We engaged a regiment that was likely trying to flee the area. They outnumbered us nearly three to one, but my Berrat soldiers would not back down. They would not run. I didn't expect we'd survive. If it weren't for the wolf-things coming to our aid..." The captain struggled to find the words, perhaps worried Kit would think him insane, speaking of such creatures.

"They're called Lupien," Kit said. She smiled to herself when the man's body suddenly relaxed. "They're often referred to as Hill Gizmos, but they really hate that name. They came to fight with you?"

"They all came," her father said. "Iba won their support. She got them all to join us."

"And you're going to need to make good on your promise, Captain." The small voice of the Tahr was unmistakable. She was standing next to Kit's bed, her chin barely higher than the top of the thin, straw mattress. Kit had no idea how long she had been there. She hadn't seen her arrive.

"Of course," Captain Harding said, giving the little Tahr a deep bow. "We are already negotiating terms with Galahdes. The Wood Nymphs aren't happy about it, but we're trying to see if your cousins can live in the Amberwood Forest."

Iba bleated. Kit took it as being a joyful noise, but she wasn't really sure. The Tahr was an enigma.

"Grams won't have any problem convincing them," Feigh said as he moved closer to the bed. He and the other sprites had come in just seconds earlier. "After all, it was we *shamed* who created it. We're letting the Wood Nymphs know they are only welcome if they can share the forest with the Lupien."

"And Grams is going to reinstate our place in the Elven Hierarchy," Midnight said. The rabbit-sprite hopped up onto the bed, fighting to find a spot for himself between Lump and Runt. "Apparently, the Council is outraged. Our return to the Elven Realm will be interesting."

"Not all of us will return," Triss said. She clambered up the side of the bed, with Feigh right behind her. The pair of mouse-sprites climbed on top of Runt and made something of a nest in his thick black fur. The dire wolf didn't seem to mind. Truth was, he didn't even move. He just kept snoring.

"Storm Cloud is going to stay behind," Feigh said, finishing the story that his mate had started. "He has chosen to stay with Lin." Kit gave the little mouse a curious look.

"Who's Storm Cloud?"

"You've met him," Triss said. She gave Feigh a look that said, in no uncertain terms, to shut his muzzle and let her speak. "He is the pegasus you met, the one who gave his feathers to you." Kit's brow crinkled as she tried to remember. Her eyes popped open. Her jaw followed a moment later.

"The invisible one? He's here?"

"He carried Lin and Feigh in battle," Triss said. She gave her mate a warm smile. "He said he was honored to fight at your side." Triss' nose scrunched up like she was trying to puzzle out an unsolvable riddle. "Storm Cloud said Lin is an anomaly. He could feel that her heart was pure, but it had a dark shadow on it. He said she is... intriguing."

The word made Kit laugh out loud. It was a deep belly laugh that raised her spirits considerably. Storm Cloud's description of Lin was so accurate. Kit's friend was wrapped in so many layers that it would take her a lifetime to peel them back. She was looking forward to that. The little priest never really thought about forever before. She had been totally focused on the here and now, and the problems that were directly in front of her. She gave Indie a smile. She liked the idea of forever when she looked at him.

"When will you be leaving?" Kit asked. Her gaze flitted between the three sprites.

"After the feast," Midnight said, his nose twitching.

"There's a feast?" Kit's stomach rumbled. She couldn't remember the last time she'd eaten. The thought of food made her mouth water. She was famished.

"Tomorrow," Indie said. "There will be a ceremony tonight to honor the fallen. Tomorrow will be a feast to celebrate the victory. To celebrate the liberation of the north."

Kit's stomach rumbled again. "Maybe we can have some food now? Please?" Kit's face heated. Tym had come to see her and, right in the middle of his story, everyone had cut him off and he was too much of a gentleman to interrupt.

"Tym, I'm sorry that I interrupted you," Kit said, trying to make up for her behavior with a big smile. "Maybe you can walk with me to the kitchens? I do so want to hear what happened after your arrival." The big man grinned and rubbed the back of his neck.

"I was happy for the disruption." Tym gave Kit's father a quick look. "There wasn't much more to tell." Captain Harding cleared his throat and nodded to the other captain. "Your father asked if I would stay on here in the city." Kit's eyes brightened. She looked at her father for more details. He raised his eyebrows and motioned back to Tym. "He wanted to know if I would stay on as the City Watch Captain." Kit's head snapped back to her father.

"What are you going to do if you're not in charge of the Watch?"

"I'm going to retire. I have a family to care for. One that I have neglected for far too long. General Wren is going to teach me how to be a farmer."

Kit snorted.

CHAPTER FIFTY-SIX

THE FLAVOR OF YETIS AND DRAGONS

Indie and the others all said they needed to get back to work. Now that they all knew Kit was up and recovered, and ready to eat something, the entire lot of them left her to accompany Captain Windspeak, Tym, to the dining hall. Indie gave her a quick kiss and promised he would return before she was finished. "I've seen you eat. You'll be there for a few hours." Kit punched him and they both had a good laugh. The boys seemed more than a little disappointed that they wouldn't be joining her for a meal.

Tym had a thousand questions along the way from the infirmary to the Temple's dining hall. It seemed like he needed to know the story behind every statue, every tapestry, every bit of mosaic tile that comprised the stone floors. He was an attentive listener. The little priest felt like she was giving the man a guided tour, but she really didn't mind too much. She liked the captain quite a lot, and she enjoyed her time with him.

Kit walked through the double doors that led into the dining hall. It was nearly empty. She could only think that the priests and acolytes were helping at the barracks' infirmary or they were dealing with preparations for tonight's ceremony to honor the dead. She wondered silently to herself if she shouldn't be helping as well, considering she had led them into battle. Surely their families would appreciate her being there. Or would they? Maybe they'd blame her for the deaths of their loved ones. She shook her head and pushed the thought out of her mind.

"Have you been to the Temple before, Tym?" Kit forced some cheeriness in her voice, even though she wasn't particularly cheery at the moment. She was sad, and she was hungry.

"Never," the captain replied. "I hear the head cook is the best chef in all of Arnnor."

Kit's heart broke. Memories of Sister Miyuki came unbidden. All the time Kit had spent with her, the love the woman had shown her, the connection they'd shared, flooded into her mind. The woman was practically Kit's mother when she was growing up. The memory of Aurora crowded into her despondent thoughts.

"Are you okay?" Tym asked. "Did I say something to upset you?"

Kit shook her head and wiped away the tears before they fell. "No, it's not your fault. Sister Miyuki was the head baker here. We were very close."

"Were?"

"She passed not very long ago. A Temple priest murdered her, a man I thought to be my friend. She was the kindest soul. The man murdered her to force my father into joining King Jordain and his lackey, Lieutenant Karr. I passed judgment upon the man. He will suffer for his actions for the rest of his life, just as we will all suffer for what he did." Kit's anger was welling up inside her. The thought of what Brother Powder, her friend, had done made her daemon want to burst out and wreak havoc upon the world. Except, it didn't. She couldn't feel the daemon's wrath within herself. All she felt was her own anger, her own fury. She suddenly wondered what had happened to Fury.

"I'm very sorry for your loss," Tym said. Kit gave him a small smile. The look on the poor man. He wasn't prepared for this sort of conversation, and yet, she could see the pain in his eyes. She could see her own anguish reflecting in them.

"Thank you," Kit said. "But now is not a time to grieve. It is a time to celebrate. I'll take you down to the kitchens. It won't be Miyuki's food, but she trained the other kitchen staff very well. We will have a good meal, and then we can go see about the preparations for tonight's ceremonies." The captain nodded, but he remained respectfully silent.

The pair took the stairs at the back of the dining hall down to the kitchens. They entered near the rear, where kitchen staff could carry their trays of food up to the dining hall above. The room was so desperately warm that Kit could barely breathe. Dozens of cooks and bakers were scurrying about as they prepared food and tended to many large pots over brightly burning fires.

"Food for the celebration?" Tym asked. "How does your city honor the dead?"

"The last time we held a mass funeral, we had to gather outside the city walls near Lake Titan." There were so many hard memories to relive. It seemed to Kit that all she'd seen in the past few weeks was death and sorrow. She would not allow herself to wallow. She could do that later when she was alone. Right now, she needed to find her inner strength. "We made large funeral pyres. My father, Captain Harding, presided over the celebration of the soldiers' lives. We didn't have time for food or consoling each other afterward. The danger had not yet passed." Kit inhaled the aromas that were dragging her deeper into the kitchens. The smells of cooked meats and fresh breads were so inviting that she could taste them. Her mouth watered uncontrollably.

"They're expecting you," one of the kitchen staff said. "They've got a few tables set up."

"Expecting me?" Kit asked. She looked at Tym, waiting for him to let her know what this was all about. He smiled and shrugged. If he knew, he wasn't saying a word.

Cheers filled the room as they rounded the corner. Fists were being banged on the tables. Feet were being stomped on the floor. At the back of the group stood Amara and Ulip, with Silverleaf wedged between them. The sound of their clapping hands was like boulders being slammed together. Amilta came scampering up, wrapping her arms around Kit's waist. Fenrir was not far behind, nor was a small pack of wolves, including the large gray that she had seen next to Amilta when Runt fought Shade. Her mother, Riva, sat at the edge of a long bench. She was dressed in light leathers and had her hands knitted together on her lap. She gave Kit an inviting smile. Without a word, Kit raced across the room and threw herself into the woman's welcoming arms.

The din melted away behind the mother and daughter. The world was filled with just the two of them.

"I don't know why I feared for your safety, Kitten, little piece of my soul." Riva stroked Kit's long blonde hair. "You look so much like your mother..."

Kit smiled at the comment. "I know. My hair looks just like yours." Riva's lip quivered. "I do hope we can spend more time together now. You don't have to leave, or anything, do you?"

"I had considered going home to Lilloet."

"But you've decided to stay here with me instead, right?" Kit gave her mother her very best grin. "At least for a while?"

"I wasn't sure you'd want me around with your new family." The woman gave Kit a one shoulder shrug.

"I have a new family, but you are my original. You are irreplaceable."

"Has life given you everything you wanted?" Riva asked. Kit gave her a sideways glance. "Do you remember what you wanted as a little girl? I think you wanted it more than anything else in the world?"

Kit thought back to her childhood and her time in her village outside Lilloet. She thought back to her arrival at the Temple and how good her new friends made her feel.

"I wanted to belong." She looked out over the sea of people who were in the kitchen. They were all there to be with her. Indie and the boys were front and center with Lin and Ormand by their sides. Sister Gale and Brother Snowpack were there, along with a good number of priests and acolytes who Kit didn't know very well. Coldforge and Slate stood with Bango, Calian, and Danny. Danny looked happy. Happier than Kit could ever remember seeing him. Behind the entire group stood Father Hoarfrost and Grams. There were even a good number of City Watch soldiers she had met while working for her father. She scanned the group one more time. Captain Harding was nowhere in sight.

"Have you seen my father?" Kit asked.

"For a big man, he's quite silent," Riva said. She motioned with her chin for Kit to look behind her. There he was, standing with his wife, her half brother, and an old man Kit had never met before.

"Hello, Kit. I know you've met them before, but I'd like to properly introduce you to Beth and Nick." Kit stood dumbfounded, unsure what to say. Her gaze fell on the old man standing a few steps behind the others. "And this is my friend and mentor, Kren Eagle Claw."

"Your mentor?" Kit smiled and her eyes widened. "Then you must be positively ancient." Kren pressed his lips together tightly enough that they almost disappeared.

"And you are your father's daughter." The retired general laughed and clapped the captain's back. "It is my pleasure to meet you."

"And it's my pleasure to meet you all." Kit looked over at Elizabeth and raised her eyebrows. "Would you like me to call you, mother?" Elizabeth's head tilted slightly to the side, like she was trying to gauge if Kit was joking with her or not.

"You would willingly call me mother, even though we've never really met before now?"

Kit took a quick look at Riva, who was beaming at her.

"We can never have too much family," Kit said brightly. She wrapped her arms around the woman, startling her badly. It took Elizabeth a moment to recover before she quickly returned the hug. Her father joined in, wrapping his arms around the pair of them. He beckoned his son, who, after several moments of indecision, joined in.

The reunion was interrupted by Sister Nevara and the row of young acolytes she had trailing behind her. A mother and her baby ducks. That's what they looked like to Kit. Every time she saw the woman with her children, that was the image that popped into Kit's mind. At the end of the row of ducklings was Iba, who was trying to keep the last few from wandering off.

"Children," Sister Nevara called out. "Children, pay attention now." The priest's hair was tied back in her traditionally tight braids, making her severe features look even more imposing. She glared down at the young novices over her wickedly hooked nose and clapped her hands repeatedly to get their attention.

The entire group of children were entranced by Lump and Runt, who were both play bowing to them, wagging their tails in quick, wide circles. The priest switched her glare from the children to Iba. Rather than helping, the young Tahr was slapping her hands on her thighs, calling the boys over to her.

Nevara finally relented. She, too, called the boys over to see the children. Lump and Runt were happy to oblige.

"I wanted to introduce the children to you," Sister Nevara said to Kit. "But things don't always go the way we plan them." Kit could only smile at the priest. It wasn't so long ago that she had taken Kit under her mother-duck wing and helped her get settled here at the Temple.

"But sometimes they turn out alright anyway," Kit said with a smile.

"So," Sister Nevara said, placing her hands on her hips. "Are the rumors true?"

"Rumors, Sister?"

"That you will take over as High Priest." Kit blinked at the woman.

"No, Sister. They are not true." The sister cocked an eyebrow. "Father asked me, but I refused." Sister Nevara's mouth formed a tiny circle and her head snapped back.

"You refused? How? Why?" The priest's gaze went over Kit's head to her family and to the young man who was quietly walking up to join the conversation. Kit reached out her hand to Indie, inviting him to come nearer.

"I have other plans," the little priest said with a shrug and a smile. "I may follow my father's lead and be a farmer. Indie has a farm a little way south of here." It was Indie's turn to look shocked. Kit had discussed none of this with him. She hadn't discussed any sort of future with him, not at all. "Or maybe I'll go north, back to where a friend of mine once lived. I'll take Lump and Runt and, if Fenrir is willing, teach them how to be good pack leaders. Maybe Runt will even take his father's place as the Alpha Prime."

Sister Nevara stared at Kit with an utterly blank expression, other than her mouth gaping open. It made Kit laugh inside more than a wee bit. "You would leave the Temple?" The words were filled with dismay and disbelief. "You are Acknowledged by Titan, the Savior of Aarall."

"The Temple will live on without me," Kit said. "But I hope to come and visit. I have too many friends here to stay away forever."

Sister Nevara spun on her heel and clapped her hands sharply together. Iba, the boys, and all the children immediately snapped towards her and gave the woman their undivided attention. "Children, listen to me," she said. The authority in her voice said this was not a suggestion they could ignore. "I would like you all to meet Sister Kit Standing Bear. When she came here five short cycles ago, she was a lost little girl. She had no friends and no family that she knew of. She had traveled many, many leagues to get here. She was called by Titan. She didn't know her purpose. None of us did. But it was within these walls that she found her way. She found her family. She found her purpose in this world and she fulfilled her destiny. Now, she looks to find a new purpose, to carve out a new path for herself and her family. That is what I want for each one of you. Do you understand? This will be your home until you decide what you want to do with your lives. We will help guide you. If you work hard enough, and you devote your entire self to it, then maybe, just maybe, you'll be the one teaching us, just like Sister Kit here."

The children all nodded in silent rapture at the tall, stark woman and the petite girl standing at her side.

"Iba," Sister Nevara said, her voice still sharp. "Will you lead these children to their new dorm room? Show them the way."

Iba gave Kit a quick gesture and ushered the children out of the kitchen. Sister Nevara gave Kit a curt nod. "May Titan guide you and keep you safe, child."

Kit crossed her arms over her breast in the traditional manner. She inclined her head slightly. "And may his grace and his light shine upon you. May his strength protect you and guide your hands in your efforts." The stern response seemed to please the old priest greatly. She snapped her fists across her chest in return. A moment later, she turned abruptly and strode off, quickly corralling a pair of wayward children.

"You want to be a farmer?" Indie whispered. "With me?"

"After we are wed," Kit said, giving her man a bright smile. "Unless that's not what you want."

Indie stood dumbstruck for several seconds. When a huge meaty hand clapped him on the shoulder, he yelped.

"Before you speak, boy," Captain Harding said. "I suggest you think this through. My daughter will be a difficult bride. She is as bold and as headstrong a person as I have ever met. You are both incredibly young and have much to learn about the world and about each other."

"And the world will be in turmoil for many cycles," Riva said. "Nothing will be easy. The world will test your resolve daily."

"Are you two trying to scare him off?" Kit asked. Her stomach was knotting up at their words. Were they talking to Indie or were they talking to her? Were they trying to scare her off? Indie wrapped his arm around Kit's shoulder and gave it a squeeze. Her doubts slowly drifted away.

"I am not easily scared," Indie said, his eyes locked on Captain Harding. "If you would allow it, Captain, I would be honored to wed your daughter."

"Are you asking my permission?" the captain said. The big man stood even straighter and pushed his shoulders back. He was huge. A huge, imposing man, and he was using every inch and every pound to his advantage. Indie maintained his grip on Kit's shoulder and mirrored the captain's posture.

"..." a pathetic squeaking noise escaped Indie's lips. His face reddened. It was quickly followed up with another, even weaker, attempt at finding words. Kit elbowed him in the ribs.

"Yes. Yes, sir. That is exactly what I am doing." The young man's face was still beet red, but he got the words out, this time with conviction. The captain laughed.

"If my daughter would have you, then that is good enough for me. But know this, young Indigo. I would be proud to call you my son." The two men stared down at Kit, as though waiting for a response. A knot appeared in her stomach. A tangle of nerves sprung up, yanked themselves into a ball, and twisted until she thought her breath would leave her. She desperately wanted to say yes, but something was holding her back. She didn't know what it was.

"Warrior chief," Ulip bellowed out. He extended his thick black hand to Captain Harding in greeting. The knot in Kit's stomach lessened slightly. Never had she ever been so grateful to be interrupted. Her father clasped the Giga's forearm in greeting. "I wish to offer my congratulations." The knot in Kit's stomach reappeared. Had the big man been listening in on their conversation? Was he congratulating her father because his daughter was getting wed?

"You fought with bravery and honor. Your people followed you into battle. They recognized a true chief. Though your losses were many, your people gave their lives in the service of others. No death can be more noble."

Thank Titan! The knot in Kit's stomach lessened a bit. She stole a glance at Indie. He was staring at her, apparently upset that she had said nothing. She gave him a shy smile. Hopefully, he got the meaning. Hopefully, he understood she loved him with all her heart, but that she wanted to discuss the matter with him. He needed to understand something that she had not yet shared with him.

"What are your plans, Ulip?" Kit asked, still intent on steering the conversation away from marriage.

"Yuka and I will remain for tonight's ceremony," he said. There was a deep solemnity in his voice. "We will honor those who fought and died. We will see them off to Gaia and to the Beyond. We will sing for their souls, that they may find peace eternal."

"And then?" Kit prompted. She hadn't gotten to spend much time with the Gigas, but she took an immediate liking to the man. Perhaps it was because he was Amara's brother, but she didn't think so. There were so many sides to him. A kind and caring side, a loving brother, and a devastatingly powerful warrior. She could relate to him.

"I will return to the home of my people," Ulip said. "I will speak with the red dragon, Spur. If he is willing, I will rebuild my clan. I will do what I can to help restore the northern realm. There has been too much pain and suffering. Now is a time for healing."

A parade of kitchen staff appeared from the back. They were loaded down with trays upon trays of food.

"Come," Ulip said, "Let us eat. We can speak of tomorrow another day. Now is the time to be with friends and family. We must honor both the living and the dead. And I am hungry."

The smell of the food was intoxicating. Roasted meats and vegetables. Freshly baked breads. The scents were so intense, Kit could already taste the food.

Her mouth was watering out of control. She was being taken away to culinary nirvana when a stench that practically knocked the little priest off her feet stung her nose.

Oh, sweet Titan. I know that smell. Kit's eyes went wide. From out of the back walked an unlikely pair, each carrying a platter of cheeses. The first was an extremely fat Nomad dressed in a white apron that was struggling to not burst at the seams. The second was a young Berrat with short-cropped sandy brown hair. He, too, was dressed in a white apron, but it hung comfortably over his slender body.

"Sam!" Kit called out. "Sammuel Larder! Karim!" The fat man's neck rolls jiggled beneath his chins as he caught sight of Kit. "Is that Blue Yeti I smell?" The little priest's face twisted as the pungent scent continued to assault her nose.

"My very best, young priest," the owner of the Cheeserie called out, his voice loud and boisterous. His many chins jiggled wildly as he spoke. "I remember how much you liked it. This is the very last of my special reserve."

How much I liked it? That stuff makes me gag.

"Greetings, and Titan's blessings upon you, Sister Kit," Karim said. He had a wry smile on his face. "Sam remembers things differently than I do. I pray you will try it, though. The flavor is worth the pain your nose must suffer."

Kit's eyes were watering. Perhaps from the joy of meeting these old friends. Perhaps it was the god-awful aroma.

"Be sure to save some room for my dragon pies," said another voice. Tears of joy sprang forth at the sight of the middle-aged man with skin like ebony. His pearly white teeth shone as he smiled back at Kit.

"Comden," Kit cried out. "I am so glad..." Her face screwed up. "Did you say dragon pies? Are they the same ones that burned my face off? Are you trying to kill me?"

"I tamped it down a little," the black man said, smiling from ear to ear. "But they're still pretty spicy."

"Come, let us enjoy this food while it's still hot," Ulip said. His insistence on getting seated suggested that he was at least as hungry as Kit was.

In minutes, everyone was making moaning noises as they made their way through the mountain of food being delivered.

Kit tried a bit of both the Blue Yeti and the dragon pies. One bite of each was two bites too many.

CHAPTER FIFTY-SEVEN

THE SECRET IN THE GARDEN

Kit tried to push herself from the table. She was so full she could hardly breathe. There were a few morsels left uneaten on this, her fourth plate of food. She peered under the long trestle table, looking for the boys. Maybe they'd want to eat the last of the Blue Yeti that sat there, smelling just as badly as she'd remembered. Maybe they could finish Comden's *toned-down* dragon pies. Her mouth was still on fire. Nothing helped quell the burn.

The boys were unconscious. Their distended bellies and the way their tongues were dangling out of their mouths, laying on the floor, said it all. They had also eaten their share of food, plus enough to feed Amilta's wolf pack. The wolves had moved off to the side of the kitchen after their presence gave one particular serving boy a minor heart attack. They were all too happy to follow a roasted boar being carried on a spit. Their meal didn't take them long to devour. Like the boys, they were all content and fully satiated.

"How's about we take a walk around the Temple?" Danny said. "I know it hasn't been so long since I was here last, but I'd really like to have another look before Calian and I head home."

"Sure," Kit said with a groan. "But I'm going to need some help to get out of my chair."

Calian grabbed the girl's chair-back and dragged her backwards. "There you go. While we're walking, maybe you can share some stories about Danny's youth with me."

"Nobody wants to hear that," Danny and Indie replied in unison. They both looked at one another, held their gaze for several seconds, and then burst out laughing. That one bit of interaction pleased Kit to no end.

"The north is safe now," Kit said. "Maybe you can stay and build your lives together here?"

Danny and Indie shared another look. They both shrugged.

"We talked about it," Calian said. "King Jordain escaped. There may still be a need for the phoenix here in Arnnor."

"The king and I will have words," Lin said. Ormand was still at her side. The man's complexion had returned to normal. The pasty white look he once had was gone. He smiled when he caught her staring at him.

"I'm not a vampire anymore," he said, like he was discussing the weather. "When Gorgaraeth was killed, whatever it was inside of me that made me a vampire died with him."

"We're going to head for Two Peaks in a few days," Lin said, "after the ceremonies are over."

"For how long?" Danny asked.

"For as long as it takes," Lin said. "I'll come back when the king is dead."

"Won't that make you the queen?" Kit asked. Lin gave her a blank stare. The little priest bowed deeply, spreading her arms out to her side. When she raised her head, a broad smile split her face. "You'd make a terrific queen."

"I most certainly would not. Could you imagine me sitting on a throne, listening to the problems of the world? Ugh, I'd rather be a priest of Titan."

"I thought we were taking a walk," Amara said, her baritone voice cutting through the awkwardness of the conversation. "I can show you my new cell."

"Our new cell," Silverleaf said, rather enthusiastically. When everybody's attention snapped to him, the half elf's face reddened immediately. "Our new cells. Separate new cells. I have mine and she has hers. Not together, well, they are together. They're next door to each other, but they're separate."

"They get it," Amara laughed, "but I hope you'll come visit me from time to time." Silverleaf staggered, his face now a deep scarlet.

"Why do you two have two separate, individual, yet connected cells?" Kit asked. Her eyebrows had been raised so high they were disappearing beneath her hair.

"Sister Gale suggested we become teachers," Amara said. Silverleaf was in no condition to speak. He still seemed to struggle to catch his breath. "I will be the new combat instructor, and Silverleaf will teach potions and scrolls. Sister Gale asked Lin to stay on as the Temple's instructor on enchantments and alchemy, but she has other plans."

"If Coldforge sticks around, Sister Gale said he could teach until I am ready to take over the roll." Slate's bright orange beard was not nearly as thick as Coldforge's, but it was twitching away in such a similar fashion that Kit was convinced they were close relatives. The similarity was just too striking.

"Are we going for a walk or not?" Amara said. She had her hand across her belly, and she was looking a little green. "If I don't get some fresh air..."

"I'm afraid you're going to have to leave without Kit," Fenrir said. "I have business to discuss with her." The crowd of Kit's friends stood motionless. Kit didn't know if they were disappointed that she would not be joining them, or because Fenrir wasn't including them in whatever it was she wanted to discuss with her. "It's family business," the wolf god added, waving the backs of her hands at them, shooing them away. "You can stay," she said to Indie. "If Kit allows it."

"Why do I need to allow it? I have no secrets from him."

"What I'm going to show you... you will not like. But it's important that you keep an open mind. I don't want either of you to overreact."

"Okay then," Indie said, moving closer to Kit. "Unless she prohibits it, I'm coming." The boys dragged themselves out from under the table. Lump barked and Runt followed suit. With considerable effort, they made their way next to Kit. Apparently, wherever it was she was going, the boys were coming, too.

⌘

Fenrir had led Kit, Indie, and the boys out to the Temple's back gardens. Outside of a couple who were seated on a bench beneath a slender tree, and the occasional songbird serenading the group, it was wonderfully quiet and peaceful. It was also a welcomed break from the joyous celebrations that were still carrying on in the kitchens, despite the amount of food that had been consumed.

"Why did you bring me here?" Kit asked. Fenrir had stopped and turned to Kit. She was staring intently into the young priest's eyes.

"Your golden eyes are gone," the wolf god said. Kit nodded, not sure what to say. "Do you still see just as well now that they're gone?" Kit furrowed her brow and nodded again.

"What's wrong with my eyes?"

"Oh, nothing, sweet child. Nothing at all. I..." Fenrir paused and stared down at her feet for a moment. "I just hope they still allow you to see with your heart."

"See with my heart?" Kit glanced around, wondering what it was the Berrat woman was getting at. Her eyes fell on the couple sitting on a bench. Kit looked harder. One of the two people was her mother, Riva. The other was a Berrat dressed in a black cloak. The cloak's hood was pulled up, hiding the person's face in dark shadows.

Fenrir's eyebrows shot up. "What do you see with your lovely brown eyes?"

"I see my mother sitting on a bench with another person, probably a Berrat."

"What else do you see?" Fenrir's voice was soft, patient. Kit shrugged at the question. "Does you mother appear to be happy?"

Kit squinted her eyes and leaned forward. "No," she said. "She looks sad. She looks worried. What's happened? What's going on?"

A smoke-gray hare poked its head out from the bushes. The boys both caught sight of it and gave chase. The hare's fluffy white tail was the last Kit saw of it before it vanished whence it had come. The boys crashed into the brush right where it had disappeared.

"Fenrir?" Kit's stomach hurt. Something bad was coming, but she didn't know what. Why was her mother out here with a mysterious stranger? A fisher darted across their path. Was that why the hare had shown itself? Had it been looking to escape from the predator?

"Come," the wolf god said, stepping quietly towards the pair. "Open your heart."

Kit clasped onto Indie's hand. She gave him a questioning look. The man's eyes widened slightly, and he shook his head. The pain in her stomach twisted. Kit pulled on Indie's hand, urging him forward. Whatever it was she was heading into, she would have his support.

Each step towards her mother made the twisting pain in Kit's stomach increase. Riva caught sight of the trio as they approached. The Berrat woman reached out and placed her hand on the knee of her companion.

"Mother?" Kit said when they were close enough to speak. "What's going on?" Riva stole a glance at Fenrir before returning her gaze to her daughter. The woman's eyes flicked quickly to Indie and then dropped. The hooded person at Riva's side ducked lower, completely hiding within the cloak's folds. Several seconds passed in silence. When Kit's mother raised her head, tears filled her eyes.

"Do you remember?" Riva asked. "When you were going through the Rite of the Way, I told you about my own experiences?" Kit vaguely remembered something about a blood-soaked sheep, but not much more. She shook her head.

"I'm sorry, Ananak. I only remember a small bit of the tale."

"That night," Riva said, "while my father watched in the distance, I was visited by a sheep. I had accidentally cut myself with my ulu, the one I later gave to you." Kit nodded. The memory was becoming clearer in her mind. She suddenly remembered about the ulu; the small, curved blade made of bone her mother had given her. She hadn't seen it in a while. Oh, sweet Titan, she had lost it.

Riva smiled and pulled the small blade from the pocket in her jerkin. She rolled it over in her hand and tested the blade's sharpness with her thumb. A thin line of crimson appeared.

"It's as sharp as the day I received it," she said. "It was this blade that set me on my path. My father, who had very little faith in me, I'm afraid, gave me the very tool I needed to ignite my destiny."

Kit rushed to her mother, taking a knee before her. The person at her side tried to turn away. In that moment, the little priest saw a man's face, a Berrat man's face. Riva took Kit's chin gently in her hand and turned her daughter's attention back towards her.

"I was bleeding badly," she said, regaining Kit's attention. "The sheep appeared to me. I didn't mean to grab it with my blood-covered hands, but I did. When I touched the sheep's wooly face, my wounds were instantly healed." Kit nodded. She remembered that part of the story. Riva had said that the cut was gone and so was the sheep.

"What I didn't tell you, my sweet Kitten, was that I was changed that night. The sheep didn't just heal my wound. It ignited my soul. It gave me the gift of far sight. It was when my visions all started." Kit was dumbfounded. Her mother had never shared this piece of herself before. But why now?

As though sensing her daughter's confusion, Riva pressed on. "I also told you of when I had been captured by the slavers. Do you remember?"

"When a guard tried to turn you into a vampire?" Her mother nodded.

"Yes. That was the night a vampire, a Berrat vampire, tried to turn me. He wanted me as his mate." Kit lowered her eyes. She had forgotten that part of the story. A shiver ran up her spine. To be joined with such a creature was unthinkable. Ormand's face popped into her mind's eye. He was not nearly as terrible as she had expected. He was just a man afflicted with a horrible sickness. Once he had controlled his blood lust, he was just a man like any other. And now, his vampire sickness, or affliction, or whatever it was, had been healed. It was completely gone.

Riva waited patiently until Kit finally looked back at her. "Something passed between me and my jailer that night. Something happened to both of us. We were... changed."

The smoke-gray hare appeared from out of the bushes once again. It hopped up to Riva and sat next to her. She was only an arm's length away from Kit, but it showed no fear. The hare looked familiar. A moment later, the boys came bounding out of the bushes. They caught sight of the hare and came racing over. When they neared, they both whined and laid down.

The fisher who had crossed Kit's path also appeared. It, too, made its way to Riva, the cloaked man, and the hare. It scampered forward, taking his place at Riva's feet.

What is happening? Kit looked for Fenrir, hoping for answers, but the wolf god was gone.

Riva reached into her pocket, retrieving something else. She opened her fist and let a small stone roll around in her palm. It was the same stone her mother had given her on the night of the Rite of the Way.

"You had left your ulu and this stone behind in Cormorant." Kit's mother gave her a bit of a smile. "Since you won't be going back there, I thought I would bring them to you."

"I'm not going back?"

Riva shook her head. "No, not anytime soon, I believe." The woman chuckled. "But then again, hardly any of my visions for you came true. So, who knows what the future will bring for you."

The rustle of feathers announced yet another animal. An eagle flew low over Kit's head, landing in the branches just above her mother. It gazed at Kit, its pale golden eyes seeming to stare directly into her heart.

Kit glanced down at her forearm. That night, during the Rite of the Way, an eagle had raked it with its wicked claws. The marks were still there. Her mother's words from that night echoed in her mind.

Listen to your heart.

From behind the tree stepped a wolverine. Its gray-black coat shimmered with each step it took. Like the fisher, it moved in front of Riva and laid down.

"Mother? What's happening?"

The man sitting next to Riva dragged back his hood. Unbraided white hair hung down his shoulders, framing his deep bronze skin. Kit's pulse quickened. She knew this man, but from where? Her quickening pace came to an abrupt halt.

"Pental."

The name came out of Kit's mouth like a curse. She wanted to end him, right there, in that moment. But... he had been helping her. His soul was black as coal.

His heart was as cold as the North Sea. Indie took a menacing step forward, but Kit grabbed his arm, stopping his progress. Why was her mother sitting next to this man? Why had she placed her hand on his lap?

"It was you!" The words flew from Kit's mouth in a hushed scream. "You were the guard who tried to take my mother as her mate."

"I loved her the moment I saw her," Pental said. "I was a fool to believe that she could love a creature such as myself."

"You are a fool to believe I will let you walk away from here," Kit said. "You..."

"I am a monster," Pental said. "I did unspeakable things. I committed horrible, unforgiveable crimes against humanity."

"He did it for a reason, Kitten," her mother pleaded. "That night. That night that he tried to turn me; he, too, was touched by Gaia." The words had barely left her mother's lips when a swarm of bear-moths appeared. They landed lightly on Pental's head and shoulders. Their wings beat slowly for several moments before they all settled.

"I don't understand, mother." Kit looked down at the hare, barely able to decern the little animal's form through her tear-filled eyes. "Gaia, why?"

The world swelled and Kit's vision faltered. She was going to be ill. Her hand flashed out to clutch onto Indie's arm, but he wasn't there. Darkness crept into the corners of her eyes. The hare was the last thing she saw before losing consciousness.

CHAPTER FIFTY-EIGHT

HEART, MIND, BODY, AND SOUL.

Kit's world swirled. In the darkness that had swallowed her, tiny lights spun about, whirling and twirling. It reminded her of traveling through the Bifrost. Everything came to an abrupt halt. She was sitting on a large, smooth rock, in a glade by a small pool. The water was the deepest, most intense shade of blue she had ever seen. No. That wasn't true. She had seen this very pool before. She was sure of it. Kit pulled her gaze away and looked up. In the night sky were millions upon millions of tiny, twinkling lights.

"Hello, Kit," said a voice. A little man was sitting cross-legged by the pool, holding a U-shaped instrument. He ran his fingers across its strings, filling the air with a most enchanting melody. The little man, with ruddy red cheeks and disheveled white hair, smiled brightly.

"Hello, Anu," Kit said. "Why have you brought me here?"

"Why? To thank you, sweet child."

"For what?" Kit gave him a puzzling look that seemed to delight the strange little man. The heavy wrinkles on his face were too cute. Had she not noticed that before?

"For teaching my children some precious lessons. I had expected the Fates to do that job, but you were a much better teacher."

Kit slid down from her rock and padded forward through the soft, thick grass. Her feet were bare. The grass was cool and moist. It smelled like honey. Anu patted the ground next to himself.

"I didn't mean to teach anybody anything," Kit said, taking a seat next to the strange little man. "I was just..."

"You were just being yourself. You showed my children what it meant to be true, and honest, and caring. Truth is, young priest, you taught me things I didn't expect to learn."

"I did?" Anu nodded enthusiastically.

"Beings, such as myself and the Fates, we're too detached from the lives that exist in our realm. I want to say they are beneath us, but that isn't the right word." Anu rubbed the stubble on his chin. "Do you ever have trouble finding the right word? You know what you want to say, but your feelings become difficult to express." Kit nodded. She really didn't know how else to respond. "Have you ever absentmindedly killed a bug, or a spider, or some other lesser being without a second thought?"

Kit nodded. She hated spiders and killed them on sight. They gave her the willies.

"Right. Just like that. I knew you would understand." Anu clapped his hands and rolled onto his back. Sweet Titan, he looked like the boys when he did that. His antics suddenly stopped, and the strange man sat back up.

"You taught me that those lives matter, that they are not insignificant. They're important. Maybe not to me, not directly, but to others, they are. The peoples who live on the planet you call Orth. They are important. I didn't know just how important they were until you showed me. For that, I wish to thank you."

Kit swallowed hard. "You're welcome?"

"What can I give you in return for your services?" Anu's eyes were bright and sparkling. Was this the reason he had brought her back here? Did he want to give her a present? "My mate suggested I restore the dragon spirit of your friends."

"Your mate? What do you mean, restore their dragon spirits?" Was he speaking of Fury? Had something happened to him?

"The being you know as Gaia. She is my mate. We are the parents of Titan and Orth."

"Gaia was watching over your children, just as Riva watched over me?" Anu nodded in response. He seemed pleased that Kit had drawn the parallel between her mother and Gaia.

"Indeed. We let others help with our children's growth, but we are never far away."

"You let others help? Like the Fates?" Anu nodded again. "But the Fates didn't want to help. They felt trapped by the burden. They told me so."

"Oh." Anu scrubbed his already disheveled hair. "I wasn't aware. I just expected they were happy with the arrangement."

"What did you mean by my friends and their dragon spirits?"

"Your friends, Indie and Lump. When they fell into the lake you named Titan, their dragon spirits perished. They are now, just as they were. A human and a wolfdog." Kit didn't know how to react. She had hated the thought of them having dragon powers, but it brought them both such joy.

"Do they know they've lost their dragon selves?"

Anu stared up at the stars as though considering the question. "Yes. I believe they knew the moment you saved them from their drowning."

"They said nothing about it," Kit said. She was perplexed by this revelation. Anu smiled and shrugged.

"Can I think about it?" Kit asked. "I want to ask them if it's what they want."

"What about you, young priest? What can I do for you? How can I thank you?" This was at least the second time the funny little man had referred to her as a young priest. He used to call her *little angel.*

"You don't know?" Anu asked. Kit's brow furrowed. Something was amiss.

"Tyche took the celestial within you and kept it for herself. She said that your life-debt was now paid in full."

"She did what? Why? How? I never agreed to it."

"But you did, little priest. Do you not remember?" Kit shook her head. "When you saved your friends, Indie and Lump, you brought them back from the dead. You poured yourself into them, to save them. You put every ounce of your celestial essence into your healing. It would have killed you, but your life was not yours to give. Tyche allowed you to complete your task and, just before you expired, she accepted your power as payment and gave you back your life. She would not allow three lives to perish when you only owed her one."

"Oh," Kit wrung her fingers in her hands. "I didn't realize. What did you mean by three lives?" Anu ignored her question.

"Would you have acted differently had you known you'd lose your powers?" Kit didn't have to think about it. She shook her head adamantly.

"Never. My powers were not important. I'd make that trade any day, every day. I'd do it without question and without remorse."

Tyr, Eris, Mephitis, Tyche, and Tiamat all appeared. They were small balls of white light, but Kit instinctively knew who they were.

"Isn't she wonderful," Tyr said. "If you would allow it, I wish to stay with her on Orth. I expect she still has much to teach me."

"Do you not wish to have your freedom?" Anu asked. "I recently discovered the five of you felt trapped, like you were being held prisoner."

The ball of light that had been Tyr morphed into a humble-looking teenage boy with shaggy, golden-blonde hair. He was perhaps fourteen or fifteen cycles. "The task you gave us was difficult and terribly boring." Tyr's shoulders slumped. "Titan and Orth. All they wanted to do was play games. Entertaining them for so many millennia, it was mind numbing." Tyr straightened and jutted out his chin. "I'm sorry for the role I played in what was a plan to destroy your children."

Anu's eyebrows shot up. "You sought to destroy them? The five of you?"

"We just wanted to be free of them," Tyr said. He looked more than a bit frightened. He likely wished he had chosen his words more carefully.

"Your plan was quite elaborate," Anu said. He gave an appreciative nod. "As well conceived as any plan I've ever enjoyed."

"You knew?" Kit asked. She was as shocked as Tyr was.

"Of course, I did," Anu said. "Well, I knew of most of it."

"You're not cross with me?" Tyr asked. His eyes strayed over to his cohorts. None seemed willing to change out of the bright orb shape they were in.

"Nonsense. There is no reason for me to be cross with you. You performed your jobs with distinction. Whatever you wish in payment..." The four balls of light brightened slightly. "Done," Anu said. Eris, Mephitis, Tyche, and Tiamat all disappeared with a pop.

Anu turned to Tyr. "And you? What do you want in payment?"

"Allow me to stay and observe," Tyr said. "I will not interfere."

"You can do that with no help from me," Anu said. "Your task is completed. You are free to do as you will." The teen boy smiled. "And I will ask you again, what do you seek in payment from me?"

"Return Kit's powers to her. It's all I would ask."

Anu cocked an eyebrow and turned to Kit. "I will not push your powers upon you. I will grant Tyr his wish, but only if you will accept his gift."

"Thank you, Tyr. Your offer is extremely generous, and I am not deserving of it. I don't think I want the responsibility of being a celestial. I just want to go home to be with Indie and the boys." The world was spinning again. Before she blacked out, she blurted, "What did you mean by three lives?"

∞∞∞◇∞∞∞

It took Kit a moment for her eyes to regain focus. She was still standing before her mother and Pental. Indie was beside her and the boys were lying quietly nearby. The gray hare and the other five aspects of Gaia were gone.

"What about three lives?" Indie asked.

"What?" Kit was still struggling with a bout of dizziness and nausea.

"You said something like, *what did you mean by three lives?*" Kit's face grew stern. She didn't know the answer to that question, and it bothered her. She waved the thought away.

"We need to talk," Kit said. "But first, we need to decide what we'll do about Pental."

"I accept my punishment," the man said. He lowered his head, refusing to look up.

"How can anyone mete out punishment to a man that Gaia herself intercedes for?" Kit wasn't speaking to anyone in particular. "She knows his heart. My mother knows his heart." Her jaw tensed. "Is this the reason you wanted to return to Lilloet? You wanted to get Pental away from here?"

Riva nodded.

"You would choose this man over your family? You would choose him over me?"

"Of course not," Riva sprang from her seat and snatched up Kit's hands in her own. "I would put no one ahead of you."

"Do you love him, mother? Even after all the things he's done? Even after all the harm he's caused?"

"I do, in ways I cannot explain. I hardly even know him, but I love him just the same." Pental remained silent. He looked up at Kit with pleading eyes.

"I will speak with father," Kit said. "If he doesn't wish to punish him for what he's done. If he believes his actions were justified... Maybe he'll let him live. Maybe he will allow him to live his life in the service of others."

"Thank you," Riva said. She hugged Kit so tightly that she feared her ribs might snap.

"If it's all the same to you," Pental said, slowly standing from the bench. "I will turn myself in to the captain. I will let him decide my fate, without intervention."

Kit nodded. She still hated the man for what he'd put her through, but she respected what he was doing. Riva gave Kit a small kiss on the cheek before she led Pental back into the Temple.

Indie waited until the couple had left. "You wanted to talk to me about something?"

"I need to speak with you and Lump both." Kit turned to the golden retriever, who was intently paying attention. Runt, on the other hand, was snoring quietly with his head on the grass. "Lump, can you change back into your human self, please?"

Lump panted. A big doggie smile was plastered on his face.

"Lump, please, I need to speak with you." The golden retriever continued to smile and pant. Kit clutched her chest.

"Are you not able to change anymore? Have you lost that, too?"

"Lost what, too?" Indie asked. "What are you talking about?"

"You and Lump, when you fell into Lake Titan, your dragon spirits were destroyed." Kit's breath hitched while she waited for Indie's reaction. She feared he would be crushed by the news.

"I know," he said easily. "I didn't know Lump had lost his dragon self, too, but I had assumed so. Ever since you saved us, I knew it was gone."

"Does that make you sad?" Kit took the man's hands in her own. She was trying to gauge his reaction, but he remained quite stoic.

"No." He paused for several seconds as though he were searching his soul for the truth. "No, I don't think I am. Now that you can control your powers completely, I'm not afraid to be with you. I'm not afraid you'll lose control..."

Kit sensed nothing. She couldn't tell if he was lying to her. The look on the young man's face said he was being honest, but she had no way of telling for sure. She would have to go on faith and trust alone.

"You won't ever have to worry about my daemon losing control. Never again." Kit tried to smile, but she couldn't find it within herself. "I have lost my celestial powers. When I saved you and Lump, I put too much of myself into healing you. Tyche thought I was going to die if I did. Anu said she wouldn't have taken three lives, so she took my power instead. I don't know what he meant."

"You spoke with Anu again?" Kit nodded. "He probably meant me, you, and Lump. She let you save the three of us in return for your powers."

Kit sighed. She didn't know the answer. "But Anu offered me something, well, offered you and Lump something. He said he could return your dragon spirits to you. You could both be dragons again."

Indie looked over at Lump. The golden retriever continued panting and smiling. He didn't respond. "I only cared about having dragon powers so I could be with you. I don't care if I don't get them back."

Kit looked to Lump, desperately hoping he would answer. He just kept panting and smiling.

"Lump," Kit said, taking a knee in front of her big boy. "If you understand what I'm saying, can you bark at me?"

"Woof!"

"You understand?"

"Woof!"

"Lump, do you want to be a dragon again?" Lump licked his lips and panted. When Kit gave him an exasperated look, he licked her face.

"Lump, bark at me if you don't want to be a dragon."

"Woof!"

Kit wrapped her arms around the wolfdog and gave him a deep hug. "I love you, boy. I love you so much."

"And that's why he'll be alive until the day you die. So will Runt."

Kit looked up to see Tyr, still in his young teen persona. "What do you mean?"

"I told Anu what you'd like to have. I said you'd never ask for it yourself, but I was certain that you wouldn't refuse." The boy had a broad smile on his face. Kit's eyes widened and her chin dropped to her chest. He looked just like Lump had in his human form. She hadn't noticed it until just now.

"Dogs and wolves have brief lives," Tyr said. He walked over to where Runt was sleeping and sat cross-legged next to him. He stroked the thick fur of the dire wolf's neck. "Much too short. They have so much love to give and so little time to do it in. I asked Anu if he could tie their lives to yours. As long as you live, so will they. You will never feel the sting of their death and they will never suffer the loss of yours."

"I want that, too," Indie said. "I want to be tied to Kit and the boys as well."

"Indie, no," Kit cried out. "Don't do that."

"I cannot live without you. I know it in my heart that you are the light of my life. I don't want to live without you." He paused and his eyes welled up with tears. "Unless you don't feel the same way. You refused my proposal. Maybe you don't want to be with me."

"You proposed to her?" Tyr asked.

"Shut it," Kit and Indie responded in perfect unison.

"Indie, my love, I didn't answer because I wanted to speak *privately* with you." She glared at Tyr, who promptly disappeared. Kit waited for several seconds, but the howl of the coyote never came. "I want you. With my whole body, my heart, my mind, my soul, I want you. I want to share my life with you. I want to share eternity with you."

Indie fell to his knees. His emotions completely overtook his ability to maintain his balance. The boys quickly pounced on him, taking advantage of the downed man.

Kit laughed deeply. She quickly covered her mouth, fearing she was about to throw up.

Chapter Fifty-Nine

Friends and Family

The following three days were barely more than a blur. The ceremony to honor the dead was a spectacular affair. Dragons and drakes filled the skies over Aarall. Fury had organized them, making sure that those who'd died defending the fate of the world were given the highest honors possible. The celebration of life that was held the following day was a somber affair by comparison.

"Are you sure you need to do this," Kit asked Lin. "Surely the people of Two Peaks now know the king for the poor excuse of a human he is? They'll likely revolt before the summer is over."

"How many times have you heard of cruel, terrible monarchs staying in power until they've passed from old age?" Lin checked the daggers strapped to her hip. She looked more like an assassin than a princess. She was wearing black leathers from head to toe, a black oilskin cloak, and her twin flaming long swords strapped to her hip. Ormand was dressed almost identically, except he had a much thicker blade strapped over his back. Storm Cloud had agreed to carry Lin to the city. They had found a kinship during the battle and the horse-sprite had offered to be her steed. Treedale was planning on riding Whistler. He and Mukale would likely arrive in Two Peaks a week after Lin, which Kit was sure was a part of her plan. Knowing Lin, she'd have completed her task and set up the throne for her little brother to ascend to. She had no desire to take the throne herself.

"And Rusty is okay with you doing this?" Kit asked, hoping to dissuade her friend.

"Oh, no. She definitely is not. I promised I would return to her in Cormorant, but she doesn't believe me. She still thinks I'm too good for her." Lin let out a weak laugh. "I just hope she'll have me when I come back. She was still dealing with her father's return to his body, so who knows?"

Kit tried to give Lin a comforting smile. "I'm glad Indie took you to find Rusty in Ravenlord. She must have been beside herself when she learned her father wasn't there."

"The city was a mess," Lin replied. "Faol's soldiers had left it in tatters. They had killed most of the Ravenlord's soldiers before leaving. The way Rusty told it, they were terminated for gross incompetence. I'm guessing they received a retributive fate when your army caught up with them on the way to Lycos."

"They're not my army. They're Rusty's or her father's, or whosoever's it will be running Cormorant. All I can say is, they'd better treat them well." The last comment made Lin laugh.

"I suppose even if you can't light up their arses, as Coldforge would say, you've got plenty of large scaly friends who would." Lin's eyes went wide as a thought crashed into her consciousness. "Do you remember the silly twins, Ashlay and Cilya?" Kit nodded. Of course, she remembered the two pretty blonde girls who didn't seem to have a brain to share between them. "Do you remember how Ashlay, or was it Cilya?" Lin waved her hands like it didn't actually matter who it was. "They said their father had a pet dragon and that they fed their enemies to it."

Kit chuckled. She remembered it well. She knew it was impossible. Dragons were locked in their mountain homes, unable to leave.

"They had one, or sort of had one. Her father had somehow captured a baby wyvern. The damned fool kept it as a pet."

"A wyvern?" Kit's face screwed up. "They're kind of like a giant bat, aren't they?"

"Kind of," Lin said. "They look just like a drake, but they don't have four legs, only two. So, yes, I suppose you're right. They do kind of look like a big, scaly bat but with a dragon's head."

"We should leave, Lady Aithlin," Ormand said. He was sitting patiently on Storm Cloud's back. Lin smiled and gave Kit a deep hug. "You know how it is. Duty calls."

"I do," Kit said, returning the hug with all her might. When they finally parted, Kit walked over to see Storm Cloud. She held out her hand and waited for him to place his muzzle in it. It was as soft and warm as she remembered. "Keep her safe for me. I would like to see her again, and you, too, if you're willing."

"I will return when the task is complete. Maybe you would honor me with a ride?"

"Seriously?" Kit asked. "Anytime. The honor would be mine."

Lin practically bowled Kit over when she went in for another deep hug.

"Bye," Lin said. The woman was trying to hide her emotions. She wasn't doing a particularly good job of it, and neither was Kit. "Until I return."

Storm Cloud carried the pair away with barely a sound. Kit watched as they disappeared into the distance.

"Be safe, my friend. Come back to me." Kit turned to walk back to the Temple and slammed into Father Hoarfrost.

"She'll be back," he said with complete confidence. "When we chose Aithlin to be your bodyguard, we knew she would grow up into a strong, independent woman."

"I had forgotten that you had picked her to be my protector." The revelation that Lin was not just another Temple acolyte still bothered Kit deeply. "It makes it hard to know if she was my friend or if she was just doing her duty."

The comment made the old priest laugh. "Oh, Kitten. I know you don't believe Aithlin wasn't your friend. Her job was to monitor you and look out for you at the Temple. We never asked her to interact with you. That was all her. When she was very young, Grams spoke with her mother. They both knew Aithlin and Treedale's lives were in peril as long as they were in Two Peaks. So, Grams invited them to come live with her at the Temple. It wasn't a life that Treedale could live, so Grams left with him and returned to Ashcroft. She took care of Treedale, and I looked after Lin. It was clear she would never be a priest, not in a thousand lifetimes. But the girl showed other skills. Her talents made her particularly well suited to watching over you."

"Oh," Kit said. She still wasn't sure if this news made her upset or not. It explained a lot about the woman, though. "I hope Lin gets what she deserves in life. She was dealt a terrible hand."

"Did her predilection for gambling rub off on you? A card reference from a priest of Titan?" Father Hoarfrost chuckled.

"Maybe. She taught me how to play and I ended up taking more chances when we were together." Kit swallowed. "I really do love her, you know. She is the sister I never had."

"You'll need to tell her that when she returns. She has expressed those same sentiments to me."

The old priest wrapped his arm around Kit's shoulder and led her back towards the Temple. They walked in comfortable silence for several minutes.

"If you don't want to live at the Temple, what do you plan to do? Become a farmer and raise your family? Perhaps you'd rather move to Fenrir's hut in the woods to raise your family."

"You seem intent on me raising a family, Father," Kit said, pulling herself away from the man. He laughed at her and took her hand. The power she felt pouring off the man was even stronger than what she'd experienced the first day they had met. He was back to being himself again.

"It wasn't I who was intent on starting one," he said. "Actions have consequences."

Kit got a queasy feeling in her stomach. She felt a sudden, desperate need to vomit.

"I hear that the feeling you're experiencing will pass in time. I don't think it's something to be concerned with."

"What feeling? Do you mean the bit of nausea I've been experiencing? What do you know of it?"

"I know nothing of it. It's not something my kind has to endure."

"What are you saying, Father?"

"I'm saying you should discuss the matter with your mother."

"Father, what are you not telling me?"

"I have no idea what you're talking about," he said. His expression was completely blank.

Kit's eyes flashed golden. "Liar!"

THE STORY CONTINUES...

This marks the end of The Priest of Titan series. If you want to read more stories from the Veil of Entropy universe, visit my website for a complete list of all my novels.

https://paulmouchet.ca

AFTERWORD

Thank you for reading my novel. Reviews are critical to the success of every indie author. I would ask that you leave a review on Amazon, GoodReads, and Book-Bub. If you have any thoughts or comments that you'd like to share directly with me, I would love to hear from you. You can email me at paul@paulmouchet.ca.

Do you want more stories? You find links to all my novels on my website. You can also sign up for my newsletter, Marvelous Mondays, which I send out every other week. They're full of fun pics, snippets of what's going on in my life, and book news.

Also, if you'd like to discuss my stories with me and other fans, in a safe, friendly environment, please connect with me on my Facebook group ~ Paul Mouchet's Reader's Group.

You'll find the link to all my social media accounts on my website. I look forward to chatting with you.

Happy Reading!

www.ingramcontent.com/pod-product-compliance
Lightning Source LLC
Chambersburg PA
CBHW050843210726
48290CB00004B/1067